REVEALING THE REVOLUTION

REVEALING THE REVOLUTION

N.M. SOTZEK

Published by N.M Sotzek

Revealing the Revolution
Copyright © 2014 N.M. Sotzek

All rights reserved. No part of this book may be reproduced or transmitted in any form or by any means without written permission from the author (except for brief excerpts in reviews).

First printing 2014

The characters and events in this book are fictitious. Any similarity to real persons, living or dead, is coincidental and not intended by the author.

Cover design by JB Centeno
Publisher logo design by Becky Carlyle

Library and Archives Canada Cataloguing in Publication

Sotzek, N. M., 1988-, author
    Revealing the revolution / N.M. Sotzek.

Issued in print and electronic formats.
ISBN 978-1-4811-9703-8 (pbk.).--ISBN 978-0-9937895-0-2 (epub)

    I. Title.

PS8637.O79R48 2014   C813'.6   C2014-905812-8
                                         C2014-905813-6

Printed and bound in the United States of America

To Ben. Even though it was always supposed to be about the sport. And the animals.

CHAPTER 1

"Dad! Dad! Didja hear?" A young boy ran from his place in front of the TV to his father sitting at the kitchen table, his little arms waving to control his balance.

"Hear what, Lucas?" His father put his newspaper down as his son tugged on his arm.

"They wanna bring Scanning to Canada! You know what that is, right Dad?" Of course he did. His dad was the smartest man in the world. He grinned as his father picked him up and placed him on his knee. Before he could respond, Lucas sputtered on. He had to show him just how smart he was.

"It's gonna work like in 'merica. You hafta scan animals for points, and each animal is worth different points because some are harder to get than others. You gotta be able to get to the animals on cliffs and underwater. But," Lucas paused to catch his breath. "But the really cool parts are the challenges! You hafta travel *all* over Canada and hike, and go on the water. I saw one challenge in 'merica, and it was a really cool rock climbing one on the Grand Canyon! You gotta use your remote console to scan things like barcodes for points to win each challenge. But...Dad, listen!" he whined when he noticed his dad watching the clock. He waited until he was once again the centre of his father's universe. "Sometimes it's a race to get the most points. Sometimes you just get points for doing the challenge, which I think is stupid. But, they still do really cool stuff!"

"Some of it is dangerous, L.J." His father set him down on the ground and ruffled his hair.

Lucas did not mind the ruffling or being called by his nickname, Lucas Junior. All that was important at the moment was what he considered to be a very serious decision.

"I'm gonna be the best!" he proclaimed, holding a small electronic console tightly in his hands. It looked similar to a thin cell phone, but with an entire touch screen surface – a very advanced piece of technology for a young child. "The challenges won't be dangerous if I'm really good! None of the best players get hurt!" spoke the logic of a six-year-old.

When the doorbell rang, Lucas watched as his father made his way to the front of the farm house. He followed his dad silently, his little fingers moving over the touch screen which controlled the Artificial Intelligence Morpher his father had given him for his birthday a few months earlier. He paid little attention to the adult conversation above his head.

"You're not supposed to be here, Henk," Lucas Senior said quietly to the man standing in the doorway. "What happened to being discrete?"

"It's happening. We're in lockdown now," Henk answered. "Trevor's finally got it into Canada. The national tournament will start in seven years to give regional teams the lead they require. We don't have much time to get our labs established before Trevor can find them, find us." Henk suddenly looked down at Lucas. He had noticed the small ball of white gel at the front door, but it had transformed into a Golden Retriever without his noticing. It was not easy to ignore the transformation of the whitish-gel, as it rippled and vibrated into the form of an animal.

"How long has he had that?"

"Four months."

"Any problems?"

"At first, yes. He's managed to keep it under control. Without my help. They seem to have bonded."

Henk's eyes widened with shock as he looked at his research partner. "He can control it?"

Lucas Senior looked down at his son with pride. "It only took him about a week to get the hang of it. I showed him how to examine the genetic codes he scans and the programming code of the chip." He turned back to Henk and his eyebrows furrowed. His voice dropped with unnecessary caution. "I don't want even your assistant to know the kind of AIM he has, or what he knows how to do. If Trevor found out that L.J can do all of this…if something happened to him, to either of them, I'd never forgive myself. L.J and Lucy are my world."

"I know. That's why we're in lockdown now. L.J's skills give me hope for our own testing, however. The first glimmer of hope since Trevor took over my initial research. And as long as you haven't told her any details, your wife should be safe."

Lucas finally turned his attention from his AIM. The boy frowned when he realized that his father was not paying attention to him.

"When's Mommy coming home?" he asked, letting the Golden Retriever jump up at him, wagging its tail excitedly as a real puppy would. Lucas had yet to discover that this was, in fact, abnormal.

"In about an hour, son," Lucas Senior answered before he looked at Henk. "It has to be now, doesn't it?"

"You and Lucy knew the consequences going into this." Henk's voice was soft as he continued to watch the boy with his AIM in awe. The bond seen between the two was incredible, but there would be time for analysis over the next few years. Discretely, of course. "We have to finish what we started."

Lucas Senior knelt down and grinned at his son. "Hey buddy. Can you do something for me?"

L.J's eyes lit up and he nodded soberly. He would do anything for him.

"If Scanning is coming to Canada, you're going to have to get started with your training right away. You have one hour to scan an animal worth more than ten points, but you have to stay in the brush on our property. Do you remember the official scanning rules you told me?"

"No animal can be scanned more than once within twenty-four hours. No scanning an animal that belongs to someone without con...contempt."

"Consent."

"Consent," he repeated.

"That means permission. That means you can't scan the animals in the field next door, okay?" Lucas Senior smiled as his son nodded once again. "Come here." He wrapped his arms around the boy who gladly accepted the embrace. "Make me proud, L.J."

"I will!" He ran out the door with his AIM trailing close behind, leaping down the steps of the front porch with the ease practice had given to him. He ran across the field and ignored the crows which were only worth one point. Not enough to make his father proud.

"It's time," Henk said once more as the two men watched the boy disappear across the field.

Exactly one hour later, Lucas Junior returned home. He walked slowly back across the field with his head down and feet dragging. He managed to only scan a deer, which was still quite a feat for a six-year-old. Most children could not stand still long enough to scan even a bird before scaring it away. But the deer was only worth five points. Not ten, and not higher. He did not want to disappoint his dad, but it was the best he could do. For now. He lifted his head, and a line of determination crossed his young forehead. When he was older, when he was a real athlete in the Canadian Scanning Tournament, he would be better. Then he would really be able to make his father proud. In seven years when he was old enough to join a junior division, he would keep his promise to his father.

Lucas had sat in the brush for almost twenty minutes before the deer, the only worthy animal so far, came across his path. From where he hid, Lucas held the Artificial Intelligence Remote Control, or AIRC as people had come to call it, up in front of his face as if he was taking a picture. His little thumb jabbed the touch screen over the area which said 'Scan' and held the console steady.

A small bar crawled across the screen but he ignored it. Instead, he focused – with an intensity far beyond that of most six-year-olds – on the deer as if it would keep the animal from moving. He had to keep the animal in view in order to successfully scan its genetic code. The boy's face broke into a grin when the words 'Scan Successful' came across the screen. There was no guarantee that his dad would be proud of his attempt, but it still was not good enough to be the best Scanner.

For the rest of the hour Lucas had climbed trees, balancing on the branches as if completing a challenge. He had jumped down from trees, his little hands raised in fists of triumph above his head to signify the successful completion of a challenge. He ran down the paths, running commentaries in his head from the American challenges, pretending to be one of the athletes. That was when his daydreams had run out, along with his time, and he started the long march home.

As the driveway came into view he began to drag his feet, despite seeing his mother's car parked there. He was not quite ready to face his father.

"L.J?!"

He stopped at the front door, hearing his mother call his name in panic.

"I'm here, Mommy!" He made his way into the kitchen hesitantly. He hoped he was not in trouble. He had stayed on their property as he was supposed to. His mom was sometimes mean for no reason, but his father always made it better. It was always better with his dad.

His mother flew into the kitchen, taking him tightly into her arms. "Oh, thank God you're alright. You scared me half to death, young man."

"Sorry, Mommy." He looked around as his mom continued to hold him. He meant his apology, but he had more important things to do. "Where's Daddy? I scanned a deer for him!"

"That's great, sweetie! Daddy-" Lucas realized his mom was crying now. Did she not like deer? "Sweetie, come sit down in the living room." She took his hand but he pulled it away. He walked himself into the other room and sat on the couch.

He wanted to show his father the scan, but he would rather delay that shame. Besides, his mother looked upset for some reason. "What's wrong?"

"L.J." She knelt on the ground in front of her son and attempted a smile. "Daddy...Daddy isn't here."

"When's he gonna be back?"

"Sweetie, he's not coming back," she explained with a soft and trembling voice.

The little boy shrugged his shoulders. His father went away sometimes on business trips. He was an important scientist. "He's on a trip? But he was just here."

"Lucas, your father won't be living here anymore." Before she could catch him in her arms, he jumped off the couch and ran around the farm house, calling for his father.

"L.J, come here. Please," Lucy called after him.

"No! He told me to be the best!" His voice faded in and out as he entered and left each room. "He told me I had an hour!" Finally, Lucas went back into the kitchen slowly. "Was I bad? Is that why he left?"

"Of course not! It's not your fault, Lucas. You're the best son we could ask for." She knelt down once more in front of him.

"Then it's your fault! You were mean to him! You're always mean! You made him go away!" he yelled, infantile anger covering his face, replacing the hurt.

"Lucas Cameron Tylar, you will not talk to me like that," she snapped. Using his full name always stopped him in his tracks. She paused before she continued. "Daddy left because he had to. It was no one's fault, especially not ours." She let him seethe for a moment before she continued. "It's just us now. It's not our fault. It's not your fault."

But he did not believe her. It was someone's fault. Maybe, just maybe, it was his father's fault. He was going to prove something to his dad. He would be the best, and then his dad would be sorry for leaving. He'd do whatever it would take, and he would be the best.

CHAPTER 2

Seventeen years later....

He looked ahead, eyes fixed on the jump ahead. He kicked his heels into the barrel of the horse beneath him, gripping the mane to keep from flying backwards.

"Cam, don't push it too hard!"

He ignored his female team-mate's advice. *What does she know?* If he did not push his AIM, it would never get better. He needed to be better. The thought of his team-mates watching him made him smirk. Time to show them what he could do. After five years on the team, he was still getting better, and it never hurt to show it.

Cam grinned as he steered the robotic horse towards one of the constructed jumps. The team had put the obstacle course together in the open field to train their bodies, and their AIMs. As usual, Cam had been the first to try the course. The horse sailed over the jump easily, and Cam hollered in triumph. The training was paying off. The more he worked with his AIM in a certain form the more accustomed it became to the animal, and the better it would perform in challenges. But it still was not going fast enough. He was grateful for the riding lessons Maria had started with him three years ago. Just another skill to add to his ever-growing list.

He eyed the last hurdle at the far end of the field. He patted the AIM's neck as it continued to canter around the course. "It's all or nothing now. Go!" The horse took off as he flapped his heels against its sides. He bent forward as the wind whipped against his face, nearly leaning fully against the up and down motion of the creature's neck. Still not fast enough.

"C'mon! I know you can go faster than this!"

"Cam, be careful!" A stern, male voice came through the AI Remote Console strapped to his wrist.

"I know what I'm doing, Owen!" he called back to his captain, his eyes still focused on the jump ahead. *Why does no-one trust me?* "Go faster!" he yelled again to the AIM, and finally felt the creature increase its speed; its legs pumped even harder. He grinned as they approached the jump.

"I must warn you," came a robotic voice from Cam's AIRC.

"Just jump!"

Cam braced himself as the horse launched itself into the air, clearing the jump with ease. He readied himself for the landing – his heart stopped. The horse was going too quickly. He swore as the horse landed hard with the sound of a loud crack. The horse's head went down and Cam was sent flying forward. He had barely enough time to tuck into a ball, but he managed to come to a rolling stop.

He winced as he sat up, and swore again when he looked back at his AIM. It was lying pathetically on the ground, pawing at the long grass with its hooves as if trying to stand.

"Worthless piece of-"

"Cam! Are you okay?"

He looked past the AIM to see his team-mates running towards him. "I'm fine. Stupid thing couldn't land properly."

"You went at the jump way too fast and you know it." Another man, a few years older than Cam, reached out helping Cam to his feet before running his hand through his dark hair. He eyed his team-mate as a warning.

"Whatever. Out of all of us, I'm the only one who'd be able to even do that, Rick."

Owen shot Cam a disapproving look as he finally came up beside him. "Maria's the equestrian on this team, whether you like it or not. It looked like you could barely stay on. What good is it if you don't even learn from your mistakes?"

Normally he admired his captain, but today Owen was ticking him off. "I don't make mistakes."

"Ha!"

Cam spun to look at Maria who wore her usual sarcastic smile. "Have something to say?"

She remained silent for the moment as she stepped towards the horse. Once it stopped trying to stand, she knelt down next to it. Cam watched as her hands, calloused from years of hard work, ran down the length of the horse's legs pausing just past the knee. With a sigh, she turned back to him.

"It feels like the tendon's sprained pretty badly, if not completely torn. Either way, this scan's ruined."

He let out a deep breath and held his AIRC in front of his face. He tapped at the electronic screen and watched as the lame horse transformed through a series of vibrations and fluid waves into a grizzly bear cub. "It was a crappy scan, anyway."

"That horse was amazing! You pushed it too hard," she snapped.

"I was training it! It couldn't handle it and frankly, if it couldn't handle the training, I'm better off without it."

"Maria, start your turn," Owen interjected quickly before she could respond to Cam's jeer. It always seemed to be his duty to split up the two, but it was part of the job description. He looked at Rick, glad that at least his son stayed out of trouble. "Why don't you and Cam go on ahead to the hunting training? Is it all set up?"

Rick nodded as a sparrow grew and formed into a horse next to Maria. "Yeah. I saw some deer up there yesterday. If they're not there, I guess that'll mean more work for us."

"Are you complaining?"

He laughed and shook his head. "Yeah right. Cam, let's get going," he said as he watched Maria mount the horse, leaving the tack on the ground to ride bareback.

The young man looked at Rick with a sceptical look. "Giving up already?"

"No, but I doubt you want to waste your time watching Maria and my dad train their horses. We can get some hunting done in the meantime."

"Anything to get away," he muttered. He swore when Maria charged her horse towards him, jumping out of the way before he was trampled. "Are you crazy?"

"Guys!" Owen stared them down until Maria continued her way around the course.

Cam followed his twenty-nine year old team-mate into the line of trees, with the bear cub ambling along at his side. "What are we going for? Deer again?"

"Might as well. They're everywhere in this forest. Most of the time. Unless you want to go for something a bit more difficult." He grinned with an arrogance he had hidden since Maria had been signed onto the team.

Every year close to the beginning of the season, Canadian Scanning team Revolution underwent a week-long training session complete with rigorous physical obstacles and camping with only the bare essentials. It was one of the reasons the team always excelled. They were prepared for everything. Somehow, the top score had eluded them, but after being in the top five for the past few years, things were looking up. The week had been successful so far, and Cam was looking forward to the beginning of the season. The tenth season in Canada, and he was part of it. Despite the computer chips storing years of previous training, the biological element in the AIM substance meant that they needed constant training to maintain their stats. Cam swore under his breath, thinking about his ruined scan. Scanners had learned years ago that if a scan is pushed too hard, trained too rigorously, it could become injured. An injured scan never recovers. Maria was right: it had been an amazing horse scan.

The two climbed the steep embankment which encircled the field, gripping onto trees and their roots to pull themselves up. Cam gazed across the field as they reached the top.

"There's still a deer down there," Rick whispered, bringing Cam back into the moment.

Cam jabbed his thumbs against the screen of his AIRC. The bear growled softly before its shape morphed into that of a blood hound. "Go get it!"

Rick raised an eyebrow as the AIM took off after the deer they had spotted down a path in the woods. "When did you scan that?"

"If you're Cam Tylar and you're at a dog park, people beg you to scan their dog."

He rolled his eyes as the two started to walk after the AIM, watching it bound out of the forest and across the field in pursuit of the deer. According to the altered robotic laws programmed into the 'brain' of the robot, the AIM could not harm an animal, so neither Rick or Cam worried that the blood hound would be a threat to the deer.

Hurting the deer was not their goal anyway. Cam was forcing and training his AIM to be fast enough to herd the animal back towards them. Not that they needed to scan the deer; off-season scanning points did not contribute to the team's statistics. Most current participants in the CST felt the scanning was a waste of time, believing that the majority of the points and ranks should be earned from the completion of challenges. They claimed that scanning for points was somewhat 'archaic.' But a team such as Revolution knew they had to be the best in every aspect of the sport. This whole exercise was all for the sake of training; becoming better.

"I'm surprised the others haven't caught up with us yet," Cam muttered as he kept his eyes on his AIM, occasionally barking orders through the sleek electronic device which he held tight in his hand, not too different from the one his father had handed to him seventeen years earlier.

"I thought you wanted to get away." Rick looked over his shoulder at the sudden drop of tree-line at the edge of the embankment. The sun was threateningly low on the horizon, sending a dusty rose colour through the sky. Their training was almost done, and soon they would be on the road, travelling around Canada for the tournament. "We should call it a night soon. I think we've done as much as we can tonight."

"No. We never do enough and our first challenges always suck," he replied through gritted teeth as he watched the deer leap into the forest at the far end of the small clearing. He swore, starting after the deer when he saw his AIM hesitate at the edge of the trees. "It needs to get used to the terrain and dealing with animals. It's a new scan. It needs to get used to pushing itself. It needs to listen to me. Follow it, don't just stand there!" Cam yelled to the hound as Rick followed close behind.

"What's with you lately?"

"Nothing. I just realized how useless my AIM is. If it can't even follow a deer, how am I supposed to rely on it to get me through a challenge?"

Rick opened his mouth just as their AIRCs chirped to life with Maria's frantic voice.

"Rick, get back here. Now!"

Cam kept going with a roll of his eyes. "Screw you Maria. We actually want to train."

Maria continued, panicking. "Rick, something's wrong with your dad. You need to get back here, now!"

"There are unconfirmed rumours that Owen Warner, Revolution captain and long-time participant of the CST, suffered a heart attack late last night." The sports anchor droned on in the special update on the television, a professionally empathetic ring in his voice. *"The heart attack was relatively mild and his life is not in jeopardy. This is a major blow to the team, who many considered one of the early favourites to win this year. With only two days before the official start of the Canadian Scanning Tournament, they may not have enough time to overcome this setback."*

"Would you just turn that off?" A stern voice came from the hospital bed.

"There's nothing better to do. Not like you're much entertainment," came Cam's unfeeling reply, a recently developed trademark.

"There's no reason to be watching it. Nothing you can't hear from my doctors."

"Like I said, nothing else to do. Besides, I love hearing what they have to say about us." Cam shifted in the chair, his legs casually dangling over its arm.

"Would you at least turn it down then?" Rick raised himself from his own chair and gave him a look of warning.

Cam glared back, but reluctantly reduced the volume a few levels with a flourish as if to prove a point.

"Thanks, I appreciate it," said the recently benched captain.

Rick walked over to the side of the hospital bed; lines of concern formed on his forehead as he examined his father. The man had never looked so old before but now as he lay there on the bed, his wrinkles were much more defined and it seemed as though the grey in his hair had spread from his temples to form a wig on the strong captain they had known. "You should be resting."

"There's no way I'm going to let a little heart attack get in my way." In an effort to show his miraculous healing, Owen attempted to prop himself up with his elbow before submitting to the force of gravity. "It was just a mild heart attack. You heard Sportcentre. You can trust them." A sly smile crossed his face as his son sighed.

"I'm not sure how Revolution is going to be able to overcome this. Warner was a key component of that team, and has been for the last ten years." Three middle-aged men who made up the sports panel stood around an elevated table, speaking as though the camera was not even there.

"Frankly, I wouldn't be surprised to see them plummet in the rankings. They have no hope of keeping up their scores."

"I have to agree with you, Gerry. It's unfortunate, but these things happen in sports. It's too bad it happened to someone like Warner, who's been a fixture of the CST since its inauguration ten years ago. Two of his original team-mates have both retired now, so maybe this is making him consider doing the same. In a sport like this, it's better to leave on a high note, and last season sure was a high note for them with a final rank of fourth in the CST."

Gerry quickly replied. *"Warner may be in his early fifties but I think he's got a lot left in the tank. Unlike other sports, we've seen elderly competitors in this tournament. They may be unlikely to achieve a top-place finish, but this is a tournament based on endurance, teamwork and luck. You don't have to necessarily be the fittest one out there to compete, though it definitely helps."*

"Exactly." The third man finally spoke as the team watched. *"But in the short term it will be interesting to see how this team responds. They're still an extremely well-rounded team with the likes of Rick Warner and Maria Kier. Not to mention their star contributor, Cam Tylar."*

"Damn, did you hear that? Star contributor." Cam grinned as he turned to look at the others in the room. He had long outgrown the need for approval, but an acknowledgement from his team would have been appreciated.

"Watch the language," Owen replied faintly.

"Haven't yet," he muttered as he turned the TV off, looking the older man over, examining him as Rick had moments earlier.

"Only like listening to them talking about you?" Rick asked.

Cam stood up and shoved his hands into his pockets, ignoring Rick as he finished his appraisal of his captain. "I have to get out of this room. I feel trapped. I don't like it." He paused at the door, not daring to look behind him as if afraid of what he might see. "I'll be back in a bit."

After a few moments, Owen stole a look at the young woman sitting on the other side of his bed, her legs crossed comfortably on the chair. "Hey Maria, mind tagging after him? Make sure he's okay? He may meet up with some media camped outside and we don't want him to say anything stu…anything we'll regret."

She flipped her dark brown hair out of her face, leaving a lone purple highlighted strand dangling in front, deliberately ignoring him as she looked through her magazine. The mindless ramblings of single women covered the pages, helping Maria to lose herself in the troubles of others.

"Maria?"

"I'd really rather not."

"Please? For me?" he asked faintly.

"Three years I've been looking out for him. I think I've done enough." She raised an eyebrow, waiting for the captain to respond or at least retract his request.

"We know. But I would appreciate it. Please."

Owen looked at his son after Maria had left. "We should talk about what's going to happen with the team this season."

Rick held his hands up, trying to stop the conversation before it began. "That's between you and the board of directors. You know I'll be fine with whatever decision you make."

"Good, because I've decided you'll be Captain."

His eyes widened and he shook his head. "Captain? No way. You know that I don't do well with things like that. Sure, I help out with the board sometimes and I've been involved with the contracts, but there's no way I can take your job."

"Well it's you or Cam. Maria's nowhere near ready. She's a great athlete, but she'd never be able to handle the bureaucratic side of things. At least nothing sport related."

"I really don't want to talk about this right now, Dad. We'll talk about it later, as a team."

"Rick, did you feel ready to be a father? No, but you've turned into a caring husband and father. It's something you're never ready for. You just have to be thrown into it."

Rick could not help but shudder jokingly. "I'm not quite ready to have Maria and Cam as my kids."

Owen chuckled softly. "Rick, you've been a part of this team as long as I have. There's no one better to be Captain than you. You're ready for this. They already listen to you, and I know they're already expecting this transition."

"Can we just not talk about this right now, Dad?"

"Fine. Mind turning the TV back on?"

Rick shot him a questioning look as he reached for the television remote.

"I never said I didn't like watching it. Cam just had it too loud."

*   *   *

"Cameron, would you hold on?" Maria swore as she nearly walked into an elderly couple, and again as a nurse almost rammed her with an empty gurney. She muttered under her breath, the frustrated tones the only thing reaching Cam's ears. It had taken her a few minutes to find him in the busy hospital hallway. She had only been able to make him out by his short, wavy blond hair, along with his left ear, pierced at its peak with a silver ring.

Cam looked at her briefly as he stopped in front of a vending machine before turning back to it hungrily. "If only Owen could hear you. And he complains about my language."

"At least I know when to keep my mouth shut."

He held back a laugh. "I really beg to differ. There's been quite a few things you've said that you shouldn't have." He slapped his palm against the machine when he realized his card would not work on the old-fashioned vender. Without a response from Maria, he turned around and headed down the hallway. A glance over his shoulder told him that she was following him, silently. He was grateful at least for that. He really did not want to talk; especially not to her.

All hospitals were the same. The technology may update as new technology is created, but the feel of it was always the same to him. And he hated it. He was anxious to begin the season and get away from the memories inside the hospital walls. It would help keep his mind from yet another loss. Cam did not need another one. Another look over his shoulder. Maria did not need it either. A brief pang of guilt flashed in him, realizing what Rick was going through. And oh how he and Maria could relate to that feeling. They would bounce back, though, and the season would begin. Revolution would be back on top soon enough.

The pair continued walking for some time before they eventually found themselves at the main entrance of the Grand River Kitchener Hospital. Cam turned a corner and they were immediately hit with a flash of brilliant lights. He winced, but managed to maintain his stride while Maria stopped, her eyes sensitive to the brightness. After a second, Maria distinguished a group of people in front of them, and realized too late what the lights were.

She swore under her breath. They stood before twenty reporters, cameras flashing and video cameras rolling. To her left were security guards and a nurse making an attempt to remove the reporters from the premises. As the media caught a glimpse of Cam, the crowd erupted with more flashes and streams of light. Reporters began to call out questions, straining to get their microphones to hover past the guards to Cam.

"Cam, can you officially confirm that Owen Warner had a heart attack?" one woman shouted.

"How will this affect Revolution?" another female reporter chirped, wearing a smile far too large to belong in a hospital.

Cam was now bathed completely in the limelight and clearly loved every minute of it. *Talk about a way to get your mind off things.* "Yes, it's true. Owen Warner had a heart attack yesterday. But we'll work through this as a team and we'll have a great year. I guarantee it. We've been through difficult times before, but nothing has ever stopped us from achieving a high score."

"Do you think this was inevitable, that Owen should take it easy at his age?"

Cam laughed. "With a team like ours, we would never dream of giving anything less than two hundred percent in every season. Asking him to 'take it easy' would be his death sentence, not this heart attack."

Oh brother, Maria thought as she stepped forward in an attempt to slow the barrage of questions. "Owen's heart attack was thankfully not too severe and is definitely not a death sentence for him or our team. With enough rest, he should make a full recovery," Maria stated as professionally as she could. Over the past three years she had acquired a decent amount of practice dealing with the media.

"Do you think he will be able to participate in this year's tournament at all, or will he miss the entire season?" Again with that smile.

Maria started, surprised by the question. Thinking about it now, it occurred to her that he would not be able to compete at all this season. "Honestly, his health comes first. He has a responsibility to himself and his family. We still have two days to submit our official roster. When decisions are made, we will give a formal press statement. Until then, we have no more comments."

Not willing to let the moment pass, Cam inserted, "Expect us to finish high even if we are without Owen this season." He reluctantly gave in to the harsh tug Maria gave on his shirt, and waved once more to the reporters before he finally followed her down the hall. "I'm not ready to go back yet."

"Well suck it up. People have to do things they don't want to all the time. We all need to be here right now. You of all people should understand that," Maria snapped. No matter what had happened, or would happen, they were all in this together. If only they would act like it. "Visiting hours are over soon anyway. Try to be here for him, okay? That's one thing I know you're good at."

"Just take a look at this clip from last year. Owen is clearly the strongest player in the challenge, with Cam close behind him. I don't think anyone would argue that Cam Tylar will take full advantage of this, but this may give Warner Junior and Kier the chance they need in the spotlight." The TV droned on as the two younger team members walked back into the room silently, but Cam's face lit up at the sight of the TV. He sat down in his chair again to enjoy the recap.

It had been a challenge out in British Columbia, and one of the tougher ones as well. They had been told they would each need to use their AIMs on the mountain, but no one had been prepared even then. The AIMs had been commanded to make a way for their team up the mountains and across a gorge, which seemed simple in theory. The animals they chose for their AIMs were carefully selected for their endurance and their natural habitat. It would be useless to use an animal not used to the snow. The first few hours had been easy; the dogs and eagle led them easily up parts of the mountain side, never needing a break. Owen's AIM had been the first to hear it.

"There is a loud rumble further up the mountain. Commands?" the AIM asked, programmed not to do anything to harm a human, or do anything without a human's command.

"Continue on. It's probably nothing," Owen replied. He had not heard anything himself other than the wind. All he wanted to do was to get to the other side of the mountain and start their descent. Even though it had already been a few hours, they were going faster than any other team so far on this challenge and that was enough to put them into first place. He had pushed his team and AIM harder than they were used to, but Owen knew that they could handle it.

"My AIM's gone!"

Owen turned around when he heard Maria's voice. She was holding her AIRC in her gloved hands, looking desperately at the screen.

"What?"

"It can't get back to us." She wiped the snow from the screen as it continued to fall gently upon them. "It's where we need to be but it's saying that way is blocked now. There was an avalanche in that area."

"Should've trained your bird to fly in winds like this instead of always training that horse scan of yours." Cam grinned playfully as she rolled her eyes. "I thought I had helped you with that bird though last month."

Owen looked forward again as the two youngest members decided that Cam had neglected that particular duty, and groaned at the faces they gave to the other. "We'll push on. We still have the dogs and they still have the scent of the trail we need to stick to."

Maria tore her eyes away from her captain, remembering how long they had been trapped on that mountain. He had pulled them through so much, and now he could barely pull himself out of the bed. The familiar sound of mechanical beeps and the smell of antiseptic made Maria just as uncomfortable as Cam. She would never let on of course. Rick needed his team. But she could tell he was worried about something more than just his father.

"Hey, you okay?" Stupid question, she knew. For months, Maria had replied to it the same way, and did not expect Rick to do anything differently.

Rick sighed as he glanced at his father. "I guess we might as well talk about it now, since it's going to effect the season."

"Yeah, your dad had a heart attack." Cam rolled his eyes. "I was there."

Rick was glad at least Cam had not lost his attempts for humour despite everything that had happened. "How do you guys feel about me being captain?"

The two shrugged. "It's pretty much assumed, Rick," Maria spoke and looked to Owen. "Do we really need to discuss this?"

"Don't look at me." Owen shook his head. "He's the reluctant one. The board already knows."

She pulled her hair back and swept it up into a bun. "When are we meeting with them?"

"Tomorrow," Rick answered. "We have to finalise the roster, so my captaincy will be official then and we'll…we'll discuss the possibility of a temp." He spoke slowly, watching their faces. He saw Cam's face twist and spoke again before Cam could fully react. "But we'll discuss it tomorrow. Right now, my dad needs to rest."

He was grateful they remained quiet, but part of him had hoped that someone would say something, anything to refute the decision Owen had made. How could he handle all of this? He was going to be the new captain while his father lay in a hospital bed. Now they needed to get a replacement. He ran his hands over his face and through his hair, nearly feeling it turn from black to grey with the oncoming stress. They still had two days to figure things out, but Rick could feel the hours slipping away before the tournament started.

They'd make it, somehow.

CHAPTER 3

Revolution sat at the large boardroom table across from their sponsors and directors. Maria and Rick had tried to dress as professionally as they could: she in a white blazer and dress pants, he in a brown suit. Cam, however, never liked the formality of dress clothes and wore a dark grey suit jacket with tattered jeans, only wearing the former after Rick's persistent requests.

The co-founders of their main sponsoring company, Jim Walker and Frank Byman, sat across from them with thoughtful faces. It had been three years since they had last been through this process to sign Maria, and it likely wasn't going to be as easy this time.

"Welcome, *team*." Jim smiled. "We were devastated to hear about Owen's heart attack. I've known him for more than fifteen years. He's a strong man, and we know he'll pull through this. We're sorry all the same, for what you're going through." He directed his last comment at Rick, who nodded his thanks. "After talking to him on the phone, and to his doctor, we've determined that there's no way that he can recover in time to participate this season. On the preliminary roster we submitted to the CST head committee two weeks ago, Owen is listed as team captain. I hear you've all come to the agreement that Rick will take over as captain now, so I'm glad we don't need to deal with the politics of that. However, we need to decide whether or not to sign a replacement.

Since we don't keep a trainer team in the Juniors, we have few options for a replacement."

This came as no surprise to the team, but the thought still didn't sit right. It was one thing to have signed Cam five years ago, and then Maria two years later, but that was due to other members retiring. Owen was the original captain. There was no way anyone would be able to replace his spot in the team, not at this critical stage of their careers. Especially not so close to when the team would be re-signing their contract with the same men seated across from them.

"We don't need a replacement."

Everyone looked at Cam with wide eyes. Rick leaned over to him slowly. "Cam, my dad can't play. Even he admitted that, and you know he's the last person who would."

"I know Owen can't play. But I don't think we need some ringer coming up and getting in our way." Cam lifted himself out of his chair, emphasizing his point more. "We're able to win it ourselves. We've finished in the top ten four of the past five years, including a fourth place finish last year. We can do this. We work well together already, and we don't need someone new to mess that up."

"Are you kidding me, Cam?" Maria shook her head. "We can't compete one man short, not with our rank."

"Why not? The fourth player is pretty much a replacement already. You should know that."

She ignored the gibe. "And what about water challenges? You haven't done one in four years. Are you really willing to take handicap scores just because you don't want someone new messing up whatever dynamic we have left?"

Cam glazed over the shot at his record and continued. "If this happened tomorrow, we wouldn't be having this conversation."

"But it didn't. It happened two days ago and we have the time to do something about it." She shook her head again and turned away. "You're unbelievable."

"We don't have anything to worry about. You guys have me. No problem," he answered matter-of-factly.

"Are you friggin kidding me?" Maria was now yelling; something which she rarely, if ever, did in front of the board, conscious enough to watch her language. "We should dump you, with all the grief you cause us."

Cam snorted condescendingly. "That's already been done. Besides, I'm practically the best in the tournament."

"Best in the tournament? Holy crap." Maria faced the board. "I motion we find a replacement for Cam."

The team had always been able to act professionally in front of the board, even Cam who could rarely keep his mouth shut in front of the media. This was something else, though, and everyone in the room sat stunned. Maria sat back down, forced out a soft apology and turned her eyes to her hands resting on the table. Cam kept quiet as he returned to his seat. Maybe words actually did mean something.

"I know not all of you feel this is the best option, but in order to keep up your current stats, a fourth player is required." Jim spoke as though nothing had happened. "A high finish means that your current fan base will stay with you. A new player, however, will bring in more fans, more ticket and merchandise sales, and a better contract next season which is definitely something you all need to take into consideration."

"Are we able to call up Wes?" Rick asked, referring to the rookie they had signed as a replacement. He started when Cam stood suddenly, his eyes narrowed in anger as he silently left the room.

"Wes was called up by the Rising Suns for a roster spot last week. It was a good opportunity for him, and his contract with us allowed it. We couldn't expect him to stick around and continue to be a replacement. He's too new for that. We've found two other candidates, though, that we thought would be appropriate."

Frank stood, drawing everyone's attention to the projected image hovering just above the table. "The first is Emily Richardson."

Outside in the hallway, Cam paced along the wall, hating himself for his rash decision. He tried to calm himself but it bothered him that he seemed to have no say in the future of his team when in all honesty, he *was* the team. He stepped back to the door and put a hand on the handle before pausing. He wasn't ready to face them again, not after that outburst. He eased the door open slightly, just enough to see the projection of a young woman's face. Cam grinned, recognizing the blonde, but his smile faded. As much as the appearance of her face pleased him, he knew she would never be on the team.

Maria didn't recognize the face, but the name felt familiar to her. "Was she a member of the Blue Phoenix?" Her forehead furrowed when Frank acknowledged the fact. "I thought she was part of that scandal last year, with the people sabotaging the AIMs. She was one of them, wasn't she?" Maria always paid attention to athletes who were not as honest as others, knowing that it affected her own career, and her team, whether certain people believed it or not.

Derek, another member of the board, paused as a frown formed on his face. Emily was an amazing athlete and frankly, they needed that now more than they needed honest players. "Yes, she was suspended for a month but that shouldn't affect how she plays."

"To be honest, I think it does affect how she plays," she commented, folding her arms over her chest. "She brought hacked AIMs, reprogrammed and potentially dangerous AIMs, into a challenge in order to hurt and destroy those from other teams. You, of all people, should know that someone who reprograms the computer chips of their AIMs is usually doing it for the wrong reason. She has a black mark, likely part of the Underground, and we don't need that kind of representation right now. I'm surprised she hasn't been black-listed altogether. Bring up the next candidate," Maria said, taking over Rick's role of authority. She usually held her tongue with the board, allowing Owen and sometimes Rick to speak but this was something she knew about. This was something she would never let go.

Derek grumbled under his breath as he flipped to the next candidate, which was no surprise to Cam standing outside. He knew about Emily's suspension, along with another member of her team, and knew exactly the offense they had committed. But he knew they were the only two to get caught, from a much more reliable source than the media. Cam focused his attention on the second candidate: a young man with brown wavy hair wearing a simple smile on his face.

"Ryan Hampton, twenty-one years old and a participant of the KWJST for the past four years." The presenter paused before continuing on to talk about the candidate's statistics. "He placed seventy-fourth last year."

Cam couldn't believe it. *Seventy-fourth?* Out of hundreds and even thousands of people it was considered a respectable finish but for a team like the Revolution, that wasn't going to cut it. A four year run in the Kitchener-Waterloo Junior Scanning Tournament was somewhat impressive, and brought Cam back to when he had been part of it himself. Each region of Canada had its own tournament, filled mostly with amateur athletes but the top three teams of the junior level replaced the bottom three teams from the National Tournament. The only other way a junior level player moved up was to be called up from their trainer team, or be signed on based on stats just as they had done with him, with Maria, and now with this replacement for Owen. For three years he had been one of the best in his region, and now he was one of the best in the country. There was no room to bring someone in who finished seventy-fourth.

"Ryan may not seem like the most qualified to be Owen's replacement," Derek continued, "but he does have four years of experience which I'd like to point out is more than Maria's one year at the junior level," Derek stated, raising an eyebrow at Maria before she could speak. "I should also mention that Ryan placed first in scans last year and placed in the top three in scans the previous three years."

It wasn't overly difficult to obtain points through scanning, but placing first nearly impressed Rick. Most of the newer generation of Scanners did not concentrate so much on the actual scanning aspect of the sport. "How does he place first in scans, but seventy-fourth overall?"

"He scored zero points in the challenge category. He doesn't have an AIM."

Rick and Maria let out an incredulous laugh. "No offense," Rick started, "but I don't think we have the time to train someone to use an AIM, nor should we even have to. We'd probably have to supply him with one as well. But he did stick with the game this long without an AIM. That's pretty impressive."

"He's your only option since we've ruled out Emily," Derek said, and by the sharp tone of his voice was still displeased. "You have two days until the tournament begins, and all other athletes who may be a more appropriate fit for this team have already been signed. I've never agreed with the decision to not keep a trainer team in the Juniors, but I'm not one to say I told you so. I don't want this to be taken the wrong way, but if Owen had had his heart attack sooner, we may have had the time to find the next *Cam Tylar*. But he didn't, and so Ryan is your only option."

"Of all the people in the in the junior level, he's the only option?" Maria asked with disbelief.

"The only one with the same potential we saw in you," he replied, bringing a flush to Maria's face.

Rick spoke after a moment, hating that he was already being thrown into the position of captain before he had officially accepted. "If it's alright, I'd like to step outside with Maria. This team makes decisions together, despite what Cam thinks." He paused. "For the record, we as a team requested Maria."

"We'll give you fifteen minutes," Derek replied, ignoring the snide comment.

When Maria and Rick moved into the hallway, they noticed Cam leaning casually on the wall next to the door as if he hadn't been listening the entire time. They both knew better, of course.

"What do you think?" Rick asked, glancing at his reflection in the long row of windows along the other side of the hall. There did not seem to be much of a decision to make. Emily was out of the question, plain and simple.

"I still think we can do this by ourselves. We're one of the top teams in the CST."

"But we would be short a player. We're only in the top because we've had four people. If another one of us gets hurt for some reason, we'd be stuck."

"So?"

He hovered over that one little word for a minute. He wished he was as confident as Cam, about anything. He didn't enjoy having the future of the team hinge on this one single moment. Where was his dad when he needed him? He realized that Owen had already given him his answer.

"We need to choose a replacement."

"What?" Cam swore. "But we can do it on our own."

"And I agree with you. We are experienced and we have the skill between the three of us to do it. But we would still be short, and you can't deny that would put us at a disadvantage. Besides, this is what my dad wanted. I can't argue with that."

Not knowing what to say, Cam turned to Maria as though the past had been erased and she would stand up for him. But she remained silent. He hesitated a moment before speaking. "I guess we're signing Ryan, then?"

Rick grinned slightly. "Like you said, we don't need anyone helping us with the challenges. We're fine in that department. And he did place tops in the KWJST in scans last year. That has to count for something."

"He's got no AIM," Cam said, throwing up his arms. He leaned back against the wall in defeat, allowing his head to hit the wooden panels. "If you think I'm going to waste my time teaching him how to use it, you have another thing coming."

"Maria and I can deal with that."

"Fine, as long as he doesn't get in my way."

"Okay, good." Rick turned to Maria, happy he had convinced the worst of them. "And what do you think about all of this?"

"Sure. I don't care." Maria's voice was toneless. "As long as it isn't Emily." She hesitated when Cam returned to the room, and kept Rick aside. "What did you mean about requesting me?"

He motioned for her to follow Cam. "It doesn't matter." As Maria passed him, he gently touched her shoulder. "Are you okay?"

"I'm fine. Don't worry about it." Maria gave a small shrug as they headed back into the room.

*   *   *

Rick glanced briefly at Cam as they sat around the table with Ryan later that evening, still unsure about the decision. It was the only one that made sense. They needed a fourth player. They had gone years thinking they were an invincible team and hadn't bothered with a trainer team to call rookie players from as most teams had. They had tried it once at the beginning, but they missed out on too many good athletes that way. It had been easier to sign people from any team they wanted. Well, Cam still thought the team was invincible. But they were here now, with their new team-mate in the same boardroom Cam stormed from earlier that day, and there was no going back.

"…a temporary contract would work best. You'll be on for the entire season, so we won't pull you out in the middle of the season." Derek looked at Rick and Cam before continuing. "I know this sounds obvious, but I'm saying it just to explain what the contract's about. Do you have any questions or concerns?"

The young player looked to his agent for confirmation and nodded slightly. "There's the issue of the AIM, since I don't own one. I was wondering how that would work. I have an AIRC though, in case anyone had been wondering about that."

"We will provide one, as well as an initial chip which we and your team-mates will inspect. Any upgrades or 'extras' beyond the basics will be your responsibility, for now at least. I'm sure your new team-mates can help you out if necessary, but officially it's your responsibility. Is there anything else?"

Ryan shook his head violently with a large grin. "No. I just can't believe you guys want me on your team. You're awesome! I mean…sorry, I'm just really excited."

Rick shot Cam a look when he heard him groan at the new member's enthusiasm, but he was glad that Maria was not there for the meeting. After the explosion earlier, who knew what Cam might do to set her off again. "Well I hope you can keep that attitude throughout the season. If that's all, I guess we're done for today. We'll meet at seven in the morning tomorrow to go over some last minute details before the competition begins. We can meet at Victoria Park, just out of convenience." Rick smiled as he shook Ryan's hand. "Glad you decided to join us. I'm sorry Maria couldn't be here to welcome you to the team as well, but you'll meet her tomorrow."

"I'm glad you decided to have me." Ryan returned the smile and moved to shake Cam's hand, but Rick noticed Cam didn't return the gesture. "I know no one likes the new guy. I don't want you to feel like I'm replacing Owen, because I know that I never could. I just want to be a new part of this team. We'll just have to get through this one day at a time. I'll try my best not to get in your way."

Rick and Derek both looked to Cam, who was silent for a moment. He looked at Rick with a sigh before shaking Ryan's hand. "You better perform as well as you can speak. See you in the morning."

When he and Cam left the office building, Rick patted him on the shoulder. "Cam, I think that's called growth. I'm not going to let you pull this team down. I know you think you're the superstar of this team and you have talent, but you still need the rest of us to win." He ran a hand through his hair, glancing up at the glass buildings around them, suddenly glad he did not live in a city such as Toronto. Their boardroom was corporate enough for him. "Look, this is what my dad thought was best; and you can't argue against that. Just try to work with Ryan, okay? You don't have to like him, but we need to make this work."

Cam shrugged and shoved his hands into his pockets. "Fine."

"Do you need a ride home?" Rick asked.

"No, I'll walk," Cam answered as he turned away and headed down the street in downtown Kitchener.

"Don't be late," Rick called after him and watched as Cam waved at his comment. With a shake of his head, Rick got into his truck and sat there for a moment. They had at least worked out the replacement issue, but he still had other things swimming around in his mind. He started up the truck and headed home for his last night with his family before the tournament officially began.

Cam walked down the street, looking around as people passed him. He should be excited about the competition starting the next day.

This was his thing. This was *his* game. He stopped when he saw a familiar sign coming up on the other side of the street. Quickly looking both ways, Cam crossed the street and entered the bar. A heavily inebriated man stumbled through the door, and Cam stepped aside to let him by. *It's five o-clock somewhere,* he thought to himself as he slid himself onto a stool near the far end of the counter. One more night, and then it would begin. After ordering a drink, Cam glanced up at the television above the counter. He grinned when a picture of his team came up, his team from last year. His grin faded when he remembered the new kid. It would be completely different this year, and without any time to even get together beforehand they were going to an have extremely rough start, especially with all the fighting with Maria. Even he would admit that had been an embarrassment in front of the board.

"Thanks," Cam muttered as the bartender slid him a bottle. He hated to admit it but Owen knew how to put him in his place, whether he liked to go there or not. He almost laughed thinking about Rick being the captain now, at least until his father was better. An entire season with Rick at the helm. "We're doomed." He turned his wrist, bringing the bottle to his lips as he first felt his phone vibrate, then heard its annoyingly bland ring. Seeing the name on the call display, he ignored the call and took another swig of his drink. *And it begins.*

Owen glanced over from his hospital bed and watched Maria fill in another word on her crossword puzzle. He reached for the remote on the TV, turning it up slightly to hear the sportscaster announce the addition of the new player to the Revolution.

"It comes as a little bit of a surprise that Revolution decided to go with a player like this to replace Warner. With a score of zero in challenges over the last four years in the KWJST, Ryan Hampton can't be much of a help to their team," the young man sitting at the sports desk pronounced.

"I'm going to disagree with you. Even without Warner, this team has always been strong in the competitions, despite tensions which seem to hinder other teams. No, if anything, Hampton will

likely be a fresh addition to this team, and it should give him the boost he needs to go pro."

Maria glanced up from her crossword when she heard the television click off. "I thought you enjoyed watching that." She closed her puzzle book and looked at her phone quickly before putting it back into her coat pocket.

"I guess this means the meeting went well. I forgot how quickly news travelled about these things. It's been a while since we've had to deal with our team getting a new player. Remember when you joined the team, just a little lass of nineteen?"

Maria laughed and threw her book at him. "Yes, I remember the embarrassment of joining this team. I never was one for the spotlight like Cam, who definitely did not make my life easy."

"You've handled the media spotlight better than he ever has." Owen nodded again towards her. "Did you hear from Rick?"

"He said he'd be over after dinner with Brittany. I said I'd watch Adam for them while they're here." She stood up to take the book back from Owen, but simply stood at the side of his bed. "I really am glad you're okay, Owen."

"I know." He looked up with an understanding smile and held out a hand to her, which she took gratefully. Three years and she was already like a daughter to him.

She stood at the side of the bed for another moment before returning to her chair, releasing his hand. "A lot is going to be different this year. I honestly don't know how Rick's going to handle it, especially with him worrying about you all the time, and him trying to deal with everything between me and Cam…"

"And of course there's nothing different with you."

Maria smiled. "Of course. I'm perfect and unchanging."

"Which is why you've had such a temper, even in front of the board."

Her smile disappeared as her eyes widened. "How…?"

"Remember, news like this travels fast." He paused. "Rick called before you came by." Maria turned away and ran a hand through her hair, using the same hand to prop her head. "What's going on with you? It's been a month now, hasn't it? I thought things were okay."

"There's just been a lot going on with the team and it's been getting to me. You should be resting," she answered quickly, trying to put an end to the topic.

"Maria?"

"I'm fine. Rest. Brittany and Rick should be here soon."

CHAPTER 4

"Ryan! You're going to be late!"

The newest member of Revolution grinned as he met his mother in the farmhouse kitchen, but the grin turned into a look of confusion when he saw the kitchen table filled with bags of food. "Mom, today's just the opening ceremonies."

"People get hungry at all kinds of events," she protested as she continued to cook yet another dish on the stove.

He laughed and turned the burner off before he pulled her away. "I'm not even leaving town yet. The first challenge for our region isn't for a few days. I gave you and Dad a copy of my schedule, remember?"

"Ryan!"

He spun around in time to catch a young girl in his arms as she hurled herself at him. "Seriously, guys, I'm not leaving yet," he said with a laugh.

"I can't believe you're on Revolution! You're the coolest brother ever! What are they like? Can I meet them?" Her bright green eyes shone up at him with awe.

"We didn't really have much of a conversation last night. Maria wasn't even there." He looked back to his mother and smacked her hand gently away from the saucepan on the stove. "I'll tell you all about it when I get back," he suggested to his sister as he set her back on the ground. "What do you think of that plan?" Ryan grabbed his pack from a chair when the girl finally nodded with a pout. He kissed his mother quickly on the cheek. Ryan paused, eyeing a plate of cheese and popped a slice in his mouth with a grin. "I'll see you guys later. Stop cooking, would you?"

He pulled his truck into a parking spot next to another just as Cam and Rick were stepping from it. *Alright, this is just like any other day. Just pretend you've always known them...and don't make a fool of yourself. You're an athlete, not a fan. You're an athlete...* He let out a sigh and greeted his two team-mates with a grin. "Good morning!"

Rick smiled. "Hey! Good to see you're a punctual guy. I have something for you." He handed a small container to Ryan. "Your first AIM."

The young man paused as he looked at the container. He knew he must look like an idiot already, staring at the silver box, but he had waited a long time for this moment. Most people were kids when they received their first AIM. Usually it was as a birthday or Christmas present, or any other holiday. Usually they got it from a special person in their family. But Ryan was twenty-one, and was getting his first AIM from his CST captain. It was a small container, but it meant a lot. He opened it slowly and examined the white-ish substance inside.

"There's already a chip implanted in it. Your AIRC should detect it automatically," Rick commented as Ryan picked the gel-like substance up out of the container and set it on the ground. "There's no memory on it yet, which you would've gotten after years of working with your AIM. But we can get it up to our rank with some training."

"Have you heard from Maria? She's late. She's never late," Cam spoke finally, pacing around the wooden park bench.

Waiting around and doing nothing was not how any of them wanted to start the first day of the competition. At least the park was nice. There were open grassy areas and a small creek flowing through it somewhere on the other side away from the parking lot. Rick and Cam knew where all of the fowl nests were along the river, but scanning them would be pointless until the tournament officially began. That would come in just a few hours. In the meantime, they had to wait.

"No, I haven't," Rick replied as he sat down on the bench while Ryan busied himself with the AIRC as it synced with the AIM. He leaned back with his arms spread out across the back of the bench, listening to the wind through the trees. One of the things he loved about his job was being able to be outside nearly all the time. "She'll be here. She didn't have a great day yesterday."

"Does she ever have a good day?" Cam muttered, earning a sharp look from Rick.

Ryan raised an eyebrow. "What happened?" He glanced away. "Was it me?"

"Don't flatter yourself," Cam replied. "We're all just under a lot of stress right now. It's still weird that she's late."

"Well, we might as well get started," Rick stated, turning to Ryan. "Maria doesn't need to learn how to use an AIM, but you do. Okay, so…" His voice trailed off when a faint voice could be heard from the parking lot.

"No…no, I don't care…yes, I know I'm a horrible daughter."

The three looked across the park and saw Maria pacing back and forth. Cam couldn't help but grin. "Three guesses who she's on the phone with. If she had a bad day yesterday…"

"No, I'm not going to come…why? Well maybe because you just told me about it…I'm sorry I have a life…the CST starts today…oh my God mom, don't start on me for not going to college. It was either this or follow dad in the Army and you know it. University was never the plan." Maria's voice rang clear with anger across the park, despite the distance. "I'm sorry I don't think your fourth wedding in two years is significant in any way. By the way, I love your version of a formal invite: a phone call at five in the morning when you're just getting home from the bar. You know what Mom, go to hell. Have a nice life."

The three looked over at Maria and watched her throw her phone, then hold her head in her hands as she sat down on the bench. Rick looked to Cam, who sighed and sat down. The waiting would continue.

Ryan watched as the two simply sat and waited, showing little concern for how long it would take despite complaining that she had been late. He may have been new to the team, but was this how they treated each other? He shook his head and made his way over to where he had seen Maria's phone land. He stood in front of Maria for a brief moment before he sat down next to her, holding out the phone.

"You're probably going to need this." After a minute he added, "She's going to find your new number anyway, so you might as well save the hassle of buying a new phone. I'm just assuming, of course."

Maria glanced at Ryan and took her phone from him. "Thanks." She wiped her face, embarrassed for the second time in two days. "I'm sorry you have to meet me this way. I'm usually pretty good with first impressions."

"Oh no, that was perfect, actually. The whole yelling thing is good. It means you have a strong voice."

She laughed. "After being on a team with three males, it's pretty much a necessity to be good at yelling."

"My hearing's fine, for the record."

"Flirting already?"

"If introducing myself is flirting, I've been doing something wrong." Ryan held out his hand, introducing himself.

Maria took his hand and shook it. "Maria."

He glanced back at the others still waiting. "They seem…different than what I was expecting. Is it always like this?"

"What? Tense and awkward?" Maria laughed, wiping away some rogue tears. "Pretty much."

He looked her over discretely. Seeing someone in person was much different than staring at an image on the TV screen. He averted his gaze quickly when Maria caught him staring.

"So," Maria started. "I hear you have an impressive history in the KWJST," she said as they began to make their way to the other men. "First in scans is pretty impressive, even if you've never competed in a challenge it's still impressive."

Ryan could only blush in response.

Maria held up her hands to stop Cam or Rick from speaking as they got closer. "I'm sorry I'm late. I hope you guys got something done. Did you give Ryan his AIM at least?"

"I was just about to show him some basic commands. Come on, then," Rick said to Ryan as he led him over to a group of ducks they would be able to scan.

He had forgotten what it was like to use an AIM for the first time. He remembered when the fad had come to Canada and how excited he had been to get his first AIM, even though he was eighteen at the time. Rick could see that excitement in Ryan. A part of him nearly resented having to teach him, but they had the time, and it was refreshing to have the enthusiasm on the team once again.

Maria, meanwhile, opened her bag and pulled out what looked similar to a cell phone. She flipped her hair back, putting it into a ponytail. Strands quickly fell to frame her thin face.

"Have a nice chat with your mom?"

"Don't."

"It sounded pleasant. And she's getting married again? That's nice. At least she found someone to make her happy." Cam grinned. He may not have enjoyed the fighting with her the day before, or ever, but it sure felt good to push her buttons now.

She stood up as she grabbed her AIRC. "Look, we're team-mates. Yesterday was yesterday. The competition starts today, so let's just be team-mates, alright?"

"Wouldn't have it any other way."

"Fine."

Cam looked over at Rick and Ryan, noticing a German shepherd sitting on the ground next to Ryan. There was no way that Ryan would be useful in the challenges, despite his background and experience at scanning. Wasn't the KWJST meant to give athletes the experience they needed to be a participant in the national tournament? He looked back at Maria and saw her leaning with her hands against her thighs with her eyes squeezed shut. "It's the first day. You can't bail on us already."

Maria took a deep breath before standing up straight and opening her eyes. "I'm fine. Talking to my mother always makes me feel sick."

"You sure?"

"I'm fine. Thanks for at least pretending to care."

Cam smiled proudly. "It's what I do best."

"Then could you pretend to care about the team and get along with Ryan? He seems like a good guy." She watched as he started to walk away without giving a reply and followed close behind, grabbing her bag as she went.

She looked up as a small bird flew above her. She walked past Cam and stood next to Rick, kneeling down to pet the German shepherd, smiling at the sight of the red blinking light, which signified it as an AIM, located on the underside of its neck. It appeared to be a small innovation – one overlooked in the early stages of the robot's development – but, nevertheless, the importance of distinguishing between real animals and AIMs was learned very early on in the production of the AIMs.

"Do you have any questions?" Rick asked Ryan, who watched another small bird flitted around his head.

"Chickadee-dee-dee!" the small bird chirped.

"Not right now. Probably as I use it more I will; seems pretty straight-forward. I'm sure I'm going to need help during actual challenges." Ryan could not restrain the large grin building up as he tested different things with his AIM through his AIRC. It looked similar to the one which Maria had slipped into her pocket, but over the years, Maria and her team-mates had upgraded their consoles: a necessity at their level of the competition. "This is amazing. I'm not just using it for a catalogue, anymore."

"Have you never even looked at the other functions?" Cam asked, slipping a pair of sunglasses on as the sun began to shine brighter in the later part of the morning.

Ryan shrugged. "Not really. I never had to, I mean, other than being in the KWJST. I wouldn't mind some help though. With your kind of stats, you must know shortcuts on this thing, like how to make things run smoother."

"Excuse me?" Cam asked.

"I'm just saying that you're probably the best person to show me the ropes. No offense to you other guys, but I've been watching you guys as a team for years and Cam is one of the quickest people I've seen using his AIRC and working with his AIM. Even though Rick's been at it longer, Cam has better personal stats."

"First of all, I don't work with my AIM, I control it." Cam folded his arms across his chest and glanced away. "But I might as well. Besides, I really am the best person to ask. We have time now before everything starts." Cam waved at Rick as if to show his acquiescence as he took Ryan's AIRC from his hands.

Maria looked up at Rick as Cam held Ryan's full attention. "So, how are you?"

"What do you mean?" he asked as they both sat down on the mostly-dry grass. It was still early spring, but the weather had been unseasonably warm and the snow had been gone since early February. The weekly rainstorms kept the field moderately damp.

"Your dad's in the hospital, which is one of the worst feelings in the world. And now you're captain. That's a lot to take in, and I know you, Rick. You get stressed easily, and you're going to constantly worry about your dad." She smiled softly. "I know what you're going through, and it's not easy. So, I'll ask you again. How are you? And don't give me the usual 'I'm fine' crap either."

Rick looked down at the ground as the AIM dropped the stick while prancing around it. It looked slightly awkward as it did so, doing something that was not natural for it. Not that there was anything natural about an AIM. He threw the stick and looked at Maria. "Tired. Worried, about a lot of things. Maria, I'm not a captain. My dad's the captain."

"You were always on the same level as Owen," she replied. "He always treated you like a co-captain. You'll be fine."

He shrugged. "And Brittany. We were talking about trying to have another baby but there's no way we could handle that right now. She's been great with my dad and I appreciate her so much. She's been helping my mom a lot too, but I know she's disappointed. I feel a little guilty about that, actually. I mean, yeah, I want to try again but...I don't know what I'm even saying. We got lucky with Adam. I don't know if I could handle another kid, but I know Brittany's already looking forward to it." He had long tuned out Cam speaking with Ryan only a few steps away, but he watched their faces. Both had an unusual stress written in lines on their faces, each for their own reasons. They were all the same in that fact.

Maria leaned back a bit on the grass. "Women feel like a mom the minute they find out they're pregnant, or if they think there's a chance. Men don't feel like a dad until they hold their baby in their arms, or find out they never will. Don't feel guilty about not being sure. You're a normal man, at least in that regard," she added with a wry smile, her hazel eyes twinkling with sarcasm.

He rolled his eyes at the comment and looked around, but he took the first part of her speech to heart. Just beyond Cam and Ryan, Rick noticed a small crowd of people beginning to form in the ceremony area. "I saw on the internet that AI protesters are joining with the Animal Rights Activists this year. I'm surprised there aren't any cops here yet, after the riot last year." He shook his head, remembering past years before the police had become involved. He glanced at Maria and remembered when she had joined the team. Usually, the participants kept their distance from the angry crowds, but that only seemed to make them angrier. He learned quickly that Maria was not the type of person to back down, and she was always the first to retaliate against the protesters, professionally, of course. Her tact with the media had always impressed him.

He winced as he remembered the rocks thrown at him and other athletes the year before while they were on a challenge, the chants they shouted, and the challenges they had tried to sabotage. No one had been seriously hurt, but Rick knew some who still carried scars from where they had been hit. And that had been a small group of protesters. If AI advocates were coming out this year, they would really have to be careful. With all of the research being put into the 'feelings' of artificial intelligence, the advocates felt they had more evidence and more justification to protest against Scanning. Why they did not think to protest at the manufacturer's headquarters, the McCarthy Company in Boston, was beyond them.

Maria peered over to Cam, watching him with Ryan. "We're going to have to keep an eye on Cam more than usual this year. With the extra protesters, we're going to have extra media all over. I'll even try to tone it down. I haven't looked into AI research enough to have anything to yell back at them, anyway. We should keep an eye on the new guy, too. He's new to all of this and we don't know how he'll be with the public eye on him." She paused when she heard Cam yell at Ryan, his words accompanied by some innovative cursing. "He's still angry from yesterday."

"No, well maybe, but I think he just feels threatened." He shrugged when she gave him a questioning look. "Think about it. We signed this guy despite his lack of experience in challenges. He's good. Cam's just trying to figure out if he's a threat. If he's a fast learner with the AIRC, Ryan could potentially learn to be better than Cam." Rick grinned. "Can you expect Cam to really like that idea? You love water challenges, and he doesn't do them. That made you a threat. And it was pretty hard to ignore the fact that you're pretty awesome at taking risks to get the challenge done. That made you pretty close to his level, even without the years of training he had. He warmed up to you pretty quickly, so I can't see him disliking Ryan for too long."

"Cam and I met before I was signed," she reminded him as she took a quick drink from her water bottle. "And he warmed up to me for a completely different reason. At least we know that he'll be able to put on a good show for the media, and make it look like we're a well-oiled machine. If we show any signs of a fracture or tension in front of the other teams, they're going to attack us. We've been through it before and it wasn't fun, or easy. Maybe this year will be different. A lot's changed."

"I like your optimism, Maria. Have I ever told you that?"

Maria laughed and smacked Rick's leg. "Oh shut up. I can always dream."

Rick grinned as he whistled to his team-mates. "We should get going to the main area. Ryan, I guess now's the time to warn you about some things in the CST. I'm sure you've seen protesters on TV before, but the media usually plays it down. I just want you to be prepared. They'll start early, and usually they try guilt tactics and throw out some false facts to throw us off. Thankfully, Maria's pretty good at fighting for this team. Cam, you need to try to stay out of the spotlight for the first while until things calm down."

"People come to our challenges for *me*. You really think I'm going to turn down interviews?" Cam retorted angrily.

"I meant to stay away from stray reporters, like the ones at the hospital." Rick gave him a look of warning and nodded when Cam remained silent. "Ryan, you can come with me to scan in. It's a good chance to meet some of the officials while they're not too busy." He walked away, resisting the urge to look over his shoulder every minute to check on Maria and Cam. They did not need a public outburst. Not this season.

"You're a prick, you know that?"

Cam peered at Maria through his sunglasses. "What happened to 'today we're team-mates'?"

"You're an irritating team-mate."

"I try to make this team look good."

"You try to make yourself look good."

"Well, I am the star contributor of this team, according to Sportcentre." Cam grinned proudly when Maria finally looked at him. "Their words, not mine, but I couldn't have said it better myself."

"If I remember correctly, they called the team well-rounded and then listed all of our names."

"Just a slip up."

"Shut up. I'm amazing." Her eyes darted to him and saw his grin falter, then reappear, when he saw her blushing – something she hardly ever did. "Shut up."

"Didn't say a word." Cam turned around, grin still intact as they headed off after Rick and Ryan. Looking over his shoulder, he saw the crowd of protesters grow and creep slowly towards the main event area. As much as he liked attention, he could not stand protesters, and he had always stayed away from them. Or at least tried to. It had been hard the year before, when the protesters had attempted to cut the ropes they had been using to climb during a challenge. Fortunately, CST security had gotten there in time to stop them.

Maria stayed silent as she walked next to Cam, walking dangerously close to a group of protesters holding signs. She read some of them, having to squint to concentrate on the bobbing posters. 'Free the AIMs!' 'AIMS are animals!' 'Stop AIM cruelty!' And then her eyes stopped on one sign. 'AIMs are slaves! Stop the slavery!' She took a few steps away from Cam to hear what the woman holding the sign was saying when she realized that she was talking to a news reporter.

"...terrible! Scientists are doing studies on the emotions of AIMs and they're proving that they do in fact have emotions and can feel pain. One even started to cry, which shows that they have free will. The CST is promoting slavery and animal abuse and I'm ashamed to live in a country that allows this. CST-like tournaments are banned in ten countries exactly for this reason!" the woman yelled into the reporter's microphone.

Maria felt her face flush with anger as she stormed toward the woman and away from the safety of her team-mate, almost forgetting to make sure none of the protesters had weapons. She knew from experience that it was a possible danger. But with a soldier for a father, she had become accustomed to war.

The woman continued, "The 'players' are simply cruel. They keep their AIMs locked up in a box when they don't need them, then work them tirelessly."

"First of all," Maria started as she got close enough. "Tournaments aren't banned because of that. There were some bans in other countries yes, but only due to environmental and economic concerns which a tournament would pose. Second, athletes keep AIMs in an animal form constantly so that we can train. When we're travelling, they're in a small enough form that they can be with us in our vehicles. The only time they're not in an animal form, is when we're on an airplane since they're still seen as pets and we don't want them to be damaged in the cargo hold. Third, AIMs are called artificial for a reason. They have no feelings, no pain receptors, and no emotions. Anything they react to is simulated. If you press a button on your computer, it'll respond appropriately. It's not real," she proclaimed passionately.

"When they started the initial research at the university in Israel, they created a chip that would only control motor skills and would not act as the part of the brain which controls emotions and pain reactors. While I admit that some seem to exhibit signs of free will, it's not. It's programmed to appear that way. Yes, chips exist in which free will is being explored, but they are banned from the CST because of issues exactly like the ones you're bringing up."

Cam grew pale and swore, realizing that he had lost Maria on his way to his team-mates. He made his way back over to her and tugged at her arm when he heard her mentioning AIMs and free will. "Maria, c'mon." That was not a good topic to bring up on TV, and they both knew it.

"Free will AIMs are a black product of the Underground and are banned. If a CST athlete is found to be using a hacked or re-programmed chip, they're suspended, and usually black-listed from competing." Maria was trying to sound professional, but more anger than professionalism was showing through. She ignored Cam and the other reporters making their way over to her.

"But people in the CST have been known to be part of the Underground and are still competing. How do you explain that?"

"That's usually because the person wasn't directly affiliated with the Underground, and it's difficult to prove whether or not an athlete is working in the Underground," she responded and felt Cam's grip tighten on her arm as a warning. She did not need the warning though, and he knew that. But it had made him feel better all the same.

"And you're telling me you don't know anyone in the Underground?"

"If I did, I would try to get them out of it," she answered quickly. "I would do whatever it took, even if it hurt them, because it's a disgrace and I wouldn't want anyone I care about getting into trouble and lose their career. I would gladly support you and the other protestors on the issue of the Underground. But know that any pain shown by an AIM is simulated. I'm all for animals, which is why I joined the CST. With the way the world is now, it's much easier to have a life and a pet through an AIM. Before, if a family had to move, they would put their pet down because they couldn't take the animal with them. AIMs can travel anywhere. And very few people are actually allergic to them in their animal form, because they don't give off dander. Maybe you guys should look at the benefits before focusing on the perceived negatives."

She finally let Cam pull her away from the crowd which had gone eerily quiet. No one had expected anyone to be able to rebut the woman's remarks. They had never seen Maria on TV in interviews before, it seemed. As they walked away, there was only the sound of the clicking of photographers with their cameras.

Maria glanced up at Cam, who was strategically keeping his eyes away from her. "They get me angry sometimes."

"Sometimes? You know they can throw things worse, and harder, than petty insults."

Maria thought for a moment. "Are they slaves?"

He shook his head but did not answer immediately. "They're robots."

"Are they? I wonder sometimes."

They were silent for a moment before Cam stopped Maria, putting a hand on her shoulder to turn her back to face him.

"I meant what I said, and that's all I'm going to say about it."

"Fine." Cam followed behind her, but sighed and grabbed her arm again. "Maria."

"Don't, okay? I know you're not going to say what I want to hear, so just…don't say anything."

"Are we ever going to talk about it?"

"If we do, this isn't the place to have that conversation." Maria gently pulled her arm away once more before she headed back to the rest of their team with Cam following closely behind.

CHAPTER 5

Rick smiled politely as one of the Waterloo Region officials excused himself. He turned to Ryan and studied him. He seemed to be composed, at least for now. Either that or he was too awestruck to do or say anything embarrassing. He could relate to Ryan's feelings. It was his first time being in the official captain position. He was the one who had to register at the main kiosk and scan his own AIRC at the computer to officially begin the season with his team.

"Well, I guess those are the only people you need to meet," he said to Ryan. "You'll probably see them again at the month end challenge in Toronto. Most of the officials for each province try to make an appearance and since this is the tenth anniversary, I can't see them changing that this year. If you ever need anything we can't give you as a team, those are the people you'll want to talk to. Paul, the first guy you met, he's always the first to know when a team is looking to sign a new player. Not in our case, of course." He grinned. "We surprised everyone by signing you. You're going to have to hold up your end of the bargain and surprise everyone with your skills."

Ryan glanced away. "Is three days enough time to train properly? I mean, I've always tried to be physically fit, but that doesn't mean I'm CST fit. If that makes sense."

"Don't worry about it," he replied as he led him away from the pavilion. "You probably won't even participate in a challenge for a while. You'll have plenty of time to train, and if Cam has anything to do with it, you'll be fit enough within a few weeks." He laughed. "Actually, get Maria to train you into shape. She's pretty intense, but it works."

He grimaced. Did they even need him? The fourth was always an extra member, but Ryan had always seen all the members of Revolution work together, and work equally. He was new, and they were all going to have to adjust.

When Ryan hesitated in responding, Rick continued. "Maria's first challenge was the month end, and did we ever hear about it. She almost quit. Had to talk her out of it myself. But it's what we do. The new player usually just sits on the sidelines for a while to get used to the team dynamics. We'll all still train together when it's not a challenge day, and that'll give you the experience you need. As long as you don't threaten to quit because of it, we'll be fine."

Ryan had to laugh at that. "I don't think I'm as outspoken, or confident as Maria. She's good. She didn't have much experience in the junior level, but she at least had some experience with challenges when she joined."

"You looked up her history?"

He shrugged. "I've been watching the CST for years. Everyone has their favourite team." He paused, and wondered if Rick even had a favourite team. He did not have the chance as a child to pick a favourite team, unless he had watched the American Scanning Tournament. This sport, this lifestyle, it was still so new but it was already so ingrained in their culture that Ryan had not even thought about the people who started everything. "I guess this team is your favourite."

The captain grinned. "Actually, there's a team in Vancouver I don't mind watching. We've never really met up because they're in a different region, but they're pretty unique. They always get top rank in scans because they go after the really strange animals. I hear that this year they're going to try to find Sasquatch or something. Just because I'm on a team, doesn't mean I can't watch others. At least I don't always watch myself on TV."

"I think I'd be afraid to. I don't want it going to my head like-" He stopped himself short, embarrassed.

"Like Cam." He gave him a reassuring smile. "You don't have to be ashamed about that. He's a great athlete, sure, but he has his issue. I don't think you have to worry about becoming like him." Rick stopped and looked back across the field when he heard a commotion near the gathering of protestors. Within moments, he could see Maria approaching from that direction, with Cam close behind her. "And honestly, I'm thankful you're not as out-spoken as Maria," he muttered as the other two finally reached them. "You're not supposed to interact with them alone, you know that."

Maria shrugged it off. "Cam was with me, for part of it. I couldn't let that woman trash the CST with false information."

"We just had a conversation about this, Maria. You know how dangerous they can get."

"I don't think that old woman was much of a threat. I was fine. You know I can take care of myself."

"That's not the point, Maria." Rick stopped, realizing he had raised his voice. "You know the dangers, especially going off on your own. I don't care if there were cameras and reporters around, and I don't care what your background is. You're not doing that again, is that clear?" He nodded his approval when Maria muttered her understanding. "Maybe we're going to have to keep an eye on you, and not Cam."

"Could all participating teams from the Southern Ontario division please make their way to the seating area. Again, could all par..." an announcer announced, drowned out at the end by the teams talking amongst each other as they moved into their respective areas. They had shown up seemingly from no-where while Revolution had found ways to occupy their time.

Rick looked around as they made their way to their seats, giving Maria another look of warning before he sat. He recognized the teams sitting nearby and noticed a few new faces, which happened every year on the national scale, but not so much in their region. He turned back to the front as an older man appeared on the low, metal stage.

The length of the ceremony had been increased to mark the anniversary and Ryan, for one, was soaking in everything he could: the speeches about the origins of the CST and retired players giving speeches about their experiences in the 'early years' which really weren't that long ago. He glanced over at Rick and wondered how Rick was handling his first season without his father. His head snapped back to the front as he realized the team spotlights had already begun which increased his nervousness. He looked over at Cam and saw him grinning, which put him at ease. At least he was not the only one excited for the spotlights to begin.

"The Raiders." the announcer spoke, after which Ryan saw Cam and Maria exchange a look before glancing over to Rick with a shake of their heads. Ryan knew rivalries between teams existed, but it was not as noticeable in the CST as it was in other sports. Any animosity between the teams had been hidden from Ryan, unless he had been completely oblivious.

"Revolution."

Ryan's head spun to the sound of loud cheers and applause. He quickly stood when he noticed his team-mates were already standing. He tried to ignore the TV cameras pointed at him and the pictures being taken. *Just keep calm.* Rick and Maria were smiling politely, waiting for the cameras to be finished. Cam, however, was a completely different person: grinning wildly, waving a bit, and making sure to look at every camera and reporter possible. It was at that moment that he realized that he was on the only team from this region that was continuously in the top ten in the CST, and just how large a fan base they had. He was going to have to become accustomed to the media. He had managed to stay away from local reporters in the junior division, but this was so much more. Everything he was used to, well, he was going to have to change it all again.

"The Rising Suns," the announcer continued, cueing the teams to switch. Cam always hated how short the time his team actually had to stand and be recognized. It seemed like every other team got double the amount of time. They were one of the top teams. They deserved better.

Maria looked around at the other teams and noticed the same look she had on the faces of other athletes: they were ready for the tedious ceremony to end and the season to begin. Her eyes stopped on the captain of the Raiders for a moment. He was dancing in his seat, similar to Cam, his grin just as wide. The two were so similar, yet so different in many areas. Important areas. She realized that he was looking back at her with a smile before she saw his eyes slide towards Cam. His smile turned into a sneer as he turned away. This was going to be an interesting season.

"I'd like to thank you all for joining us. I congratulate new and old players alike for starting yet another season. Thank you, and good luck!"

"So this is it? It's officially started?" Ryan asked, taking a deep breath to calm himself.

"Well, scans don't count for another three hours and challenges don't start until tomorrow. But yeah, this is it," Maria replied. She gave him a slap on the shoulder before rising from her seat. "Get some practice in, Ryan. You're going to need it. Anyone need a ride home?" She glanced to Cam quickly but shook her head as if to retract the offer. "I'll see you guys in a few days."

Ryan watched as Maria and his captain walked away, heads leaning together as they spoke. He looked over to Cam with a sheepish smile as he shrugged. "I know you and Rick already kind of showed me how to do some stuff with the AIRC, and I get all of that. I guess, well I never really had an AIM, even when I was younger. My family's old fashioned and they still believe in having real animals. Both sets of my grandparents are farmers, and made their living from real animals. When AIMs were created, my dad was dead-set against any of us having one. He thinks the whole thing is corrupt, and a danger to society." He laughed lightly. "Guess that comes with coming from a small town."

"There's nothing wrong with real animals, or coming from a small town. I lived on a farm until I was seven." Cam glanced around as the field slowly cleared of people, officials already taking down the stage which had been erected just that morning. "It's why AIMs were created in the first place, to work with real animals. Do I really need to start from the beginning?" He eyed the rookie when he shrugged. "The fundamentals are simple. It's going to take some time to get to know your AIM, but everyone goes through that."

Ryan pulled his AIRC from his pocket and looked at it, examining the boxy console in his hands which looked quite different from the sleek ones he had seen Maria and Cam use. "I guess I should get a newer version."

"Eventually," Cam agreed. "The type of AIRC you have doesn't slow the connection between the AIM, but it has less memory for scans, which you should know, and doesn't always work well in a team setting. We need to be able to have GPS and Wi-Fi at all times to work together, and communicate." As much as he hated the idea of a rookie, Cam did not mind being able to show off his knowledge of the game or the AIMs. It would be good practice for him once he eventually retired and became a coach, his only retirement plan so far.

"Okay, well, treat me like I've never worked with an AIM before, which isn't too far from the truth," Ryan requested, holding his AIRC carefully.

Cam rolled his eyes but grinned. Good practice for teaching toddlers. "Easiest way to start is to think of the AIM as a real animal, as much as I hate to say it. The substance it's made from deteriorates, but obviously much slower than flesh. The biological component of it allows that, and in some ways it's the biggest flaw of the AIMs, but there's nothing *they're* willing to do about it," he said with a slight twinge of anger. "Because it deteriorates, you can't just abuse the AIM. If you tell it to jump off a cliff, it's going to get damaged."

"Guess that's why the protestors think they're real animals," Ryan interjected thoughtfully.

"Right, but we know they're not because real animals aren't controlled with an AIRC. *Imagine that.* Since the AIMs are just a copy of an animal, they need to be trained to act like a particular animal. That's the biggest downside to just getting your first AIM: it doesn't have any memory. I've had mine since I was six, so it has quite a bit of memory to work with."

"So I have to teach a bird to fly, and a fish to swim?"

"Essentially. But, thankfully you have a super star as your trainer, so I'll help you out." Cam flashed the charming smile he reserved for interviews before he got back to business. "Each AIM will react differently to commands and the AIRC. None of them are perfect, and each has their own little quirk, so you have to look out for that. No matter how they're initially programmed, something's bound to go wrong."

Ryan was quiet for a moment as he stared at the small bird resting on the ground next to his feet. "Does it freeze?"

"In the cold? No. It'll get slower because of the biological element in it, but no it won't freeze."

The rookie shook his head. "No. I mean, it's essentially a computer, right? Computers can freeze. Do they ever get stuck in a single animal form? How would you reset it?"

Cam's face turned to stone, and his hands gripped his AIRC tightly. He glanced around; his eyes narrowed when he noticed The Raiders still mingling in the field. "Just make sure you keep changing your AIM every so often in the off season and you'll be fine." He looked back to Ryan and when he saw the confused look on his face, he shook his head as if to get rid of his team-mate's confusion. "Please tell me I don't have to explain the rules of the sport to you. You've been in the junior division long enough to at least know that, right? You've been alive long enough, right?"

At that, Ryan seemed to perk up, which told Cam that the rookie was nervous about using an AIM for the first time, and not about the challenges. He better be nervous, working on a team as good as Revolution. "I know all the scanning component of the rules, of course, at least for the juniors. Is it much different? I...I never really paid much attention to many of the challenges. I never needed to."

He shook his head. "Nah. Still have the same basics ones, like you can't scan the same animal more than once within twenty four hours, and you can't scan an animal that belongs to someone unless you have permission or a deal worked out with the person. All scans made before the opening ceremonies can't be used during the tournament."

"That's a new one."

Cam nodded after a minute. "Yeah, well technically that rule's in the juniors, too, but you never used your scans in challenges. Some challenges have even more rules about which scans you can use. Sometimes they're specie specific, so you're screwed if you don't have the right kind of scan." He looked over to Ryan, and figured he looked as though he needed to write everything down. "Why don't you go home? We can get together tomorrow, get some scans, and I can show you how to train your AIM."

"I really appreciate all of this, Cam," Ryan said as the two walked towards the parking lot. "I know you'd rather not waste your time on this, and I know you didn't even want to have a fourth this season. But I appreciate this."

"It passes the time."

As Ryan got to his truck, he paused and faced the star. "Can I ask, what's the deal with Maria? I mean, I've watched you guys on TV for years. You all always look so intense and awesome, but you guys barely said anything to each other."

"It's been an eventful off season. Everyone's a little off their game right now. We just...we all have to learn how to work as a team again."

"You need a ride?"

Cam realized he had arrived with Rick and he swore. "My ex has the car today. I don't live far. Don't worry about it. Get some rest to get ready for more training tomorrow." He started to walk away but turned around with a grin. "Just so you know, we train for the entire off season to be ready for the challenges, and you're only going to have a few days to train. Think about that as you try to fall asleep tonight." He grinned to himself when he saw Ryan's face pale. He had exceeded everyone's expectations for being friendly, but he had to get at least one shot in.

And he was going to need to get his car back. Eventually.

CHAPTER 6

Rick pulled to a stop behind a truck in the long driveway which led to a farmhouse. It was painted a light green with a wrap-around porch; unique in an area of traditional farmhouses, and Rick liked that. Stepping out, he noticed a middle aged man coming from around the house.

The man looked Rick over with a furrowed brow. "Can I help you?"

"I'm here to pick up Ryan. Do I have the right house?"

"He's inside."

Rick nodded and started for the door, fully aware that the man was following him with his eyes. Before he had the chance to knock, the door was flung open and two young boys showed themselves at the door.

"It's Rick Warner!" one yelled with excitement.

"You're awesome! I can't believe you're here!" the other yelled, attempting to push his brother away.

Rick took a step back and glanced behind them into the house. "Is Ryan around?"

"Yeah! I'll go get him!"

"No! I'll do it!"

He watched the second boy push his brother into the wall before he ran off, just as Ryan came out from a different room. "I'm glad I only have one brother." He laughed as the two shook hands in greeting.

"Those are only two of my brothers. I have another one running around somewhere. My two sisters are at a sleepover." Ryan grinned at Rick's shocked expression. "After I was born, my parents waited a while to have more. I was enough to handle for a while. Just give me a second. I have another bag upstairs. Come on in. Mom! Gather the troops!" he called out as he bound up the wooden staircase.

"Kids! Your brother's leaving! Where's your father?" an older woman called as she came out from the kitchen, drying her hands on a tea towel. "Well, you must be Rick." She smiled as she held out a hand.

"Pleasure to meet you," he said as they shook hands. "I think I saw your husband outside."

She nodded and looked out the window in the front door. "Sorry about that. We've always supported all of our children in everything they do. We've always supported Ryan's love of Scanning, or tried to, at least. Ryan and his father are close, and it's hard to think of him leaving."

"We're able to come back pretty often. I don't think I'd be able to have a family if we didn't."

Ryan's mother grinned, putting a hand to her chest. "Oh! You have a family! That's wonderful!" She looked down as her three youngest sons came running towards them. Two of them held onto a piece of paper. "Ryan's not the only one who enjoys the CST. Would you mind?"

Rick laughed and knelt down. "Of course not." He took one of the papers, now that the two boys seemed to be much calmer. "You know, you can get your brother to sign this. He's going to be famous too, and you're going to be able to tell all the other kids at school that your brother is Ryan Hampton." He grinned and looked to Ryan's third brother who looked older than the other two, but obviously younger than Ryan. "You're not a fan?"

"I find the idea of Artificial Intelligence Morphers quite interesting, especially when looking at the evolution of the initial research conducted in Israel," the pre-teen stated simply. "I find it ironic that a sport evolved from an experiment in which the motor skills of humans could be restored to those who had suffered brain damage. Last year, more money was put into Underground AIM research than into neurology research. If you would like, you can sign a piece of paper for me, marking your personal achievements in this sub-culture form of entertainment."

"William, what did I tell you about all that smart talk?" Ryan's mother whispered, patting the pre-teen on the back.

"No, he's right. But the McCarthys are the highest donators to the Boston Neurological Research Association. They get their money from Scanning. It's funny how the world comes full circle sometimes. I have a feeling you'd get along with Maria," Rick said.

"Sorry to keep you waiting!" Ryan called out as he finally came back down the groaning wooden stairs.

"Miss Kier's arguments are valid, and it is clear she has done her research," William continued. "However, she seems to be driven by personal motives rather than to spread awareness of the truth. It makes me question her integrity, but there is no doubt she is a talented athlete. If that counts for anything."

"And what did we agree earlier? No talking about Maria," Ryan said as he ruffled his younger brother's hair. "Ready to go?"

"Oh! Wait! I have something for you two to take with you," Ryan's mother said before she hopped into the kitchen. After a moment, there was a scream from the kitchen. "Ryan! Get this squirrel off my kitchen table!"

"Crap. Sorry!" Ryan ran off into the room and came back holding the small animal. "What did we talk about last night? You agreed to stay out of the kitchen," he said quietly to the AIM before giving his mom an apologetic smile over his shoulder.

"I was about to hit it with my rolling pin. I'm never going to get used to this," she muttered as she followed her son, holding a flat box in her arms. "This is for the team. Athletes always need food for the road."

Maria finished tying her hair up in a messy bun just as she heard a knock on her apartment door. "Just a minute," she called out as she buttoned a plaid long-sleeved shirt over her tank top, looking around her apartment as if to make sure it was presentable. She heard another knock and let out an irritated breath. She made her way to the front hall. "I said I'm...coming," she paused when she opened the door. Cam stood in the hall. "What are you doing here?"

"Rick asked me to pick you up. He went to pick up Ryan in Elmira." Cam looked into the apartment, examining the nearly empty living room, and the empty dining room through the kitchen. He didn't take the time to question why she hadn't bought more furniture. "Do you want me to wait in the car?" His voice was uncharacteristically kind, Maria noticed. No tone of sarcasm for a change.

Maria shrugged and opened the door wider to let him in. "I'm almost ready. You might as well come in." She stepped back into her apartment, letting Cam close the door behind him. "I'll just be a minute. Help yourself to the kitchen," she called over her shoulder as she went back into her bedroom. She tried to sound as natural as she could, but she was not sure how successful she was. She heard him move into the kitchen and grab a glass from the cupboard, so at least he ignored it if he noticed. It was strange to hear someone else in the apartment again, and she was very aware of the fact that it was Cam.

She shoved the last pile of clothes into her duffle bag, zipped it up and threw it to the ground. A few thin strands of brown and purple highlighted hair fell out of the bun and in front of her face. She brushed it aside when she heard Cam at her bedroom doorway. "I'm done packing. I'll be right there," she said without turning around.

"Are we going to talk?" Cam's voice sounded forced, nearly cracking.

"Well, we're talking now." Maria moved towards her window and pressed on it, making sure it was fully closed and locked.

"You know what I meant. We didn't talk for a month."

"What's your point?"

"Isn't it about time we did? You didn't even let me explain, not fully."

Maria turned around and shook her head. "It's fine. I don't care what, or who, you do. It's your life."

"The competition just started and we need to make sure there isn't anything interfering with that. Things need to be cleared up."

She picked up her duffle bag and the backpack she had packed before Cam had shown up. "There's nothing to clear up. We're team-mates. We'll work together, and travel together, and we'll kick butt like usual."

Cam swore under his breath. "I'm sorry, okay? I'm sorry," he said, raising his voice defensively.

She should have stopped. She should have taken more notice of the fact that he apologized for nearly the first time she had known him. Apologized for something he had not done. Instead, Maria tried to push past him. When he stopped her by putting a hand on her shoulder she let out a sigh. "Cam, what do you want me to say? That I forgive you?" she pleaded with him. "There's nothing to forgive."

"I just want to talk about this."

Maria glanced away, not being able to help but notice this was the closest she had been to him in quite a while. "Cameron, it's fine. I'll be fine. Just let me be your team-mate, okay?"

After a moment, and without a word, he took the bag from her hand and stepped backwards out of the doorway, heading back to the front door.

Maria slipped her shoes on and lifted a small cooler. "This'll last us for the day, depending on how much Ryan eats. Can't be much more than you." She tossed her keys to Cam. "Lock up." She was going to burn out if she tried to be this friendly with him all the time, but she had to at least try. She didn't know which was worse: having to try so hard, or that Cam did not even seem to need to.

Cam caught the keys and picked up her guitar case near the door but paused when he saw an empty picture frame on the table next to the single couch in the living room. He stepped towards it and picked it up, his thumb running along the edge of the frame.

Maria heard him make a noise, almost a sigh, when she saw him with the frame. She cleared her throat and pretended not to notice.

"Hurry up. We're going to be late." He moved away quickly from the frame as if caught committing a crime before he herded her out the door.

She raised an eyebrow. "Not with the way you drive," she muttered, as she stepped out of the apartment. It was almost like he cared. Almost.

"Sorry about that," Ryan said as the two drove to Rick's house. The team had agreed to leave from there and head to Owen Sound for their first challenge of the season. "This all happened so fast. No one really got a chance to get used to the idea."

"Don't worry about it." Rick grinned as he pulled off the Kitchener Expressway. "My mom and Brittany never really get used to me and my dad leaving all the time. Your family seems like a lot of fun, especially that one brother of yours."

He laughed. "Yeah. Will's a smart kid. He doesn't really like the CST, but he loves to scan. He and I go out scanning all the time, then he would go back home and research all the animals we found. I think that's a big part of why I never really cared about the challenges. It was just something for me and my brother to do together. He doesn't like anyone coming between that, but he likes this team because of Maria. So he's allowing me to go." Ryan grinned and looked out the window. "I'd be afraid if Will became as outspoken as her though."

"I would be too. Before I forget." Rick shoved a small box towards Ryan that had been sitting between them in the front seat. "Can't be part of the team without the proper attire. And we signed you just in time, too. Our sponsors just changed our design. Best one yet, I think."

Ryan opened the box and pulled out a thin black jacket, the red letters of his team name scrawled along the back. Underneath he found a few more shirts along with a hat, each with *Revolution* printed on it, along with small logos of the team's sponsors. A grin cracked along his face, but he stayed silent. Now he was starting to feel more like a part of the team. He looked up as they pulled into a driveway. He examined Rick's house which seemed to be a fairly good size. No porch, but there was a nice large yard, neatly trimmed. A large bay window stuck out from the front of the house next to the front door. He noticed, though, that they were the only ones there.

"Where are Maria and Cam?"

"I sent Cam to pick her up. They should be here soon." Rick opened up the door of the RV sitting in the driveway and went in briefly, bringing in the food Ryan's mother had sent with them. When he noticed Ryan's uncertain look, he shrugged. "They're going to be stuck together in a vehicle as we travel around. They're capable of putting things aside to play the game. If anything, they'll get into fights just from cabin fever. None of us are really that great with travelling, but we deal with it." Rick watch Cam and Maria pull into the driveway and he hoped he told Ryan the truth.

"Are we set then?" Rick asked as the last two team-mates stepped from the vehicle.

"Yep," Maria answered shortly and began to pack her belongings into the truck.

"Cam, you and Ryan can take the truck. Maria will take the car and I'll take the RV. We'll see how that works until we get to Owen Sound," Rick announced as he dug the keys to the RV from his pocket.

Cam didn't say anything, but gave a look to Ryan as he walked towards the truck, handing Maria the keys to the small silver car. "Let's get going then." He took the truck keys from Ryan and hopped into the driver's seat. Having to spend an entire day training the rookie had been enough time to already get sick of him, which did not bode well for the rest of the season. Ryan found a bright side to everything, even losing a few valuable scans or having so little time to train. But there was something about him, Cam noticed. He was very cautious with every decision he made, as if he was unsure. As long as it did not interfere with their stats, that should not be a problem.

Rick looked at Maria as Cam started up the truck and revved the engine. "Drive safely, would you? We don't need another accident,"

"Hey, that guy crashed into me. I'm an awesome driver." Maria jogged back to the car with a grin and got in, adjusting the seat and mirrors to suit her. She pulled out of the driveway, taking note of the time as she headed for the Expressway. She looked into the rear view mirror and saw Cam and Ryan in the truck behind her. She couldn't see it, but the RV would be following close behind. Maria normally rode in the truck, and was used to being in the truck for long distance driving, but felt more comfortable driving the small car. Maria laughed as she remembered her first time driving around with Cam. She had almost quit because of the fighting. And for other reasons. Some things never changed, she supposed. Maria turned onto the Expressway, put on some music, and let herself relax for the long drive ahead.

Ryan glanced over at Cam, who was concentrating intensely on the road. "So...what music do you want on?"

"Doesn't matter."

"Country?"

"Doesn't matter."

"Techno?"

Cam simply looked at Ryan and then back to the road. "Just pick something and put it on," he said, glancing over his shoulder quickly before changing lanes.

Ryan played it safe and turned on a generic radio station which he would likely have to change soon after leaving the city. He watched the small car they were coming up beside, able to see Maria singing along with whatever music she was listening to. He felt Cam looking at him and he looked back to the road. "So what, are you going to give me my ground rules? I don't want to fight. I just want to be a part of this team."

"If that's all you want to be, then I don't need to lay any ground rules."

"Right."

Maria pulled up next to the truck in a hotel parking lot nearly three hours later and got out slowly, groaning as her muscles finally got the chance to stretch. She smiled at the familiar smell of the Georgian Bay. "How long have you guys been here?" she asked, seeing Cam sitting on the edge of the truck bed.

"About twenty minutes; long enough to scan a ring-billed gull," Cam answered, jumping off the truck and walked around the truck. "Ryan went in to get our keys but he's taking a long time. Rick called and said he'd be about another hour."

She smiled. "With that old RV he still has to fill it with gas. Only he would keep something so old, just to say he had it. He's going to be in trouble when the last gas stations close. I'm just waiting for him and his dad to realize that it slows us down on the road." Maria grabbed a few of her bags from the bed of the truck. She paused as though to say something, but shook her head and headed into the hotel.

Looking around the small lobby, she recognized a few people from their division but could not find Ryan. She walked to the front desk and asked for the team's room numbers. Normally, they would not get a hotel in Owen Sound but with recent events, they had needed rooms last minute. Waiting for a response from the receptionist, Maria continued to look around before she finally noticed Ryan speaking with a rather tall man. "Oh crap." She thanked the woman behind the desk quickly and made her way over to her team-mate.

"Thought you got lost," Maria said brightly as she stepped up beside Ryan.

"Yeah, sorry. I got side tracked," Ryan answered, his smile showing that he was glad she had come to interrupt.

"Maria Kier. Nice to see you looking so well. What's it been? Just about a month now?" the man asked with a large smile. "I heard what happened. It's a shame. You two were *perfect* together." His voice dripped with sarcasm and Maria was sure she heard joy somewhere in that deep voice of his. It almost sounded like genuine joy. How people could act so different one-on-one was beyond her.

"Thanks, but I don't need your fake pity, Jack." She held a hand out to Ryan. "I'll take mine and Cam's key cards."

Ryan nodded and passed her two cards. "Nice to meet you," he said before heading off to the elevators, glancing behind him to make sure Maria was alright.

Maria started back outside to give Cam his key but stopped when Jack gripped her elbow. Her eyes glared up at him as she wrenched her arm away. "Don't touch me, and don't go near Ryan, hear me?"

Jack laughed and stepped towards Maria, towering over her as he looked down. "What, are you afraid I'll turn him against you guys or something?" He swept away his light brown hair from his face, his eyes singing with mockery.

"No," Maria snapped. "But nothing good comes from associating with you."

"You sure?"

She would have been taken aback by the kindness in his voice if she had not heard it before. "Very sure. If anything, it's less than exciting."

Jack rolled his eyes and turned his head when he heard someone calling his name. "That's not how I remember it." He grinned as her eyes began to fill with anger. "I'll see you later."

She did not wait for him to finish before she went back outside to the truck. Maria found Cam sitting in the driver's seat with the door open and radio on. "Here," she said, throwing a key card into the truck which hit Cam in the shoulder.

"Whoa, watch it," Cam snapped as he turned the radio off and his eyes went to Maria knowing her moods with precision. This was not a good one. "What happened?"

"Jack Tyson's in there, because apparently there are no other hotels in this town for him to stay at."

Cam swore, then picked up the key card from the floor of the truck. "Just what we need. Maybe he'll get lost in the hotel."

"We'd never be that lucky." She picked up a bag from the back of the truck and hoisted the strap over her shoulder. "Rick can get his key from the front desk." She started back for the hotel with Cam close behind. When she noticed his proximity, she sped up.

Cam slowed his walk to let Maria get far enough away. If he had learned anything, it was to let her walk away. It made it easier every time she did it.

The hotel was not very large, but the top two floors had been reserved for CST teams. After an awkwardly silent elevator ride, he watched Maria fumble with her key card before getting it under control, then get her door open and slam it behind her. He smiled to himself as he got into his room and dumped his bags onto the floor, nearly setting them down on top of his AIM.

"Shall I stay out of your way, then?" came a robotic voice.

"Sorry," he muttered. He sighed, realizing he had carried one of Maria's bags. He picked it up and went back into the hall. Maria was already there.

Almost startled, the two stared at each other.

"I have one of your bags," Cam said, holding it out to her.

"Oh, thanks." Maria took it and tossed it into the room behind her quickly. "I still have bags out in the truck."

"Sure."

They stood there for a minute until Cam motioned back towards his room. "I'm going to just rest until Rick gets here."

"Okay, good," she said and started to turn away but stopped with a groan. Jack walked down the hall towards them.

"Well hello, Cameron," Jack said. He smiled as he watched a gull hobble around Cam's feet. "How precious." He motioned with his head to his AIM as he continued walking. A small fox followed close at his heels, eyeing the gull hungrily as it trotted. Jack looked at Maria as he passed her, slowing down. "And hello again. Looks like your room is next to mine."

"Lucky you," Maria commented with a roll of her eyes.

"Definitely lucky me." Jack looked her up and down, not bothering to hide the gesture. He looked at Cam and smiled. With a final look at Maria, he turned into his room.

Cam stared at Jack's door. "I hate that guy." He paused. "He got a fox already," he muttered under his breath.

"Everyone hates him. And we both know that foxes hunt around garbage." Maria started down the hallway, but stopped when she realized Cam was walking with her. "What are you doing? I thought you were going to rest?"

"I figured I should get the rest of my bags. Is that alright with you?" Cam asked, walking past Maria.

Neither said anything more while they made their way back to the truck. As they were taking out the last bag from the truck bed, they saw Rick and the RV pulling in. They waited for Rick to park and make his way over to them.

"Where's Ryan?"

"I killed him," Cam said, his face straight, perhaps showing too much desire.

"Well, I believe that. I'm not sure that's a good thing."

"The Raiders are staying at this hotel instead of the campsite," Maria explained.

"Crap. Did you see Jack then?"

"Oh yeah, and he definitely saw us," Cam said, looking pointedly at Maria.

She rolled her eyes and started back to the hotel. "I'm going to just get my own dinner. I'll see you guys in the morning."

Rick picked up his bags before heading into the hotel with Cam. "We're going to need to show Ryan the ropes before tomorrow. He knows how to scan and use an AIM, but he's going to need to know how to switch between animals and communicate with it in a challenge setting."

"I can show him in the morning."

Rick was surprised the younger member would even suggest such a thing without being told to do so. He had already started to train Ryan, but Rick had not thought Cam would follow through and continue the training.

At his captain's confused look, Cam shrugged. "I want to help the team, and he's going to need to know how to do it eventually. Besides, I can always talk about my generosity in the next interview," Cam explained with a grin, entering his room.

Rick rolled his eyes and entered his own room, not looking forward to the next day. The Raiders were notorious for smack talk and scandals. Nearly everything bad associated with the CST could be indirectly associated with The Raiders and Jack Tyson. It would not surprise him if that Emily girl was associated with Jack as well. He was a sore spot with Rick's team: a constant threat and one of the only teams which actually gave them much of a challenge. It did not help that they were both from the same region.

After arranging some of his things in his room just the way he liked them – a by-product of his OCD – he went across the hall to what he assumed would be Maria's room, straight across from Cam's, just at the same time as Ryan.

"Hey, you made it," Ryan said with a smile.

"Yeah, at the speed limit. And with a fill-up on the way." Rick laughed. "How was the drive with Cam?"

"Awkward. But I did manage to scan a red-tailed hawk on the way."

"Oh yeah?"

"Cam was pretty upset about it, too. He couldn't get it first because he had to drive."

Rick laughed again and knocked on Maria's door. "That sounds about right." He looked to the door once Maria had opened it.

Maria raised an eyebrow questioningly. "This is a first. Two men at my door. What's up?"

"Just wanted to make sure you were okay. Did Jack say anything to you?"

"I'm fine, and no. I just don't like the fact that we ran into him. Thank you for checking. Now go call your wife. Let her know you got here safely."

He nodded after a brief moment. Sometimes he acted too much like an older brother, but despite his unease of having a female team-mate she was like a younger sister to him. "Alright, well, have a good night then. See you guys in the morning."

Maria waved a bit to Rick before turning to Ryan. "Your turn, I guess."

Ryan gave a shrug. "I don't really know what there is to do in this town, and I'm not one for adventure, not city adventure anyway."

"What? No scanning?"

"Well, I should, but it was a long, awkward trip and it's getting a little late – sleep is always nice. Actually, I'm not going to lie, I'm drawn in by your guitar."

She laughed and opened the door wider. "Come in."

*   *   *

"Now's not a good time," Cam muttered into his phone as he stood in the hotel's lobby. "Our first challenge is tomorrow. Keep the AIM sequestered for now, and make sure no one goes in with it. Has Mark tried to control it yet? ... I figured. He's useless. Okay, give me a few days and I'll see if I can get away long enough." He slipped the phone into his pocket and looked around the lobby. He saw a few people milling about, but not the person he was looking for. He turned around walking right into Rick who was still holding onto his cell phone.

"Sorry, hey, have you seen... Ryan?" Cam asked, realizing Rick had probably just finished a call with Brittany.

Rick nodded his head back towards the elevator. "Yeah, he's in Maria's room last I saw."

Cam rolled his eyes at Rick's grin. "Don't give me that look. It doesn't bother me," he said as he headed for the elevator. What bothered him was that Ryan wasn't trying to spend his time with him. He had asked to train under him, and Cam supposed he hadn't been the nicest to him, but if Ryan had wanted to spend time with Maria, he should have just asked Maria for help.

Ryan, meanwhile, strummed slowly on Maria's guitar, frowning as he fiddled around with the head, tuning the guitar gently. "I would've thought you'd keep this in tune. I mean seriously, this is a *Martin*."

Maria shrugged as she lay behind him on the bed. "I haven't played it in a while. Haven't really been in the mood."

"Was it a gift?" Ryan strummed again before continuing to tune the instrument, gently turning a peg to change the pitch.

"Hm? Oh, yeah, a few years back."

"Birthday?"

Maria propped herself up on her elbows. "Is this you trying to get to know me?"

"You're making it difficult, but yes." He played a quick scale and with a grin he slid the guitar to Maria. "All set."

"Thanks. I've never been good at tuning it by ear. Didn't even realize how bad it had gotten." She sat up and crossed her legs, pulling the guitar onto her lap. "Anniversary gift," she said as she played a few chords. "My only one, actually."

"Anniversary?"

"Gift. Our anniversary was in the middle of the season, so there was never really any time for gift exchanges," Maria said absently as she strummed.

Ryan leaned back a bit, watching her fingers move and he smiled at her use of the past tense. "Must've been hard, not seeing him for most of the season. I'm surprised Rick's able to do it especially with his son, despite our time off. Was it hard for you?"

"Was what hard?"

"Being away from him?"

Maria stopped playing, hearing a knock at the door. "Just a sec." Ryan seemed like a sweet guy, but she was not sure she wanted to open up to him. Not yet. Not so soon. She had made that mistake before. She opened the door and groaned when she saw who it was. "Yeah?"

"Can I talk to Ryan?" Cam asked.

"And this is where you look for him?" Maria asked, opening the door.

"Rick told me he was here," he answered as he walked into the room. "I was thinking I'd drive to the reserve in the morning to get some scanning and practice in. Interested?" he asked Ryan.

He smiled and stood up. "Yeah, definitely! That sounds great!"

"I'll meet you in the lobby at five."

"In the morning?"

"Best to get an early start to the day. You should probably get some rest," Cam said with a nod.

"Yeah, sure." Ryan turned back to Maria and pointed at her briefly. "I'm going to be on your case about that guitar. You know a Martin deserves better than that."

Maria shook her head and folded her arms across her chest as Ryan left the room. "Five in the morning? You've never been up that early. Are you trying to keep him occupied?"

"No. I'm trying to keep myself occupied. We're going to have to kick butt at the challenges and Ryan's going to have to participate at some point, and we're already lagging behind other teams in scans." Cam kicked the doorframe gently as he looked back into the room, noting the faded wallpaper. He expected nothing more from an Owen Sound hotel. "We've only got twenty-seven points in the first few days – not our best start – and we've wasted today driving straight through small towns-"

"Because of what we can get in the country and you know it. We'd never get the same scans on the highway," Maria said sharply. "Besides, you started that practice, remember?"

Cam shrugged. He turned to leave but hesitated, turning back to her. "Are you going to visit your dad?"

Maria's eyes widened with surprise but she shrugged and glanced away. "Tomorrow. I figured I'd go before the challenge."

Cam raised an eyebrow and glanced around the room. "Is Rick going with you?"

"No."

He paused and looked straight at Maria. "I can get back early if you want me to go with you."

Maria hesitated briefly as if considering his offer but she shook her head. "No, it's okay."

"You shouldn't go alone. I'll come back early."

She shook her head again. "No, really. I'll be fine."

"I can just leave Ryan in the forest, see if he can make it back on his own." Cam smiled.

She laughed. "I'll be okay. Thank you though, Cam."

He nodded as he turned to leave. "Let Rick know before you go, at least." *So far, so good.*

CHAPTER 7

"You want it to do what?"

"Not get caught." Cam watched his AIM shift from a gull to a barn owl as he grinned. "It'll help you and your AIM train and work together. But it's just mostly for my entertainment."

"You have a barn owl already? That's pretty cool." Ryan looked down at the grey squirrel in his arm and had to remind himself that it was a robot, not a real animal. He set his AIM onto the ground gently. "It hasn't been in this form long."

"Even better. It can learn how to move in this form." He glanced up at the owl flying overhead. "You better hurry up. It'll attack without notice."

"But AIMs can't hurt each other, right?" Ryan looked to Cam when he did not reply immediately, and his AIM stayed close to his feet. He looked down at his AIM and nodded. "Go ahead. Don't go in a straight line. Go!" He watched the squirrel dash off as the owl swooped down mere inches away.

Ryan looked to his team-mate hesitantly, worried by the smile on his face. "How exactly does this train me?"

"It helps you two build a relationship. It needs to learn to listen to you. If you tell it to dart one way, it needs to learn that if it doesn't listen to you it'll be in danger. Besides..." He grinned and tapped the screen of his AIRC, looking at the energy level of his AIM. "I think it'll be fun to see my owl scoop up your little squirrel."

He did not respond as he watched the squirrel run across the grass, but he noticed that it was not moving as quickly as it could be. "Is everything okay?" he asked through the AIRC.

"Attempting to adjust to the form."

"Dart left!" he yelled suddenly as Cam's AIM once again swooped down. He saw his AIM obey and continue running in the same direction. This time when it ran, it seemed to make much more fluid movements. He was glad that it was learning so quickly. He felt his heart race as he watched his AIM move, feeling the panic he knew a real squirrel would feel.

"Yes!" he yelled when his AIM jumped onto a tree, but Cam was the one who was more excited when the AIM fell, losing its grip of the bark. "Come on! Dig your claws in deeper and go up the tree in circles! Go!"

"Go, come on!" Cam called out to his AIM. The squirrel could not get away, not so easily. "Fly around the tree! No! The other tree!"

The owl flew around the side of the tree as Ryan's AIM finally found a way to grip the side of it and clambered up. The owl did not need to wait for Cam's instruction before it landed on a branch and watched the rodent as it attempted to stay out of sight.

"Use your tail for balance and jump to the next tree!" Ryan said through his AIRC as he watched intently. He grinned, seeing the squirrel ready itself to jump. He watched as his AIM awkwardly lunged itself from a branch towards a nearby tree, flying through the air.

"Yes!" He paused and winced. "No..."

Ryan groaned as Cam's owl landed on top of the squirrel where it had fallen from its failed jump, and flew back to the athletes with the rodent in its talons. "So much for training it."

Cam grinned with a shrug. "You did. Not well enough, but it's a start. Why don't we take a break from this and do some scanning? Maybe you'll be able to do that."

He opened his hands to catch the squirrel as Cam's AIM flew by and dropped it. He followed Cam back down a trail towards the water, looking at the AIM in his hands. He stroked its fur gently, and smiled when it seemed to enjoy the gesture. At least he had experience scanning. Maybe he had some hope to succeed at that.

Ryan caught himself in time as he felt himself fall forwards, nearly landing in the lake. He gripped his AIRC tightly as he stepped back from the edge of the decrepit dock.

"I know how to scan, you know."

Cam shrugged, pacing back and forth on the dry, solid ground. "You need to learn how to scan and then quickly transform your AIM. There've been times I've needed an animal, but didn't have it. Luckily I managed to find one during the challenge." He pointed at Ryan with a nod. "You won't be so lucky. So, try it again. Scan a fish and then quickly use it."

Ryan sighed and stood on the edge of the dock once more. "This would be easier if we were in a boat."

"Just hurry up."

He looked down into the water again, grateful that people were still fishing close by. He did not understand why Cam would not let him in a boat and fish to get the scan. If he was trying to get him to do everything the hard way, it was working. Ryan held the AIRC in front of his face when a turtle popped its head above the surface of the water. He jabbed at the screen to start the scan and held the console steady as a grin came to his face. Now, the turtle just had to stay above the surface long enough…

"Crap." Ryan glanced back at Cam to see him looking at his watch. "I'll get it…"

"We don't have time. We better get back. At least you got some scans earlier."

He paused for a brief moment, his AIRC still in front of his face as Cam walked back to the truck. What was his problem? He knew he could scan, and he usually did it on the first try. He had done it thousands of times before. He had been ranked first in scans. But that was at the junior level. Maybe he just was not cut out for this level of competition. He could barely hold his AIRC steady when his team-mates were around. Maybe it had all just been a big mistake.

"Keep practicing when we're at the challenge later," Cam said, bringing Ryan out from his thoughts. "We'll do a team practice tomorrow once we get to the next city." He looked to Ryan sitting in the passenger seat and raised an eyebrow. "Are you kidding me?"

Ryan looked away from his AIM in the form of a turtle on his lap and gave Cam a shy smile. "I couldn't just leave it there."

"Well, good job on the scan, I guess."

His voice did not sound kind, but at least it was mostly friendly. That was something. He looked around as farm fields passed by, and Cam made a turn down another dirt road. Ryan was not good with directions, but he knew enough to know that Cam was not driving back to the hotel after their time at the reserve near Tobermory.

"Are you going a different way back to the hotel?"

Cam leaned over the steering wheel to read a road sign before turning down another small street. "Nope."

Ryan waited for a more detailed explanation, but soon realized he was not going to get one. "Where are we going?"

"We're going to pick up Maria."

"Where is she?"

Cam sighed from frustration. "Visiting her dad. You ask too many questions."

"Well if she's visiting her dad, she might not want to be rushed. We still have some time before we have to be at the challenge," Ryan said. He was surprised that Cam was offering to do something for his team-mate, but he supposed it made sense. He was the outsider, not Maria. Despite the tension he had felt earlier, Cam was close with his team-mates and there was no reason he would not do nice things for them. When he thought about it, Cam was doing Ryan a huge favour in training him. Then again, that was all just for the team's benefit. Not Ryan's.

"There's no rush. It's not like her dad's going anywhere. I wouldn't mind seeing him, too." Cam pulled in through a gateway onto a nicely paved road surrounded by manicured lawns.

Ryan opened his mouth to make a comment, but stopped, looking at the surroundings. "Oh," was all he said as the truck came to a stop. "Should I come?"

"I'll go get her." He turned the engine off and stepped out of the truck. He walked around to the other side of the vehicle and leaned against it for a minute, watching Maria sit in the grass.

She did not look up as he came up next to her, but wiped her face quickly. "You didn't have to come."

"You'd sit here all day if someone didn't come bring you back to the hotel. Besides," Cam said, stepping towards the granite stone and kneeling next to it, "I visit every year. Nothing would change that." He glanced back at Maria, who was still holding a small container of flowers, a garden trowel on the grass next to her. He grabbed the trowel and began to turn over the small patch of dirt in front of the grave. He held his hand out to take the flowers from Maria and planted them in a row.

She watched him as he finished, wiping the dirt from his hands onto his jeans. "He liked you, you know."

"I know. He was a good man. The least intimidating father I've ever met."

"How many fathers have you met?"

"Only yours." Cam ran his hand over the engraved letters and gave his head a small nod. "Owen's going to be okay, Maria. Your dad had two massive heart attacks in a row. Owen had one mini heart attack and he's pretty much recovered already. He didn't even need the surgery your dad did."

Maria silently nodded, leaning her face into her hands. After a minute she shook her head and looked back at Cam. "Thank you, for coming."

Cam shrugged and stood up. "I would have come whether or not you were here."

"Do you have to ruin this, too?"

He looked down at Maria and shook his head. "You're welcome." He glanced back at the truck and nodded towards it. "Are you ready?"

Ryan stepped out of the truck to let Maria sit in the middle as she approached with Cam close behind. He said nothing as they got in and as Cam drove into town.

"So, find anything good out there?" Maria asked, looking back and forth between the two men, which was when she noticed the turtle on Ryan's lap. "Cute."

"We don't have to talk about it if you don't want to," Ryan said quietly.

"Got a few," Cam answered casually, "but I gave up trying to help Ryan. He needs to get a new AIRC. His is so slow when it scans. Oh, we got a few fish, which should help. I know fish weren't usually one of our priorities-"

"Your priorities," Maria interjected.

Cam rolled his eyes, but continued, "Not really worth the hassle of actually fishing for them, but I figured I should show Ryan how to use some more functions on his AIRC. There's a good chance the challenge today is going to involve water for some part of it, so a fish will be good."

Ryan noticed Cam speaking as if it was a regular conversation. He assumed that Cam knew Maria enough to know how to speak with her, but it still did not seem right to him, to be speaking in such a carefree manner after being in a cemetery.

"I'm glad you're at least doing something. Maybe we can take Ryan to get a new AIRC soon, but his will work well enough for the first challenge which, by the way, we need to figure out," Maria said, looking out the side window, not really looking at anything, at least not until Cam stopped at a red light next to a house.

Cam glanced at Maria, watching her view the people sitting out on the patio of the house at the corner. "Are we going to need to visit them too?"

"No, I told them we didn't have time. I don't want to make a big scene. You know how my family gets, and how they talk. I don't want to have to explain things."

"You're going to have to tell them eventually. Unless you're holding off for some reason."

Maria turned to Ryan, ignoring Cam. "I hope Cam wasn't being too much of a jerk to you today. He gets like that. A lot."

Ryan shrugged, now regretting letting Maria sit in the middle. "Not overly. I'm not the greatest student, so I'm assuming for now that his anger was justified. He did somewhat convince me I need to get a new AIRC. And it was kind of cool at the reserve."

"I love it up there." Maria's eyes lit up for the first time that day. "I used to go all the time. I have to say, though, I'm surprised Cam brought you out to get fish when there's so much more to scan. Did you go out on a boat or just stay on the dock?" she asked with a smile, looking at Cam before back at Ryan.

"Just on the dock. We got what we needed though, I guess."

"Oh, well that's strange. Cam, you've been there plenty of times. Did they move the boat rentals?" Maria teased.

"Hey look, another house I'm sure you find familiar. Want to stop in?"

Maria shot an angry look at Cam before looking out the windshield. "You're right, though. There's a good possibility that this challenge is going to involve water. There's usually at least one stage of the challenge that's in the water around this area."

Cam nodded as they pulled into what was now a mostly empty hotel parking lot. "Well, we'll just have to wait and find out." He hopped out of the truck as he pulled to a stop, followed close behind by Ryan and Maria as Rick approached them. "Ready to go?"

"Yeah. Is Maria okay?" Rick said, standing next to the driver side door of the car.

"She's fine," Cam said. "Let's go." He paused and raised an eyebrow at Rick, who sighed and tossed him the keys to the car.

Once again behind the driver's seat, Cam drove down towards Harrison Park in the centre of the town. Having eyed Cam and Rick awhile, Ryan spoke up, "You don't like Rick's driving?"

"I don't like anyone driving my car."

"You let Maria drive it on the way here."

Cam looked at Maria through the rear view mirror and shook his head, not replying to Ryan's comment. He glanced around at the park as they drove by, noting the cars making their way out. While this was the starting point for the challenge, it seemed like most of it would be away from the park, which was usual for challenges, even small ones such as this.

As they got closer to the middle of the park, near where the river was, a few other teams could be seen, and Cam's face fell. "You're kidding me. This is our first challenge?"

Maria grinned and glanced at Ryan. "Guess you're up, rookie."

Ryan raised a confused eyebrow as he looked around. "Do you really think I should participate in the first challenge?" He examined the starting area for the challenge and among the CST officials were crowds of fans grouped around the docking area. His eyes widened and he felt a sudden jolt of panic sweep through him. It was one thing to be in front of the media at the opening ceremonies, but now he had to face fans, face the people who kept teams like his going. He was not sure he was ready for that quite yet, but he was going to have to deal with it.

"Don't have a choice, looks like we're on the water. Cam won't do it," Maria said matter-of-factly as Cam pulled into a parking lot next to a docking area, which was fully dressed up for the CST, indicating the starting point.

"It's not my strong point," Cam muttered, slamming the door as he got out.

Rick grabbed his pack quickly and went silently to the check-in area. He had seen his father in this position for years, and it was still so strange to think of himself as the captain of this team. How could he possibly be responsible for the actions of his team-mates? He could barely control his toddler, let alone three grown adults.

"So what kind of fish did you get?" Maria asked Ryan, closing the truck of the car and moving closer to the water.

"Some trout, I forget the species, but I got a Chinook Salmon," he said, flipping through entries on his AIRC.

"Is that model waterproof?"

Ryan nodded and shifted the weight of his pack. He looked to the river and noticed only one other team was there, already getting into three kayaks. Although all the teams from their region would be attempting the challenge that day, they would not all start at once and by the look of it, the teams were staggered quite a bit. "I guess we only need three people for this challenge."

"Yeah, all of the regular challenges are like that, which is why some people think a team can do well with only three players," Maria said, looking pointedly at Cam. "But the fourth player is necessary, especially in situations like this."

For the first time, he was beginning to feel as though he really was part of the team, and a necessity. It helped that he was wearing his team's jacket. An excited vibe ran through him as he imagined what he looked like, standing with his team-mates in similar clothing. His face fell when he remembered failing to scan the yellow perch earlier that morning, even though he had scanned the two other fish. Sure he was needed on the team, but they needed anyone. They had not been picky when they had chosen him. He was all they could find. With a sigh, he watched Rick come back over to them and drop his pack at his feet.

"The challenge is completely on the water," Rick said. "We're kayaking down the river and into the bay; no idea how far. We have to find a submerged buoy somewhere along the coast, and there're three stages but only two really worthwhile. They said the intermediate stage has a gold buoy, and the advanced has a red, like usual, worth seventy-five and one hundred points respectively. The other one is only worth twenty-five points. Depending on how we feel once we get through the second stage, we can go from there."

"I say you just go for the advanced. It's only the first challenge. It'll be nice to get that kind of a lead in stats," Cam suggested, folding his arms in front of his chest.

"We also have a new member who's never competed in a competition before and this is going to be an all-day challenge." Rick rummaged through his pack before zipping it back up and handing it to Cam. "Fourth player keeps in touch and picks us up at the rally point somewhere on the beach."

"I know the drill," Cam muttered.

Maria grinned as she looked around. "This should be good. The rapids in this river are awesome. I'm surprised they don't just start us at the regular dock near the mouth of the river. We'll likely have to portage once we get to the fish ladder. I have to agree with

Cam though, as much as I hate to say it: going for the advanced stage would be best for us. Our scanning scores are low, and we're already at a disadvantage. No offense, Ryan."

Rick nodded. "Like I said, we'll see how it goes."

"Let me know where you guys are as you go. But I don't need updates every minute." Cam watched them start for the dock before calling out. "Hey, be careful would you?" He headed back to the car and dumped Rick's pack onto the ground in order to open the trunk.

A familiar young woman with blonde hair leaned against the car, grinning at him. "You know where you're going?" she asked, not seeming to care that he did not even bother to look at her.

"No, but my team will tell me. I don't need your help. I think you've already done enough damage to this team," Cam growled as he threw the pack into the trunk and headed to the driver's door.

"You're the one damaging your team, Cam," she said with a grin as she put a hand on his arm.

He snatched it away as he glowered down at her. "Don't you dare touch me. I didn't want it before, and I don't want it now. Go find your team."

"I don't need to. I know where they are, and where all the buoys are. You know, Tylar, you have so much knowledge in that handsome head of yours. You should use it sometime for something that really matters. Trevor could use someone like you. Think about it." She smiled, stepping from the car as Cam got in and pulled away.

CHAPTER 8

Ryan watched Maria and Rick put on their lifejackets as he fumbled with his own.

"He really doesn't like the water, does he? He barely let me stand on the dock at the reserve."

"Everyone has their quirks," Maria replied, surveying the kayaks, not paying much attention to Ryan. "He had a bad experience with the water, and doesn't want to repeat it, is all."

He nodded and looked around. He motioned towards the growing crowd at the edge of the parking lot. "They're not going to be allowed much closer, right?"

Rick turned to see the protesters held back by police officers. "After all the injuries last year, I can't see them getting too close to us. They're not even letting many people along the river. I guess the tickets to stand along there were pretty expensive. If it's just one or two protesters, there's not much they can do while we're paddling down the river. I wouldn't worry about it. We'll stick to the middle of the river. Even if they try to throw rocks, most of them won't be able to hit us."

Ryan eyed the group again. He tried to think back to when he would watch CST challenges on the TV, and he had never seen as many protesters as what he had experienced in the few days on the team. Owen's heart attack was not the only change that year, it seemed. He looked back at Maria after a moment when he remembered something she had mentioned.

"You said rapids?"

She nodded. "Yeah, but it's really not that bad. I'll give you some tips before we get there. You'll be fine." She gave him an encouraging smile before she went over to Rick to help him into his kayak.

Ryan looked back at the parking lot and saw Cam's car already gone. "Guess he doesn't waste any time."

"We shouldn't either," Rick said, slipping into the kayak as Maria held it steady. "Keep an eye on him, alright? The river will be fine, but if he's tired after that, open bay kayaking will be really dangerous for him," he said quietly. "For all of us."

"I know, but I refuse to get just twenty-five lousy points for this challenge when we know we can get at least seventy-five," Maria said, glancing over her shoulder.

"You sound like Cam," Rick said with a laugh.

"I hate you. Come on, let's get going," she said, hearing Rick push out behind her and into the river. She waited until Ryan got into his kayak. "Have you done this before?"

"Not really. I've tried it a few times, but I've canoed, if that counts for anything."

"Canoeing is much different." Maria took the paddle away from him and pulled the boat into the river, glad she had thought ahead and worn her bathing suit under her outfit. She shivered suddenly as the cold water wrapped around her legs. Even though the snow had been gone for a few months, the temperature was still relatively low. Being in the water was not going to be as much fun as it usually was. Nothing she couldn't handle.

"If you tip over in a canoe, you fall right out. You need to know how to get out of the kayak if you flip over, because if you flip over in the rapids, you're going to smash your head, and no one wants that." She laughed when she saw Ryan's eyes widen while she held the boat steady once the water was just to her chest. "Paddling isn't that difficult and you can learn that as we go, but you need to be comfortable doing a wet-exit before you set out."

He looked at her hesitantly, gripping onto the edge of the kayak. "Are you sure I can do this?"

"You'll be fine. When you tip over, you should just slip out. Don't panic if you don't, but you'll want to tuck up against the kayak to get as far away from the bottom of the river and the rocks. And this is going to sound stupid, but make sure you're fully upside down and in the water. I've flipped before in rapids, but wasn't actually fully in the water, and it turned out bad," Maria said with a smile but it faded as she remembered the situation.

It had been in her first season as a member of Revolution. She knew she had to prove herself as a new member, and it was only her second time participating in a challenge. After convincing Owen that she was an experienced kayaker, he had given in. Cam had likely spoken to him on her behalf. There was no way any of them could have taken the protesters into account. They had been paddling down a calm river, and she remembered commenting on the serenity of being out on the water. Then the first rock came from the bank of the river, landing in the water near Rick's kayak. The second caught Maria's arm and when she attempted to duck from the third, she tipped.

Despite the calmness of the river, she had thought she was fully submerged and attempted to slip out from the vessel. When she had trouble, she panicked before attempting to right herself. Thankfully, Rick had been close enough to help her, but those ten seconds were the longest in her life. Cam had been so upset with her that day, and it was probably the first time she realized that she would need to relax and work with her team rather than trying to be the main focus. Cam still did not seem to grasp that concept.

With a shake of her head, Maria pushed Ryan's kayak a little bit as the current pushed it against her. "Once you're fully over, you're going to pull this loop here, pull it off and then push the kayak off of you," she said, pointing to the spray skirt around the opening of the kayak. "Got all that?"

"I think so," Ryan said as he attempted to visualize what he was supposed to do.

"Okay, I'll be here the entire time, and Rick is staying just over there in case you're brought down the river. Just tip yourself over. Don't worry about doing it as fast as possible; just make sure you're comfortable with the motions you have to make."

Ryan nodded as Maria stepped away from the boat. He waited a minute before flipping himself over. Panic shot through his body, but he let himself hang upside down, feeling the kayak start to head downstream. He moved through Maria's steps and managed to free himself before he travelled too far. He smiled as he surfaced and laughed. "Well, I survived."

Maria laughed, too, catching the kayak before it got too far away. "You feel okay with it?"

"Yeah, that was pretty easy."

"Well you're in a calm part of a river. That wet exit should be a last resort. If Rick or I can't get to you quickly, and if you can't roll yourself over, you'll need to do that. For the most part, you'll want to do a buddy roll." She waved her hand at Rick, calling him to come a bit closer. "Rick'll be your buddy since he's already in a kayak."

After a few more practice manoeuvres flipping over on his own with and without his paddle, Maria and Rick agreed that Ryan knew enough to begin the challenge. Rick almost hated himself for thinking that it was a bad idea having a new member, but there was no way they could have done this challenge with Cam. In the past, Cam had argued that they should take a handicap for the water challenges, but Revolution had never needed to do that. It surprised everyone when Cam, of all people, suggested taking the minimum score so they would not have to attempt the challenge. They would never do that. Not as long as they had people who could attempt the water challenges.

A part of Rick was nervous for Ryan's first challenge. Another part of him was excited to start another season: he wasn't necessarily a huge fan of kayaking, but as their first challenge, it was going to be fun and enough of a challenge to force them into the competitive mode none of them seemed to have yet.

Rick looked over his shoulder, staying in place as much as he could in the river. "That salmon you caught earlier might actually be the best to use for this challenge. Have you used it yet?" he called out to Ryan, knowing that salmon commonly swam up this river; if Ryan had scanned a salmon from this area, it would likely be good for a challenge here. He himself had been able to take a quick fishing trip on the Grand River before they had left, scanning a couple of fish before they had left Kitchener, but a local fish might be best to use.

"Not the salmon, no," he answered. "I started to train it with another fish I got back in Kitchener, though."

"That should be good enough. The training you need to give your AIM is pretty much the same for all fish. Besides, it's not too difficult for the AIM to just swim down the river. It'll be a good way for you and your AIM to get used to challenges. Nice and easy first challenge." Rick grinned as if his smile would lend the rookie support and encouragement he needed.

Ryan glanced at Maria as if asking for a second opinion. He felt fine when he was scanning. He knew how to do that. He knew how to hide out to wait for shy animals, and he knew where to go for the rarer animals thanks to all those times he went scanning with his younger brother. But this was new territory for Ryan. He had expected to feel out of place, but this was as though he was learning to walk all over again. If he could remember that far back. He reached into his lifejacket's pocket to pull out his AIRC while keeping balance in the kayak. He grinned briefly when a chickadee landed on the bow of the kayak and watched as the small bird morphed smoothly into the form of a salmon, flopping on the bow of his kayak before slipping into the water.

"Do you guys have any fish, just in case?"

Maria grinned, pushing her kayak away from shallow water effortlessly and tucked some hair back up into her helmet. "We'll have our AIMs as fish too, but yours will be the one attempting the challenge with us. We might as well train ours at the same time. You're okay communicating with your AIM?" She glanced down into the water, felt something run into her kayak, and sighed. It was definitely a good thing she would use this challenge to train her AIM. It seemed to have lost all memory of how to swim during the off-season. "Stupid AIM…"

Ryan nodded and watched as the salmon swam around the boat, easily moving against the current. He took a few tentative strokes with his paddle. He smiled once he realized just how easy it actually was.

Rick laughed as he watched Ryan catch up with him slowly. "Are you ready for this?"

"As long as I don't lose sight of you guys, I'll be fine. I'm just worried about those rapids."

"Don't be. I'd be more worried about the bay. Open water is always rougher."

"If that's your attempt to make me feel better, that was great. Let's get going," Ryan said, noticing Maria had already gone ahead of them. "I guess she likes to kayak?"

Rick paddled slowly beside him. "It gives her a release. That and rock climbing, but I don't know how often she does that. We all have our favourite thing. I like swimming challenges." He glanced down into the water, noticing the salmon sticking close to the boats. "If you want, you can send it further down the river to look for buoys. When we're doing a challenge like this, it's usually better to send our AIM a little bit ahead so it can get an idea of where we're going, especially once we get into the bay."

Ryan nodded. "I really appreciate all of this. I know you have to do it with me, but I guess thanks, for the chance."

"If you want to show appreciation, how about trying to go a bit faster," Rick suggested. "It's not a timed event, but this'll give you practice too. The sooner we finish the challenge, the sooner we can either head down to Sarnia or have the rest of the day to rest and scan."

The two caught up to Maria around a few bends, although she had slowed down a bit. Once she realized they had caught up, she spun her kayak, letting the river take her down as she faced the other two. "How's it going? How do you feel?"

"Not as good as you, I bet." Ryan laughed. "But it's good so far. Less nervous, I guess."

"How's it going so far?" a voice called from their pockets, startling Ryan. He had nearly forgotten they were able to contact each other through their AIRCs. He had never needed to use that function before. Everything was so new to him.

"It's fine. We spent a bit of time showing Ryan exits but we've been on our way about half an hour now I'd say." Rick spoke up, raising his voice to be heard over the sound of the river. "How is it on your end?"

"Boring. Teams are already starting to bargain, which is a little pathetic. It's only the first challenge in our division. Even with Ryan around, we're still in good shape if that's the competition we're up against this season," Cam said. "Everyone's doing okay though?"

"Everyone?" Rick asked, looking at Maria with a grin.

"Just making sure no one's flipped over yet, but if you haven't even hit the rapids I shouldn't even bother asking. I'll call you guys again in an hour. Hopefully you've at least hit the bay by then." His voice held a hint of frustration and impatience, which was not unlike Cam really.

"You really like to antagonize him, don't you?" Maria asked, still going backwards in the kayak.

Rick shrugged. "I would call it subtle teasing." He nodded towards her in the kayak before glancing down the river.

Ryan looked back and forth between his team-mates. "What did Cam mean when he said teams were bargaining? Bargaining for what?"

He looked around, as if the trees along the edge of the river would take over his position. "It usually doesn't happen until a few months in," Rick began. "Some teams bargain for information about challenges. For example, what AIM is best to use, and especially where landmarks are."

Ryan's eyebrows furrowed as he thought, nearly forgetting to paddle. "What do they use to barter, then?"

"Money, usually. Or scans. There's nothing really wrong with it, but it's definitely not honest. Sometimes not-so-legal items are bargained. Those teams are the ones to watch out for." Rick paused with a sidelong look at Maria. "They'll do anything to win." As if that ended the conversation, Rick turned his full attention to Maria. "I'm surprised you didn't bring your own kayak. You never know when you'll get a chance to do this and you're always so prepared for absolutely everything."

Maria turned her kayak around with a fluid motion of her arms and hips. "It's in storage right now. Someone else has the key. Besides, we never really know what the challenge is until the day of and it's not the easiest to always have all of my equipment."

"When has that ever stopped you from bringing equipment for every possibility?" He could not just tease Cam. He had to save at least some for her.

Ryan raised an eyebrow. "Who else would have a key to your storage unit?"

She hesitated briefly. "My old roommate. This is where the rapids are coming up. They're nothing difficult, but let's be prepared for anything."

He gave Maria a second glance when he noticed the look she gave him. He remembered his mother giving him the same look whenever she wanted a topic left alone. He figured it was something females had perfected.

"Let's just get through this." Rick spoke. "We don't need to make this challenge any longer than it already is by taking a detour to scan."

Ryan looked around when he heard a rapid beeping sound and a voice coming from his AIRC, but it was not Cam's voice.

"Buoy sighted."

"Oh, okay cool." It was still a strange idea for him to be communicating with the AIM. He communicated with it often, sometimes having full conversations with it, but it was still just another thing he had to become accustomed to. "What colour?"

"Green."

"Thanks." Ryan was slightly pleased with himself for the first time. "Hey, I guess they put buoys down the river," he called out to his team-mates.

"Yeah, the officials always plan that. It's not much of a big deal in a river like this, but it'll come in handy in the bay," Rick said, now beginning to concentrate a little bit more as the rapids came into view. "You ready?"

Ryan nodded. The rapids did not look as bad as he had imagined: it seemed like a bit of a stretch, but they were not the giant white water rapids he was used to seeing on TV. "Well that doesn't look too bad."

"It's not, really." Maria paddled backwards to go alongside Ryan. "You don't even really need to paddle, because the river will just bring you along. Have you ever skied?" She smiled when Ryan nodded. "Alright, a lot of it is just to keep your balance. You can use your paddle to help you, like you would use your ski poles, but the majority of it is in the hips and your legs. I'll stick next to you the entire time, okay? Rick, want to go ahead?"

"Sure." Rick paddled a bit and pushed himself into the choppy water, barely putting his paddle into the water as he was taken down by the current.

"Alright, well, there's no going back now." Maria grinned as their kayaks were caught by the faster current. Her hips moved easily as her kayak was tossed from side to side with the water. She looked over at Ryan; every once in a while, his paddle went down into the water to keep his balance. Ahead, she could see Rick was through the rough waters and waiting for them along the edge of the river where the current was slower. Not even a minute later when they were through, she glanced again at Ryan and she saw him trying, unsuccessfully, to hide the grin on his face.

She could remember the first time she had been through rapids, and suddenly realized that this was not just a short stretch of rapids to Ryan. This was his first challenge. She was glad for some reason that she could share that with him.

"Well?" Rick asked once the two had caught up to him.

"That was sweet!" Ryan said, raising a fist in the air at about the same time he noticed a string of people along the river, cheering as the team passed. He brought his fist down slowly with a sheepish smile.

Maria laughed and gave a small wave. "Hey, Cam?" she said, leaning her head down a bit to her life jacket. "Cam?" she said again after a minute.

"Yeah?"

"We're through. Everything's fine."

"Alright. I'll talk to you guys later." Shortly after, her AIRC spoke up again with his voice. "Thanks."

"Go back to sleep." She heard a laugh, which surprised her. Before she thought too much about it, she turned her attention back to Rick and Ryan as they continued down the river. "That's the worst of it until we get to the bay," she called over to Ryan.

"Well, I feel pretty good, so hopefully we get to the hundred point buoy."

"If you're not up for it, don't worry. We can make up for it in other challenges. I'd rather take the hit now than have you do something you're uncomfortable with."

Ryan smiled at Maria. "It's good to know I have people looking after me."

"Someone's going to have to. I'd let Rick do it on his own, but with the way he looked after me, I don't know how much I trust him."

He could not help but laugh at the thought. "What trouble did he let you get into?"

"That's a different story for a different day. In his defense, he warned me numerous times along with Owen, but I didn't listen," Maria said as she sped up a bit, leaving Ryan back with Rick. She missed this town. She had lived here her entire life but when she joined Revolution, it made sense for her to move to Waterloo to be closer to her team. What she missed the most was her dad, even though he had not been around much. She knew that was not his fault. As a soldier, he had been called overseas when the war began years earlier. Since he died, it had been hard for Maria to come back here. Being on this river allowed her the chance to enjoy the town for its natural beauty.

"So, do we know how long the challenge is going to take?" Ryan asked after another fifteen minutes. He almost had to remind himself he was participating in a challenge and not simply leisurely paddling down a river. He had to step it up. Rick and Maria were going so much slower than he figured they usually went.

Rick shook his head. He watched as a different team passed them on the river and he felt his morale drop. With a single look at Maria, he knew that she was feeling the same. Despite having to teach Ryan how to kayak, it was almost as if the three of them had worked together for years. The team passing only reminded them that they still had a long way to go before they could call themselves a team.

"No," he answered. "That would defeat the purpose. The mouth of the river should be coming up soon, and from there we have no idea. Has your AIM found anything yet?"

"I don't think so. It just passed the mouth of the river a few minutes ago. I think it tried one side of the coast and now it's going to the other, looking for a marker buoy," Ryan said, making a mental note that he should check in with his AIM.

"Hopefully it finds something soon. How're you holding up?" He did not want to rush Ryan, particularly because this was his first time out in a challenge, and first time in a kayak, but Rick still wanted to finish with some points.

Ryan caught the hint. "Really well, actually. I guess I can speed up a bit. You guys've been saying that the bay is going to be worse, so I might as well start doing some power strokes to work up to it." When Rick nodded in response, he began taking faster strokes. The voice from his AIRC startled him again.

"Right hand coast line, there is a green buoy ten minutes north of the river."

"Good job." He winced, not really knowing if that was proper or not. What was he supposed to say to a robot? 'Hey, you did what you were programmed to do! Good for you!' "Hey guys, stick to the right hand coast; there's another buoy about ten minutes past the buoy at the mouth of the river," he called out.

Maria looked over her shoulder, letting the river carry her. "Do you need a break at the mouth?"

"No, let's just power through it. We'll get to the second stage and see how we feel from there." He could never admit he was already starting to tire, or that his legs were beginning to cramp. *Power through, Ryan. Just power through it.*

Less than ten minutes later, Maria looked over her shoulder at her two team-mates. "Last chance," she called out, slowing her paddling as the river opened up into the bay. Her hips moved along with the medium waves as the two currents clashed against each other. The bay was closed to all incoming vessels, but the high concrete walls of the dock were lined with boats parked until the challenge was complete.

"Let's go!" Ryan smiled as confidently as he could. He glanced to the side of his kayak, noticing a salmon swimming alongside the boat near the surface. He was beginning to warm up to the AIM which almost seemed like a pet. Most people did, in fact, keep an AIM as a pet. But it was nice that although it was programmed to do so, his AIM stayed at his side unless he asked, almost as a dog would.

Rick pulled up alongside Maria's kayak with a bit of difficulty. She should not be putting this much force into it, especially if they did not know how far they still had to go. "Hey, Maria, ease up, okay? We don't need you exhausted." Maria rolled his eyes at him, but he winced when he heard a shot of thunder. "That's never good." He motioned back towards Ryan. "Stick next to him, okay? You're the stronger paddler if he gets into trouble."

"Guys, hurry up," Cam's voice said through their AIRCs. "A bunch of teams are saying that there's a massive storm coming up. Shouldn't be here for another hour – at least not full force – but officials are re-scheduling the rest of the teams for tomorrow. They only let five teams start after you. Please tell me you're close to the second buoy at least."

"I don't think so. Should be at least another forty-five minutes. Ryan's AIM hasn't reported anything yet but there are marker buoys every so often," Maria replied, already bracing herself for the wind to pick up.

"I hate to say it, but if this storm gets bad and you're still on the water," he paused as more thunder rumbled in the sky, "don't go for the last stage."

"Yeah right. As long as we stay close enough to the coast, we'll be fine," she answered.

"No, you won't, especially not with a rookie paddler, or those rocks along most of the coast. And you know you're not the greatest swimmer, Maria."

"I know these waters, Cam. I'm saying we'll be fine." Her eyes narrowed as she spoke into seemingly thin air, despite the fact that Cam could not see her.

"Maria, he's right." Rick looked at her briefly as they continued on. "If the storm is only about an hour out, and we still have another hour or so to the next stage, we're not going to be able to make it to the last stage. You said you know these waters, so you of all people should know how quickly things can change. I'm making the decision. If we can get to the third stage within an hour, then fine. Otherwise, we end at the second. Cam, we're along the east side of the bay, on the side of the hotel. I'm guessing the second stage buoy is going to be somewhere around the conservation area."

"Which one?" Cam asked, knowing not to gloat about his victory. Not yet at least. There would be time for that when they got back safely.

"Hibou," Maria chimed in, using her knowledge of the area. "There's an inlet they use as a swimming area. We could get in there. You remember it? It has the playground."

"I remember. Ryan, send your AIM further ahead and tell me where it finds the buoy. Rick and Maria, maybe you should do the same. I'll try to figure out how long it'll take to get there. Oh and Rick, make sure Maria doesn't get herself killed. I'm keeping you guys on speaker so I can listen in."

"Is Cam usually this concerned with your safety, or does he just not like thunderstorms?" Ryan spoke directly into his AIRC as the sound of the waves and wind drowned out his voice even though he was paddling next to Maria.

"They made such a big deal about having four team members; I'm just trying to make sure we still have four at the end of the day. That's as far as my concern goes," Cam snapped, listening in as he had said.

"Well, if we die on the water, he doesn't have a team. But I'm sure as the *star contributor* he'd be fine on his own," she replied, surprised Cam did not make a retort.

"How about we just save our energy for when we really need it?" Rick needed to keep his team on track. It was bad enough they fought in person; he did not need them to be making shots at each other through an intercom system.

Maria growled under her breath, frustration dripping from her mouth as she tried to send her AIM up with Rick and Ryan's. It was having trouble swimming in the dangerous water in its current form, even more trouble than it had simply swimming in the calm river. "Go back to shore and meet up with Cam," she yelled at her AIM, switching it to a hawk as it rose to the surface of the water. She watched as it flew away. At least it could fly in the gale. With a sigh, she glanced at Ryan and nodded forward with her head.

"Think you can speed up a bit? We'll all need to stick as close together as possible, but we need to try to get ahead of the storm," she said as a wave jerked her sideways. She was able to keep her balance with her hips and noticed Ryan had done the same. She noticed the worry lines on his forehead and gave him a small smile. "Come on. Everything will be okay." She hoped.

CHAPTER 9

The clouds darkened above the team as they stabbed the water with their paddles, trying to stay ahead of the impending storm. The three stayed in a near-V formation as they paddled along for another half hour, with Cam chiming in every so often to make sure they were still safe; in Maria's opinion, he liked the sound of his own voice. Ryan gave his team-mate the benefit of the doubt, deciding Cam was actually concerned for their safety: if Cam was not comfortable on the water, it only made sense that he would be concerned. When he thought about it, Ryan could not remember ever watching him attempt a water challenge in the last four years he had been on Revolution.

The storm thundered above their heads, but the wind had fortunately not grown too severe. Maria continued to watch the storm clouds build over the bay, pushed by the wind towards them. The main storm cell could get to them in less than fifteen minutes, and they were still too far from the coast to be able to swim, even for Rick who was the best swimmer on the team. The sky had grown uncomfortably dark and by looking over to her captain, she knew he was just as uneasy with the situation. She could see on the coastline lines of lights where CST officials lined cameras and spotlights to keep the team in sight. But they were too far away. If anything were to happen, all they could do was watch as the team went under.

"Ryan, send your AIM ahead to find the buoy. That storm can get here in minutes, and if that marker is more than fifteen minutes away, we're going to be in trouble," Maria said.

Ryan nodded and sent the salmon up ahead. It had been reporting every time they passed a marker buoy, but there had been no mention of a gold one. He took a few deep breaths, trying to relax his legs which were growing stiff and sore.

"Cam, have you found somewhere to stay until we figure out where we're going?" Rick called through his AIRC, looking with nervous eyes to the coastline as he watched the waves crash onto the beach.

"Yeah, I'm up at Hibou. There's a group of officials here waiting and some teams have rallied together to watch you guys come in. The last team showed up almost half an hour ago, and they left twenty minutes behind you. I told you that a rookie would slow us down."

"At least we're doing the challenge. Do you want to get out here?" Maria snapped, as a round of thunder clashed.

"Nope, I'm fine. Just get here quickly, alright?"

"Gold buoy, one kilometre ahead."

Maria swore and examined the coastline up ahead. "Did you hear that Cam?"

"Yeah. Where do you think that puts you?"

"Most likely the swimming area I mentioned. I don't know if we can get there before the storm really hits us. These winds aren't letting us get anywhere." As she spoke, her eyes squinted against the spray which was being picked up by the wind.

"That's pretty much where we're all waiting. Just step it up. I'll bring the car in closer to the inlet."

"Just don't AIRC and drive," Maria said, trying to hide her concern for the growing waves with what she considered a joke.

"Just get here."

Ryan drove the paddle into the water with significantly more force than before after listening to their conversation, but was still only going about the same speed against the wind.

"Think we'll make it?"

"We're going to try." Rick's face filled with determination. "Good first challenge, eh?"

The waves continued to grow and the team was able to stay upright for most of them, tilting in unison for the rest of them. Ryan understood what Maria had been talking about, feeling as though you've flipped, but you're still half out of the water. He supposed it would have been easy to hip check out of a half flipped position, but with the waves and current as strong as they were, he found himself using his paddle to stay upright. Even though it had cost them almost twenty minutes, he was glad Maria had taken the time to show him how to do so. But now he was beginning to think that if she had not had to show him, they would be out of danger from the storm. His attention turned to Maria who was pointing ahead to a beach with her paddle. There he could see a group of lights which shone across the bay towards them.

"Cam should be up there," Maria said, smoothly stabbing the water with her paddle. "If we pick it up a bit, we can get there in about half an hour." She swore when another clap of thunder finally induced the rain.

"Yeah, I'm there. We have all of the spotlights pointed out towards you guys," Cam yelled to make sure he would be heard above the wind and waves. "I can see you guys with binoculars, but barely without them."

"Fifteen minutes to the buoy," Ryan's AIM chirped; it suddenly bothered Ryan how uncaring it sounded. Did it know, or even care, that they could potentially be in a lot of trouble?

Maria and Cam swore at the same time. "We don't have that!" she yelled against the sound of the rain and wind.

"Just head for shore. You won't be able to make it all the way. Get off the water while you can," Cam said.

Rick looked to his team-mates in the dim light and motioned towards the beach. "Don't let this go to your head, Cam, but guys he's right. Let's just-"

Maria saw the wave before Rick had the chance to react. She watched as it pushed him over sideways, cresting on top of him. She yelled out to him as the water swallowed him before the same wave pushed her over and interrupted her screams.

Cam slammed his foot down onto the gas pedal when Maria's voice was replaced by the sound of rushing water. *Come on....*

Maria remained upside down for a moment, feeling the waves push and pull at the boat attached at her hips. She shook her head, glad she had managed to grab a breath before going over. She reached up with her paddle and drove it downwards as she rotated her hips, but felt another wave hit against the kayak just as she began to right herself. Her throat began to burn and she attempted another go immediately after another wave. At the feel of rain on her face, Maria took in a deep breath, coughing at the sudden burst of fresh air. The rain was warm on her face compared to the icy temperature of the lake. She knew that if they did not get to shore soon, the storm would be the least of their concerns.

"Maria? Maria, answer me!"

She coughed again before replying to Cam. "We all flipped." Maria looked around and saw Ryan's arm up at the side of his kayak, trying to signal for someone on the surface.

"Are you okay?"

"Hang on." Maria coughed, bringing air into her lungs as she paddled desperately towards the flipped kayak, looking around for Rick at the same time. She hit Ryan's hand with her paddle when she got close enough. When he pulled himself up, sputtering, she grabbed his paddle to catch his attention.

"You okay, Ryan?" Maria ignored Cam's inquiries while she waited for Ryan's reply.

"Yeah. Yeah I'm good." Ryan glanced around and saw Rick's overturned kayak. "Where's Rick?"

Maria looked around, not seeing any arms around the kayak. Her eyes went back and forth across the choppy water frantically before she saw Rick bobbing up and down in the waves. She made her way towards him with Ryan close behind. She pulled up next to Rick, keeping her balance as he clung to her boat.

"And you were worried something would happen."

"Maria, is everyone okay?" Cam's voice was choppy with the sound of rain on his end, but its pounding volume could not hide the desperation and concern in his voice.

"Rick's out of his kayak so we have to get to the beach quickly. Ryan and I are fine." Maria reached down into her cockpit, pulled out a bit of rope and tossed it to Ryan. "Hitch Rick's boat up to yours and drag it in. I'll make sure he gets to shore. Rick, can you hold on long enough?"

"As long as you don't flip, I'll be fine." Rick tried to smile but was unable to hide how quickly he had become tired from treading the stormy water.

She waited for him to get to the back of her kayak before starting ahead. She could almost make out the car on the beach amongst the crowd, but she concentrated on going as straight as possible to get to the coast quickly. At least the waves were helping to propel them towards their goal. She glanced behind her every now and then to make sure Rick was still hanging on. Maria was going significantly slower than Ryan, who made it to the shore within a few minutes, and she saw Cam in the water helping to pull in the kayaks. She turned suddenly, feeling Rick let go of the boat and slip a bit under the water.

"Rick!" Maria spun her kayak around and grabbed at his hand, pulling her towards him, hooking his fingers onto the edge of the cockpit. "We're almost there," she said to him.

Cam watched as Maria paddled towards shore backwards with Rick hanging on beside her. He saw her leaning far to one side to compensate for Rick's weight and the small strokes she made. Within a few more minutes, they were close enough to wade to, at which point he and Ryan got back into the water quickly to each get a shoulder under Rick's arms to help him get his feet grounded.

Maria un-looped the spray skirt from her kayak and began to slip out when Cam went back and steadied the kayak for her. She stepped out and into the water, stumbling against Cam as a wave hit against her legs. She threw her paddle onto the beach, her chest not able to move fast enough to pull in the air she needed, so she frantically pulled off her life jacket to permit deeper breaths as two medics rushed over to her with thermal blankets after taking care of Rick and Ryan. The choppy April water of Georgian Bay was unforgivingly cold, and the storm did not make it any easier to handle.

"You okay?" Cam took a step back as the medics worked at finding the answer for themselves. He saw her nod as her chest continued to heave.

"Yeah. Just need to rest," she answered finally after the medics left her alone concluding she was, in fact, healthy. She walked up beside Cam and smiled tiredly. "So, why are you afraid of the water again?"

Cam did not smile but nodded ahead to the car which Ryan and Rick had already entered. "He did good."

"That was a hell of a challenge." Her voice was raspy from yelling.

"I could have done that on my own." Cam grinned a bit. He reached an arm to drape her shoulders, but stopped himself suddenly and let her get into the car before he took the driver's seat.

Maria turned in her seat to Ryan who had taken a backseat. "Hey, did you get your AIM?"

Ryan nodded, lifting his hand to show a small turtle. He closed his eyes and rested his head back. The last ten minutes replayed in his mind. The rush of the water was still fresh in his ears, literally, and he still felt the pressure of the waves against his body. It was only the first challenge and there had been the very real possibility of death. His parents had told him of their concern, but this was what he wanted, was it not? The first challenge…this was only the first challenge. If he had any hope of continuing as a Scanner, he either had to carry on and train harder, or just give up now.

He took in a deep breath, trying to get his body to relax. He would train harder. If this was the challenge in a small town, the larger competitions he knew would be much more difficult. At least he now felt justified in calling himself an athlete.

Cam glanced over at Maria who had her eyes closed like Ryan. "What happened to your arm and knee?" he asked, driving slowly in the torrential rain.

"Oh." She rotated her arm. The skin was red, and it was only a matter of time before it turned a deep purple and blue. Her knee was already multi-coloured. "I must've hit it when I flipped, and my knee bashed against the brace."

"Why didn't you bring your kayak?" He kept his voice low, noticing that the other two seemed to be passed out. He ignored the fact that the seats were now completely soaked.

"It's in storage and I didn't have the key," she replied looking out at the water streaming down the side window.

"You could've asked for it."

"Well, you were busy moving out," Maria snapped, but regretted it immediately.

Cam pounded a fist on the steering wheel. "That wasn't my choice, so don't you dare get mad at me for that." He had always sounded more threatening with anger in a low voice, rather than when he yelled.

She was silent for a moment as she kept her eyes out the window. "Honestly, I didn't want to bother."

"I'll get a copy made."

"Thank you."

"What would you do without me?" Cam asked with a small smile in an attempt to ease the tension.

"I've been doing fine for the past month." It scared her how easily she could lie and say that she was alright, and how hard it was to not tell him how much it hurt.

"Yeah? Well that's good. I've been great."

"Me too."

"Great. Glad we're in the same place then," Cam said sharply.

"Awesome."

The rain had lessened by the time they arrived at the hotel. CST officials re-opened the challenge briefly, but closed it again when no teams came forward to attempt it, none having the courage or skill to even complete the river portion of the challenge after the storm.

Maria knocked on Rick's door a while after the team had settled and gotten a chance to clean up, and almost knocked a second time before he opened the door. "Did I wake you?"

The captain shook his head slowly and rubbed the side of his face, stubble already growing dark. "No, I just got off the phone with Brittany. She flipped out, but she's glad we're back safely."

"Guys!" Maria was interrupted by Cam charging towards them with a grin on his face. "Hey, have you guys checked your AIRCs since the challenge?" His grin grew when they both shook their heads, and he held up his AIRC. "A hundred points! I can't believe you guys landed right at the marker point."

Rick frowned and took the AIRC to look at it closer. "I thought we were aiming for the gold marker, not the red."

"I thought so too, if we were even aiming for anything but shore at the end." She glanced at Cam, whose smile was slowly fading. She had seen that look before, the look that told her there were two stories: the truth, and the one he let others believe without correcting them.

"I don't remember what it said, but you guys got full points." Cam shrugged and glanced down the hall. "You guys have been through a lot today; you might be remembering it wrong."

"But-"

"I'll go talk to Ryan and see what he remembers," Cam interrupted Maria. "You guys need your rest. It's fine, I'll check it out." He raised an eyebrow at his captain. "Seriously, guys, you almost died. Get some rest."

Rick nodded as he passed the AIRC back to Cam. "Yeah, sure. Most of the challenge is a blur right now anyway. I'll see you guys in the morning."

Cam looked at Maria as Rick closed his door. "Go on." He ignored her stare, but waited until she left as well. Before he could knock on Ryan's door, Ryan opened it but stepped back quickly, startled at the sight of his team-mate. "Hey! They're talking about us on Sportcentre! This is so awesome! There's even a video of us doing the challenge." He grinned, while holding the door open for him as the TV could be heard from inside the room.

"I was sure that bringing Hampton onto the team would slow them down, but apparently not even the weather can slow down

this team," a young broadcaster said, wearing a very shocked look on his face.

"With Tylar's track record for water challenges, I'd say Revolution definitely did better with Hampton than without," an older one said.

"What I want to take a look at is this team's determination. First of all, having to find a short notice replacement for their long time captain, and now a very difficult first challenge. If we look back to Kier in the video, she attempted twice to get above water before going over to help her team-mates. And the junior Warner managed to tread water the entire time in that storm." As the third broadcaster spoke, the video was shown of the team at the point when the large wave washed over them.

"I honestly can't believe that they were the only team today to get the full hundred points, and I think this doesn't necessarily show their determination, but their desperation. They braved this storm to get those points, and they got them, the only ones to get them today despite the Raiders who were slotted to attempt the challenge about an hour before Revolution, which was quite a sur..."

The broadcaster was interrupted as Cam turned off the TV now that they were done talking about them, not that he had liked what they said about him. If they looked at his stats overall, they were better than anyone else's. There was no need to point out a small flaw he had. If they looked at his history, they would be more understanding...

"Do you remember what your AIM said the colour was of the buoy? The last one?"

"I thought the gold one." Ryan paused. "But, maybe it said red. We got the full points, so maybe I heard it wrong. It was pretty loud out there with the wind."

Cam nodded. "I remember red, but if you think it said gold maybe it did. I doubt there'd be anything wrong with your AIM, but it's a possibility."

His head snapped to look at his team-mate. "Something wrong? It's brand new."

"That's true." He stroked his chin as if in deep thought. It was a cliché move, he knew, but it was dramatic at least. "Hey, what do I know, right? I'm sure everything's fine."

"Well, what would be wrong with it?"

"Oh, nothing. You may not have a competition level chip yet, but I'm sure if I train you well enough, you won't even notice." He guessed that if Ryan had never had an AIM before, he would never know there was no such thing as a competition level chip. All AIM chips were created and programmed the same. Those that weren't were products of the Underground.

Ryan paused and looked at his AIM. "Well, could you take a look at it and make sure? I don't want to make more work for you, but I'm sure this is less work than having to train me twice as hard." Cam was right.

He shrugged. "I could get Rick to look at it for you. He's the captain, after all."

"I don't want to bother him. Could you...could you just look at it, and maybe not tell Maria or Rick?"

Perfect. "Sure, don't worry about it. You guys almost died together. I'm sure he wouldn't mind, especially being your captain, but I'll do it."

"Thank you." He did not want to sound so desperate, but he was still so new to using AIMs. He knew what the basic code of an AIM looked like but he had no idea how to look for problems or glitches. They were rare anyway, so there had not been any opportunities for him to see any different programs. He handed the turtle to Cam along with his AIRC. He did not like the idea of someone else handling his AIM. He was already beginning to like it, and he was afraid of what Cam might do to it, but he did not really have any other choice.

"Don't worry about it. Have a good night. Hey, you did good today, Ryan."

Cam went back to his room and as he stepped in he heard Maria behind him.

"Oh, I don't think so." She put her foot in the door before he could close it, putting her weight against the door to open it again.

"I thought you were asleep."

"Tell me what's going on," Maria said, looking up at him with anger burning in her eyes.

"I don't know what you're talking about."

"I know that AIM said gold buoy, and I know you're hiding something because that's what you do."

Cam glared down at her. "I don't know anything. He asked me to take a look at his AIM, so I am. I'm not going to tamper with it. Why would I do something to jeopardize the team?"

Maria raised an eyebrow and glared back at him. "Your existence jeopardizes this team and puts us in danger. You don't have to tell me what you know, but you at least owe me the truth."

"I haven't even looked at his chip yet, so how could I know anything about it?" he said through gritted teeth, towering over her. "And I don't appreciate your accusations."

"Well you're the most logical person to blame." Maria knew better than to be intimidated by him- they had fought too much, known each other too well for her to be afraid of him. "I'm sure your Underground co-workers can help you look at it."

"Who I associate with isn't any of your concern anymore."

"It concerns me when it gets my team and their careers in trouble. I'm also the only one who knows you're part of the sorry excuse of an organization, so I'm the only one who can keep an eye on you."

After a minute, he finally looked away with a sigh. "I'll work on it. There's probably nothing wrong with it, but when I find out I'll let you know. I can't do anything more than that." He looked back at her, suddenly feeling as though she was judging him with her eyes. Even after all these years, he still could not stand the thought of disappointing her.

Maria nodded and stepped back from the door. "Well, it's more than I expected. I'm glad you're at least starting to think about the team." She muttered a good night and headed back to her room.

Cam sighed with frustration and tried to slam the door, not realizing that the door was designed not to, being in a hotel. He sat on the edge of his bed and placed the turtle on the bed next to him as his AIM in the form of a snake made its way over to inspect the creature.

"Behave. Both of you. And be quiet when I'm on the phone." He watched the two for a moment before he picked up the phone, dialing another room just down the hall.

"Hey. We need to talk."

CHAPTER 10

Ryan glanced at Cam as they drove down the highway to the next challenge city, Sarnia, a border town at the south end of Lake Huron. They had not said a word to each other for the two hours they had been driving, and all he could think was that he had done something wrong. Cam had looked into the programming of his AIM and had said nothing was wrong with it, but it just made Ryan realize that he had absolutely no idea what he was doing. If something happened again in the future, he needed to know what to look for.

"I'm not going to be kicked off the team, am I?" Ryan asked, his nerves apparent by the slight waver in his voice.

Cam raised an eyebrow in confusion. "What are you talking about? I told you, I didn't see anything wrong with the programming." Of course, that had been the problem. After the conversation he'd had with Ryan's AIM, Cam definitely should have seen something in the coding. Then again, there was nothing in his own AIM's coding that would explain its behaviour, but Cam knew his AIM was a one-off. Something was wrong with Ryan's, but he did not know what. Not yet. Other than the fact that he had a full conversation with a robot which should not even have the capability of having a conversation.

"I know, but if there had been something in the programming and I used it in a challenge, could the officials take away our points?"

"We'd be disqualified and you'd be suspended because only people in the Underground change chip program codes." Cam looked at his team-mate and saw the shame on his face. This guy really needed to get some confidence. He always looked like a puppy that thought it was in trouble. "You won't be kicked off the team for having bad hearing. Everyone heard different things. It's really no big deal. I've done much worse and I'm still here. If anything, we'd kick you off for being a pain in the butt."

Ryan looked at him hopefully, as if Cam's failures would redeem him. "What'd you do?"

"None of your business." Cam looked in the rear view mirror of the truck before changing lanes.

"Well, did you get into any trouble?" He did not want to press for details unless they were offered, but he was still curious.

"My girlfriend broke up with me."

"Sorry to hear that."

"It's not a big deal," he muttered.

Ryan looked at Cam, noticed the frustration in his eyes and decided to drop the topic. He should have known better, though. From what he had seen on television, and what he had seen in person, Cam was not one to back down. Then again, Ryan had not pictured Cam to be the type of guy to be in a relationship in the first place. "So, Maria's pretty awesome."

"Excuse me?"

"Kayaking, she's pretty awesome at it. Taught me in less than half an hour, not that I'm great or anything but still. Has she been doing it long?"

"Why don't you ask her?"

"Well, we could always talk about your ex if you prefer."

Cam tapped on the steering wheel impatiently. "What do you want to know about Maria?" He rolled his eyes again with a sigh when Ryan shrugged. "Maria Kier, twenty-two years old. Her parents divorced a few years back and her mom's been married four times since. Her dad was in the military, but he died from a series of heart attacks during her first season on the team. She's into stupid sports like kayaking, horseback riding, and rock climbing. She's even a certified guide. She played on her high school's soccer team so I guess that's pretty cool. She was in army cadets until she went into Scanning." Cam smiled and looked at Ryan. "She loves to hunt, so you should definitely talk about that."

"What got her into those sports?"

"Why do you care?"

"It says a lot about a person, their motivations," he said, looking out the side window as they drove down to Canatara Park in Sarnia. "So, why are we coming here?"

"You ask too many questions," Cam said with a sigh and did not bother answering, but pulled out his AIRC instead. "Maria, are you on a trail?"

After a pause, she spoke up. "I'm at the car now. I parked it near the beach. I already did some scanning on the trails, and Rick's uncle won't be back until tomorrow morning apparently, so I figured I'd do some training. Alone."

"I'm dropping Ryan off with you. I have some stuff I need to take care of."

"Take him with you."

"I have people I need to see."

There was another pause before she sighed. "Turn right when you get onto the beach. There's barely anyone here. The car won't be hard to find."

Cam slipped his AIRC away and drove onto the sand slowly, swearing lightly under his breath. "She knows I hate the car in the sand."

"You let her drive it."

"I wasn't talking to you." Cam slowed more as he pulled the truck next to the small silver car Maria was leaning against. Remnants of a storm system similar to the one in Owen Sound brought cold winds to the park. He looked at her hugging herself in an over-sized sweater, and jeans before he got out. He found himself trying to find her shape beneath the baggy clothing before he could stop the instinct.

Ryan followed, much like a child caught in between divorced parents. "Sorry I'm being dumped on you."

She grinned and shook her head. "Don't worry about it. If you want to take the car and explore, I can just let you know when

I want to be picked up. Unless you want to do some training with me," she added with a friendly smile. An addition which Cam did not miss in his brief glance.

"I don't think so," Cam snapped. "He's not driving my car."

"My car." Maria shot back. "Check the registration."

"Are you really playing that card?"

"Right now? Yeah, I am."

"You know, I've never been here before. I'll just stay here with you, Maria." Ryan stepped between the two. "Besides, I could use the extra training."

Cam waved his hand at them and went back to the truck before driving away as Ryan watched. "I'm learning more and more about this team every day. He drives your car but calls it his, and he drives you crazy."

"Is it that obvious? And here I tried to make it subtle." Maria flipped the hood of her sweater over her head as a gust of wind pushed it down, throwing her hair around like a toy. "I'm sorry you're always getting caught in the middle of things."

"I guess I understand why he's always kind of a jerk. If I was dumped I'd be ticked too, especially if I wanted her back. Cam doesn't seem to be the kind of guy used to girls leaving *him*."

Her eyes opened wide with surprise. "He talked about his ex to you?"

"That was all he said, really."

"He's not the type to go crawling back," she said with a determined shake of the head.

"You never know. Stranger things have happened, I'm sure, such as him being a boyfriend in the first place."

Maria waved the comment away and looked down to the other end of the parking lot. She thought about what he had said. He was right about that, at least. "I'm sorry. I really shouldn't be talking about it." Her eyes squinted as she tried to see what the group of people were doing in the parking lot. She glanced back at Ryan and pulled out her AIRC from her pocket. "You need to let the paddle spin."

Ryan gave her a confused look. "Um, what?"

"When we were kayaking, you had the paddle in a death grip. Nice and loose, spin it in your hands when you need to turn quickly, in the river at least."

"Oh, okay. Thanks."

"It was bugging me and I didn't get the chance to tell you while we were going. So don't do it again."

"I'm still better than Cam." Ryan smiled.

"I don't know about that."

"I do." From the shocked look on Maria's face, it was clear both were stunned by his forwardness. He cleared his throat and began to walk with her.

"Have you guys talked to Owen at all?" He stopped when they stood next to a flock of seagulls sitting on the beach and as he smiled he slid out his AIRC. They were just seagulls, but every scan counts. There was no harm in it. He touched the screen and held the AIRC in front of his face, keeping one of the gulls in focus while the progress bar crawled across the screen.

"Yesterday I called him. Rick calls him every night after he calls his wife."

"And Cam?" He grinned when the screen showed 'Scan Successful' and he looked through the stats of the genetic code he had just scanned. Not too bad. Gulls were not the greatest bird, but at least now he had one. He scrolled through his database of scans and chose the German shepherd that Rick had let him have. He smiled as the dog formed next to him and reached down to pet the rough hair.

"Cam asks us how he's doing. I think he's scared to call. He doesn't like hospitals, even just calling one."

"And how have you been holding up? Cam told me what happened to your dad. I'm really sorry. I figured he died after we went to the cemetery, but I didn't know what had happened."

Maria shrugged and looked at him, glad he had changed the topic but not so glad of his new choice. "I'm okay, I guess. Not so good on the first day. Since my dad died, Owen's kind of taken over that role. I think what bothers me is that I know Owen won't relax after this. And knowing what a heart attack can do, what it can take away from me makes all of this worse."

"It was just a small one though. If Cam can sit out from water challenges, Owen can sit out from the really physically demanding ones." He briefly put a hand on her arm. "Owen'll be fine. When he comes back, you guys will figure it out."

She looked up at him with an appreciative smile. "How do you feel, being a temp?"

Ryan shrugged. "I see it as a contract to be honest. And you never know, maybe another team will see me in challenges and pick me up." He grinned. "Maybe I'll be a Raider." He noticed his AIM look up at him, and he swore that he saw the dog's head shake as if to say no.

Maria laughed. "No, you'd have to become mean and broody."

"I can do that."

"Nah, you're fine the way you are."

"Thanks. You're pretty fine yourself." He laughed when Maria flicked his arm playfully. "Oh, what? You didn't mean I'm good looking? Well fine, I take it back."

"No you don't. You're too nice."

"There is that." He looked at her as the wind pushed her hood down once again and laughed when she pouted in frustration. It was nice that he was able to be so open with her, but it was not natural for him; at least not with someone like Maria.

"Now it's my turn to ask about you," Maria said, holding her hood in place. "So, spill. I want to know everything."

"See, you're hooked already." Ryan grinned. "Well, I'm a year younger than you, which you already know. I've lived in Elmira my entire life. Parents are still happily together after twenty five years and I have three younger brothers and two sisters. I go hunting every now and then with my dad-"

"You what?"

"Hunt. Not too often though. Why, have you ever been?"

"Why would I ever want to go hunting?" Maria cried. "I can't believe you've gone hunting!"

"Wait, what?"

"You seemed like such a good guy. For someone who was raised in a family that appreciates real animals, I can't believe you would do something so completely horrible and disgusting!"

"Whoa, wait, hold on!" Ryan said, holding his hands up defensively. "You don't hunt?"

"No, of course not!"

Ryan stared at her for a minute before laughing and rubbing his face. "Cam…"

She raised an eyebrow. "What?"

"Cam told me you love to hunt, but I should've known better. You love animals, don't you?"

Maria closed her eyes and covered her face, shaking her head. "Oh my God. I can't believe he would tell you that. I'm sorry, but really, you hunt?"

"I don't have to anymore, if you think it's really that bad."

"I do."

"Okay."

Maria dropped her hands to show the confused look on her face. "Wait, what?"

"I'll stop. I don't need to hunt."

"Just like that? Because I said I didn't like it?"

Ryan shrugged. "Sure, why not? But that was your only wish, and you can't get me to do anything else." His smile faded when Maria covered her face. "Did I say something?" He stepped towards her when she brought her hands away and wiped away a few tears. "I'm sorry, I didn't mean to upset you," he said quietly.

"No, you didn't. You just…you just agreed to stop doing something simply because I said I was against it. My ex didn't even do that for me."

"Then he's an idiot."

She took his hand briefly. "Thank you, Ryan. You don't have to stop hunting."

Ryan shook his head. "Now what kind of friend would I be if I went back on my word?" She did not need to know he never enjoyed hunting in the first place. They remained quiet as they continued walking until a group of four people stopped in front of them.

"Hey, Maria!"

She smiled lightly with that professional smile she had. "Hey, Todd. Did you guys just get here from Owen Sound?"

The man nodded as his team-mates laughed. "Yeah. Seventy-five points. Even in good weather, we can't keep up with you. I'm not looking forward to having to compete against Cam this season if this is the level you guys are at now."

"I'll remind you that Cam sat out of that challenge." She glanced at Ryan and motioned to him. "Sorry, Todd, this is Ryan Hampton. The rookie we got after you signed Wes on us," Maria said with a joking scowl.

Todd held up his hands with a laugh. "Hey, you weren't using him. How were we supposed to know Owen would be benched? Besides, Wes is our best shot. If you guys thought he was good enough to keep as back-up, it means we have a chance."

Maria nodded in agreement before turning her attention to her team-mate. "Ryan, this is Todd Hannigan."

"Yeah, captain of the Rising Suns." Ryan grinned shyly. "Nice to meet you."

"I meant to come over and introduce myself at the opening ceremonies. Got any good scans so far, anything better than the German shepherd there?"

He shrugged and looked at his AIM. "Well I got a Northern Goshawk, and I tried to get a turkey vulture today but it had already been scanned."

"Northern Goshawk?" Todd nodded with approval. "Not bad. I should've guessed that you'd have good scans with your performance so far. You guys were incredible last night." He took a few steps towards Maria. "But if you think you're going to continue to beat us, you have another thing coming."

She laughed and stepped around him. "Yeah, well miracles do happen. After ten years, this might be the year you beat us. See you around." She waved with a smile as she continued walking with Ryan. "You really get star-struck, don't you?"

"Sorry. I'm starting to get used to you guys, I think. It's like moving to Hollywood for me." He paused. "Actually, I think that'd be worse. At least we're sticking to the country for most of the time. I don't think I'd be able to handle a big city like Hollywood."

"I don't think so, either. You have that whole 'country boy' feel to you." She looked down at the dog. "I can't believe you used to hunt."

"Yeah, yeah..."

Cam unzipped the front flap of his tent when he heard a vehicle drive up and park next to the truck. He stepped out and stretched his arms above his head as his two team-mates climbed out of the car. *This should be good...*

"So you can't be too upset about my first time hunting," came Ryan's voice.

"No, but the other times, that was just reckless killing."

Maria sounded less angry than Cam had expected. When he actually looked at them, he realized they were smiling.

"Have fun?" he asked.

She looked around with a shrug. "Didn't get much done. Saw Todd. Looks like they have a pretty good team this year, for once. Where's Rick?"

"He wanted fast food for dinner."

"The meal of champions." Maria looked at him finally. They had not spoken at all, really, since their argument in Owen Sound. She knew where he had gone today, well, not the exact location but what it involved. It disgusted her just being around him, and hurt her enough to take a few steps towards the line of trees behind the tents. "I'm going to do some more scanning. Let me know when Rick gets here."

Ryan watched as Maria walked away before he turned to Cam. He had decided to not be angry with his Cam's attempt of sabotaging his conversation with Maria. *Kill them with kindness.*

"Hey, thanks for the advice."

"What advice?"

"Talking to Maria about hunting. It gave me the chance to get to know Maria. I had no idea she was so passionate. I mean I saw her talk to those reporters, but she knows so much about everything to do with hunting. She's not just another crazy animal lover. I respect that about her. Even convinced me to stop hunting, not that I did it that much anyway."

Cam turned to the new member. "You're going to stop? Just like that?"

Ryan shrugged. "Sure. She got really upset about it."

"You did that for her?"

"I guess. I didn't want to cause tension on the team because of it. It's not worth it."

Cam smiled angrily. "Unbelievable."

"What?"

"Screw you," he snapped and went after Maria.

Maria looked over her shoulder after a few minutes to see Cam close behind her. "What do you want?"

He stopped and looked around as if to make sure no one else was around. "I checked out his chip, and everything's fine. Ryan said he'd let me look at it whenever I needed just in case I missed something. I don't think I did, but I've been wrong before. I had some other people look at it too to be sure."

"Did it tell us gold?" When he glanced away, she let out an angry groan. "Are you kidding me, Cam? Something's obviously wrong with it."

"It's not dangerous. It's not even Underground material. I checked out where the chip was made and the code says it was made in a McCarthy lab. Unless someone hacked the code to make it look legit, I'm not going to take it away from Ryan. There's nothing wrong with it," Cam said, looking back at her defensively, but he knew he could not say much more than that. "It could be something wrong with the substance, but I can't check that here."

"But it *is* part of the Underground, Cam! What about this are you not understanding?" she asked, raising her voice in frustration. "We could be disqualified!"

"It can't be traced back to the Underground. It's not all that bad, Maria."

"Yes. It is, and I can't even express how disappointed and ashamed I am for you. You know it's wrong and you still do it. I've talked to you about it for years and you still made me out to be the judgemental girlfriend." Maria's voice rang through the forest. "I have one stupid conversation with Ryan about him hunting and he said he'd stop, just like that, because he didn't want to cause tension in our friendship. He's known me for a total of four days and he already appreciates me more than you ever did."

Cam rolled his eyes. "This is not the same thing. Ryan gets nothing from hunting, so it's not like he's losing anything."

"Oh, and what do you get?"

"Respect," Cam spat at her. "Challenges. My talent's actually being put to good use."

"Oh, and I never respected you?"

"Not the way you should've."

"So what, you wanted me to worship the ground you walked on? No, maybe I didn't fully respect you and I'm sorry for that, but how could I when you didn't even respect yourself? Cam, you are so talented. You're an amazing athlete, and a huge competitor. I probably wouldn't have made it in this competition if I had to go up against you." She shook her head and stepped closer to him, looking up at him. "Cameron, the Underground doesn't offer you anything the CST doesn't, and at least you get recognition through the CST. The Underground, it seems like it's just made you lose more than you've gained," she said, her voice finally low.

Cam looked down at her with a look she had not seen in over a month. He drew in a breath and sighed. "Are you going to tell me if that's why you broke up with me?" He looked at her, hoping for some form of affirmation, affirmation he had not even sought but felt that after a month he should probably have.

"One of the reasons, yes."

He nodded and glanced away. "At least you finally told me a reason, although I probably should've assumed. Well, I just wanted to let you know what I found out." There was more. He could have argued, he could have told her more of what he got from the Underground, that in reality he actually helped people, but now was not the time. If he ever could tell her.

"Cameron, you deserve better than to have your life ruined by this," she said softly, trying not to plead the way she had so many times before. She was tired of pleading, tired of trying to make her case. Tired of trying to make him care.

"And you just deserve better. Clearly you've realized that," Cam said with a sad smile. "Ryan's not too bad. At least he seems to like being on the water. Maybe not in Owen Sound anymore, but at least he was willing to try." He turned to go back to the campsite, but he stopped and turned back to Maria. Before she could say anything, Cam caught her lips with his briefly, an arm wrapping around her waist.

Maria was caught off guard, and glad he pulled away when he did before he finally left. She watched him walk away as she leaned her back against a tree and held her face in her hands.

CHAPTER 11

Maria came back from the forest to see the three men already sitting down and eating. She sat next to Rick, grabbing the last bag of fast food. "Thanks for letting me know you were back," she muttered with a grimace. She hated being so emotional. It didn't usually hit her this hard.

"Cam thought you might want to be left alone," Rick answered after swallowing a bite of his hamburger. "Sorry." If he had been offended by her tone, he didn't show it.

"When have you known me to wait around when there's food to be eaten?" Her eyes caught Cam's briefly. She looked into the bag before closing it again. "Actually, I'm not really hungry right now." She gave the bag back to Rick before she stood. "I think I'm just going to go for a ride. When do you think your uncle is going to show us the horses tomorrow?"

"As soon as he gets back in the morning. He said he'd be back in plenty of time for us to get to the challenge. I guess he has some good horses this year for us to scan."

"Alright. I'll see you guys later."

Cam watched as she walked away and disappeared quickly into her tent. He crumpled up his wrapper and put it into a larger bag. "Are you sure we're going to be able to get to the challenge in time tomorrow? Your uncle likes to talk."

"We'll be fine. If it's on the water again, you won't need to worry about when we get there." Rick grinned as Cam shot him an angry look. He knew that Cam hated when someone pointed out his flaws and shortcomings, and he should not antagonize him like that, but they needed to get their dynamics back to normal. This was the best way he knew how.

"Isn't this a little like cheating? Scanning horses at a breeder's farm?" Ryan dipped his fingers into a pile of ketchup, trying to rescue a drowning fry once the fire lived without his coaxing.

"It's strategic. It's fine as long as we have his permission and the horses haven't been sold yet," Cam replied. *With consent...* He leaned back in the camping chair and listened to Maria shuffling around in her tent. "I'm going for a hike, maybe do some scanning." He started towards the forest, the heat of the fire leaving his body quickly as he moved away from the circle. He stopped suddenly as Maria came out of her tent holding a helmet and bridle in her arms. They both stared at each other awkwardly for a moment.

"I'm going to go for a ride," she said.

"I'm going for a walk."

"Good. Walks are good."

"That's what they say."

Maria nodded and pointed to her AIRC. "I'm going now." She paused, looking down around her feet, and saw her AIM as a cat crawl out of the tent. With a quick glance at Cam, she walked away as the cat rippled and shifted into the form of a quarter horse which continued to follow her obediently down the dirt path.

Cam ran a hand through his hair, realizing he had not even bothered to gel it that day. At least no one had wanted to take his picture. He headed into the woods which were already dark with the dusk, and slipped his AIRC from his pocket. He looked down quickly when he saw a Golden Retriever at his side. "I don't want to hear it," he said quietly, as if assuming the AIM would speak out of turn. He smiled lightly when it remained silent, but it faded when he thought about his attitude so far this season.

He had done well by simply concentrating on the game. He did not have to think about her, or anything else that had happened, and he was fine. But now his concentration slipped. Cam shook his head as if that would help. *Just stay focused. Get some scans, and get prepared for the challenge tomorrow. One day at a time.*

Ryan glanced at Rick, watching him finish his dinner a while after Cam and Maria had left. "Hey, Rick?"

"Yeah?" he answered above the crackling of the fire between them. He started as one of the logs popped in the heat, sending a wave of sparks into the air.

"How are you doing? I don't mean to pry, and I don't want to get all personal or anything. I'm only asking because you....you just seem a little out of it."

Rick leaned back in his chair and shook his head. "I'm fine. It's just...I'm responsible for everything that happens to this team. I have no idea how my dad did it, but I'm pretty sure he never had to deal with any of this kind of stuff. At least as far as he let on. He was always the strong one."

"Well, you seem to be a pretty strong leader to me. You're keeping Cam in line so far." Ryan grinned a bit when Rick made a motion with his hand, forming it into a gun and held it to his head. "Alright, well it seems you're doing a pretty good job to me." He paused, shoving a stick into the fire to push some wood around. A log crumbled at the touch, sending a wave of sparks into the air.

"So, I remember Maria mentioning something about the Underground when she was talking to those reporters." Ryan looked at his captain, hoping for a facial reaction. "What's the deal with that? I never really heard about it until now, at least not much. I've just heard some rumours, so I thought you might know something more."

Rick shrugged. "It started up around the same time as AIMs were created, about twenty years back. A group of people started doing some experiments on the gel substance, and then began fooling around with the programming on the chips. After that, they traded and sold what they created. Most people treat it pretty much like a mafia or something. I've even heard of animals being imported to create different genetic codes and programming specialty chips."

"So what's wrong with it? Other than mafia type operations."

"Well, it's almost impossible to regulate, especially if it's brought into the CST."

"Makes sense, I guess," Ryan said, slurping the last of his drink. He shook the cup and set it down once he was convinced there was nothing left.

"And most of those people just do it for money or to try to screw over teams."

"Has that ever happened to you guys before?"

Rick shook his head and folded his arms across his chest. "No, at least not that I know. I can see them doing it this season, though, because we're disadvantaged. But you never know. If you keep training, you might even be the next Cam Tylar."

Ryan smiled sheepishly. "I'm trying hard not to slow you guys down. I know there's a lot on the line."

"Well, we'll see how that turns out." He stood and walked past Ryan, clapping him on the shoulder on his way to the RV.

Ryan sat around the fire for another half hour, watching the flames lick at the chilled air. The next Cam Tylar. He threw a clump of dirt into the fire and leaned his elbows on his knees. Sure, he had done well in his first challenge. He had worked harder than he had ever worked before, but it was his fault they had been caught in the storm. He shook his head before he stood and headed down the dirt path Maria had taken. He walked slowly, not wanting to get too far away from the fire. He needed to just stop thinking. Ryan had learned that the more he thought, the worse he performed. Distractions always helped. He stopped walking after a few minutes when he saw Maria's outline in the dark. She was heading back towards him on the horse but she stopped just in front of him. He waved to her as she dismounted.

"Not a bad looking scan you got yourself."

She grinned and ran her hand down its neck. "Yeah. It's a scan of a horse I had when I was younger. She was great. See her face? The shape shows she's spirited. I've never used her in a challenge though. She'd be good, if we could get her personality into a scan."

Ryan laughed. "Wait, the shape of her face?"

"Don't laugh." Maria smiled with a shrug. "I haven't gone wrong yet."

"Can you read humans the same way?"

"Unfortunately not. They're even more complex and confusing." Maria looked at the horse longingly. "The AIM is never able to replicate her spirit. It's a good copy, but not close enough," she said softly. "AIMs do absolutely everything you tell them to. They don't spook or buck you off. It's always easy to tack up and you never need to groom them. Completely predictable."

"You sound a little bitter."

"It's just been a long time since I've ridden a real horse. I doubt I'd even be able to handle it." She paused as she took the bridle off the horse. "My horse died a few years before my dad. Haven't ridden another since."

"Maybe a chip that allows free will, maybe it wouldn't be so bad. Never know if the Underground is doing experiments like that. It could actually be a good thing if they are," Ryan suggested with a shrug.

Maria's head snapped to look at Ryan, her eyes wide and her eyebrows furrowed in anger. "I can't believe you just said that!" she hissed, looking around as if worried someone would hear. Unfortunately, someone had.

Cam came out from the forest next to their path after listening to the two for a moment. He stayed near the line of trees, not expecting to see them but he was not in the mood to really talk to either of them. Rather than go back into the forest and go the long way back to the campsite, he waited until his two team-mates continued down the path.

"Why not? You were just saying that AIM's aren't close enough to the real thing!" Ryan said defensively.

"Exactly! And that's how it should be! There has to be that difference, that line between an AIM and a real animal or there's no point in having both. We still need real cows for milk and chickens for eggs. If people develop AIMs that could produce those-"

"It would allow every household to support itself," Ryan interrupted gently.

"Are you kidding me? Then there'd be no more farms."

"Maybe not dairy farms, but agricultural farms would still be around," Ryan said with a shrug. "I'm just saying that whatever the Underground might be working on, maybe it's not so bad."

Cam grinned as Ryan unknowingly defended him. He began to step out from the edge of the trees when Maria spoke again.

"I can't believe I'm hearing this from you!" she said, running her hands through her hair.

"What do you want me to say? Good things can happen even from bad intentions. Look what the World Wars caused."

"The death of millions of people."

"Global unity," Ryan declared, raising his own voice as he stepped towards her. "The Human Rights Act. The creation of the United Nations."

"But at what cost? I know you're new to the world of Scanning, I get that, but you have no idea what you're talking about."

Ryan paused. "Sometimes things have to go through hell and back to get to something amazing," he said softly.

Maria shook her head, fighting back tears she knew would fall anyway. "I just...I can't justify it. Any of it. I don't think the cost is worth it. I'm part of an organization that deems it irresponsible and dangerous, and I agree with them. The government has even made Underground products illegal because of the dangers. Not that I'm a fan of the government, but at least they were smart enough to see the dangers. I don't think it's worth losing your job, or the ones you love. I just don't."

Cam did not hear anything for a moment, but then he heard Maria's soft sobs. He looked at the ground before stepping out onto the path to see Ryan holding Maria as she cried into his chest. He walked over to them slowly and stopped when Ryan noticed him. He looked too comfortable holding her like that. Cam had never seen her like this talking about the Underground. Yelling and screaming was something he had seen many times. But never a break down. He noticed Ryan motioning to him with his head, trying to switch off but he shook his head. He needed to try to rebuild his concentration.

Ryan gave him a confused look and glanced down to Maria and he shook his head to silently disagree with Cam, putting his hands on her arms around his neck to switch her over. He stepped away quickly when Cam finally came over to take his place.

Maria only briefly looked up, feeling Ryan move away from her and felt familiar arms wrap around her. She tensed quickly and forced back her sobs. She felt his mouth near her ear and heard him whisper, "It's okay," before she let herself cry again.

He should not even be like this. What happened to focusing on the game? *She's a team member. She's a team member who's upset. That's all. And because she's a girl, this is how she feels better. So this is helping the team.* Cam felt her begin to move away from him after a few minutes of sobbing and he looked down at her. "You don't need to..."

"No, I'm okay," Maria said quietly, slipping her arms from his neck to her face, wiping it dry. She glanced around to see that Ryan had walked away. "Guess I made Ryan a little uncomfortable. Men never seem to know what to do around a crying woman." She gave him a rueful smile.

"I think he figured you'd want to be comforted by someone you've known longer."

"He thought I was mad at him."

"Well, you did a good job taking your anger out on someone. Nearly had me convinced, even."

Maria glanced up at him, noticing his arms still loosely around her. "How much did you hear?"

"Enough to like Ryan a bit more." Cam gave her an arrogant smile before he could regret it.

Maria swore and tried to back away. "You have to ruin everything, and everyone, don't you?"

"Hey, I'm kidding," he said with a laugh. "Come on."

"No, you come on, Cam."

His face darkened as he looked down at her, lines of anger crossing his face. "You know what, he barely knows anything about the Underground and he already understands its benefits."

"Cameron, don't," she said as she turned away from him in his arms.

"He's just like me, Maria. Just like how I started out."

"He is *nothing* like you," she snapped at him.

"Yes, he is, Maria. He's all sweet and says what you want to hear when you want to hear it, but he's on the same path I took. I'm not saying that it's a good thing, I'm just saying that he's like me." He lowered his face, trying to get her to look at him. "Maria."

"No, Cameron. No," she said, finally pushing away from him. "We're not talking about this. We've talked it to death, and I'm not changing my mind about it. Clearly you don't have any intention of changing your mind, so the conversation's over."

"Maria."

"No," she said with a definite tone of finality. She began to walk back towards the campsite as she switched her AIM back into a cat form.

"Maria, it's not that easy."

"Sure it is," she called over her shoulder.

"You really think I could just leave? You think they'd make it easy? With my skills? With everything I know?" Cam called after her.

Maria turned around, her eyes wide with concern. The thought had never crossed her mind, but in that split-second, fifty different scenarios appeared along with a realization that she had no idea how much he knew. "Did they threaten you?" she asked, her voice barely above a whisper.

"No." He barely held back a laugh. "I've never been stupid enough to try to leave." He squeezed his eyes closed when Maria began to storm off, immediately regretting his words. "I didn't mean it like that. Maria! Think about it."

"I'm done thinking about it, Cam! I'm done with all of it. I've been done with it for over a month now." Leave it to Cam to find a way to ruin everything.

"Maria, come on," he said, taking quick steps to catch up.

When he grabbed her elbow, she spun around, wrenching her arm away from him. "Just tell me I wasn't worth it. Tell me I wasn't worth losing whatever place and reputation you may or may not have with the Underground."

"Maria..."

"Say it."

"You're not worth it."

Maria nodded. "I guess that's closure then."

Cam stared at her before looking away. "I guess so." He could not say anything more. Over the years, he had told her too much, and he could not risk telling her that if he left the Underground, it would be worse for not only her, but everyone involved in the CST. It was better she was angry with him. It was better she hated him. That was his mantra, at least.

"I'm taking my car back."

"I paid half!" he said, surprised at her sudden childishness.

"I'll buy you out."

"Fine!" Cam let her walk a few paces ahead as they strode angrily to the campsite. He watched her jump into her tent quickly before he grabbed his stuff from his tent and whipped the RV door open. "I'm taking the truck," he said shortly but paused when he noticed Ryan in the RV with Rick. He waved his hand in frustration and left the vehicle without bothering to address Ryan or explain.

"Hey, what?" Rick let his book fall as he jumped from the bed, scrambling after him with Ryan close behind. "What the hell happened?"

"*She* happened," Cam yelled, pointing to her tent as she swore at Cam through the canvas enough to make even Rick cringe at the words. "I'm going to a hotel. I couldn't care less what types of horses you guys scan. Call me when you're done and I'll meet you for the challenge."

"You're not going anywhere." Rick put a hand on Cam's shoulder to stop him from getting into the truck. His words came out strong, authoritative. The way he would speak to the board when a decision needed to be made. "Take my bed in the RV if you can't be in a tent next to her, but you're not leaving this campsite." Rick moved to Maria's tent and opened the flap.

"Get out here." He waited for a moment until she sighed and crawled from her tent. He looked at her as she folded her arms over her chest, not bothering to wipe the tears of anger from her face. "Both of you need to stop acting like bitter exes and start acting like team-mates. You knew the risks of being together; my dad and I warned you guys, so now you have to deal with it. Your relationship was never private. It always included the entire team, and it didn't hurt us until now so quit dragging me and Ryan into it. Both of you go to sleep, and all of us will go to my uncle's farm tomorrow, together. Is that clear?"

Both Cam and Maria muttered some form of affirmation, neither of them looking at the other or at Rick.

"Good. I'll see you in the morning." He looked over his shoulder to watch Cam enter the RV. He shook his head and turned in for the night, taking the tent Cam had abandoned.

Ryan stood awkwardly next to the door of the RV and caught Maria's glance. He should have figured it out sooner though, that Cam and Maria were together, or had been. He saw her shake her head at him slowly, as if saying she did not want to talk, before she crawled back into her tent, zipping the flap closed slowly. This was going to be a long season.

"I don't know what to do. I mean, they've been broken up before. We've all dealt with stresses but I don't know what to do." Rick lay back onto his sleeping bag in the tent as he waited for his father's response over the phone. He kept his voice low. Maria was still awake in the tent nearby.

"Think about when you and Brittany had rough patches when you were first married. Even you couldn't manage to keep that away from your performance." Owen's voice sounded much stronger than when the team had left. His father was making an easy recovery, but it would be a while until Owen would be back on the field. "Besides, you still sometimes have trouble keeping control of your son. Heck, I can barely control you."

Rick thought about that. Dating Brittany had been fine, but he remembered the struggle they'd had when they were first married. It had been a huge adjustment, made harder with his career in the CST. She had never once asked him to quit, even though he knew it had been on her mind, especially once Adam was born. They pulled through, of course, but he could not imagine the adjustments Cam and Maria were making.

"If they could just separate the personal from the team, it'd be better. I'm afraid of when they do a challenge together."

"Maybe that's what they need to do to work through this. They've always worked well together, even before they dated. Cam's ego is too big to risk failing a challenge just because of Maria."

Rick paused, listening to his father wheeze slightly. While he was recovering well, he was still in fact doing just that: recovering. "How are you feeling?"

"Like you guys need to keep up with the other teams, that's how. Have you used the AIM I gave you yet?"

"No. It doesn't feel right. Maybe I'll try it out on a day I'm sitting out from a challenge but I don't think I could use it officially."

His father didn't say anything for a moment. While he had been in the hospital, Owen had given his son his own AIM to use for the tournament. While the AIRCs were the same, each AIM seemed to perform slightly different from another, and Owen had told Rick to use his while he had to sit out for the season. For some reason, he knew that he was not ready to use his father's AIM. Not yet. Not in this situation. If he used the robot it would be as though he was admitting his father was not coming back into the tournament, even after he had recovered.

"You should get some rest. I'll say hi to your brother for you."

"Take care of yourself, Rick. Don't go worrying like you usually do. Things will work out."

Rick closed his cell phone before turning off the dim lantern. He knew things would work out, but he had no idea if they would be for the better.

CHAPTER 12

Ryan watched Maria as she ate her breakfast around the empty fire pit. Cam was still in bed when he had left the RV, and there had been no movement in Rick's tent but even so, there was still a heavy tension in the air from the night before. The sun had barely risen, which should have given him a clue as to why Cam was still asleep. He cleared his throat, sending a puff of steam into the frigid morning air. He spoke hesitantly.

"I'm sorry about yesterday." Ryan continued when she gave him a confused look. "Even though I can see some potentially positive qualities to whatever they do in the Underground, you were right." He folded his arms over his chest, either to hide from her reaction or in an attempt to get warmer. "It's not worth losing my career, or my place in this team. If it makes tension in this team and with you, then it's not worth my time." Ryan paused when Maria only nodded. "I'm not going to pursue it. Okay?"

Maria set her empty paper plate down and looked at Ryan for a moment. It was their first time camping this season and already the meals were becoming bland. "I want to believe you."

"Then believe me."

"I believe that for the moment, you mean it."

"I'm not stupid enough to risk my career. I'm just starting. I'm not looking to screw that up." His voice sounded so much like Cam's with that declaration.

She wanted to believe that he would keep his word, but it was not until the previous night that she realized how little she trusted people. Everywhere she turned she was reminded of the tendrils of the Underground which had sprouted in the CST. She frowned when Cam stepped out from the RV. She watched him pause and look over at Ryan before he walked towards the truck.

Ryan watched Cam sit in the truck alone before he looked back at Maria. He tried to hide himself within his sweater.

"So...you and Cam..."

"Me and Cam."

"The guitar?"

She nodded.

"The roommate who moved out and has your kayak in storage?"

Maria sighed and stood, making sure to grab all of her garbage. "Any other way you'd like to qualify him? The guy I lived with, the guy I slept with, fought with, competed with? That's Cam."

"I'm sorry, I'm just processing it."

Maria leaned her elbows against her thighs, her eyes closed tight as she went through her usual waves of nausea. "Yeah, well it's still processing with me, too."

That was new. "Didn't you break up with him?"

"I didn't break up with him because I stopped caring about him. But you already knew that." She looked over at Ryan and saw him looking down at his feet, nodding.

He looked back up at her and smiled. "I'm just going to pretend you guys slept in different rooms." He saw her copy his smile but it did not last long and he glanced at Cam sitting in the truck. "I'm not him. Whatever Cam's doing that you don't agree with, I'm not going to turn into him. People keep saying that I could be the next Cam Tylar, but I don't want to." He picked up the turtle AIM that had finally caught up with him from the RV. "He's a great athlete, but I don't want to be him. I still have a lot to learn, and I know I'm not that great right now, but I want to see how far I can go as myself."

She looked at him quickly. Had they been putting too much pressure on him? She had tried not to treat him like a rookie or a fan, but she realized that comparing him to Cam had made it harder. And now she was putting her experience with Cam on Ryan as well. She nodded and put a hand on his arm gently. She opened her mouth but hesitated when Rick came out from his tent and she gave Ryan a soft smile. "Come on. You can ride with me."

In the early afternoon, Maria leaned against her car, waiting for Rick to come back from the scan-in kiosk to give them details about the challenge. It never usually took so long. All that was needed was for the team's captain to scan the barcode on the screen of his AIRC at the kiosk to mark the time they began. She looked at her AIRC and the new horse scan she obtained at Rick's uncle's ranch. She had to admit: she always loved going to the ranch. Jim, Owen's brother, bred hunters and jumpers and he had set aside horses with amazing potential for the team to scan. It was beneficial for everyone, really. They were able to use great scans, and Jim was able to sell the horses quickly. They were horses scanned by Revolution, after all. At the ranch, it was the first time she really noticed a major difference with Ryan, other than his inexperience.

When they had each chosen a horse to scan and pulled out their respective AIRC, she had taken a quick glance at each one. Cam's looked the sleekest, which was usual for him. He always needed the newest models, and always was very protective of it. It was also the fastest at scanning, and had finished scanning his horse a few seconds before Maria and Rick. They had newer models as well, but not quite as intense as Cam. Ryan's, on the other hand, was bulky and looked like the model she had used in the junior division in Owen Sound. It impressed her that much more when she remembered his rank in scans, especially when she saw that his AIRC took a full ten seconds longer than the others to scan animals. Despite the older and outdated model he used, he was still keeping up with the rest of his team.

She glanced over at Ryan and saw him messing around with his AIRC, likely looking over the new scan. She looked at Cam who was still sitting in the truck, refusing to get out until Rick came back. She rolled her eyes, folding her arms over her chest. She really hoped it was another challenge in the water. She was not quite sure if she would be able to work well with Cam, not today at least. Walking around the trails the day before had refreshed her memory of the park, so she would at least be physically prepared for an on-land challenge.

Rick walked back from the kiosk and looked around at the other teams milling around, waiting for their starting time slot. He hit his palm against the hood of the truck a few times, getting Cam to come out finally and he waited until Maria and Ryan came over.

"There's no guarantee there isn't a section in the water. There's a marker we have to get to, but it can only be seen from the sky looking straight down. Cam, I'm assuming you don't want to sit out twice in a row, so you'll be participating. I think Ryan needs more practice with his AIM before the four person challenge in Toronto too."

"I'm okay with sitting out," Maria said, slipping her AIRC back into the pocket of her jeans.

Rick looked back at her and shook his head. "No. You guys need to work this out, and the sooner the better. You guys work well together; you always have, despite your continuous arguments. We need to keep up our scores if we want to have a shot this season, which means we need to step it up. Alright?"

Maria glanced at Cam and nodded. "See, my problem has never been working together. I've always been a team player."

"Oh yeah, which is why you've never actually stuck to anything right?" Cam snapped, glancing at her only briefly.

"Enough! Just get out there and don't waste any time, okay? It's a timed challenge and you're likely going to need to use all three AIMs at once and work together. If you guys actually do your job, it won't take long. The park isn't too big, and we've been here before so the trails shouldn't be too confusing for you." Rick's voice was thick with frustration.

Maria swung her backpack onto her back, adjusting the straps until the weight sat comfortably enough for however long this challenge would be. "Are you guys ready then?"

"Yeah." Ryan watched as Cam grabbed his pack and started ahead of them before looking at his captain with a small smile. "I'll try to keep them from killing each other."

"Well, as long as the challenge is finished, I don't really care who comes back alive." Rick shook his head with an off-handed wave and got into the RV to wait for them. Might as well be comfortable. If he needed to, he could keep an eye on them through his AIRC, or at least through the tracking system. He did not expect this kind of challenge to take too long. Cam and Maria were pretty good at the timed challenges; it gave them more motivation to work together as a team. Hopefully this would force them to step it up and work as team-mates again.

Ryan looked around him on either side of the trail, looking up at the tree tops and the sun shining down through to him. The sun was warmer this afternoon, which was a welcome change from the weather during the previous challenge. He looked up ahead at Cam before looking beside him at Maria. "So how should we do this?" He tried to speak loud enough for Cam to hear as he walked ahead of them.

Cam turned around, took a few steps backwards before stopping. "I don't care what you do, but I'm going up ahead to get further into the park."

Maria rolled her eyes as he continued further down the path. "Cam, you can't do it on your own. Would you just get over yourself and work with us? You know we can do this with a better time if we work together."

"Well, you've made it clear you don't need me around. Besides, I can do this on my own. Go find a bench to sit on. I'll be back soon," he called over his shoulder. He glanced behind him briefly, but quickly turned his attention to his AIRC.

"Are you a one man team, now?" came a robotic voice.

"I always have been," he muttered under his breath. He did not have to worry about anyone hearing him speak with his AIM. No one was really around, but it was better to be safe than sorry.

His AIM, in the form of a hawk now, flew above his head. "And that is how you got into this situation in the first place."

Cam stepped off the trail and paused just inside the treeline. He hated it when the robot was right.

Ryan heard Maria swear and throw her pack down onto the ground with a loud thud. He walked over towards her as she sat down, continuing to curse Cam while slipping her AIRC from her pocket. "He doesn't actually expect to do this challenge on his own." More a hopeful statement than a fact.

"Oh, you bet," she grumbled. "If Cam pulls it off, good for him, but we all need to do it. So, what do you think?"

His eyes widened, realizing that he actually had to figure out this challenge. He walked over towards her and leaned his back against a tree. He watched his AIM hop towards him in the form of a frog and he picked it up. He had already grown attached to the robot, although he was sure it was ridiculous. They had good conversations. He noticed that no one else seemed to talk to their AIM, probably because it was more of a private thing. It had been a long time since he had felt he could speak freely. Except when he was with Maria.

"Well, there's a marker seen only from the sky. Obviously we need a bird. We don't know what kind of marker it'll be, so having two birds up there means it'll be easier to search."

Maria nodded as a teacher would when a student gave a correct answer. The only hint of her anger now was the clench of her jaw and the severe look in her eyes. "Hawk or another bird of prey would be best. Do you have one?"

"Yeah, I got that Northern goshawk, so that should be good for this."

She eyed him carefully. "You mentioned that yesterday to Todd. I meant to ask you how you got it."

He shrugged. "Sat in a tree for a while. Got a few red-tails in the process, but I'd seen a goshawk there before, so I knew to wait. Unfortunately, they weren't too happy about me sitting on their nest," he said with a grimace, showing her the back of his arm which sported fresh scars from the attack.

Maria watched as her AIM turned into a red-tail hawk. "Impressive. You're just full of surprises, aren't you? Let's get this show on the road." She sent the bird up into the air, watching it disappear above the trees as Ryan slipped out his own AIRC.

Ryan looked at his AIM as it shifted into the shape of a Goshawk. His eyes followed it up into the sky, joining with Maria's above them. "Cam seems like a good guy, and I know he's an amazing player, but does he ever actually come around?"

She picked up her bag again and started further down the trail, walking slowly enough for Ryan to walk with her. "He used to, after some time to cool off. Now, it's like he's always trying to prove how great he is, which means it's going to affect this challenge. The worst part is that he'll find a way to do the majority of this one on his own, which ticks me off. But I guess that's what you get with a team like this."

"No marker found," Maria's AIM called through her AIRC, which made her frown and look at her console to see where her AIM was flying around.

"Do a full sweep of the park, starting on the eastern side," Maria commanded.

"Do the same, but start on the west," Ryan spoke after a minute to his own AIM. He looked at Maria. "Might as well have them split up a bit, maybe get more ground, or air space covered."

"Line found out over the water near the beach," chirped Ryan's AIM after a brief moment.

Ryan looked at Maria with a raised eyebrow. "Just a line? Is that what we're looking for?"

Maria's eyebrows furrowed once more. "Shouldn't be. It's usually an exact spot for us or our AIM to get to. It could be looking for two intersecting lines maybe. Like 'X marks the spot.' They do that occasionally. We had that kind of challenge out in BC a few times in the mountains and let me tell you, that was much more difficult than just here in a park."

"Why don't we just wait until they find something?" Ryan asked, putting a hand on her arm to stop her from continuing. "There's no point walking down one trail when we might have to get to another on the other side of the park."

Maria held up her console, looking at something sitting on the branch of a tree and she grinned after a moment, showing

Ryan the screen of her AIRC which showed the stats of a newly scanned Northern cardinal. "We can scan, at least, in the meantime." She frowned as she looked at Ryan, who was grinning. "You already have a cardinal, don't you?"

"Yeah well, you haven't been doing much scanning yet. I have a lot of animals you don't, or Cam, for that matter. It's the only thing I'm used to, so you can't really blame me. Speak of the devil…" He nodded his head, motioning down the path ahead.

Cam stood in the middle of the trail, his face looking up to the top of the trees. He was walking slowly as if trying to line himself up with something. His team-mates watched with amusement as he nearly walked into another team as his focus stayed on the sky. He was speaking, most likely to his AIM, but they could not hear him from where they were.

Maria rolled her eyes after a brief moment and started towards Cam until her AIM's voice startled her by speaking.

"Second line found. Possible intersection?"

Maria nodded, but realized her AIM could not see her. "Yeah, probably. Can you and Ryan's AIM find out where the lines intersect?"

"One minute," came the reply, and then silence.

Ryan nodded towards Cam before looking at Maria. "Should we let him know?"

"Not yet. We'll let him wander around with his nose in the air a little while longer. Even if he can figure out the intersection with only one AIM, he still has to get there. It could be in the water for all we know. Unlikely, but possible," she replied.

"At intersection of the two lines," Ryan's AIM said. "Land?"

"Sure, might as well," Ryan said and hoisted his pack a bit to relieve a bit of the weight from his shoulders. "We can just track them through our AIRC, right?"

"That's the plan." She stared at the screen of her AIRC for a moment, waiting until the two birds landed, hoping they landed in a tree and not just randomly on the ground. Although, that may not be possible, wherever they were. Once the small blip on her screen remained stationary, she looked back at Ryan. "Alright, I guess we have a location. Shouldn't be too hard, especially after that kayaking challenge."

Ryan laughed, starting in the direction of his AIM. "Yeah, if all we have to do is hike to the spot, then I'm pretty sure I can handle it." He glanced down at his AIRC, trying to figure out where they were going. "So, you said you hiked around here yesterday. Any clue where the marker is, or how long it'll take to get there? It can't take more than half an hour."

"Well," Maria said, stopping suddenly at the side of the trail. "To get from one end of the trail to the other can take over an hour. Cutting through will be our best option, especially since you can likely bet that the marker isn't going to just be on a trail. It's going to be in the wooded area, if anywhere." She glanced around, her eyes moving slowly at first, but then frantically looked around. "Did you see where Cam went?"

"No, but he's probably thinking what you are and got off the trail." Ryan stepped off the trail and up a small hill. "You're not going to let him get there first, are you? C'mon, you can't tell me one of him is better than two of us." He gave a playful smile, watching Maria roll her eyes and hurry after him. "There are no…cliffs, or lakes or anything in this park, right?"

"No, it's actually a small park compared to other challenge locations, so I'm a little surprised. For Sarnia, I was expecting something a little more challenging," Maria said as they walked through the trees, each stepping over roots which grew on the surface of the ground.

"See, now that you've said something…" He paused as he regained his balance after getting his foot tangled in a patch of tall grass. "Now that you've said something, a huge cliff or chasm's going to appear out of nowhere and we're going to have to climb it with our bare hands. Thanks a lot, Maria."

She laughed, pushing a branch aside as she walked by, holding it long enough for Ryan to catch it behind her for himself. "Oh sure, blame me." Maria glanced down at her AIRC to make sure they were still on the right path. Even just fifteen minutes walking in the wrong direction could add to their total challenge time.

"We should really pick up the pace. All three of us are required to scan whatever's there, and if we get there before Cam, we have to find him. He's not always great with directions."

"Who is he going to ask? A chipmunk? Men don't ask humans or animals for directions, Maria, and we just never will," Ryan said with a smile but it disappeared when Maria gave him a look. "Sorry."

"He could always ask other teams, and I'd rather he not," she said, letting herself slide down a small embankment.

Ryan followed close behind, almost running into Maria. "What do you mean? Why would he ask another team? Like, a bargain?" He remembered Rick mentioning something along those lines while they were in Owen Sound.

She shrugged. "Not necessarily a bargain." She paused, formulating the proper answer. It was like introducing Scanning to a child. "Asking directions in a challenge like this encourages friendliness, and teams working together. We don't really do it that often. Never really needed to, to be honest. But you really need to know who to ask. Just because you ask, doesn't mean they'll tell you the truth," she said, glancing back at him as they crossed a street.

"Oh my God, it's Maria and Ryan!"

Maria turned back around suddenly and came face to face with a group of teenagers with backpacks. She flashed a smile and a bit of a wave before trying to hurry Ryan past the group.

"Wait, can we get an autograph? We're from Kitchener!" one of the girls said, starting to rifle through her bag.

"Oh! They're probably doing the challenge! Cam just came through here, you're trying to catch up to him right? Man, isn't he awesome?" another girl said, a little too sweetly for Maria's liking.

"Yeah, he's great," Maria replied with only a slight tone of sarcasm. "And yes, we're doing the challenge. We're heading to Windsor tomorrow if you want to chat then," Maria said. "We really have to catch up to Cam." She flashed another smile. In all honesty, she never really minded talking to fans. It was still a strange feeling to have a complete stranger address her by her name, rhyming things off about her history and past challenges, sometimes even things about her personal life. But at the same time, it made her feel justified. People actually took notice of the hard work she had put into this sport. It was not just a hobby. For some fans, Maria knew they flipped on Sportcentre, supported whoever was doing best, and turned the channel. Others followed stats for each player and team, and followed stats of rival teams just to make it seem like they could struggle against the team as well. People paid attention. But she did not need them paying attention while she was trying to complete a challenge.

"That's a good sign that Cam's already been through here," Ryan said, glancing back over his shoulder as Maria pushed him across the road.

"Good and bad, I guess. Let's go." She ducked underneath another branch before coming out to the edge of Lake Chipican within the park and she swore. "Are you kidding me?"

Ryan sighed and took off his hat to wipe his forehead. "So, what now? Kayak across?"

She shook her head. "No, it's not across, it's on one of those two little mounds out there," she said, pointing to what looked like small islands just off to the side. She glanced down to the edge of the lake and laughed when she saw Cam standing on the shore, at a 'safe' distance from the water. "Time to knock some sense into him."

Ryan looked to where she had been looking and shook his head, not liking how he was imagining this would end up. *Hey Rick, so, Cam drowned after Maria pushed him in the water. On the bright side, we completed the challenge!*

"Did you run into a bit of a problem?" Maria called out to Cam, her feet sliding into the water every few steps as she made her way along the edge of the small lake towards him.

He glared at her before looking out to the island where his AIM was likely waiting for him. "Just trying to concentrate, and you're not helping."

"Think if you concentrate hard enough, the island will move towards you? Wow, Cam, I knew you were good but I did *not* know you have magic powers." Maria teased as she finally reached him with Ryan close behind.

"Shut it. And how do you think you're getting over? Just going to swim?" Cam asked dryly. "It's April. I don't think you really want to get in. The water's still freezing."

"Thanks for letting me know. I had no idea what April water was like while I was upside down in my kayak the other day," she replied. "Fly up so I can see you," Maria said into her AIRC while watching the air just above the small islands. She grinned when she saw a red-tailed hawk fly up into the sky and catch a wind current before landing back onto the smaller of the two islands. She dropped her pack and grinned to Cam. "Ryan, are you much of a swimmer?" she asked while still looking at Cam.

"I can swim," he replied, dropping his bag as well.

"Then I guess we're just going to swim. Shouldn't be much colder than up in Owen Sound," Maria said as she took her sweater off but left her t-shirt on, glad she had at least thought to wear shorts in spite of the cooler weather. "At least we're choosing to get into the water this time." She turned. "Give me your AIRC," she said to Cam as she slipped off her shoes and socks.

"I don't need your help."

"Cam, don't be an idiot. There's no way you can get across."

"I'll figure out a way," he snapped, staring at the island.

"Cameron..."

"Don't call me that. I hate that."

"We're almost at the hour and a half marker. I am *not* going to do poorly at this challenge because you're too pigheaded to admit you can't do it alone," Maria yelled, finally noticing the people in canoes taking pictures. She rolled her eyes and held her hand out. "I know what you're thinking, and your AIM can't do it for you. But I can."

Cam looked to the people furiously taking pictures of them and he tossed her the console. "Someone has to look after the bags anyway," he muttered and leaned back against a tree as he watched Maria and Ryan slip into the water and make their way over to the small island.

Almost as soon as she was immersed in the water, she regretted swimming, but it was the quickest way to get there. It was not that far, so at least she did not need an amazing swimming ability to finish the challenge. She stopped suddenly, almost to the small island Ryan had just reached, and felt her pockets. With a sigh of relief, Maria felt both AIRCs after thinking she had felt one slip out.

Ryan looked around the small mound of earth, not quite sure what he was looking for. There were three hawks milling about, and he knew they were his team's AIMs. "What am I looking for, guys? Er, AIMs," he asked. He watched as his goshawk flapped over towards a small patch of grass and pecked at something on the ground. Almost like a real bird, although Ryan knew actual birds of prey did not really peck, but struck from the air. He glanced back at Maria and held out a hand to her as she finally made it onto dry ground, although with the storm that had moved through the few days previous, it was not so much dry ground as it was a mound of mud.

"Find it?" Maria asked, slipping a bit in the mud with her bare feet. She smiled with relief as she pulled out the AIRCs, seeing a small strip of metal in the mud where Ryan's AIM was standing. "Well, at least we don't have any trouble with other teams right now," she said as she scanned the small metal strip with both AIRCs and stepped aside for Ryan to do the same. "It's times like this that I'm glad we have staggered starting times."

"So, that's it?" Ryan asked. "That's all we have to do?"

"Pretty much. Once it's verified, which is immediately usually, we get the points." Maria looked down at the AIRCs for a second before she grinned and showed Ryan. "Challenge complete. Not the greatest time, but at least it's finished."

"And both you and Cam are still alive."

"For the moment." Maria slipped the consoles back into her pockets before heading back to the water, waving to the canoeing group with a grin before beginning the short swim back.

She climbed up the bank at the edge of the lake, taking Ryan's hand which he offered and she looked to Cam. "See, that wasn't too hard."

"I would've found a way," he muttered, holding his hand out to take back his AIRC. "Can I have it back?" Always so protective.

Maria glared at him and rolled her eyes. "You wouldn't have found a way, because even if you had asked those people over there for help, they would've just bombarded you with questions you're too impatient to answer while in a challenge."

"I could've done it on my own," Cam repeated, raising his voice until he was nearly shouting at her.

"Like we didn't need a fourth player?" she snapped and moved towards him quickly and pushed him into the water before he could brace himself against her. "Get out of that on your own, *star contributor*," she yelled down at him as he splashed in the water, sputtering.

Cam regained his footing in the soft mud around the edge of the lake, but even standing, the water came up to his shoulders. He looked up at Maria, glaring at her as he worked his way back out of the water. He slapped Ryan's hand away as Maria turned and grabbed her pack. "Go to hell, Maria," he called after her.

He watched as his team-mates walked ahead of him, with Maria in front. They had worked well together, Ryan and Maria. Cam remembered when he had worked like that with her, with everyone. When they had been on speaking terms, there was not a challenge they could not handle as long as they worked together. It was why Cam had been so insistent that they did not need a fourth player. They could do it with just two. Well, maybe before. A small ache stabbed at his chest. This was what he missed most of all: working as a team.

"You work better on a full team, and you know it. Even a rookie performed better than you on this challenge," his AIM spoke quietly through the AIRC.

Cam glared down at it. "You sound like Maria." He really hated it when his AIM was right.

Maria pulled out her AIRC after ignoring Cam's comment to her. "Hey Rick, we're done and heading back."

"Everyone still alive?" came Rick's reply through the console.

"Unfortunately," she muttered, glancing back over her shoulder as Cam and Ryan trudged behind her. Maria opted to take the road back to the main parking lot rather than walking through the trails again. She took her hair from its ponytail and squeezed some water from it as Cam walked past her.

"I think that was uncalled for," Ryan said quietly as he came up beside Maria.

"Well, it sure made me feel good. It's not like he got hurt or anything. He knows how to swim, he just doesn't like being in the water," she said angrily. "He actually thought he could complete the entire challenge on his own. It's not like he's part of a team or anything. Oh no, it's just Cam against the rest of the CST, that's what it is. We're just here, getting in his way."

"I'm sure he doesn't actually think that," Ryan replied, walking awkwardly in his wet shorts.

"When I joined, he told me to just sit out of all the challenges because I was just there to look at. Didn't even care about my own stats, he just knew that his were good enough to make the team great, and hated the fact that I'm good," she said, attempting to retie her hair back out of her face, but gave up and put a hat on. At least it would keep the sun from her eyes while they made the walk back to the parking lot.

"Did he choose me because I look pretty?" Ryan asked with a charming smile.

"He stormed out of the room when we brought up bringing on another player."

Ryan looked down at his feet as they walked a little ways behind Cam. "He didn't want me at all?"

She heard the hurt in his voice. But it was the truth. It hurt sometimes. "Only your scanning stats were good. To be honest, you're a long shot. Cam's good, and unfortunately, he knows it. He sees everyone as a liability. Don't take it personally. I got the same treatment. At least he's trying to get along with you, and took you out scanning with him, to the lake, no less. Don't let what I say about him change your opinion of him." Maria shrugged with a sigh. "He's a good guy, just rough around the edges. Definitely doesn't like to be told what to do, but other than that he'd be a good mentor for you."

Ryan nodded. "Maybe it's my being friendly with you that ticks him off."

"Probably."

He laughed a bit, but he felt slightly bruised. He knew Cam had a bit of an ego. Anyone watching his interviews or challenges knew that. But knowing that Cam did not even want to talk about the possibility of him joining the team, he could not help but take that personally, despite what Maria had said. Ryan looked up ahead and saw the parking lot. Cam walked faster to meet up with Rick.

"Are you going to get in trouble with Rick about the whole pushing Cam into the water?"

"Only if Cam makes a comment," Maria said as they got closer to the RV. She winced when she saw Rick standing outside the vehicle and leaning against the side of it with his arms folded across his chest. "Or maybe he already knows." She didn't see Cam say anything to Rick, but he still did not look too pleased with any of them.

"An hour and a half?" Rick said as they got closer. "Really?"

"Yeah, really," Maria said, slipping her pack off of one shoulder, letting it hang from her right shoulder. "We thought we'd take a nap, like you."

Rick shot her a disapproving look. What else was a fourth member supposed to do on a day off? "How did it take you guys, two experienced players, two good players and a new guy an hour and a half to go across the park and scan something? We've done something like this in forty five minutes," Rick said, trying to keep his frustration from his voice. He knew it was not like him to get like this, but he knew they could be doing better, and he did not want to think that Ryan was slowing them down.

"We tried the whole 'Cam's awesome and can do it on his own' thing, so it took us a while to catch up to him standing at the edge of the lake." Maria folded her arms over her chest, mimicking her captain defensively. "Although I'm impressed he actually got that far."

"I could've done it," Cam muttered under his breath.

"And what about all three of you scanning the chip? Did you think about that?" Rick asked Cam, his voice softening now. Cam had never acted so irresponsibly before. Sure he thought of himself as a rock star, but he usually worked well with Maria, even with the other break ups they'd gone through. He sighed and rubbed the back of his neck. "Let's just start down to Windsor and cool off. You don't have to like each other, but you do have to work together. Is that understood? I'm tired of acting like your dad." He paused. Cam and Maria both looked at him, and he knew the words hit home. Neither of them had a father. "I'd like to start being your captain, but you're making it pretty difficult."

Maria glanced away, suddenly feeling guilty for the way she had acted. Rick was right, but it was hard to mend a bridge from one side of the river. "Cam and Ryan can take the car," she said, fishing her keys from her pack. She held them out, along with his AIRC, to Cam. "Haven't driven the truck in a while."

Cam took the AIRC but not the keys, leaving them in her hand. "The truck's better off-road if we want to scan." He nodded towards Ryan, motioning towards the truck and started towards it, but stopped when Rick put a hand on his shoulder.

"Are you okay?" Rick asked quietly as the other two headed to the vehicles.

"Why wouldn't I be?" Cam looked around impatiently.

"Because you've never been this stupid when it comes to a challenge. We need you to be clear-headed, okay? You're good, but not when you're stupid." Rick leaned his head down a bit to the shorter player, to him at least. Cam and Rick were the tallest on the team, and even then there was only an inch difference. "If you need to talk…"

"I'm fine. Just getting back into the swing of things. We'll get better." The corner of Cam's mouth twitched lightly before he headed towards the truck. "Star contributor, right?" For the first time in his career, he was beginning to doubt that.

CHAPTER 13

Ryan walked into the dining room of the hotel in Windsor the next morning, rubbing his eyes a bit and stayed near the door to look around. He did not see many other teams at the hotel, but he supposed most teams alternated between campsites and hotels, just as they were. He was glad they had opted for the hotel rather than the campsite for the night. Not that he did not enjoy camping – because he enjoyed it thoroughly – but he was not so sure he was ready to camp with the team in the state it was in right now. Not for a second night in a row. The others had agreed, especially with their interview later in the evening after they completed today's challenge. They did not want to bring any more tension to the team before they had to speak to the public.

He was nervous about the interview, and knew it was a good thing that he would be sitting out from this challenge. Ryan doubted he would perform well with the thoughts of the evening's events on his mind. The team needed to perform well, and he just wanted to make sure they had the best chance of that today. He knew he should not be so nervous, though. Cam would be doing all of the talking, as it usually happened in the team's interviews. Ryan was just the new guy, so he doubted he would get much attention.

After another quick scan of the room, Ryan saw Cam sitting at a table with a half-finished plate of food in front of him and he went to join his team-mate. "Hey," he said as he sat down across from him.

Cam glanced up briefly and muttered a quick good morning before going back to his breakfast.

"Is it that hard to be her team-mate and work with her?"

He looked at the rookie with a sharp look. "Excuse me?"

Before he realized what was happening, Ryan's mouth continued to move. "It's been a month. Yeah, I'd be bitter if she broke up with me, too, but you're Cam Tylar. Your life is this team, and I can't believe you're letting this break-up affect your performance. You're better than this." His heart thumped in his chest as he watched Cam's face turn from apathy to confusion, and finally settled on fury.

"You know what?" Cam glared at him, shaking his head with disbelief. "You think you know what you're talking about, but you don't. You don't know the first thing about being on a real competitive team, so don't go lecturing me about being someone's team-mate and working with someone who frankly couldn't give a damn about me and has made that very clear. I don't have time for people like that, or people who feel the need to lecture."

Ryan looked at him as his face flushed before he stood. "I'm sorry. I don't have experience with working with team-mates, but I at least have experience working with ex-girlfriends. I was just trying to help."

"Well don't," Cam snapped before finishing off his plate.

He clenched and unclenched his hands, not from anger, but embarrassment. "Tell Rick I'll just meet you guys at the studio later. Good luck on the challenge," Ryan said softly. He made his way back up to his room before realizing he had not grabbed anything to eat. He could eat later. He was likely sticking his nose where it did not belong, but didn't it belong? This was his team now, too. Sure, there was history and maybe he had not been a part of it, but he was a part of it now, and was finding himself stuck in the middle of more than a few arguments. Should he not get a say? No. He was just the replacement. There was not a real place for him in this team.

Maria swore as she bumped into Ryan as she rounded a corner. "Hey, you almost ready?" she asked, wincing a bit from the run in.

Ryan shook his head. "I'll meet you guys at the studio later." He looked her over quickly and noticed she was wearing workout clothes, again. He did not see the need to work out on challenge days, but she seemed to work out every day.

"What, don't want to see us off?" Maria asked jokingly, but his body language made her frown with concern. "Are you okay?"

He nodded and forced a smile. "Yeah, I just figured I'd get out of your way today."

"You're not in our way, unless you ate all the food already at breakfast." She paused, watching his face. "Ryan, you're not in our way. You're part of this team. You proved that in the last two challenges."

"It's fine. There's no point in me coming to the site just to come back here anyway. I can say my good lucks here. So, good luck!" Ryan said, patting her on the shoulder.

Maria looked up at him, unsure if she should let him go, but maybe it was best. They were already putting him into an awkward situation with all of their internal drama. She knew it was tense, and likely inappropriate, but it was not going to be fixed overnight. "Thanks. See you at the studio. Wear something nice," she instructed with a playfully warning look. She paused as she looked back up at him again. "Thanks for the other night. I didn't mean to get so upset, not with you." Before he could respond, she headed to the dining room with her pack slung over one shoulder.

Ryan looked behind him as he walked down the hall, watching Maria find Cam and sit down at the table next to him rather than sitting with him. This interview was going to be interesting. Now he knew without a doubt that the obvious tension would be the main topic of the interview. When he entered his hotel room he smiled gently at his AIM, waiting patiently in the form of an Eastern chipmunk on his bed.

"At least you seem to like me," he said, before falling face-first onto the mattress.

"Did you reach that conclusion because I talk to you?" came a robotic-sounding response.

"Well, yeah. That may not be the best way to judge things, though." Ryan's voice was muffled by the comforter. He rolled onto his side to look at the robot. "No one else seems to talk to their AIMs like I do. I figured AIMs only respond to nice people."

"Is Maria not a nice person?" When Ryan turned his face back into the bed, it hopped a few steps closer to his body. "Your crush is entertaining. You have asked me to remind you that she is your team-mate. She is your team-mate." It paused. "She is your team-mate." It reminded him once more. With no response, it hopped onto his head, gripping his hair with its small paws. "You are concerned about something else."

Ryan sighed, or tried to as his face pressed against the comforter. "Don't you ever sleep?" He thought he heard the AIM grumble as it clambered off his head and back to the edge of the bed. If he was going to be a part of this team, he would need to be prepared for this interview. Public appearance was important to a high-standing team, and he needed to look the part, even if he didn't feel it.

A few hours later, Ryan sat in the local TV station's dressing area, regretting his decision to come alone instead of waiting at the hotel for the rest of his team. He had not been waiting long, in reality, but it felt like forever, especially since everyone working there seemed to ignore him. So, he sat there in the room alone, waiting for the rest of his team. He looked up from his lap when he heard familiar voices coming towards him, and turned his head towards the sound.

Rick came in first wearing a suit jacket with dark jeans, knowing that while he should dress nicely, it was not going to be as important as going in front of the board. They were a sports team after all. People would understand if they went on the air wearing what they wore during a challenge, especially since they had finished the challenge just half an hour earlier. Cam walked in after him, wearing almost exactly the same as he would in front of the board: sport jacket with his tattered jeans.

Even if it was not exactly professional, Ryan supposed this was what people had come to expect when it came to Cam. And Cam probably assumed he could get away with it as long as people let him. He smiled when Maria came in next, wearing a black blazer on top of a purple blouse with black dress pants. He was surprised that she would go through this trouble for an interview, although he supposed he had seen her like this in interviews before. She had even taken the time to curl her hair, which he noticed right away and had to keep from staring.

He smiled as they got closer and more attendants seemed to come from nowhere to take care of them before they went on the air. "Hey. How'd it go?"

"Didn't keep up on your AIRC?" Cam asked, not looking at him. He grinned at the staff, who seemed more than happy to cater to his whim.

"Well, yeah, but I was asking more how it went for you guys. I know the points we got, but I wasn't really there with you guys. Never mind." Ryan looked back down at his lap as his team-mates were prepped for air.

"It went pretty well," Maria said, despite the woman sweeping her face with makeup. "Pretty much the same level as Sarnia, but still didn't get that hundred points. I wonder why."

"We're not going to talk about that right now," Rick said with a flat voice. No one wanted to make a scene in front of the people working at the studio. They did not want to give the interviewer anymore to question than they already had.

Maria glanced over at Ryan and gave him a reassuring smile. "I'm glad to see you know how to dress for TV interviews. You should be the one training Cam."

Ryan winced and from the corner of his eye he saw Cam glare at him. He had chosen a similar outfit to Rick after watching interviews the team had given over the past few years. Never had studying been so enjoyable. "I'm sure Cam knows how to dress. I think he wants to be his own person," he said, choosing his words carefully. Cam's glare eased. Apparently they were the right words.

"They're ready for you," a stout woman said. She had a headpiece in one ear and a thin microphone around the side of her face. She flashed them a smile as she led them to the stage. They were greeted by applause which grew when the team became visible to the studio audience.

Cam grinned as the applause washed over him. All of the fights he had had with Maria lately completely disappeared. None of that mattered. What mattered to him was hearing those people shout out his name. His smile did not falter as they sat down across from the middle aged man already sitting in a high chair on the brightly lit stage.

"Revolution! It's great to have you guys here," the man said, shifting in the seat to lean towards the team.

"It's good to be here," Rick replied, giving the audience a small wave which resulted in them erupting into cheers again and he laughed.

"How's your dad doing?" This first question set the tone for the interview. This was going to be personal.

"Much better, and recovering well. He'll be out of the hospital at the end of the week, which is a good and bad thing for my mom." He smiled lightly, trying to joke. They all knew to keep the topic light as much as they could.

"It's always interesting to see how new captains handle the responsibility, but you and your dad have worked closely throughout your careers. How has it been without him to guide you through this?"

"It's different. Every change is always a challenge to overcome, but we're pushing through and accepting every change with as much enthusiasm as possible."

"And what a change you have. Ryan Hampton!"

Ryan and Cam's head snapped around when the man said the new member's name. "Hi?" Ryan said, unsure, but he forced a smile anyway.

"I'm not going to lie, a lot of people were expecting you guys to really bomb, but Ryan, you're definitely better than everyone was expecting. Granted, you guys aren't doing as well as you've done in the past, but better than any other team with a new member. Maria, how do you feel about that?"

She shifted in her seat, leaning closer to the interviewer. She had long ago learned what it meant to be a female athlete, and what was expected of her. "Honestly? I'm used to winning, but my first few challenges weren't that great either, but I learned quickly as Ryan seems to be doing." She flashed a lip-glossed smile at the audience. "We started out extremely strong this season, especially with Ryan being so new. We got a hundred points in our first challenge, which no one else managed to do. It was one of the most difficult challenges I've ever participated in, and it was a great way to start. I think so far that we're holding our own."

"So, how is this affecting how you guys act with each other? It took some time for this team to become adjusted to you. Can we expect to see the same issues this time?"

Maria glanced at Rick as though asking permission to speak. "Every time you add a new person, it's going to shake things up a bit. When Cam joined, well, we all know how he likes to shake things up." There was a polite, knowing laugh from the audience. "When I joined, the guys had to adjust to not only a female teammate, but one with little experience in the Juniors but strong stats. And a bit more discipline with my military background. I was a bit of a drill sergeant," she said and Rick laughed in agreement. "We've all dealt with it before, so we'll get through it this time. The hardest part is trying to immediately have that connection we had with Owen. Unlike other sports, because we only have four active team members, we need a quick connection, and a good dynamic. We're travelling and seeing each other twenty-four-seven, so we need to learn how to deal with changes. There really isn't much alone time in this sport."

"Ryan, what's it like being on one of the top teams in Canada?" the man asked with a grin, clearly excited to be talking with the newest player.

"It's…incredible. These guys are amazing and to be picked up by them is pretty much a career goal for anyone. Even if I'm only here for one season, I'm set," Ryan said with a grin, trying to ignore the audience and multiple cameras staring at him. It was definitely an adjustment, to have cameras and fans facing him at once. He just had to concentrate on the interviewer and each question. If he ignored everything else, he imagined he would get through the interview.

"You participated in the first two challenges which, to be frank, no one really expected. Even when Maria joined, her first challenge was the month end one in Toronto. How has this prepared you for the rest of the season?"

Cam stared at Ryan as he answered the questions while barely hiding his unease with the cameras on him. He looked over at Maria and Rick, who seemed glad that they did not have questions being directed at them. Cam knew that Rick was likely glad that Ryan was responding so well to the questions and was answering them professionally. They were asking a lot of him, but he was living up to the standards of being on a team such as theirs, so far. Cam was glad Ryan was able to put up a good face for his team, but he was still fuming inside. No one had even so much as greeted him. Ryan would only be around for one season, and Cam had been around for five years!

He hid his impatience as well as he could, and tried to find a time to jump in and get involved with the interview, but the questions were too specific to Ryan. He had helped to train the guy and he did not even give him a 'hey, thanks Cam! This guy is great!' Cam kept a smile on his face as they went to commercial and thanked the team for coming to the interview. The middle-aged man came up to each of them, shaking each of their hands.

"It was really good to see you, Cam," the man said. "Sorry we didn't get much of a chance to ask you questions. Good luck with the rest of the season."

Cam managed a polite reply as he followed his team-mates from the stage. Waving to the audience again to a response of a louder applause made him feel a bit better at least. Usually this kind of high would last him longer, but there wasn't much of one this time. The best thing about the CST, for him, was the recognition as Maria had said the other day. With Ryan around, he did not even get that. *Is there even much of a point anymore?*

"Hey Rick, do you think I could take the truck to Niagara Falls tonight? I have some buddies there who want to get together," Cam said as Maria drove the team back to the hotel. Once again, they had agreed to stay in a hotel in Niagara Falls rather than a campsite. The challenge, they knew, would be in the heart of the city and it was much more convenient than staying outside of town. But normally they would not leave until the morning.

Maria looked over her shoulder to Cam with a look. "Buddies?"

"Yeah."

She looked at him skeptically. "Who are these *buddies*?"

"You don't know them."

"You have friends I don't know about?"

"Are you really going to complain about a night with Cam away?" Rick asked, glancing over to Maria.

She glanced at Rick and paused, thinking for a moment. "I might as well go tonight then too."

Cam's eyes narrowed when Maria gave him a look. "You know someone in Niagara Falls too?"

"No. I was thinking of doing some shopping for supplies in the morning before the challenge, and it's too late tonight to do much of anything," Maria said simply, staring at Cam pointedly through the rear mirror. "I can drive. We'll take the car."

"That sounds fine to me," Rick said as she pulled up to the hotel. "You want to go too, Ryan?" It almost sounded as though Maria was trying to make things work with Cam. Everyone knew that tensions rose when people were stuck in a vehicle during a long road trip. He hoped Maria knew what she was doing.

Ryan, who had been silent since the interview, shook his head. "I was thinking of doing some scanning tonight. There are some good spots in this area I wanted to check out." He should have done that earlier in the day while his team-mates were attempting the challenge, and he found it strange that he was already slacking in that area. Ryan was so used to scanning, and he was surprised how easily he was letting that slip now that he was participating in challenges.

"I think that actually sounds like a good idea, and I think I'm going to tag along if you don't mind," Rick said as they finally parked. "I'm just going to call Brittany and my dad first if that's alright."

"Yeah, no problem. Just come get me when you're ready." Ryan stepped out of the car as it turned off and walked back to his room, watching as Maria and Cam stormed past him. Obviously he had missed something in the car, and he definitely did not know if it was a good idea for the two of them to drive any long distance together, alone. Sure Cam thought the team would still succeed with three players, but if both Cam and Maria were killed off, they had no chance.

Maria slipped her key card into its slot, opened the door, but spun around when someone grabbed her elbow. She stared up at Cam who had no hope in hiding his frustration. "Something wrong?" she asked sweetly.

"What the hell was that? Shopping? What are you trying to do, babysit me?" he snapped, surprisingly attempting to keep his voice low.

"Shopping, yes," she answered as she folded her arms across her chest. "I hadn't planned on doing it at the Falls, but when you brought it up it sounded like a good idea." She glanced back into her room with a sigh and looked up at him. "Cam, honestly, I'm not trying to babysit you. I don't want to be around you, frankly."

"But you'll sit in a car with me for four hours? I know you know where I'm going."

Maria nodded. "Yeah, I know. Just, let me do this."

Over the past three years she had never wanted anything to do with this part of his life, other than trying to get rid of it, and now all of a sudden she wanted to?

"Why?"

She shrugged with a small laugh. "Because I've gone crazy. Maybe it's my way of still trying to keep control of you."

Cam laughed at that and stepped back. "You wish you ever had control. You could barely control cooking dinner, and you think you can control someone like me?"

"Someone like you? What's that supposed to mean?"

"Uncontrollable. I do what I want, and you always knew that about me."

"Please," Maria muttered and stepped further into her room. "Just meet me out at the car when you're ready." She closed the door before Cam could try to say anything more. What was she thinking, offering to drive him to the last place she wanted him to go? She had to admit, she had not so much offered as much as she had told him she would drive.

After gathering her belongings, Maria brought her key card down to the lobby to check out. She thanked the receptionist before starting out to the parking lot, but a familiar voice stopped her. She looked around and found Rick sitting in one of the lobby chairs set aside from the others.

"I have no idea how Dad did this," she heard Rick say into his phone. "I mean, I've seen them fight before, and our challenges suffered because of it, but it's never been like this. I warned her, I warned them both, and with our contract coming up for renewal, they're screwing everything up…No, I know it's hard, I just, it's hard for me too. I don't think I can do this anymore, Brit. It's hard trying to be my dad, and it's hard being away from you. I could probably handle it if we even had a chance doing well at these challenges, but the way we're going, I almost just want to give up, and you know I've never felt like that before." Maria heard Rick laugh lightly. "I know. You know I'd never do it. It's just harder than I thought to deal with all of this."

Maria glanced at the door before stepping into Rick's view with a small smile. She shook her head and just gave him a small wave when she saw him get up to go over to her. "I'll call you when we get to the hotel," she called out to him with another wave as she finally went out to the car. She saw Cam leaning against the driver's side door and dumped her bag into the back seat.

"I'm driving. Move." She grabbed the handle next to his waist and pulled the door open, shoving him out of the way.

"You're actually going to do this?" Cam said, looking down at her, lines of concern and confusion crossing his face.

"Just get in the car," she said, starting up the engine.

CHAPTER 14

Rick looked over at Ryan and watched him for a few moments. The rookie was staring intently into the darkness as if he could actually see something. His AIM was in the form of a Southern red-backed vole at his side, waiting patiently for instructions. They had been sitting up in the tree for just over an hour and had barely spoken. It was slightly awkward to be quiet for so long, in Rick's opinion, but it was giving him the chance to see Ryan in a new light. They had signed him onto the team knowing that he had top scores in scanning, but they had yet to see him in action.

"So, is this what you do?"

Ryan turned to his captain quickly. He gave him a sheepish smile as he shrugged. "Pretty much. Usually I would research an area first before I had a stakeout, but this is pretty much what I do. Most people scan during the day and miss the nocturnal animals." He looked back out into the night. "My brother and I, Will – the smart one you met – we would go camping all the time and just sit up in trees together. He can identify every bird call and every sound from an insect. It's strange, but I've learned a lot from him, even though he's younger. He was never really into scanning, but it was something just for us, you know?"

Rick nodded in response and leaned back against the thick trunk of the tree, pulling a blanket up around his body. "My dad and I were never really that intense. We would go camping and do some scanning, but my brother never really liked it, so he would stay home with my mom. It's probably why we're not really close. He's two years younger than me. He's lived over in England for a few years. He wanted to come home to be with Dad after the heart attack, but we convinced him not to." Rick shrugged. "Probably pushed him away even more, but there was no need to spend the money. If it had been serious, we would've gotten him to come."

"If anything happened to my dad, I'd be pretty ticked if I was told I wasn't needed. I like to think we're a close family, even if we don't agree about everything. Sunday mornings are always a hassle in my house." He laughed lightly as he suddenly brought his AIRC up from his lap and began to scan a flying squirrel as it climbed on the branch above them. He held a finger up, telling Rick to stay silent until a grin came across his face as the animal leapt away.

"I haven't found one of these in a while," Ryan said happily as he flipped through the stats of his new scan. "Look at that!" He lit Rick's face with the bright screen of his AIRC as he turned it towards his captain.

"Not bad! You're right about Scanners. I don't do much scanning at night. In the first few years I did pretty often, but not as much anymore."

Ryan continued to look through the stats. When he was satisfied, he placed the AIRC back onto his lap. "Can I ask you something? What is your AIM like?"

"What do you mean?"

Why did I even bring it up? "I mean, what is your AIM to you? Do you view it like another team-mate, a pet, a friend?" His heart fell when Rick laughed.

"I never thought of it, honestly. I guess a form of team-mate during the season, and a pet when we're alone or during the winter. When I first got it, it was sort of a friend the way a dog would be." He shrugged thoughtfully. "But you know, I never named it. Not sure why."

"How's your dad doing?" Ryan asked, satisfied with Rick's answer. *So, I'm not the only one, at least.*

"Pretty good. He's angry a lot of the time, my mom says." He stared off into the darkness, his voice turned sober. "He's not used to being stuck in the house. I get why he's mad, but it's hard on my mom too. He's not the only one who's stuck doing something he doesn't want to do."

Ryan looked at his captain, trying to see the details of his face in the dark but he had turned away from him. "I know I don't have anything to compare it, but you seem to be a good captain to me. Cam and Maria respect you. That's easy to see. They're going through their own stuff, and I don't think anyone could handle them any better than you are."

"Thanks." Rick gave him a grateful smile, as if he had yet to hear those words from a team-mate. "You'd think that ten years on this team would teach me how to be a better captain, though. Most people I started competing against are retired now. It's like...I'm supposed to be carrying on this torch, but I keep dropping it. I don't think I can do this much longer."

Ryan was silent for a few moments. "I think that maybe there is no torch. Scanning has changed so much even in the past ten years. Newer models of AIRCs are being produced, different rules are needed, and the challenges are harder. Now, it seems like every season there's at least one more person accused of being in the Underground, some people even being arrested, and it's become so complicated. It was hard to see that on the outside, but I'm starting to see it now. Things keep changing, and I think to become better, we need to adapt to the changes."

Rick gave him a small smile once again, not sure if he could see it. "Like us bringing you onto the team."

"I meant your dad being benched, but I guess me, too."

He nodded and looked at the rookie for a moment. "Are we pushing you too hard?"

Ryan's forehead scrunched with confusion as he returned his captain's look. "What do you mean?"

He shrugged. "I just want to make sure...I don't know, are we putting too many expectations on you? The media keeps trying to decide if you're the next *Cam Tylar*."

How do I feel? Ryan thought for a moment. "I think...well, Maria made a comment that Cam didn't want me on the team, that I'm a long shot because of my stats." He paused, collecting his words. He kept his face clear from looking at Rick. "I know I'm a long shot. I don't think you're pushing me too hard for my situation. I need to be pushed so I can get better at challenges. I don't mind the challenges, but I feel…yeah, maybe everyone's trying to get me to be like Cam. I'm not well-rounded. I know that. But it seems to be working, for the most part. I'm doing what I can to keep the spot warm for your dad to come back."

Rick nodded again, taking in the honesty. He had never needed a conversation like this with Cam. He had a similar one with Maria, but it had been the complete opposite with her. No one had pushed her at all, and that had nearly led her to leave the team. Only Cam had truly seen her potential from the start.

"You're doing a great job, Ryan," he started, which surprised the rookie. "And you're right. You're a long shot. But you're a great Scanner in the literal sense. If you play to your strengths, I think you'll do really well in this sport. You have a way with people. You fit in well with us without even trying. And you have a way with animals. But seriously, Ryan, you need to stop thinking of yourself as a replacement." Rick's voice was forceful now. It was about time he acted like a captain. "You're on this team, whether Cam likes it or not. It's not Cam and the rest of us. We're all part of this team, and working together will barely cut it. We need to fight, as a team, to get to the top. Which means we each need to bring our best to the table, whatever that might be. We signed you for a reason. So, take your shot."

Ryan gave a soft smile to the darkness, glad for its blanket. "You think I fit in with the team?" he asked after a moment.

"Well, as long as you don't start dating Maria. We don't need any more drama than we've already had the past three years. She's a great person, and an amazing athlete, but it's difficult having a female team-mate, no matter what her stats are."

"I don't think it's so bad," Ryan stated with a grin.

He laughed. "Don't even go there, Ryan. Both Cam and I will kick your butt."

Ryan paused. "Noted."

*   *   *

"Hey! Rick!"

He turned, hearing his name called as he and Ryan walked back into the hotel after another hour of scanning. He grinned when he saw a group of middle-aged men sitting around a table in the restaurant. "I'll see you in the morning," he said to Ryan quickly. "Thanks for letting me tag along."

"For the record, I let you scan that raccoon," Ryan replied with a laugh.

Rick walked into the restaurant, not questioning it being open so late at night and shook hands with the men at the table. "Hey guys. Haven't seen you around lately."

"We're always around. It's you who disappeared." One man lifted a beer bottle to his lips and sighed with satisfaction. "We thought maybe you became a recluse."

"I've been busy, Jeff." He pulled over a chair from another table and sat down, dropping his pack on the ground next to him. "What's been going on with you seniors?"

Another man laughed. "I'm only five years older than you, so you better watch it. The twins were born last month, so Vicky took this season off to be with them."

"Twins? I don't even want to congratulate you for that, Matt." Rick shook his head with a smile. "Adam gives me and Brittany enough trouble as it is."

"The guys and I were just saying how different it is without Owen, Vicky, and John in this season. We knew Vicky was going to be out for at least a season, but no one expected John or your dad to retire," Jeff said softly.

"My dad didn't retire," he said shortly. "He'll be back next season. You really think he'd be able to stay away? Mom's about ready to just let him out into the wild. He's driving her up the wall. More than usual, at least."

Jeff shrugged. "That sounds like your dad, but I don't know, Rick. Owen's good, but you know he'll push too hard. You remember the first season?" He laughed as he attempted to speak. "He wanted to get the season to start a month early because he was so impatient."

The other men laughed and Matt spoke up. "He was after us for the entire season. 'I technically have a full month ahead of you guys. I don't care what your stats are. Mine are better.'"

"Hey, we scored in the top twenty," Rick retorted. "Your team came in last in all of Canada."

"Yeah, but *my* team came in first," said the third man. His thick grey beard hid the grin on his face. "But according to your dad's way of scoring we came in second. He kept that going for three seasons. Do you remember?"

Rick nodded. "Yeah. Luke, you were always a sore spot with my dad and you know it."

"Had to have some fun, didn't I?" Luke scratched his beard before he slammed his hand on the table. "Do you remember the third season? When Owen broke that horse's leg?"

"We didn't even know that was possible," Matt muttered as he finished off his beer. From the looks of the cluttered table, it seemed to be his third. "At least he was able to get a different horse scan afterwards after ruining the first one."

"That was Owen though: always pushing AIMs and himself past the limit. You'd think those scientists in Boston would have figured out that AIMs could get hurt earlier." Jeff nodded as if agreeing with himself. "Owen was a pioneer in many ways."

Rick shifted a bit in his seat. "Cam did nearly the same thing the day my dad had the heart-attack. He went over a jump, and the AIM landed a bit too hard. Tore the tendons, Maria said."

Luke laughed. "That kid's gotta learn to cool it. He's got too big a head already. One mistake, and he's going to crash and burn, disappear forever."

Rick ignored the comment. It held too much weight behind it. "Did you guys hear from Marshall? He's retiring this year."

"Then it'll just be us left in the division, and Owen if he comes back," Matt said as he looked at the other athletes.

Rick nodded slowly, wishing he had a beer of his own. "First people to compete in the CST. I can't believe it's been ten years." Maybe Ryan was right. Maybe it was better to adapt to the changes rather than hold onto the past.

* * *

Maria had gone two hours without looking or speaking to Cam, but she decided she should probably start. That was how things had always worked with them.

"I think we need to figure some things out."

"Oh, you think so?"

"Our contract is up for renewal, which pretty much makes what you do incredibly stupid and irresponsible, but we can't keep going at the rate we're going. You know we're not doing as well as we could be, and it's because we're fighting so much, not because of Ryan."

"And you think we can figure this out in the next two and a half hours?" Cam asked, looking back out the passenger window.

"We can at least start to talk things out, at least for the next challenge. I heard Rick talking on the phone with Brittany, and he's really not doing well. You've known him longer than me, you know how much he loves this game, and we're making him hate it." Her hands tightened around the steering wheel. "If you're not willing to work things out between us personally, then we need to at least find a way to make things work between us professionally."

She dared a glance at him. "We're not together anymore and honestly, I think it sucks, and it sucks how we're handling it. I'd rather not be around you and work things out on my own, but we're team-mates and we need to work things out together."

He paused a brief moment. "I never said I didn't want to make things work between us."

She kept her eyes on the road in front of her and bit her lip as if it would hold back what she wanted to say. But they needed to get along. "Well, do you think you can act a little less like a jerk during challenges? I admit, you're amazing." She smiled lightly when he grinned and shifted in his seat. "But you're honestly even more amazing as a part of this team, and when you work as a team member. We were amazing, both in and out of challenges."

Cam nodded and paused, thinking it through. They were a top ten team, and he was a top ten player. There was no reason for them to be getting anything less than perfect scores at every challenge. The friction between him and Maria was causing too much trouble.

"Even if I can do the challenge on my own, I guess two other people have to do it with me. Might as well work together, huh?" he said with a small smile, but it faded quickly. "This team was always based on trust. We have the reputation of taking risks, especially you, but we can't do that without trust."

"I do trust you, but only as a team-mate. I don't know if I trust you as a person yet."

"Well, try. You know I didn't cheat on you with her," Cam said, looking straight at Maria and saw her nod. "When I tell you everything's going to be okay, that what I'm doing isn't that bad, you need to believe me." He turned away when she remained silent. "If you want this team to work, you need to learn how to trust me again."

After a quiet moment she gave a soft sigh. "It's hard when you talk about things that I'm against. You have to realize that. And it didn't help that you told me that you *wanted* to cheat on me."

"I know, but you've still got to trust me enough to work with me. I was being honest with you. Being open for once about my life. You can't always have this in the back of your mind. I'm sorry, but I'm not going to be stopping any time soon. I'll be more careful since our contract is so close to renewal. I've never even been close to getting caught, so unless you tell someone, I'll be fine." He looked over at her.

"While I'm being open, I might as well tell you that I may have found something with Ryan's AIM. It's nothing illegal," he added quickly when her head snapped to look at him. "Everything's clean. I may have misread the code, but I thought I just saw a blip or something. I'm going to the lab tonight to see if there's anyone who knows about a similar case. But I couldn't find whatever it was a second time, so I'm sure it's nothing. I just wanted to let you know, and be open."

Maria nodded before looking back towards the road. "Okay." They had never been so open about his work before. He was trying to make her understand, but a part of her wished he had not told her. Less knowledge is always better when it came to things like this. "Thank you."

"I don't sell anything," he said without warning. "We don't import animals. That's a completely different group."

"Cam, I really don't need to know."

"Yes, you do. I do research. That's it. I don't use any of it during challenges. I don't buy, sell, or trade anything I find. I just research. And train."

So much for less knowledge. "So, what's the plan? You'll be less of a jerk, and I'll trust you?"

Cam leaned against the door of the car. "Guess so. Think you can handle it?"

"Oh please. You'll give in way before I do." That had always been the way.

He laughed. After a few moments of watching her concentrate on the road, he spoke again. "Seriously, though. Shopping? Was that the best excuse you could come up with?" When she paused, Cam turned to her as much as he could in his seat. "You hate shopping."

She flicked her eyes towards him briefly, debating whether to explain herself or not. If they were going to start being open again… "Most of my clothes don't fit anymore." When he did not seem to understand, she let out a harsh sigh. "I've gained weight, okay? Happy now?"

Cam held back a chortle, barely. "Too much post-break-up ice cream?"

Maria bit her lip. "I've changed my diet, I'm working out twice a day, and I'm still gaining weight. I didn't bother asking for the kayak because it was made for my specific weight, and I didn't want to bother practicing with it. It's why my balance was off in Owen Sound. I've never been this heavy in my life."

He looked her over, finally realizing it was a bigger issue than he thought. "You barely look like you've gained weight. You couldn't have gained that much to throw off your training."

"Eight pounds so far."

In the three and a half years he had known her, Maria had never shown concern over her weight. She was not the typical female in that sense. But she was an athlete, and anything that affected her training was upsetting. He shrugged and sat properly in his seat again. "I wouldn't worry about it. Athletes gain weight all the time. Just change your training routine," Cam said dully.

Maria smiled. Leave it to him to calm her with indifference. She could expect nothing else.

"Want to come shopping with me?" she teased.

"Actually, I have plans to throw myself over the Falls."

They were only about half an hour away from the building and Cam began to fidget in his seat. He had always made sure to never involve Maria with anything regarding the Underground. Now, she was going to see one of the places he worked, and likely going to see some people there too. He realized this was not going to be as easy as he thought. No one there had any idea that Maria knew what he was involved with, and he had planned on keeping it that way.

"Take a right at the next turn," he said as they drove down a country road. He looked out the side window, but his own reflection blocked his view of the dark scenery outside. "There's going to be something that looks like an industrial park a while down that road along the canal."

"That'll be it?"

"Yeah, then you just come back out to this road, and continue down the way we're going now. It'll take you straight into the city. Think you can remember that?"

Maria rolled her eyes with a smirk. "I'm the one who got us back on track when we drove out West last summer after *you* got us lost. Yeah, I think I can remember directions."

"It was the scenic way," he muttered. He should have seen her bringing that up again. Men and their directions, she would say.

Maria looked around at her mirrors and out the windows, not seeing much in the dark. She could see the glow of the city off in the distance which helped to give her a clue of her surroundings. She was thankful for the dark, so she would likely not be able to find it again in the daylight. She made the turn as Cam had instructed and watched for the industrial park. She slowed as they drove up to a group of buildings and her eyes flickered towards Cam for some affirmation.

"This it?"

"Yeah, just pull into a space," Cam said, not looking at her. His eyes scanned the parking lot and the entrance of the building, looking for anyone who might see Maria with him. He finally glanced at Maria as the car pulled to stop. "I'll get a ride back with someone, so you don't have to worry about it."

Maria nodded and stared at the steering wheel. "Alright. I'll see you tomorrow then for the challenge."

He unfastened his seatbelt but kept his eyes on Maria. He paused when he saw the strained look on her face. "What is it?"

"I'm just-" she began, but jumped in her seat when she was interrupted by a tapping on Cam's window. She swore when she saw a man waving in at them.

Cam repeated her curse. "Stay in the car." He opened his door, pushing the other guy out of the way in the process. "She's just dropping me off, Mark." He looked him in the eye, standing eye to eye with him.

"I wasn't aware that we allowed this kind of escort service," Mark said, walking around to the driver's side. He opened the door before Maria could lock it. He leaned down with a friendly smile and a tilt of his head. "Hey there, how're you doing tonight?"

Maria looked at Cam, standing behind the man. "I'm tired, I just want to get to a hotel and sleep."

"Why don't you visit for a minute? Hm?" Mark opened her door wider, giving her room to get out.

"She's just dropping me off." Cam stepped forward as Maria got out of the car slowly, keys in hand. His eyes narrowed as he heard the sound of a metallic gear clicking into place from the hand Mark had behind the open car door. Cam took a step in between Maria and the other man.

"You really want to rethink this situation," Cam growled, looking at Mark who had never taken his eyes from Maria. "You want to walk back into that building and wait for me there. She's going to go to a hotel, and that'll be it." When Mark did not move, Cam stepped towards him. "You really don't want to make this worse than it has to be. I'd love to see you piss me off, and then watch you try to find someone else who can do my job."

Maria stood behind Cam, trying to press herself up against the car. She tried to hide her uneasiness and fear of the sound of what she recognized as a gun being cocked on the other side of her car door. She watched Mark finally take his eyes away from her and look at Cam for a moment before heading back into the building.

Cam turned around once Mark was gone and looked at Maria. "You should go."

"You can't be serious." She looked away and brushed her hair from her face, swearing as she looked at the building. "He had a gun. He had a gun, Cameron."

"He wasn't going to do anything." Cam put a hand on the side of her arm and looked down at her. "I wasn't going to let him do anything to you."

"That's not the point. He had a gun. You're at a place that has to be protected like that. I can't even just drop you off without being threatened." She kept her face away from him and bit her lip. "I don't like you here. I don't want you to be here. If you're only doing research, they shouldn't need guns."

"Maria, the research is exactly why we need to be like this. We need to be this protective of our space. There are plenty of people who don't like what we're looking into. I'm sorry. I shouldn't have let you come here."

She shook her head. "You couldn't have stopped me anyway." She moved out of his grip and went to get back into the car. "Let me know when you get to the hotel, alright?"

"I'll be fine."

"Please? I'll feel better when you get to the hotel," she said. When he nodded, she got into the car. She gave him a final glance before she let him close the car door.

Cam watched as Maria drove away, making sure she was out of sight before he stormed into the building, slamming open the metal door. All eyes were on him as he looked around, whipping the door closed behind him as he stepped forward, letting his eyes adjust to the florescent lights of the warehouse. With another glance around and his eyes finally adjusted, he found his target.

He shoved Mark against the wall and then again when he tried to get away. "What the hell was that?" Cam yelled, now pressing him against the wall. "She was just dropping me off. What the hell was that about?"

"She's not one of us." Mark finally pushed Cam away and straightened his clothes, as if that would bring back his dignity. "I would've done the same if it had been anyone else."

"That's bull. If you *ever* go near her," he growled.

"You'll what?" The other man raised an eyebrow.

"You really want to push me? Who do you think Henk would rather replace? Me or you? And the gun? Would you rather work for the McCarthys?"

"No, but we need to start protecting ourselves better. Besides, I know Maria has a military background."

"Yeah, she'd have no problem kicking your-"

"Cam?" a woman called out, interrupting him. "Dr. Baxter needs you in here. Things are getting out of control in the training room." Her head hung out a door on the far side of the room. "You were supposed to be here yesterday." The woman winced as the sound of loud growling came from behind her, and heavy thumps against the walls. The sound of a very large, and very angry, animal.

He turned, letting go of Mark as the woman called his name again. "Don't you dare go near her again, or else her military background will be the least of your worries." Cam walked through a row of desks, picking up an AIRC from one of them as he passed it. It looked a bit bulkier than the one he used during the challenges, but it did what was needed.

"And how are you this evening, Sandra?" He grinned, turning on the AIRC as he stood at the doorway.

"Busy. Hurry up."

He eyed the older woman. She had always been somewhat bossy, but being the assistant to the head of the project, he supposed she had earned the right. But not with him. Only Henk had that right. "Five minutes. I have my own work to do. I wasn't even supposed to be in tonight, remember? I said I would come in when I wasn't busy. I'm sorry I'm trying to keep my cover."

"Yes, we're all so glad you've graced us with your presence. Now do you mind fixing the rogue?"

"Alright, time for some damage control," he said with an arrogant smile, scrolling through the AIRC as he stepped into the training room.

Maria rolled over quickly in the bed when she felt a light touch on her arm. Her hand flew to the bedside lamp and winced at the sudden light as she looked up at Cam. With a groan, she lay back onto her bed. "What time is it?" Her voice croaked with drowsiness as her eyes fluttered against the lamp's glow.

"Almost two."

She groaned again and threw the covers over her head. "I dislike you."

"Yeah, well, like me again for the challenge tomorrow. I'm back, safe and sound." He turned the light out again and moved from the side of her bed back towards the door. "You don't have to worry about that guy. Everything was cleared up."

"Good night," she said, rolling back away from the door.

"Have fun shopping." He closed the door before the pillow could hit him.

CHAPTER 15

"Forty-four…forty-five," Maria breathed with her final reverse crunch. She let her body relax, allowing her legs to hit the floor of her hotel room. Her abdomen burned, but it was necessary. It did no good to train the AIM if her body got out of shape. With a groan, she stood and looked at herself in the full-length mirror. She turned sideways with a frown, sliding her hand over her abdomen. No matter what she did, she kept gaining weight. It was not an issue now, but it was beginning to affect her stamina. That was never a good thing for an athlete.

"What was my count yesterday?" she asked her AIM.

"Fifty reverse crunches, and thirty sit-ups." Much lower than when she had been in cadets. This was pathetic for a soldier, let alone an athlete.

She let out a frustrated breath and sucked her stomach in. It barely made a difference. Her shopping trip had been a disaster. She went up two pant sizes in the past few months. Cam could never know. Maria smiled to herself. He could probably already tell just by looking at her. He was like that. "Okay," she addressed the AIM once again. "Update my nutritional diet for weight loss and endurance training."

"Updated."

Maria cast a sidelong look at the robot. It was worth a shot. "Do you think these shorts make me look fat?"

"I have no qualifiable data to answer your request."

She rolled her eyes. "Why do I even bother? It's not like you could give me an answer even if you wanted to," she muttered. "Come on." She grabbed her pack and headed for the closest coffee shop to the hotel, her AIM following close behind.

Maria slid from the hood of her car as she saw her team's RV and truck pull into parking spaces near her. She picked up a tray of coffee cups and carried it over to her newly arrived team-mates, taking a cup out as she greeted each one. "Almost thought you weren't going to make it."

"We stopped in a few small towns on the way," Rick answered as he took the offered coffee. "Ryan had a bit of the scanning bug, which is fine. I haven't been doing as much scanning as I should be so it was nice to catch up. And I needed to fill up the tank. I know, I know. Gas is the way of the past. I like my vintage things." Rick grinned and nodded towards the hotel. "Cam ready to go?"

"Yeah, he said he had to make a call first." Maria had surprised herself with her reaction, and she guessed Cam had been just as surprised when she had not given him a hard time about his mysterious phone calls. She had to learn to trust him again at some point. "How'd it go last night with the scanning?"

Rick grinned and pointed towards Ryan. "You should see this guy. We were up in the trees for hours just scanning."

Ryan shrugged, but his face flushed with the attention. "It wasn't anything special. You just have to have patience. It's all I did before in the KWJST, so it's really no big deal."

"I gave him the choice of sitting out and scanning today, but it might be good for him to get used to participating at least for the first little while. Besides, I'm the captain and I get to boss you guys around."

"Well, look at you, embracing your new role." Maria grinned. "It's about time. Good to see you finally in the driver's seat."

"Hey, you all set?" he called out to Cam as he walked towards the group.

Cam took the last coffee from the tray, nodding his thanks to Maria. "Yeah. I was talking to another team in there and they said the Raiders have the same time slot as us."

Rick swore and looked at the coffee cup in his hand. Maybe it would not be such a good idea for Ryan to attempt this challenge. Not that he doubted Ryan's abilities, but Rick did not want to take a chance. Five years earlier, the Raiders were rumoured to have sabotaged another team at the Niagara Falls challenge, almost sending two of the team members over the falls. Of course, it was just a rumour, but it still left a bad taste in the mouths of many contestants, including Rick.

"I know what you're thinking," Cam started. "They won't be a problem. We've been in close quarters with them before. We were stuck on that mountain last season for five hours with them. We were fine then, we'll be fine today. Don't worry about it. Besides, they'll have to deal with you if they try anything." He grinned and eyed Maria. His smile grew. "You *have* gained weight, haven't you?" He was like that.

Maria hugged her torso. She had only had enough time to buy new shorts, and only realized when she got back to the hotel that her shirts were beginning to feel, and look, snug as well no matter how much she worked on toning her core.

"Shut it. Let's go." She dumped her cup and the tray into a nearby garbage can.

Less than ten minutes later, the team stood together at the entrance to Dufferin Islands. They stared at an LCD screen with the official CST logo on it. It was a good spot to start a challenge: off from the main road, a quiet river which surrounded a tiny wooded island, but not much of a physical challenge if they had to actually do anything there. The roar of the falls was nearby, and if it had been any other day, Rick would have thought of just sitting at the park and scan, not having to worry about anything else.

"Since when have they had rules like this?" Cam asked with a hint of disgust in his voice. "I feel like they're talking to children."

"They've put restrictions on AIMs before; it's not that bad," Maria said, stepping towards the sign as if it would help her see something she may have missed.

"Only one AIM to be used. Only two animal scans may be used, but each must only be used once. Animals chosen can be no taller than three feet," Ryan read out loud quietly. "Well, that's fine to only use one AIM, but why the height restriction? If we need to find something small, we'll use a small animal anyway."

"To slow us down, most likely," Rick said after a moment, looking around. "It's another timed challenge. Small animals slow us down, especially if we have to follow them or get them to find something. But three feet is still quite large, especially if we want to use birds again. We only have two animals we can use, so you guys better think it through, and decide when you're going to use them. I really don't think this is going to be much of a problem."

Cam rolled his eyes as Rick went back to his truck. "A bird would be good for some point of the challenge, but I don't think we should use it yet."

"Well, we need to figure out where the marker is first," Maria said. She looked around, taking in her surroundings. This was completely different from the challenges that had been here before. Usually it was more of a tourist attraction than an actual challenge, but maybe they were trying to step it up for the ten year anniversary. More likely, it was to make it look better for the tourists who had been constantly photographing them since their arrival at the park on the side of the island.

Looking around, she realized just how many police vehicles were around. "Guess they're expecting more protesters here. That's not a good sign. I don't see many areas for ticket holders either. That won't be good for revenue."

"Yeah, I noticed that. Unless they're at the last stage. I'm not looking forward to that," Cam muttered.

"That's a first." She grinned, glad they were able to jest with each other. *Finally.* The first time they had spoken after their breakup had been during the training session when Owen had his heart attack. Actually, it had been the first time since he had moved out that either had even seen the other. For the length of time they had actually been speaking, she thought they had come a long way. She was proud of that, despite the fighting that had brought them there. It finally felt as though they were a team trying to win the CST and not simply trying to get along.

Ryan stood across the street, looking out across the river. Something had caught his eye a minute earlier, but he could not see it anymore. It had been a faint glint, so he was not sure if he had actually seen something or not. He wanted to say it was somewhere over on the other island, the much larger Goat Island. Why it was named that, he had no idea. He had never actually been to Niagara Falls before, and he was trying desperately to not look like a tourist himself.

There. He had definitely seen it that time.

"Hey guys, I think it's over there," he called over his shoulder. "Over the river, but I can't see exactly."

Cam and Maria crossed the road, both thankful that it was not busy, and stood beside Ryan. After a few moments, they saw the glint Ryan had mentioned and Cam swore.

"It's a moving marker. Probably going to need another fish. It'd be nice if we could use different animals than the ones we've used before," he grumbled as he leaned against the railing.

"Moving marker?" Ryan gave Maria a confused look. He had never heard of moving markers before, and had not even really seen them on TV.

"It's not something you see at the junior level, and it's not common in the CST either," Maria explained. "It means we need to lead the AIM to the marker because they won't be able to see it while they try to get to it, and in the water, that's going to be even more difficult."

"Alright, who has the best fish?" Cam looked at his teammates.

"Would the salmon work, the one I used for the first challenge?" Ryan asked tentatively.

"What kind of birds have you scanned?" While Ryan's variety of fish was not impressive, a salmon would work well in this turbulent water. Cam did not want to ask about Maria's fish, assuming she had not trained it much since Owen Sound and that had been a bust.

"I have a few hawks, and I got an eagle last night," he said quietly. "Nothing too great, but it might work."

That caught Cam's attention. "You got an eagle?"

Ryan shrugged. "I tried to get the pair of them, but they flew away before I could get closer on their branch. And Rick scared them away."

Maria smiled, watching them. Cam was right: Ryan was like him in many ways. He was passionate about the sport and went to crazy extremes to get the best scans. There was something else about him too. Then again, there was something else about Cam too, and it ended up being the Underground. "Guess it's your AIM again, Ryan. Let's get this show on the road."

Ryan changed his AIM quickly into the salmon, letting it get used to the current of the river. They were extremely close to the Horseshoe Falls and the water was quite rough in that area. "You guys are going to have to help," Ryan said, looking up from his AIRC's screen.

"It doesn't help that we can't see it all the time," Cam muttered and looked out over the river. "Alright, just go straight towards...what is that? Looks like a set of rocks before the island."

"It can't be that far. That's American ground over there. We have to stay in Canadian water," Maria said as she rummaged through her pack. "It looks like just a pole in the water somewhere." She pulled out a pair of binoculars and passed them to Cam, who took them without even looking at Maria.

Ryan watched as the other two stayed silent for a few moments, trying to get the bearings of the pole and he realized something. This was how he had seen them on TV: working together without even needing to speak to each other. Maybe things would work out. He looked back at the river and he squinted. "I see another thing out there."

"Yeah, I saw that too. They look the same to me, so I'm assuming we'll find out the next stages at the same time." Cam's eyes remained glued to the binoculars. "Means we get to decide if we want to go for all three or not."

"It'd be a good chance to catch up in our scores," Maria suggested. "I'd rather go for all of them. We're not the type of team to back down."

"I say we go for it," Ryan agreed, and the other two nodded.

"Okay, the AIM has to go a little to the right now. It's going to get caught in a current," Cam ordered. "How does it look on your screen?"

Ryan looked at his AIRC, following the small moving blip on his map carefully. "It looks good, far enough away from the falls." After only a moment, he heard his AIM chirp to him that two sets of co-ordinates were found. "Okay, plot them and send them to me." A second passed before a map showed up on his screen and Maria and Cam looked over his shoulders. "Those are the next two stages, I guess."

"Looks like they're both around the whirlpool. You going to be okay with the water, Cam?" Maria asked, hurrying back across the road, holding her hand up for a car to stop. She had to wait for the other two as they let the car drive through. "Come on! This is timed."

"I'd rather die by drowning than by getting hit by a car," Cam muttered as they piled into the silver car, waving to Rick as they sped off down along the falls and the river to the next stage.

After what felt to Maria like an extremely long fifteen minutes, the three of them stood at the top of a lookout point which overlooked the whirlpool down river from the waterfalls. They could see one of the stages clearly: a wire going from the Canadian to the American side of the gorge.

In the middle was another rope hanging down with a flag, which they guessed had something to scan attached to the end. They could not see the final stage, but its GPS location was almost directly across from them on the other side of the whirlpool, and they guessed it was somewhere on the side of the cliff. A good hint was the number of holes they had seen in the ground near the edge, indicating some form of climbing system which had been put in by other teams earlier.

"Should we be worried that we haven't seen Jack's team around?" Maria asked, looking around as if the team would pop out from the bushes.

"Are you worried about me, Maria?"

She spun around, a glare ready on her face as the Raiders stepped up beside them. "I'm worried you're going to survive," she quipped quickly.

"Now, what I have done to deserve that kind of talk?" Jack sneered and looked at Cam. "I'm surprised you're here with all this deadly water around."

"Cram it, Tyson," he growled. "Don't make me push you over the edge."

"I'd watch what you say. There are cameras flitting around all over the place."

Every season, Maria managed to ignore the floating cameras that were set up around the challenge sites. Until someone pointed them out, of course. There had been very few in Owen Sound, likely due to the storm. "Come on. We need to figure this out with clear heads," Maria said and led her team-mates to the side of the lookout point.

"I'm getting my AIM over here now. Would the eagle be alright?" Ryan asked.

"Yeah, it's fine," Cam replied, eying Jack as he was led away. He looked around, staying silent. Sometimes the CST provided some form of equipment, as they had at their first challenge with the kayaks, and they had done it minimally at the Windsor challenge in the form of a pointless map. But there did not seem to be anything at this stage. That was never a good sign.

As he continued to look around, he noticed Maria take off her pack and pull out her climbing gear. After her first season on Revolution, she had gone all out and bought what she would need for later years. All of it had come in handy, but it almost made her seem like a fanatic. But she would never admit to it.

"What do you think you're doing?"

Maria jumped a bit as she pulled the harness up her legs and around her thighs. "I'm going out there. Give me your AIRCs." She fastened the harness snugly around her, and frowned when she could not tighten it as much as other years. When the two paused she held out a hand. "Are you kidding me? Like you can do this, Cam. Maybe going down the cliff you can do, but there's no way you can hang above the water and I'm not going to let Jack get out there first. Ryan, do you think you can do this?"

"Well, maybe..."

"Have you trained for something like this?" At his hesitation, Maria grabbed his AIRC along with Cam's and slipped the wrist bands onto her arms, pulling gloves on afterwards. With a grin, she climbed over the railing of the lookout point and sat down, letting her legs dangle over the side of the gorge. Quickly, she attached both carabiners to the wire before sliding off the edge of the gorge. As she fell, she hooked a leg over the wire which was a few inches thick, and gripped it with her hands. She took a breath, letting her second leg dangle for a minute before she brought it up and hooked her ankles together. She began to slide herself across, knowing enough to trust the metal clips which attached her securely to the wire.

Jack stepped towards the railing and stared after Maria. "She's crazy. Why wouldn't she just get the AIMs to do the challenge?"

"Because she's a better athlete than you, that's why." Cam watched her as she moved across the wire, one hand over the other, too quickly for it to be safe.

Ryan glanced at Cam and saw the apprehension on his face. "Hey, slow it down! We're making good time!" he called out.

Cam folded his arms over his chest as he continued to watch his ex-girlfriend slide across the wire. "Come on Maria!" Cam yelled out as she reached the hanging rope, almost sounding as though he was rooting for her, but more as if he was trying to rush her. But not too much.

She paused as she neared the middle of the wire and the rope which hung down a few metres. Her legs were beginning to cramp from their position and the strain of her weight. Her arms were fine for now, but she had no idea how they would feel afterwards. Maria slid the final short distance to the rope and let her head drop to look at the flag hanging below her.

She hooked her ankles tighter and, although Cam would likely kill her later for doing it, she released the wire from her hands and let her upper body dangle upside down. She grabbed for the rope twice before finally pulling it towards her as an eagle flew by and perched on the wire.

"Mind pulling the rope up a bit?" Her voice was strained from being upside down. She waited for Ryan's eagle to pull the rope up with its beak enough for her to grab the small strips of metal and swiped them across the three AIRCs. "Thanks," she managed to get out as she let go of the end of the rope and took the wire back into her hands.

Maria avoided looking at Cam once she made her way back to the side of the gorge, knowing she would get a lecture if she did. Instead, she tossed the guys their consoles and picked up her pack. "Two down, one to go," she said, breathing heavily. She started for her car but stopped and faced Jack. "And that's how it's done."

"You're out of your mind," Cam shot as they piled into the car. "You know that, right?"

"But I'm awesome," she grinned and looked at Ryan. Slipping her gloves off, she re-tied her hair into a tighter ponytail. "You ever been rock climbing?"

"Not enough to get down and back quickly."

"Alright, it's you and me, Tylar. You better have practiced."

"There was no way I could get out of both rock climbing *and* kayaking after dating you," Cam said with a grin as he drove back along the edge of the whirlpool, back to where a group of fans and media were waiting for them. Police officers held back the line of protesters they had predicted would be there. With the police and the amount of media at the challenge, he felt safe that nothing would go wrong. With the bad press they had received so far with their poor scores, Cam was going to make sure this was the first thing that Sportcentre talked about that evening.

And it was going to be good.

CHAPTER 16

By the time Revolution arrived at the third stage, CST crew members had set up a belay system, which confirmed thoughts of rock climbing. Cam smiled and waved to the cameras quickly before getting his own harness on. Sure he loved the limelight, but he was in a challenge now. He did not need to talk to them. He would let his skills speak for him. He glanced hesitantly towards the group of protestors who were inching their way towards the staging area. Great job the cops were doing, keeping them back. At least the protesters were only throwing insults.

He attached himself to the rope and, even though he had promised himself he would not, Cam looked over the edge and took a deep breath. They were directly over the rapids which led to the whirlpool. With jagged rocks along the side and at the bottom, a person was just as likely to survive going over the falls as they were falling at this point.

"Hurry up, Maria," he called up to her as he leaned backwards over the edge, his harness safely holding him in place. He concentrated on his memories of rock climbing; memories which did not include water at the bottom.

She glanced up at the nearby crowd of protesters. If it had been any other time, she would have thrown her own insults right back. *When are they going to research so I can have a proper debate with them?* With a sigh, she clipped herself to the line and took hold of the belay device which would slow her descent.

"Ryan said it's about halfway down, according to his AIM. You okay with this?"

"We'll see," Cam said with a grin and began walking backwards over the side of the gorge, stumbling a bit as some rocks gave way. He caught himself quickly before continuing.

Maria smiled as she followed and the crowd erupted in cheers as the two disappeared over the side of the cliff. She looked over at Cam as he slowly propelled himself down the face of the cliff, looking as though he was sitting with the harness tight around his thighs and waist. "At least you're not actually in the water."

"For now." Cam looked up as if to inspect his rope, but she knew it was to distract himself, and to see if the cameras were looking over the edge. "Good coverage in this leg. We should get some sweet shots."

"Maybe they'll highlight me during the second stage." She laughed when he shot her a look. "Good thing we're not fighting."

"Good thing that rope can support you with your weight gain," he shot back at her.

"So much for not fighting," Maria muttered.

They continued their descent, taking one step at a time down the rock face, gripping their hand breaks as they went. Despite a quick descent, their arms began to burn from the work. After a few minutes, Maria stopped suddenly, motioning for Cam to do the same. "It's on my side," she called out to him. The dominating sound of the rapids and the rush of the water echoed in the gorge, acting as a constant reminder of the danger that lay below. "Can you swing over here to scan it, or do you need me to?"

Cam snorted and put his feet solidly against the rocks before walking towards Maria, his AIRC ready around his wrist. "I can do it myself, thanks. You know, I was part of this team two years before you came along."

"According to your stats you had never participated in a rock climbing challenge before I joined." Maria grinned. "Admit it. You were threatened by my abilities. You thought you were signing just this hot chick, and once you found out that I'm pretty much your equal, you became threatened." Her grin grew as Cam shot her another look as he scanned the strip of metal sticking out from the side of the gorge. He scanned the barcode with Ryan's AIRC and checked it to make sure it was successful.

"Just hurry up, would you? And so you know, I knew you were good even when we first met," he commented, getting back into position to begin the ascent. As soon as Maria scanned the barcode, they would officially complete the Niagara Falls challenge, and in less than an hour, too. That was impressive, even for them. With the sound of a soft ping from their AIRCs, signifying Maria's scan, they were done. Cam grinned and looked at his team-mate. "Ready?"

"Yep," she answered, putting her AIRC away but she stopped suddenly. She saw Cam catch her freeze and he turned to her as best as he could.

"What?"

Maria did not say anything, but felt her rope jerk slightly. She looked up to see if anyone was adjusting the metal spikes and pins which held her rope in place. No one was there.

"Cam," she said quietly, as if speaking too loud would make the situation worse. Maria swore when she felt herself lowered with a jolt. "Cam, my rope."

"Get over here." Cam stepped towards her quickly.

"My rope's breaking," she said, her voice flustered with the sense of panic as she took a step sideways towards Cam. With a simple repel, they had not needed to place safety hooks. No one could have seen this.

The rope give way before she actually felt herself fall, the line slackening above her as if moving in slow motion. She squeezed her eyes shut. There was no time to scream. Her lungs contracted as her stomach rose into her throat, and she felt herself plummet down the rock face.

Seven seconds. That's all it would take.

Seven.

The wind whipped around her, the broken rope long gone from her harness.

Six.

She barely felt the rock-face scrape the length of her body as she fell.

Five.

The sound of the water crashing against the rocks below echoed louder than the thumping of her heart in her ears.

Four.

Everything stopped. Maria felt a familiar pressure around her, and her stomach lurched to its regular place in her abdomen. Confused, she opened her eyes slowly and looked straight into Cam's face.

"You okay? No, don't look down," he said when she attempted to look below her. "Are you okay?"

Maria's legs were somehow wrapped around his waist and she felt one of his arms wrapped tightly around her. She looked between them to see both of her carabiners attached to his line. She finally allowed herself to nod and rested her head against his shoulder, closing her eyes. She wrapped her arms around his neck and gripped his shirt. "I'm okay."

"I'm not going to let you fall, alright? I've got you." He felt her nod into his shoulder as she managed to wrap her arms around him. He manoeuvred his AIRC as close to his face as he could while still holding the lock on his rope. As he had fallen after Maria, he'd attached her to his line, and it took all his strength on the locks to keep them from descending further. He did not want to look to see how little line he had left below him.

"She's safe and secured to my rope. You're going to have to pull us up. Can you get some help up there?" Cam called into his AIRC.

"Yeah. We have a medic ready for you," Ryan's voice came through the AIRC as the two were pulled up in slow spurts. "They have an emergency belay system hooked up now to get you guys up. Do you think you can hang on until then?"

"Just keep the medic standing by," he said, his voice strained. With a grunt, he shifted his head a bit to look at Maria. "You sure you're okay?"

"I'm fine." Her voice was muffled against his shoulder. "Are you? Aren't you going to get tired hanging onto me and my extra weight?" Whatever pain either of them felt was masked by the adrenaline pumping through their system.

He looked upwards to see a group of people looking over the edge. "You needed a few extra pounds anyway. You looked sickly." He kept his legs out slightly to bounce them away from the rock face as they were lifted up. "What happened to not pulling any more stunts today?"

"I never agreed to that."

When the two were pulled up and over the edge, they were greeted with cheers from a much larger crowd than what had been there when they descended. Maria winced at the lights of the cameras and she gave a soft smile as she let someone take her harness off of her. It was not until the harness slid down her legs that she noticed the gash running from her thigh to her calf. She began to turn towards Ryan as he approached his team-mates but a reporter stepped in front of her.

"Maria, how do you feel after that stage of the challenge? What were you feeling when you were down there?"

She winced slightly, and took a confused step backwards. She clenched her fists to stop them from trembling.

"Give her some space!" someone yelled.

"I don't even know what happened," she started slowly. "I closed my eyes for most of it. Cam would be the best person to ask. He's the one who was able to think and, thankfully, act quickly." She turned to Cam and stepped to the side as if to make room for him. She gave him a pleading look, asking him to take the pressure from the media.

"We'll get you to the medic," Cam said, putting a hand on her back as if to lead her away but stopped when Maria pushed him towards the reporters.

"Talk to them. It'll keep them occupied. Besides, you're the hero." She gave him a smile as more reporters circled around him, giving her the chance to step away with Ryan as the medic came over to her. She could hear Cam talking to the reporters, of course not mentioning her stunt at the second stage but instead talking about how, being the more experienced climber, Cam instinctively knew what to do. Only Maria could hear the concern in his voice and she smiled until she heard one of the reporters pipe in.

"Do you know who did it?"

Confusion crossed his face. "Did what?"

"The rope was cut," the reporter said as someone brought the top end of the rope forward.

Cam held it, looking it over. It had clearly been cut, or at least a cut was started. The rest of the line was frayed, which was likely the ripping feeling that Maria had felt. He shook his head and looked back to the cameras. "I have no idea. You guys were the ones up here, and unless you were trying to make even better TV, we're going to have to assume that this is an old and damaged line, which the CST should have checked before letting us use it." His eyes went to a group of protesters that had made their way to the edge of the gorge. "If it turns out someone tried to sabotage my team–" he stopped himself quickly before he said something he and his team would regret. *Always a first time for everything.* "I guess this just shows that nothing can stop Revolution. Nothing," he confirmed forcefully.

Just beyond the protesters, Cam saw Jack standing with a familiar blonde woman and his heart began to pound. "If we find that someone tried to sabotage my team, nothing is going to keep me from them." *Well, I tried.*

Ryan looked towards Maria, his eyes wide. "No one went near your line. I didn't even see the rope fraying until it was too late. I promise you, I didn't see a thing."

"It's alright," Maria said as she shut her eyes while the medic bandaged her leg, ignoring the way the woman pressed on the sensitive parts of her wound. "It was probably an old line, like Cam said. That happens sometimes. It's my own fault."

Once the medic ensured Cam was not injured anymore beyond a few bruises – while he continued to speak to reporters, of course – he joined his two team-mates.

"Ready?"

"Yeah, I'll drive," Ryan said and then paused. "If that's alright with Cam." He smiled when Cam rolled his eyes and made his way to the car.

"So, did that media coverage make up for the interview yesterday?" Maria asked as they walked behind the younger player.

"I'd say. I'm almost glad I had to save you. I should be getting that kind of attention all the time." He forced a smile, but could not shake the feeling there was more to this than an old rope.

Maria paused as he got into the car, looking back to the group of protesters who had now begun to heckle Jack's team. She caught Jack's eyes and saw his unexpected look of concern before she slipped into the car.

Rick watched as his team-mates walked into the hotel then paused. He had seen the live coverage of the last stage of the challenge and had tried to contact his team immediately. They had never come so close to something so dangerous before. For the most part, Cam had actually been professional during his short interview, or at least more than usual. For that, and much more, Rick was grateful. He walked over to the three and held his hand out for a hi-five as he smiled.

"Our first full score since Owen Sound. Glad to see we haven't lost it yet," Rick said, glancing between Maria and Cam. "Think we have a shot?"

Maria looked to Cam who returned her look before shoving him playfully. "As long as hot-shot over here can keep his ego in check, I think we've got a shot. I'm going to get some rest. Let me know when we're heading out." She gave a faint smile before she started to head off to her room, but Rick's hand on her arm stopped her. Before she knew it, she was pulled against his chest in an embrace. She closed her eyes briefly. For three years, Rick had been like an older brother to her. It could have been gone in three more seconds.

"We can wait until morning. You need to get that leg checked out again tonight," he said, his voice lowering. He had seen her almost fall; he had seen Cam catch her. Sure, she seemed playful and joking right now, but Rick knew her. She needed time.

"No." Maria pushed herself away from him before emotions caught up with her. "We can travel today and get someone to check me out before we go," Maria said strongly, now finally showing her shock through a bit of frustration. Before Rick could say anything else, she headed up to her room. She let the door close behind her as she slid down against the wall, wincing as she bent her bandaged leg. Her head tilted back to lean against the wall and her hands came up to cover her face. Finally, she was alone.

With Maria off to her room, Rick walked with Cam and Ryan to theirs. "You guys...you really impressed me. Cam, I haven't seen you and Maria work together like that in a long time," Rick said with a largely monotone voice, but Cam could hear the appreciation in it.

Cam shrugged. "It was a good drive last night. Got some things worked out." He glanced to Rick and saw his look. "Some, not all. Whatever, just let me know when you want to head out." He gave a half wave before quickening his pace.

"At least they're not fighting. And they were working amazingly well together today. It was almost the way I've seen them on TV before," Ryan said as Cam walked away.

Rick sighed as he ran a hand through his hair. "Maybe. I knew something bad would happen here though."

"It wasn't the Raiders," he said with a strong shake of the head. "They didn't even get to that stage of the challenge until we were done."

"Unless they were at that stage tampering with the rope before they started." Rick looked at the new member and realized he had completely forgotten to check out the results of other teams with everything that had been going on. Pulling out his AIRC, he flipped to team statistics and saw that the Revolution currently had the highest scored points for the Niagara Falls challenge. If the Raiders had in fact tried to sabotage them to get ahead, it hadn't worked. Not much could, save for internal pressures.

"I'll give you guys a few hours to rest up. I'll come and get you." He began to turn away but stopped and clapped Ryan on the back. "Good job, rookie."

"I barely did anything during this challenge."

"It was your AIM used during the challenge. That means you participated." Rick shrugged, his voice remaining monotone as usual. "And you survived another challenge with Cam and Maria. That should count for something."

Maria lifted her head from her knees when there was a knock on her door. With a groan she stood slowly and opened the door, the corner of her mouth twitching into a brief smile.

"Hey."

Cam glanced down at her leg and nodded behind her, into her room. "Can I come in?" He waited as she stepped out of the way before walking into the hotel room, Maria closing the door behind him. "Just wanted to make sure you were okay. It's been a big day. We both suppressed fighting with each other, and you kind of almost died."

She gave a small laugh as she followed Cam further into her room with a limp. "Not fighting with you is easy when," she paused, "when I realize how much you still take care of me. It's hard to hate someone who saves your life."

"Was it easy before today?"

Maria shook her head and sat down on the edge of her bed.

"Do you want to talk about what happened?"

"Cam, it's not that big of a deal."

He stared at her now with his arms folded across his chest. "I know you, Maria. Just talk to me."

"Honestly? I'm a little more freaked out about some guy threatening me with a gun than having my rope cut today." She closed her eyes briefly, her stomach rising once again. She was not sure she was telling the truth. She had never felt more helpless than these two times in her life.

"I told you that I took care of it."

"You think that changes anything? God, Cam," Maria looked away, wiping her face before she stood up again. "I've never even seen a civilian holding a gun before. Trained soldiers I'm fine with, not some random guy in a parking lot. All I did was drop you off." She shook her head violently, stepping back as Cam reached out to touch her arm. "No. I trust you, I do, but I can't feel okay about this, about you being in the Underground." She took in a breath, calming herself. She held her hands up to interrupt Cam before he could speak.

"I understand that whatever you're doing there needs to be protected, even to the point of threatening people, but if I can't even come near the building without a gun being involved, then it really is a good thing we broke up. When will it get to the point that I can't even be near you without being in danger? And what happens if any of your…colleagues…if they find out that I know what you're a part of?"

"They won't," he said with certainty.

"They will, eventually." Maria paused as she looked at his face. So much had happened in less than an hour. He had saved her life, and now she was throwing it back at him as if it meant nothing. "What if today was planned? What if my rope being cut was supposed to be a warning?"

"It's been three years. I don't plan on telling anyone anytime soon. Maria, come on," he said, attempting to get close to her again but she backed up even further. He would never resort to begging. Never again.

"I don't want to take that chance. Probably the only reason why I haven't been threatened before now is because we kept our relationship relatively secret from the public. Maybe it's good now that you can say you're single in interviews, truthfully. Might even get you more publicity. You'd love that, wouldn't you?"

Cam looked away. He had heard this before, many times before, but it never hit him quite like it did now. He was proud of how he came across to people, how he handled himself: cool, composed, a superstar. He never showed too much emotion unless it was pride, or passion for the game. He was not about to change that any time soon.

"So that's it then?" But then again, it never hit him quite like this before.

"It's always been up to you," she said softly.

"Don't." Cam raised his voice. Now he was angry. He was fine with showing that. "Don't you dare put this on me. You made the decision. You broke up with me."

"You knew the consequences of staying in the Underground."

"You didn't have to follow through." He waved her off as he stormed towards the door. He stopped suddenly and made his way back to Maria who was staying as stoic as he was. "You know what? I'm getting really sick of this. You either want me, or you don't. If you don't, then fine. Good riddance. If you do, you need to learn how to work through this, because I'm not quitting. What I'm doing isn't dangerous." This would be the closest he'd get to asking her to take him back.

"Isn't it? You said yourself the guns are needed to protect whatever you're doing. I am *not* going to learn how to work through someone threatening my life, or yours. Had you cared about me, you'd have quit the minute he pulled out that gun."

"No, if I cared about you, I'd stop people from pulling guns out on you. And I have. Did you think I was going to tell you every time you were threatened?" His voice grew louder as he spoke until he was sure people would be able to hear him through the walls. "*I* kept people in line. *I* kept people away from you, from this team." Her face was still blank, but Cam could see her emotions flicker through, if only for a brief second. He turned then and opened the door to her room. He paused as he glanced back at her. "I'll send a medic up to check out your leg." Without another word, Cam let the door close behind him.

Maria heard the soft click of the door closing as she sat back down onto the bed, just before she heard another knock at the door. Her eyes narrowed as she stormed with a limp, and swung the door open. Her face immediately softened, her eyes wide in surprise. "Sorry, I thought you were Cam."

Ryan shook his head. "I heard yelling and almost got trampled by him. Everything okay in here?"

She nodded and gave her best smile. "We got the best scores yet at this challenge. Of course I'm okay," she said as she opened the door a bit for Ryan to step in.

He turned to her once the door had closed. "Maria?"

Why was it so easy for her to break down in front of him? She had barely known him two weeks, and already she had done this twice. Why was it so easy for her to let him take her into his arms as tears streamed down her face? She let Ryan try to calm her down as she rested her head against his shoulder. She could hear him whispering to her, but she was not paying enough attention to really hear what he was saying. She just needed that attempt at comfort, and somehow she knew that Ryan did not mind standing there with her until they had to leave.

"I'm sorry for being like this," Maria muttered as soon as she could speak through her sobs.

"Don't be sorry." He could not help stroking her hair, but caught himself after a moment when she looked up at him, catching his eyes. "It's been a rough few days. First, you had to survive a car ride with Cam, and then everything today. It's a lot to take in. I have to say though," he paused as he looked down at her with a grin. "You were really impressive. I mean, I've seen you on TV and yeah you were good, but that wire stunt…most teams would've tried using their AIM before going out over the edge. But you, well, you were right on top of it."

She gave a small laugh as she wiped her face. "It was stupid. I shouldn't have been so reckless," she said as a loud knock came from the door. "I'm popular today." She gave a brief smile before moving away from Ryan slowly, feeling his grip stay on her as if not wanting her to leave his side. She opened the door and let the medic in. "I'm fine. Really. It barely even hurts anymore."

"We still have to make sure you're fit to compete. I doubt you want to compete tomorrow, make it worse and then have to sit out for the rest of the season," the male medic said with a grin.

Maria sat down on the bed as the medic began to un-wrap the bandages on her leg, wincing slightly as it pulled at healing flesh.

It was nearly twenty minutes before Ryan walked into the lobby with a limping Maria. She had changed into baggy pants, which were something she tried to never wear.

"I was planning on giving you a few hours," Rick said, taking Maria's pack from her without much argument.

"This is best. Means I can get to my interview on time," Cam said, hefting his own pack onto his shoulder.

Rick turned to him quickly, his face twisted as he tried to remember Cam mentioning the interview. "What are you talking about?"

"Got a call from a TV station in Hamilton. They want me in for an interview at six," he said with a grin. "Apparently I'm a hero. It's about time the calls started coming in. I know we don't usually do individual interviews, but I didn't think you'd mind." He looked to Maria and paused.

They had both been angry, or they had at least sounded it. He was not going to be the first to admit they still had a lot to work out, but he may as well put himself in a situation that it was a possibility. He was too proud to admit he said things he did not mean, and it was clear they were never going to work everything out, but after that challenge it had felt like they were a team again. He would admit to missing that, but nothing more.

"You want to ride in the truck with me? I'm sure Ryan would love to drive the car."

Maria glanced to Ryan as he looked down to his feet, suddenly finding them overly entertaining. "Actually, Ryan's already going to be driving the car. I thought I'd go with him."

Cam's eyes shot to Ryan who was still examining the laces of his shoes. He gave a small nod. "That's how it is then." When she did not respond, he turned and headed for the doors.

"Cam, I can't drive."

He turned back around, knowing Rick was giving her the same curious look.

She sighed, finally showing a bit of emotion. It wasn't pain, it was...shame? "The medic didn't clear me to compete." She bent slightly and rolled up her pant leg to show a brace on her leg. Cam and Rick both swore. "I guess the puncture was pretty deep, and if I put too much pressure on it, it won't heal. I can't bend my leg too well, which is why I need the car. There's not enough room in the truck to stretch out."

Her team-mates were quiet for a moment. Rick had no idea what to think. First his dad, and now Maria. Granted, her injury was not life threatening and she would be able to compete again, but did it have to happen so soon? It seemed as though every challenge they obtained a perfect score, something bad happened. He was beginning to think they would need to try not achieving perfection, as though it was that simple.

"How long are you out?" the captain asked.

"At least a week. Wherever we are at that point, I have to have an official medic do a full physical to make sure the rest of me is healthy." She took her pack away from Rick, almost as if to prove a point, before nodding towards Ryan. "For a while, I might be more comfortable with someone I've driven with before," she said, glancing to Cam, looking for some form of agreement.

Cam looked to Ryan, but took the chance before the younger member could speak. "I guess it'll give me something more to talk about at the interview. C'mon," he said to her, leading her out to the parking lot.

As Maria passed him, Ryan swore he saw her mouth an apology. He had clearly heard them argue, and Maria had been obviously upset because of it. She had let him comfort her, and he knew he had not imagined that moment between them, however brief it had been. Sure, maybe she was more comfortable with Cam's driving, but was that it? Was he willing to get in the middle of them, to deal with her obvious uncertainty? He was startled from his thoughts as Rick handed him the keys to the truck.

"Let's get going then. I guess Cam'll go straight to his interview, and flash Maria around like a prop. As long as they don't argue on the air, I'm happy."

CHAPTER 17

The two were silent as Cam drove down the highway. He kicked himself for getting into this situation. Normally, he would have left her alone. Normally, he would make some snide remark about not needing her at the challenges anyway. He would have let her go off with Ryan. He saw Maria glance at him every now and then, looking just as troubled and uncomfortable as he felt.

"We don't have to talk about it. We'll just go to the interview, get to the campsite, and that's it," he said curtly.

"Why did you want to drive with me?" she asked without hesitation, as if she had been holding her breath.

"Lack of sleep makes me say stupid things, apparently."

"Then maybe you shouldn't do the interview."

Cam smirked, letting himself glance over at her. "You wish, woman."

She shot him a cold stare. "I hate it when you call me that. Remember, I have plenty of names I can call you that you'd rather not hear."

"And there are some I know you wouldn't. Without a *very* good reason. Like death." He looked back towards the road, his face blank once again. "Like I said, we don't have to talk."

"Fine."

*   *   *

"I'm here with Cam Tylar of the Kitchener-Waterloo CST team, Revolution. Welcome," the lead sports anchor said in the studio of the Hamilton TV station.

"It's great to be here," the team member replied genuinely, a grin on his face.

"You guys had a rough start to the season. With Owen's heart attack, and some really low scores for most of the challenges, I'm sure that hit you hard."

He shrugged. Without Rick to control what he wore, Cam was happy enough sitting in the studio wearing his team jacket over a plain t-shirt, and of course he wore his tattered jeans.

"It did. After years of being at the top, it was hard being kicked down to the ground. Owen's been a great captain, so it was tough admitting we needed to replace him for this season." If only they knew the half of it. "Every team goes through an adjustment phase. I work well with pretty much everyone one on one, but it's a little tougher when there's a third person added to the mix. Ryan's been great so far. I've pretty much taken him under my wing, teaching him what I know."

"Think he'll soar above you?"

Cam laughed at the idea. "Not a chance, Ken. He's a great kid, but he has a lot to accomplish to get to my level. He only got a taste of what it means to be on this team today and back in Owen Sound."

"So, then, let's talk about Niagara Falls," the anchor said as he shifted slightly in his seat as if indicating that this is where the real interview began. "It happened just earlier today. Can you walk us through it?"

Cam relaxed in his chair. He could play it cool, but he was dancing on the inside. "It was a really good challenge. It was a multi-staged timed challenge which isn't too common for a regular city one, but we've gotten over the initial shock of a new member so we knew we'd blow it out of the water. It suited all of our strengths. Ryan scanned the salmon while I was training him back in Owen Sound so we were able to use that. That's his strength: finding and scanning animals. Maria and I were able to handle the rest."

"What do you think went wrong during the last stage? You weren't the first team to attempt the challenge, but you were the only ones to complete all three stages so far in your division."

"The CST is always really careful with equipment," Cam started slowly. He could give a false idea, but he had not really thought about it too much. *What happened out there?* He collected his thoughts briefly before he continued. "We got there, we got harnessed up. Everything was going fine. We had scanned the strip and were about to ascend back to the top. And then she just…fell." He paused; the studio went silent. Cam shook his head slightly and grinned. "Guess my training paid off. I had practiced recoveries so at least I was prepared for anything to happen."

Maria watched from where she sat just off camera. He was smiling now, but he had paused. Even he could not hide how all of this had affected him. He had thought there was a chance she could have died. It was only now she realized what this must have been like for him: seeing her fall, not knowing if he would catch her in time. Seven seconds was all it would have taken. He saved her in four.

"How is she now? There she is, hiding behind our cameras."

Her eyes widened, and she gave a sheepish smile as the camera swung around to face her. The camera did not swing away until she gave a small wave. She sank into her chair when it did and looked back at Cam, who surprisingly did not seem to mind her small bit of spotlight.

"Well," he paused, realizing they had not come up with a formal media release. Cam glanced at Maria who gave a small nod. "She's alright. She's agreed to take a week off from challenges, but we only have two more scheduled for this week before we have some time off. She has yet to sit out from a challenge, so it honestly won't affect us at all. It might even be nice to have just the guys compete for a change."

The two laughed and Maria rolled her eyes. He could bring it back quickly; she had to give him that.

"It's been great talking to you again, Cam," Ken said, proffering a hand to the athlete, which Cam shook enthusiastically. He turned back to the camera. "Revolution will be competing in the Hamilton challenge tomorrow afternoon. Steve, what kind of weather can they expect tomorrow?" The sports anchor expertly transitioned into the weather segment of the news broadcast.

The glowing red light above the TV camera faded and Ken leaned towards Cam briefly, Maria could see. The two laughed again and shook hands before Cam walked over to Maria.

"Told you you'd be bored. I should've dropped you off at the campsite," he said as they made their way to the exit.

"You need to be monitored, and no one else is willing to do it," she replied coolly.

He rolled his eyes as he opened the door leading out to the parking lot, where they were greeted by a small crowd of people who began to cheer when they saw them. Cam's face lit up into a grin as he waved.

A group of teenage girls reached Cam first, swooning. "Cam! Cam! Would you sign this for us?" They giggled in unison as he gladly took the pens and CST magazines from them. "Oh my God, that was so amazing, what you did today. You're, like, a hero."

"You bet I am," he said with a wink. They squealed but stayed hovering around Cam as he continued to sign autographs.

Maria kept her distance, but she still found herself cornered into a few photographs with some fans. After a brief conversation with a young girl, her eyes wandered back to Cam, who was kneeling down on the ground. A few people were trying to get his attention and blocked her view. After a few painful steps, she was able to see what had finally gotten Cam's sole attention.

"What's your name?" Cam asked in a tone Maria rarely heard him use.

"Derek," a young voice came out softly. The young boy looked no more than four years old. He clutched a piece of paper tightly in his small hands as he rocked back and forth, his eyes glued to Cam's feet.

"That's a cool name. Do you have an AIM? Yeah?" he asked when the little boy nodded his head. "I didn't get one until I was a bit older than you, so you have a head start. You need to practice really hard, okay?" He smiled when the boy again nodded, his face serious, taking Cam's words to heart. He slipped his AIRC from his pocket, ignoring the crowd which was trying to push up against him as he knelt. "See, this is mine."

"Cool!" Derek's eyes lit up and his little hands trembled with the piece of paper.

"Yeah, it's pretty cool." Cam pointed to his car. On the trunk sat a crow. "That's my AIM. Do you want to change it into something?" He laughed when Derek's eyes grew wide and he turned the console around so the boy could hold it. "Pick whatever you want."

The boy seemed unsure for a moment, contemplating between the AIRC and the paper which Maria had noticed Cam had already signed. But Cam took the piece of paper to free his hands, and the boy readily took the AIRC. He stuck his tongue out the side of his mouth as he tried to manoeuvre around what would obviously be a different AIRC than his own. After a moment, Derek spun around to look at the car and saw a raccoon where the crow had been.

"I just scanned that the other day," Cam said, taking the console back when the boy offered it.

"I know! I saw online!"

Cam grinned as he exchanged the console for the paper and looked around quickly. "Who brought you here?"

"My dad. He's...over there," Derek said, pointing through a forest of legs to the other side of the parking lot.

Maria saw Cam's face change as he looked over at a middle-aged man standing quite a ways off from the crowd, talking busily on his cellphone.

Cam stood and held his hand out to Derek. "Can I meet him?" He tried to smile when the boy took his hand, apparently losing his earlier hesitation, excitedly dragging him over to meet the man. He stood in front of the father, keeping hold of Derek's hand as the boy tried to get the man's attention. He stayed silent as he stared.

After a minute, Derek's father sighed, angrily ended the call and looked down at his son. "Are you done now, Derek? Can I go back to work?" Finally, he noticed Cam and raised an eyebrow. "Can I help you?"

"You can help yourself and pay more attention to your kid," Cam said calmly, not noticing Maria limping up towards them.

"Excuse me? Who are you to tell me what to do with my son?"

"I'm the guy he watches on TV, the one he looks up to instead of you. You need to stand beside to your son next time, rather than being in the background, or else you're always going to be in the background."

"I don't have time for this. Derek, we're leaving." But the boy didn't let go of Cam's hand. "Derek, get in the car!"

"Can Cam come too?"

Cam knelt down, letting go of the boy's hand reluctantly. "Sorry buddy, but I can't. I have to get ready for the challenge tomorrow. You're gonna be better than me someday, so I have to train really hard tonight. Okay?" The boy nodded but looked down at the ground. "Hey, give me a high five for good luck." He grinned when Derek obeyed, matching Cam's grin. Satisfied now, Derek jumped into the car and waved through the window. Cam stood again and looked the man in the eye, stepping in his way from getting into the car as well.

He felt a hand on his arm, turning quickly to see Maria there. He looked back at the man, who was now fuming but at least restraining himself in front of the child. "At least bring him to the challenge tomorrow." The man passed him without a word, and Cam waved to Derek as they drove away.

After a minute, Cam realized the rest of the crowd had left. "Let's get going," he said as he started back to the car, walking slowly to match Maria's pace.

Once in the vehicle, Maria finally turned to him. "You have to stop trying to save them. They're not you, Cam. All those men, they're not your dad."

"They might as well be. At least my dad...at least he knew what an AIM was."

Maria started to reach out to cover his hand with hers but stopped when Cam put his hand on the clutch and pulled out from the parking lot. "You were good with him." But he shrugged off her comment.

She was used to this from him, though. It was a strange sight for her when she had first joined the team. Cam went from being this flirtatious, good-looking athlete to a soft-spoken, kind role model. He rarely spoke about why, and Maria had never pressed him, but she knew he had not told the rest of their team-mates about his father abandoning him and his mother. "I'm proud of you. You didn't make yourself look like an idiot on TV."

After a minute, the corner of his mouth pulled up into a smile. "Yeah, well, I'm just that good."

"How are you, really?" Rick sat beside Maria around the fire he had made at the campsite. He would never say so in front of Maria, or to anyone else on the team, but he always felt more comfortable on an all-male team. Having Maria around was great, and she was definitely an amazing athlete, but he felt driven and reckless with two other males attempting a challenge. Maybe that had been Cam's problem. He had gone from an all-male team, to the introduction of a female. He had started dating said girl, even lived with her, and then eventually broke up. It was like having to get used to her all over again. Maybe that was what had happened, and now it was like old times with the guys.

"Annoyed by people asking me that all the time. I'm fine. Ticked off that I can't compete, but I'm fine. My leg only hurts if I put weight on it, but the medic said that should heal soon." Maria barely looked at Rick as she spoke. "Cam doesn't seem to be doing well, though."

He shrugged, shaking his head slowly. "Well, we were all a little shaken. I can understand him being the worst of us. Have you talked to him about it yet?"

"You really think he needs to talk it out before the challenge? He'd much rather just ignore it and focus on winning, and bringing up our stats," she said as she finished the last fork-load of food from her plate. She slowly stood up, keeping her balance on the uneven grass around the fire-pit. "Good luck tomorrow."

"Have a good night. And hey, Maria," he said, stopping her as she turned. "I'm glad you're alright."

She gave him a shrug. "Then thank Cam." She started for the RV, listening to the various night-time sounds. If there was any benefit to travelling so much and camping, it was the continuous sounds of crickets during the night and birds during the day. It calmed her and let her appreciate the experience of the CST even more. If it had not been for the tournament, the only travelling she would have done would be in a war zone. She stepped back suddenly as she started to enter the RV when Cam came out from the door. Maria swore as her eyes closed, wincing as her weight went down onto her bad leg.

"Sorry, didn't mean to scare you. You okay?"

"I'm fine." She was really getting sick of that. "Can we talk?"

Cam looked away, looking for something else to take up his time. "Actually, I was going to do some scanning, maybe go for a swim, paint a picture, do my taxes..."

"Please?"

Cam stood awkwardly in the RV. She had wanted to talk, but she had not said a word for a few minutes. Just as he was about to just shrug it off, which he should have done in the first place, she finally spoke.

"Are you okay?"

"You're the injured one."

"No, I mean, I could've died today. I thought that maybe we should talk about it."

Where was she going with this? Things had been dangerous before, and would be again in the future. This was not new for the team. But it had never been quite so dangerous before. Even with the first challenge, and the storm on the lake, it still did not seem as dangerous as this had been. Her death did not seem as imminent. He shrugged, uncaringly.

"But you didn't, so there's nothing to talk about." He turned to leave, but looked back at her suddenly. "You know, for someone who's against the supposed dangers of the Underground, you don't even look at the risks of the tournament. You almost drowned in Owen Sound, and you almost died today. One gun's pointed at you and that's all you can think about." His breathing quickened, and his face began to flush with anger.

"You make me listen to you as you flip over in your kayak. You make me watch you fall and I have to catch you. But when I keep a gun from firing that's the worst of it?" He stepped towards her, his face full of illogical anger. "And you pull stupid stunts like hanging from a wire. What the hell was that about? I almost think you're trying to get yourself killed, and for what? To prove a point? To prove how good you are without me?"

"Cameron?" she said softly, opposing his raised voice.

"What?"

"I'm alright," she told him, reaching out to take hold of his arm. "Nothing happened to me, other than my leg. It could've been a lot worse, but it wasn't."

"You think I don't know that?" He pulled away from her, his face twisting as if disgusted by her touch.

"Cameron." She was surprised that he let her step so close to him, and surprised even more when he did not pull away from her embrace. "I'm okay."

He was silent for a moment, not moving to return the embrace. She had seen his face during the interview, and had heard the waver in his voice. It was not until she felt his arms around her that she fully realized what had been going on inside his head. Maria felt his breathing deepen and realized he was trying to calm himself down. He would not cry in front of her. He had only done it once after his mother had died, but only that once.

"I don't think I can stand the thought of knowing I could never be with you. Never talk to you." His voice was soft in her ear, but Maria knew he was struggling to keep from showing too much emotion. It was likely already too late for that. "Breaking up is one thing, but watching you die..."

"I didn't. You saved me." She pulled back slightly to look him in the face to drive in the point further. "You saved me."

"If I had been a second slower..."

"But you weren't."

"It came that close, Maria."

"Actually, you had three more seconds."

By the time she noticed Cam leaning down towards her, she was already reaching up to him, their lips separated by a brief second. The second passed, and was filled, instead, with the incessant ringing of Cam's cell phone.

He swore and backed away as he answered the phone angrily. "What?...Now's not a good time. I'm in Hamilton right now and I don't really feel like driving back." He noticed Maria look at him. "Tell him to get someone else to do it for a while...I don't know, a week or so...I know we're behind schedule but I said I can't come in...no, he's not as good, but you'll manage with him...yeah, it's important, but so is this...I couldn't care less about my own research right now." He swore again as he shut off his phone, shoving it back into his pocket.

Cam looked back at Maria to see her staring at him. Usually he took calls like that elsewhere. He looked her face over, seeing disbelief and something else he could not quite put his finger on. His face hardened. "I'm not quitting."

"I know."

He paused and listened to the rain that was beginning to come down lightly, tinkling off the metallic roof of the RV. "I can at least take some time off." He watched her nod as they continued to stand in front of each other awkwardly. "I'm glad you're okay."

"Me too."

He smiled lightly. As if there was any other answer for her to give. He began turning away but stopped when Maria stepped towards him, pressing her lips against his. It took him a moment to register the feeling but he found himself with his arms around her, holding her close against him.

The rain had grown louder, falling more consistently on the RV by the time the two broke away from each other. Cam kept his face close to hers, looking at her as she kept her eyes closed. "Don't you ever pull a stunt like that again. Because if you end up dead, I'm going to bring you back to life just so I can kick your butt. You hear me?"

She gave a small laugh. "I hear you." Maria finally looked up at him. "I'd feel bad about you guys stuck in tents and me in the dry RV, but I'm disabled so I deserve it."

He laughed and before he could think, his lips pressed against hers once more briefly. Cam stepped away then, widening the gap between them. "You wouldn't feel bad even if you weren't. Enjoy the RV."

"Good luck tomorrow." Maria smiled lightly as he nodded his thanks before heading out into the rain. He was not quitting, but at least this was a start. Maybe good things really could come from the bad. *Just maybe.*

CHAPTER 18

Maria leaned against the tree, trying not to rest too much weight on her leg. It hurt less than the previous day – the rest really had done its work – but the pain was nowhere near the level of tolerance to do any form of training. So, she scanned. Even at that task, she felt useless. She had been slacking in scans this season and she scolded herself for it. After trying unsuccessfully to perch herself in a tree to get some of the rare birds which flew in the region, Maria had resorted to staying at the base, hoping to see through the thick branches to scan something.

She had heard the trill of the Northern Hawk Owl the night before, and knowing it was only partially nocturnal gave Maria hope that she may hear it again in the daytime. Unable to climb any of the trees, it was going to be difficult to know where to even start. The tree she was using for support was a fairly large one, likely a good spot for the owl to nest. Maria smiled to herself, thinking of Ryan stuck up in a tree all night just to scan a single bird. *Have I lost that?*

Her breathing stopped. She heard it again, the ki-ki-ki trill of the owl. It was not above her, but the sound echoed around the forest, bouncing off different trees. Maria kept her breathing light as she stepped forward, trying to get a bearing on the sound. The bird continued to call, which helped her, but only barely. A fluttering of wings and leaves made her turn to the left to see the owl land on a nearby tree. She was grateful that these birds did not seem to mind human contact.

Maria lifted her AIRC, waiting for the console to register the presence of the bird. She frowned, not able to get a clear shot of it. She took a few tentative steps backwards to get a different angle before she noticed that the bird looked as though it was about to take off once again. She swore inwardly and quickened her pace, nearly tripping backwards over an exposed root. Maria held in a squeal as pain shot through her leg. As the pain radiated up and down, she continued to keep her weight on the bad leg while she brought the console to her face again and smiled weakly, having a perfect view of her prey.

After only a few seconds, the scan was complete, and just in time before the bird took flight again. Looking at her AIRC, she scrolled through the stats of her new scan. It was a young owl, but it seemed to be in pretty good condition. Its speed was not the greatest, but its dexterity made up for that.

She limped her way back from the forest towards the campsite. An hour was long enough trying to scan. Her last check in with her team told her that they should be finishing soon, probably only giving her enough time to get back to the RV and pack things up before they headed off towards London.

With the tent taken down and the rest of the equipment away, Maria started for the RV, hoping to rest in whatever time she had left before the rest of her team arrived. Before she could get too far, she heard the sound of a large vehicle coming down the pathway. "There goes my nap," she muttered and stood in front of the RV to wait. Her eyebrow rose in suspicion when an unfamiliar truck stopped in front of her.

"Well, hello there."

Maria swore, folding her arms in front of her defensively. "What are you doing here, Jack?" She eyed the blonde girl who got out of the truck along with Jack, remembering her as Emily, one of the athletes presented to her team as a replacement for Owen.

"Just came to say hi. I thought that maybe I had earned that right. You came looking for me once, now I come looking for you. Even trade." Jack gave her a smug smile and glanced around. "All alone, are you?"

"Not for long. They'll be here in a few minutes."

"Guess you'll be going to London right when they get here. Well, I think I'll just wait for them. You don't mind, right Emily?" Jack asked as he leaned against his truck, mimicking Maria's arm position.

She eyed him warily. As he leaned, an Eastern Massasauga rattlesnake slid across his shoulders, tasting the air. Only he would actively use the only venomous snake in Ontario for his AIM. "Just leave, Jack. None of us have anything to say to you."

"I have some business with one of your team-mates. I think you're just nervous around me." He grinned with amusement. "Your knees are weak just being near me, aren't they? Tell me, have you told Cam yet?"

"It's not something I'm about to shout to the world, no." Her eyebrows furrowed. "Wait, what kind of business?"

"Not yours." He looked at Maria for a moment, and stepped towards her as her face changed. "What?"

"I didn't say anything," she said softly, taking a careful step back. Jack was looking for Cam. She should have assumed that Jack was in the Underground as well. He fit the description. But if they worked together, why did Jack not tell Cam what had happened? He had not even tried to blackmail her, at least not yet. "I'm surprised you haven't told him yourself."

Something strange flickered across his face: compassion. "Not my place to tell. I don't know why you're surprised. I'm the one who told you Cam was innocent, remember?" he said softly. "Or-" Jack was interrupted by the sound of another truck coming up the path. Cam was the first to get out of the truck, scrapes running up and down his arms and legs. "Looks like the challenge got the best of you."

"Screw you. We got full points. You barely made it past the first stage," Cam snapped as he stepped between Jack and Maria.

He had not spoken to her since the night before in the RV, and now she wondered what it had all meant, what he was thinking.

The group was silent for a moment. Maria noticed the way Emily looked at Cam, with hungry eyes. It was not the first time she had seen someone look at him that way, but there was something more to it with her. She had never asked Cam who it had been he had thought of cheating with, but the tension was too obvious to not make an assumption now.

"Got a minute?" Jack finally asked as though he had satisfied himself with examining Cam.

"Not for you."

"What about for me?"

Cam whipped his head in Emily's direction. "Definitely not for you, for either of you." He turned around and put a hand on Maria's back to lead her away. "Let's get going."

"We don't want to interfere, but you're making it difficult," Jack said, pulling Cam back towards him.

"Then interfere with someone else." Cam's voice was low and threatening, his eyes showing the same anger.

"I already have." Jack grinned again, glancing towards Maria briefly before motioning for Emily to follow him. "You have two days, Tylar," he said before they pulled away, ignoring the other Revolution members.

Cam glanced at Rick and Ryan, a sudden jolt of panic flowing through him. Jack had never done this before. No one had ever thought of appearing in front of his team members. No one had ever been that stupid, with him at least. It was an unwritten rule that everyone stayed discrete. Apparently Jack thought he was above the rules. *There's nothing going on in two days. It was all for show. But why?*

"I can't believe you lost that much money to him in poker."

Cam turned around quickly to look at Maria, who had a smug smile on her face.

"What?"

"He told me all about your little game. You were never good at poker. Stupid idea. Especially playing with Jack." She gave a shrug and motioned towards her captain and Ryan. "Well, are we ready to go? Everything's pretty much packed up."

Rick nodded as he approached Cam and Maria. He hated the idea of Jack coming around, and even being near him sent his skin crawling. "Was that Emily Richardson?"

Cam shrugged as he looked at the scrapes on his arms. The wind smarted against the broken skin. At least it would not keep him from competing. "Probably another one of his girlfriends."

Years ago, Jack and Cam had come to the agreement that they would stay away from each other. They worked in different areas on different projects for different people, and dated different girls. Of all the people Cam had told about his relationship with Maria, Jack had been one of the first. Initially, it had been a way to boast superiority over the older player, but after knowing Jack's intentions, Cam made clear the boundaries: he was to never come near his team. Why, then, did Jack say he had interfered with someone else already to get to him?

"Alright, let's get going then." Rick clapped his hands together, satisfied that the situation had cleared itself. He was trying not to let anything ruin the high of another fully completed challenge. It had not been an easy challenge, either. Going down into the caves of Eramosa Karst had been tougher than the year before. Parts of the cave had collapsed, and it did not help that Cam had forgotten his head lamp, resulting in quite a few tumbles.

Thankfully, the majority of the challenge had been completed by their AIMs, all of which needed high levels of dexterity to maneuver around the complex passages. Most of the other teams attempting with them did not have as much luck, or skill.

As Maria headed for the RV, Cam put a hand on her arm. She stopped and turned back to him, but was careful to avoid his face. "I'm going to ride with Rick in the RV. I'm going to try to get some rest before we get back to Kitchener. Hopefully that'll help heal my leg sooner. I'm really sick of it hurting."

"Did he say anything to you?"

"Why is everyone so concerned about him talking to me? Besides, he's not stupid enough to say anything that would incriminate either of you, as much as he hates you."

He paused for a moment. He did not want to ask, mostly because he was tired of being angry, but he was fine with the idea of having yet another reason to hate Jack. "Did he threaten you?"

Maria pulled her arm away. "He wouldn't hurt me, despite what he says."

"Since when have you given Jack Tyson the benefit of the doubt?" he asked incredulously.

"I know he isn't stupid. At least not that stupid." She paused. "And I've seen the way he looks at me."

She began to move away again when Cam stepped in front of her. His closeness was unnerving and threatened to tear her apart, and the night before only made her more confused. "You said I wasn't worth it. Doing it less is never going to be enough for me. Let's just leave it at that, okay?" She did not want to talk about what happened, despite having it run through her mind for the entire day. In the moment, it had felt like nothing was wrong between them. Just in that moment.

He let her walk away this time, knowing that Ryan was watching them. Watching Maria, actually. With a glower shot towards Ryan in the truck, he headed for Maria's car, pulling out quickly before the other two vehicles. She was right. Jack was not stupid, but he clearly needed a reminder of the boundaries. He pulled out his cellphone and dialed a number quickly, being sure to keep his eyes on the road as much as possible.

"Hey, Mark? Did you get a chance to look at the AIM's programming? …I said I was taking a break, not that you were allowed to have one. Just do it, alright? And bring some people with you and have a chat with Jack. He's starting to go public, and we can't have that right now." He threw his phone onto the passenger seat with a curse. Having two full-time jobs was beginning to be too much. He always had to do things himself.

The campsite just outside London was relatively quiet with few campers. Most teams enjoyed staying in hotels in the downtown centre of the city, but the site was in the middle of a few small towns and only twenty minutes away from a wildlife reserve.

Ryan sat down next to Cam, watching him flip through different screens on his AIRC. He noticed that the older member was looking at his own scores and statistics, which did not surprise him. He had been in the top ten in Canada for the past five years. Even when he had been a participant in the KWJST, Cam had been one of the top players.

"Why don't you scan as much anymore?"

Cam sighed and slipped his console into his pocket. "What do you mean?"

"You used to be good at it. I just wondered..."

"Excuse me? I *used* to be good at it?"

Ryan held up his hands, realizing his mistake as soon as he saw anger growing on his face. "No, I didn't mean it like that. I'm just saying your scores have dropped."

"So, you're saying I'm not as good as I used to be? Like I've peaked or something?"

Ryan's face flushed with embarrassment. "No! I'm just saying you were more well-rounded at the junior level." That did it.

"More...more well-rounded at the junior level." Cam gave a laugh and stood up. "You really think that the junior tournament means anything here? You think that any talent gained there does you any good? We're at the professional level."

"My scanning scores haven't fallen. Isn't the junior level where you learn what you need to know before moving up?" Ryan moved away quickly to stand when it looked as though Cam was about to attack him. "I really didn't mean any offense."

"You think you're better at scanning than me?"

"That's not what I-"

"Fine. If you're so great, then I'm sure you can get more points than me. In three hours we'll meet back here. Whoever gets the most points in scans is clearly the better player. Just remember that *I've* been the one training *you*."

The two stared at each other for a few moments. Ryan tried to decide the best thing to do. He did not want to make Cam angry, but he had only ever been confident in his scanning abilities. It had been why they had chosen him as Owen's replacement in the first place, so he had hoped that they had the same confidence in him.

"What is this, a staring contest?" Rick asked as he came out from the RV, his hair still wet from his shower.

"Ryan and I are going to have a scanning contest. Whoever gets the most points in scans in three hours can call himself the best scanner."

Rick raised an eyebrow towards Ryan. "Neither of you are the best, or we'd be in first place."

"I'm closer to it than he is, that's for sure," Cam snapped as he motioned towards Ryan. "Well?"

The rookie sighed and slipped out his AIRC. "Fine. Three hours." He gave a glance towards Rick, trying to show his reluctance as he headed for the truck and drove away.

Rick watched as Cam sat back down on the grass and picked a few blades of grass as if it actually entertained him. "What are you doing?"

"Relaxing. Hey, how's your dad doing?"

"You'd know if you actually called him. I thought you and Ryan are having a competition."

"Please. Do you really think I'm concerned about that? I was just trying to get him out of my hair. Might as well send him out to do something productive."

"And what happened to helping to train him?"

"Trust me; this'll definitely be a lesson for him." He glanced away, noticing Maria coming from the RV finally. She had been asleep since the team had left Hamilton and for the few hours they had been in London. He saw Rick look towards her as well. "She'll be fine," Cam said. "She's already doing better than yesterday."

"We could use her tomorrow, though. London is usually a bit rough."

"I'm sure it'll be fine. We were fine today."

Rick did not reply before heading off towards Maria, smiling at her as he passed.

She returned the expression before continuing on towards Cam. She stood beside him for a moment, deciding how to sit without too much pain, but he stood up before she could make a decision. "Look…"

"I don't work with Jack. He works for different people, even worse than the Underground, although I'm sure you could've assumed that. He's not the saintliest of people."

Maria folded her arms across her chest in an attempt to keep herself warm despite the sweater she was wearing. It was only mid-April, and she knew that there was still the possibility of snow. The bitterness of the evening made the threatening seem more like a reality. "I think I always thought that about him. But I guess now I know who *she* is. She's pretty." She looked at Cam when he did not reply. "Guess it would've been awkward if we had chosen her as Owen's replacement." She held her hand up to stop Cam from speaking, seeing him want to defend himself.

"Let me just get this out." When he stared at her, she took a breath and continued. "I know nothing happened. But honestly, it may as well have. Wanting to be with someone else, to me, is nearly just as bad as actually following through with those feelings. The fact," Maria paused. She had practiced this speech so many times over the past month. Not once did she become upset. Until she actually had to say it. Saying it to his face was much harder than saying it to his picture. "The fact that you wanted to be with someone else killed me, Cameron. I honestly hated you for it, because you treated me like I wasn't good enough. I know I am, and I know I didn't deserve that. But I know you don't think the same, especially if I'm not worth leaving the Underground for."

"I didn't do it because I wanted you more," he replied, half desperate. "I told you, I was upfront with you, because I wanted you to trust me, to know that I wasn't hiding anything from you, other than what I do in the Underground. I was trying to share my life with you, Maria. If you had only let me." Cam looked down at her, watching her become more upset the longer they were silent. "You really hated me that much?" He watched her turn away, holding herself again. "I didn't, and don't, have feelings for her."

"That doesn't make it any better."

"At least it's not worse. It was always you, Maria."

Maria looked back, staring up at him. Normally, it would make it better, knowing he did not have any feelings for Emily. But here was this girl in his life who he did not have to hide anything from. They worked together, or had similar jobs, and they were able to really share their lives together. When Cam had been with her, it was as though he was living two lives. Maybe that was not fair to him. It was definitely not fair to her.

"I thought I hated you. I knew that I wanted to hurt you, at least."

"Guess you did."

Maria shook her head. "Our relationship had been going downhill for months before I actually ended it. You don't even seem to really care we're not together."

Cam sighed with a shrug. "Then I guess you're the better person for not hurting me. I couldn't even do that." His eyebrows furrowed when Maria began to cry, stepping away from his advances. "Maria?"

"I slept with someone." The words came out quickly and hung in the air.

He stared at her, his arms still half extended towards her. He watched her attempt to hold back her sobs as she waited for his response. He blinked, shaking his head. He opened his mouth for a brief second before closing it.

"You...you slept with someone," he repeated it as if it would help to process the statement. "When?" *Is that why she's been so upset? Maria's spent all of this time blaming me for wanting to be with someone else when she had wanted the same and followed through?*

"The night we had that fight, when you told me about Emily." Her words were slow. She had managed to control her tears now, but barely had control over her breathing.

The night they broke up. It was not technically cheating, but they had broken up only hours earlier. He was not sure that made it any better. But she had not asked him to move out until the morning. After she had slept with someone else. Cam swore and ran a hand through his hair, glad for the coolness of the London evening. "Is that how you thought of hurting me?" If it was, she did it. Not that he would show it. He had hidden any pain over the break up, and this should be no different.

"Sleeping with someone? No. It was...the person I was with was what would hurt you." Maria closed her eyes.

"Who got the honour of pissing me off?" he said after a brief moment.

Her face turned down towards her feet, hidden with shame. She had wanted to hurt Cam, to make him feel as badly as she had. And she chose the one man who had always wanted a way to one up Cam, in everything.

"Cam..."

"Who was it?"

"Don't do this."

He moved towards her, towering over her, and he pulled her face up to look at him. "Who?" he growled.

"Jack."

Cam swore again, and continued as he turned away from her. His hands went up to his head, balled fists resting on top. "Are you kidding me? Are you kidding me, Maria?" he yelled, inserting more curses as he spoke to her.

"I knew it would hurt you the most. Cam, I'm sorry. I'm so sorry." But it was much too far past the point of apologies.

"You're *sorry*? You screwed him, and now you're sorry?" Cam swore again, cursing her. "I hope to God you're sorry, because he will be." He shook his head as he walked past her, wrenching his arm away from her when she tried to stop him. "Don't you dare touch me. Don't even come near me."

Maria watched as he stormed towards the car, and sped away. After a minute she wiped her face as she headed back for the RV. She smiled lightly at Rick watching TV.

He glanced up briefly as she stepped in, but gave her a second look when she noticed her wet cheeks. The honeymoon was over, it seemed. "What happened this time?"

She shook her head as she sat down next to him. "I screwed up. Cam left. I don't know if he'll be back before the challenge tomorrow, or to compete at all."

"He'll get over it. He'd never give up a challenge."

But Maria shook her head again. "No. He's not going to get over this." She took a deep, shuddering breath as she once again attempted to control her sobs. She knew Rick would not ask any questions, but he was at least a comforting presence.

"He'll be back. Apparently he's teaching Ryan a lesson."

"He may want to teach me one more."

Ryan drove back to the site only five minutes before the time Cam had told him to be back. The sun had since set, and in the darkness he did not notice anyone around the fire at first, but could make out Cam's figure on the far side of the fire as he parked. When he got out of the truck and made his way towards him, he noticed Rick was there as well. He smiled lightly as he reached the fire. For once, he felt as though he had actually accomplished something, and had done it well.

"Well, I think that went relatively well."

Cam looked up at him with a sigh. He had only recently returned after a phone call from Rick. It had been the thought of winning against Ryan that had brought him back. "So, how'd you do?"

"Twenty." His smile faded when Cam laughed and stood up to face him.

"Twenty. Not bad. You were gone for pretty much the entire three hours. Did you take a break at all?"

"Not really, no. I didn't go too far away so I'd make the most of the time. I learned that from the KWJST, even though you said what we learn there doesn't mean anything."

Cam's face turned from slightly amused to fury as he thrust his AIRC into the new member's face for him to see. "I was gone for an hour. Thirty-five points." Ryan's face dropped. "You really thought you could do better than me? Sure, you were good at scanning in the junior level, but let's get this cleared up right now." He stepped close towards him, his voice going threateningly low. "You will never be better than me. You will never be able to do what I can do. We signed you for scanning, but what good are you when I can do better than you in less time?"

"Cam," Rick said as he stood. His voice held its own threat.

"You know what? I don't need any of you if I can get those kinds of points on my own. Stay the hell away from me from now on." He eyed Ryan. "Find someone else to train you. I'm done."

Rick and Ryan watched as Cam walked towards the car and got into the back seat, clearly finding it to be a suitable place to spend the night. The captain stepped towards Ryan and put a hand on his shoulder. "He and Maria had another fight. Don't listen to him, okay?"

Ryan shook his head. "He's right. I bust my butt trying to even get the scans that I did for three hours. He went out and came back with more in less time. You guys signed me because of my scanning scores. But I couldn't even beat him.

"I wouldn't worry about it. Cam's made it his life goal to beat everyone. Just let him work it out on his own. We signed Maria because of the risks she takes, but it's gotten her injured a few times. Everyone's got their faults." Rick shrugged as if to show there was nothing else to say. "Tomorrow's a new day. He'll have calmed down, and we'll get another hundred points at the challenge." *If Cam doesn't kill someone first.*

CHAPTER 19

"Whatever's going on with you right now, can you at least put that towards the challenge?" Rick glanced over towards Cam as he drove to the London challenge. "We aced the last one, and I know we can keep it up."

"Of course we can. As long as Ryan keeps it up. His luck can't hold out forever," Cam muttered, watching the farmland pass as they drove around the outskirts of the city. He could not wait until the challenge was finished and they were on their way back to Kitchener, which was a first for him. In the past, he would hate having to go back home, wanting to continue with the challenges instead. The few days away from the team, away from her, would do him some good.

The challenge was located in the West end of the city, right in a residential neighbourhood which made the team slightly nervous. Thankfully, Cam had heard that there was no water involvement in this challenge, but he had no clue what they would be doing in that kind of area. Usually he would have at least heard a hint at this point. The silence of other teams usually implied a heavy reliance on their AIMs, which Cam was not going to complain about. It was about time he was able to fully use his AIM in a challenge rather than relying on his own athletic strength. The area around the museum, they knew, was kept close to how it was at the time when the native settlement was still there. If anything, the team knew that they would be in a very small area, likely around the embankment of the site.

The truck pulled into the small parking lot which had been made smaller by the other teams and local residents who had gathered to watch the excitement. The team stepped out to survey the area. They were at the edge of a thin forest surrounded by houses and a steep embankment, but not steep enough to need climbing equipment. Just enough to make it difficult. Dangerous, even, if one was not careful.

"Guess we should get going." Rick called over the other two team members. "If it's not a timed challenge, we'll take our time. We don't need to be rushing through things with this kind of terrain. We don't want another climbing accident."

"No, that would be a shame."

The team spun around, hearing Jack's voice. He was standing next to the path into the forest, his team-mates milling around, waiting for their time slot. Rick rolled his eyes, wanting to ignore him, when he noticed Cam heading towards Jack.

Cam's eyes glowed with angry flames as he made his way towards the opposing captain. Each step he took his anger grew, Maria's words repeating and echoing in his mind. He watched as the man's face turned into a smile, and his mouth opened to speak. Before anyone could stop him, before Jack could mutter his mockery, Cam's fist flew into his face. He ignored the yells from the people around him as he landed another one before the man could regain his balance.

He managed to dodge the full force of a return blow, but Jack's fist clipped him briefly in the jaw. He swore as he put his full body weight into his shots, barely feeling the few hits Jack landed back on him. Another shot to the side of Jack's face nearly sent him backwards. Cam ignored the shouting of his team-mates, but could not ignore the three men holding him back who grabbed him suddenly, pulling him off the other man. None of the restraints subdued the urge to continue the fight.

"You slept with my girlfriend!" Cam screamed, throwing his body against his restraints.

Jack shoved away his team-mates, wiping the blood from his lip. He grinned at Cam as he kept a few fingers pressed against it to stop the flow. "She loved every minute of it."

Cam threw continuous curses at the man. "I told you to stay away from her, you son of a -"

"I couldn't even if I tried. She begged me." Jack grinned again, watching the fury on Cam's face. "Give it up, Tylar." He shoved Emily away when she tried to take a look at the cut above his eye.

Cam finally escaped from the grip of the men holding him, his arms at his side to show he was not about to throw another punch. Not yet anyway. He took a few steps to look Jack in the eye, glowering at the man's grin. "If you go near her again, I *will* kill you. I will destroy all of your work, I will destroy the company, and I will kill you." Cam saw the faint flicker of what he hoped was fear in Jack's eyes before he let the man walk away.

As his team-mates finally joined him, he wiped his face to clear the blood. He was not sure where it was coming from the most, but he knew that he looked better than Jack. At least that gave him a small amount of contentment. He looked at Rick and Ryan, seeing their faces. He and Maria had always managed to keep the contents of their arguments private. It was humiliating to have them know about Maria had done, to have them think that he had not been enough for her.

"Let's just get this over with. I'm really not in the mood to screw this up, so it'd be great if you could actually do something right for a change, Ryan." Cam picked up his pack from where he had let it fall and led the way into the forest, going around the palisade which surrounded the museum grounds while ignoring the trespassing signs which meant nothing to a CST player.

The other two athletes looked at each other, a look of understanding passing between them. As long as he put the same passion into the challenge as he had put behind his punches, they wouldn't have to worry about Cam. At least now they knew why he had been so angry. There was always something deeper, it seemed.

Maria did not look up as she heard the sound of tires coming towards her. Only when she heard the truck doors close did she dare a glance away from her guitar towards her team-mates. She had seen her AIRC update with yet another full score but she was hesitant to say anything to them until after Cam had gone off on his own. Cam was leading them in, of course, but her eyes grew when she saw the state of his face. His bottom lip was busted open, swollen. His right eye was no better. There was a cut just above his eye, and the skin around it was beginning to turn a yellowish black colour. Her mouth dropped open as he walked by but she remained silent. For once, she would listen to what he asked of her and would keep her distance. When Rick and Ryan made their way over to her, she nodded her head towards Cam who dove into the tent he had claimed as his own.

"What happened to him?"

"The Raiders were at the challenge when we got there," Rick said dryly.

By his tone and the look of disappointment on his face, Maria realized that he had found out. If the Raiders were at the challenge, that would explain Cam's face. At least Cam had not wrecked the car. Unable to look at her captain, she tilted her face down towards her guitar again. She watched from the corner of her eye as her AIM hopped up onto the log next to her in the form of a cat and sat down, content with its seat.

"You just had to choose Jack, didn't you? Couldn't have found someone else to cheat on Cam with? He can be a jerk, I know, but he doesn't deserve that. There's nothing he could have done to deserve that."

Other than cheat himself. She shook her head, holding her instrument closer to her body. "It was a stupid mistake. I know he doesn't deserve that, so you really don't need to tell me," she said shortly. Maria had no intention of telling Rick about Cam's own offense, but she did not need a lecture from him. Not tonight.

"Be ready first thing in the morning. We'll head back to Kitchener then." Rick looked Maria over with a disapproving shake of his head before going to the tent he would share with Ryan.

She glanced up as Rick walked away, and noticed that Ryan was still standing next to her. "Don't even bother try to make me feel worse than I already do."

"I wasn't going to." Ryan paused before going off to the tent after Rick, reappearing after a moment with his own guitar. He sat down next to Maria, and his AIM in the form of a cat climbed up after him. He glanced at her leg and realized she was not wearing her brace. She had given up with it out of bitterness, despite the medic's advice. He strummed a chord before nodding towards her injury. "How's the leg?"

"You don't have to make small talk. I'm really not in the mood."

"I'm not making small talk. I want to know how your leg is doing."

She paused, looking at him. In the dim light, it was difficult to determine if he meant his words. He had never given her a reason to doubt him, not yet at least. But they always did. "It's getting better, but the medic won't clear me any sooner than the end of the week."

The two watched as Ryan's AIM moved cautiously across his lap and stood next to the other AIM. It paused and sniffed the cat and after a brief moment, found it acceptable and sat down.

Maria smiled lightly. "You trained it well. It's almost like a real cat."

"It does that a lot, actually. It's pretty easy to train it to act like an animal."

They were quiet for a few more minutes before Ryan sighed.

"I don't agree with what you did. I just want to get that out of the way. I don't hate you, but I think I know you well enough to know that you don't do anything without a reason. I won't ask what it is because it's none of my business. And I don't judge you. It's not my place." He paused, picking at the strings of his guitar. "But if you want to talk about it, then I'll listen."

"I don't want to talk about it."

He nodded, noticing her tone change. She was much less defensive, but sounded more defeated. "Do you regret it? Only question, I promise."

"Yes."

He nodded once more, signalling the end of that conversation. He began to strum consistently, the chords turning into a familiar song. When Maria gave a small laugh at his version of *Kumbaya* he picked up the beat slightly, waiting for her to join in. Whatever her reason had been, Ryan did not think it was good enough to cheat on Cam. Granted, Cam had not given any details. They assumed she had cheated, but she did not seem to be the type. All he could do was sit there with her, play the guitar with her, and be there when she did want to talk. Ryan would have to brace himself for the next few days against Cam. As much as he did not want Maria to be left without a friend, he wanted to go against Cam even less. *I'd be out in one blow*, he thought as they continued to play in the dark.

After a while Maria turned to Ryan, her fingers slowing over the strings. "You should go sleep. You're not helping yourself by being here, associating with the girl with the Scarlet Letter. Cam dislikes you enough. Trust me, it's not fun being on his bad side."

He shrugged. "I'm never going to make him approve of me, and I don't know if I want his approval really. I mean, Cam's awesome at what he does but, I don't know. It's like it's the team plus Cam at these challenges."

"He's always been independent, always needed to step up and be the man, I guess you could say," she said softly, looking over her shoulder as if Cam could hear her talking about him. "He wasn't always like this, you know." She gave a soft laugh as she thought for a moment. "You must think I was crazy to even date him for as long as I did." When there was no response, she shrugged.

"He's been through a lot; lost a lot of people. He had to create a wall to protect himself. But when he lets you in…" Maria's voice trailed off as it caught in her throat. "He'd lay down his life for the people he cares about. He makes sure you know that. He isn't perfect, and his ego gets in the way sometimes, a lot of the time actually, but for the most part…it was pretty great being with him." She looked Ryan over for a moment.

"Truth is, you guys are a lot alike."

Her statement struck him momentarily dumb. "I didn't think I was that good."

She smiled genuinely for the first time all night. "You both have something deep down that you won't let out. I don't have that in common with you guys anymore. My skeletons are dangling from the trees for all to see. Can't wait to see what the tabloids will say about this." She swore as her fingers finally came to a rest. "We have the signing tomorrow. Cam looks like crap."

"Injury from the challenge. He took quite a bit of a tumble down that embankment today." Ryan gave her a quick glance. "No idea how that tree branch managed to get him right in the eye."

"Anyone ever tell you that you should go into politics? You lie too easily."

He shook his head with a serious face. "No. It's not easy. I don't like doing it, especially not to people I care about." He gave her another glance, her eyes flashing up to meet his before he gripped his guitar tighter and stood. "See you in the morning."

She watched as he walked away with his AIM following close behind as they disappeared into his tent. She rested her face in her hands. It would be easy to take a longer leave, to give them space. The medic would only clear her if she was completely ready. She knew her leg was healing well. She was ready. But her team? No. They weren't ready.

Ryan watched with a sigh as the last of the team's fans trickled from the Memorial Auditorium in Kitchener. It had been a long day, but he felt more satisfied than after completing the challenges so far. Despite being new to the team, and being the replacement for the previous team captain, Ryan had a surprising number of fans who had requested his autograph and a picture with him. Of course, he did not have anywhere near the amount of the other three, but that was expected.

"Well that was a pretty good turnout." Rick stood, stretching his limbs after a few hours of sitting behind the long table. "Nice break from constant travelling and competing."

"Says you."

Rick glanced at Cam, his eyebrows furrowing. "I thought you liked the attention. Most of the people came to see and talk just to you. Are you really going to complain about that?"

"No, but I don't like one more than the other. I'd rather do all of it all the time." Cam stood up and pushed his chair in carelessly. He leaned against the table as he looked at Ryan. He had avoided speaking to the younger player since the challenge the previous day, not necessarily because he was angry with him, but he was just angry in general. "You need to get a new AIRC. You've been able to get by with your old one, but while we're in town you might as well get it now. Rick will be too busy with Brittany and Owen to take you, so I guess it's up to me. Who better to help you with it, anyway?"

"I can't help him?"

He did not even glance towards Maria. "You're currently inactive, and pretty much useless."

Ryan looked at her and saw the flinch of her face at Cam's words. "You'll be busy meeting with medics anyway. You might as well rest while you can. Besides, Cam will get me the best one. He won't let me get anything less than that." He hoped that he had lightened the tension, if only slightly.

She stood slowly, wincing less than the previous few days. Her leg was almost healed, but there was still stiffness from disuse. She had forgotten how quickly a body could get out of shape. "Fine. I'm taking my car." Cam began to protest and she held out a hand to take the keys, her head raised in defiance. "I'm well enough to drive now. Unless, of course, you'd like to drive me to my appointments." The keys were quickly flung into her hand.

"Actually, I wouldn't mind doing it."

Her eyes went to Ryan quickly, as did those of her other team-mates. "What?"

He shrugged. "I can't imagine taking long to get a new AIRC, and even though you're inactive, your scans still count so you might as well do that too. You haven't been doing much, so I'm going to use you training me as an excuse to get more scans. Besides, Cam said I should get someone else to train me from now on. He also said Rick would be busy. Why not spend some time with you?"

She braved a glance at Cam, but did not get much of a reaction from him. She turned to Ryan, intending to turn him down. "I'd appreciate that." Not what she had been thinking.

"Just let me know when you need to go in." Ryan stood finally. Despite what Maria had done, no one's closet was clean. Maybe the skeletons were different shapes and sizes, but they were there nonetheless.

"Cam, you'll let me know when we're going to get my AIRC then?" He did not get a chance to say goodbye to Maria before she left, not even glancing behind her to say goodbye to the others.

"I'll see you guys later." Cam stood, working his shoulders to stretch them. "Have a good time with your family." He nodded towards Rick, showing the most camaraderie towards him since Owen's heart attack before leaving. He was glad Ryan would be out of his hair for the most part. He had to make sure Jack did not approach him in public again. Officials were already beginning to ask questions. If too many eyes turned to him, he would be forced to give up either his place in the team, or in the Underground. He was not ready to make that decision yet.

After a long few days of doctor's appointments, Maria stepped out of her car and watched her three team-mates pack the truck with supplies they would need to get them through the rest of the Ontario challenges. They would be leaving the RV behind, and then leaving the vehicles at the airport before heading out from there, renting cars for the rest of the tournament. All paid for by their sponsors. They had agreed to meet early to try to beat the Sunday afternoon traffic of people coming back from wherever their personal weekend had brought them. Her limp was almost gone now as she walked towards them, still unnoticed. It had been close to a week now, so she was glad for that at least. She smiled when Ryan caught a glimpse of her and waved her over. The other two turned as she got closer.

"We're going to have to put some bags in the car too. This is going to be our long stretch of the season," Rick commented without looking at her as he moved towards her vehicle.

"I wasn't cleared."

Her team froze, moving in perfect unison after a moment to turn towards her as her eyes dropped to the ground.

"I thought the stitches meant you'd be fine. Your leg looked fine last night." Ryan glanced at Cam as he realized his mistake, but his eyes went back with a questioning look at Maria.

She sighed as she folded her arms over her chest. "They want to run more tests. They found something in my blood samples, or a number was high that shouldn't be, or whatever. They said my leg's fine but they don't want to risk something else being wrong with me. It might be an infection or something. They're not sure what it is, but I wouldn't worry about it." It scared her how easily she could lie.

"Does it have to do with your nausea? I thought that had gone away too." Ryan seemed to be the only one with questions. Maybe he was the only one who really cared.

"It has for the most part."

Ryan had been so good taking her to the appointments and simply hanging out with her when she needed the company. Cam, well, his face was a mixture of concern and frustration, the latter marked by the lines on his forehead which she had always found endearing.

"You guys will have to just go ahead and finish the Ontario schedule without me. As far as I've heard, there aren't any more water challenges. And then you'll go on out East according to our challenge schedule and when I'm cleared, I'll get to you guys on my own. I should be cleared before you head out West."

Rick nodded and made his way back to the truck. "We'll cram into the truck until we get to the last Ontario challenge. We'll rent a car at the airport, and you can rent a truck. We'll need the space even before you get to us, whenever that'll be." He paused before getting into the truck. "Good luck with the appointment."

Ryan stepped towards Maria, tilting his head a bit to look her in the face. "Don't miss us too much."

She smiled as she placed a hand on his chest. She had appreciated the time he had spent with her, and surprisingly, she had not felt uncomfortable when he fell asleep at her apartment the night before. "I'm more worried about you travelling alone with those two."

"I think I'll manage, but it'd be nice to have you around." He took a step back, awkwardly aware of Cam's stare. He cleared his throat before he joined Rick in the truck, Cam close behind him.

Cam had simply nodded to her, but it was better than nothing. She knew he would not say anything to her, even if he was concerned. He would not allow himself to, and she knew that any trust he had found in her was lost. With Cam, that meant she may as well be dead. Maria sighed and walked to Rick's front door once the others were out of sight.

Brittany opened the door slowly as if expecting the team member. "Well?"

"You were right."

She nodded with a sympathetic smile as she looked down the road. "Come on in. You can borrow some of my books."

"Thanks." Maria stepped into her captain's house but paused at the door. "Brittany, it's not just that."

The woman turned around with a raised eyebrow. "What do you mean?"

"I got a letter from the army."

"I thought you didn't go through with Basic Training."

"I didn't. After Cam and I broke up, I applied for a job working with military AIMs. I wasn't sure I'd be able to compete again. My dad wrote a letter of recommendation based on my background in cadets before he died and they've kept it on file." She shrugged. "Anyway, I got a response. They want me to start Basic at the end of the season."

Brittany nodded towards her. "What are you going to do?"

She shrugged. "I have no idea. I guess I have to tell Cam first. One step at a time."

CHAPTER 20

"It's been nearly one month since the tenth season of the CST started. Let's take a look at some of the highlights so far," a sportscaster announced before the TV flipped to video clips of various teams. *"An early highlight was the unfortunate benching of Owen Warner, captain of Revolution. He was replaced by rookie Ryan Hampton and, so far, he's proven to be a surprisingly up and coming player. The team's been a roller coaster ever since, acing their first challenge and then gaining miserable points for the next few scores. A heroic gesture by Cam Tylar in the Niagara Falls challenge gained his team another perfect score, but resulted in Maria Kier sitting out for almost two weeks now. We've yet to confirm her status with the team, although sources say she will be cleared soon to re-enter the tournament."*

Ryan tossed the remote control onto Cam's hotel bed and lay back onto his own. "Do they really pry like this all the time?" he asked as the hotel room phone rang for the eighth time that day. The team, along with their agents, had been inundated with calls from reporters about the Niagara Falls challenge, the fight in London, and any news of Maria.

"Once they find out some news, they don't back down." Cam flipped the TV off, a gesture noticed by Ryan, and answered the phone. "What?" He paused, looking at Ryan before turning away. "Sure. I'll be there in a minute."

The rookie watched as Cam hung up the phone before grabbing his coat. "Where're you going?" Twenty minutes in any direction from their hotel in Charlottetown, Prince Edward Island, landed a person in the middle of farmland. There was nowhere Cam could possibly be going.

"Out."

"Out where?"

"God, you sound like Maria." Cam swore as he tugged on his shoes. "It doesn't matter. I'll be back when I'm back, too." He slammed the door behind him, ignoring Rick coming up behind him. He glanced over his shoulder to make sure Rick would not bother following him as Jack come out from a side hallway, pushing him against the wall with a thud.

"You really think you can just hide from me, Tylar? Think I'd really back off just because you got some lucky shots?" the man growled, pinning Cam with his forearm against his chest.

Cam glared at him, seething. "And do you really think I need a reason to hide from you? Your funding's gone." He gave a smirk when he noticed the man's eyes flinch. "Oh, thought I didn't know that *Mr. McCarthy* has lost confidence in you? That you're a mere babysitter now? I have a few more friends than you know, Jack. I'd watch your back if I were you. We're not backing down. We're going to finish our research, despite your pathetic attempts to ruin it." He shoved Jack away from him after a moment, straightening his clothes as he noticed a woman coming down the hallway.

"Stay away from me and my team, Jack. I already have a good enough reason to kill you. If you bring this to the public, you know we have more the press would love to hear about the precious McCarthys." Cam stared at him briefly before he followed the woman down the hall, catching up to her easily with his long strides. "Is everything ready, Sandra?"

"For two days. I know things are a little screwed up on your team right now with Maria inactive, but you were the one who wanted this extra research done on this chip you won't tell anyone about. First of all, that's extremely unprofessional-"

"My association with you is unprofessional."

"Second, we can't help you if you don't tell us where you found this chip. If you tell us, we could use it in our main research and testing."

"Why don't you just do your job?"

Sandra raised an eyebrow as she walked with Cam out to the parking lot. She stopped at her car and got into the passenger seat. "You need to learn how to separate things. You're upset about Maria and I get that, but you need to stop taking it out on your team-mates and co-workers. And you were absolutely out of line when you brought Maria to the lab."

Cam swore when he noticed Mark in the back seat. "That doesn't mean Mark should have pulled a gun on her." He noticed her spin her head towards Mark who shrugged. "Yeah. I can be mad about that. I don't care if I did something you don't agree with, but he had no right to threaten her."

"You know I wouldn't hurt her, Cam," Mark said. "I'm probably one of the few people who knew how much she meant to you."

"I don't care what Mark did," Sandra continued. "I care about what you did. You absolutely cannot bring her that close to our facilities. What if one of the projects escaped? How would you explain it to her? What if it attacked her?"

"I get it, okay? Just drop it. I screwed up. I think I'm allowed one slip up in four years. You really think you're much better with your history?"

She paused and sighed, continuing to watch as the town turned into farmland. "Well, your mistake could have cost a life. Just drive."

The three men of Revolution gathered at the start of the Charlottetown challenge. Ryan watched as Cam yawned, standing to wait for their turn to sign in.

"You were out late."

"And your point?" Cam rubbed his eyes as if it would help to wake him up. At least this time he was not hung over, unlike the entire last week. For some reason with Maria away, he felt the need to go back to his old routines. Well, most of his old routines.

"It's a water challenge." Rick walked back to the other two, rubbing the back of his head. "Have either of you heard from Maria? It'd be nice to know when she's coming back. I don't want to take another handicap score for this challenge. We did it for the one in Halifax. Cam, I don't want to do it twice. We're better than that."

Cam swore as he looked around, noting their surroundings. He could have guessed they would have to do something on the water, since the challenge began at the harbour of the city. "Do you really think she would contact me? She hasn't talked to any of us directly, just some messages through Brittany."

"Actually," Ryan started quietly. "We've been talking a bit. She called me last night while Cam was out."

Rick looked at Ryan, his eyebrows raised in surprise. "Has she been cleared?" At least she was speaking to someone.

"She didn't say."

"Well, what did you talk about?"

Ryan looked quickly towards Cam before looking back at his foot. "Just stuff."

"Cam, you're going to have to do a water challenge at some point in your career."

"Why don't we just skip it then? Forget the handicap, just forget the entire challenge." Cam folded his arms across his chest. In all his years, he had never suggested to skip an entire challenge. It was bad enough he accepted handicaps, but to skip one entirely was borderline career suicide. And they all knew it.

"Is the almighty Revolution backing down from a challenge?" came a female voice from behind Ryan. "What planet are we living on that Cam would forgo a full challenge?"

Ryan spun around, grinning as Maria came into view. "Well, hello there stranger." His grin grew as he pulled her into a quick embrace. Two weeks was all he needed to learn how much he missed her.

She laughed and pulled away awkwardly as Rick and Cam watched. She glanced at them, clearing her throat. "You guys can't seriously be considering backing down from this challenge. It'll ruin any chances of winning the tournament."

"Are you cleared?" Rick asked. He sighed with relief when she nodded. "I wasn't considering it at all. If I had to, I'd push Cam into the water myself. Seemed to work well for you in Sarnia."

"Just get the challenge over with," Cam snapped. Grabbing the other men's packs, he threw them down where Maria had put hers. He glanced at Maria but looked away before she could address him.

Maria looked at Cam as the other team members walked to the kiosk to scan in. Cam did everything he could to avoid her gaze, but her sigh made his eyes cautiously flicker towards her.

"I'm okay."

"I figured, since you're here." His signature unfeeling tone.

"I should've let you know what was going on." She paused, trying to look at his face. "It's not cancer. They were just worried about an infection. I should've thought that..."

"It's no big deal," Cam spoke, his voice soft enough to contradict his words.

"I didn't call because I knew you wouldn't care, but I still should've told you it wasn't cancer, or that it was nothing serious. The spiked labs, they were nothing."

Cam finally looked at her fully, his eyes narrowed in a familiar anger. "Do you think I hate you that much that I wouldn't care? After what happened to my mom?" She remained silent. He hefted up the bags onto his arms when he saw his two other team-mates start back towards them. "You should know better than that." His look lingered on her momentarily before he walked back to their rental car.

"Ready?" Ryan asked, putting a hand on her back to lead her towards the start of the challenge. "Looks like it's going to be an interesting one. Some of the teams are swimming parts of the challenge, so hopefully we'll be able to keep up. I don't know about you, but that Owen Sound challenge didn't make me like swimming all that much."

Maria nodded in agreement as she slipped her AIRC from her pocket. She had been out on rough water before, but she would be remembering that challenge some time. "So, what's the goal?"

"It's a timed challenge." Rick fumbled with his AIRC, flipping through his various scans. "We're starting at the Hillsborough Bridge. We have to go down the supports to find a barcode to scan. We have no idea how far down we have to go, but all our AIMs are allowed to do is bring us air."

She looked out to the bridge. "What do you mean?"

"Officials will have oxygen at the surface. Once we're down, we can't surface or else we fail the challenge. We'll be starting on the worker's foot bridge under the cars, which is closer to the water." He led his team to the entry to the foot bridge. "We need to get this done quickly." Rick stepped to the side of the bridge as a rather wet team passed by them, frowns on their faces. "And safely. Maybe we'll have two AIMs going to the surface for oxygen and then one guiding us down. I noticed you did some scanning, Maria, while you were on vacation."

"Vacation? I was medically benched." Maria's voice rose a register with disbelief. During the conversations she had with Ryan over the past few weeks, he had mentioned that Rick had said some rather unsavoury things about her offense. It grated on her, but she had said nothing to Ryan. If things were being said behind her back, it would make it hard to work together as a team.

"You were on my case about working with Cam for the good of the team, so now you have to suck it up and work with me. If you make me out to be this terrible person who slept with another guy *after* breaking up with Cam, then fine." She shook her head at Rick's look of shock and embarrassment. "Yeah, you didn't bother to ask for details. But get off your high horse and stop acting like you've never made a mistake in your life. Just be my captain, Rick."

Rick continued walking to the starting area crowded with CST officials and medics. He stopped at an empty platform and slipped his shirt over his head, ignoring the officials who had swarmed around his team to ready them. "Have you had a chance to train your Brook Trout?" Sometimes the best way to work through things was to push through and focus on what was directly ahead. Right now, directly ahead was water. He nodded in response to hers and waited for his team-mates to get ready. "Your

AIM can lead us down, Maria. My AIM will go in unison with Ryan's to get the oxygen."

"What's the current like here?" Ryan asked, eyeing the water below. After Owen Sound, even he was hesitant to get into deep water once more.

"Fast enough to make this hard," Maria muttered as she flipped through the list of scanned animals on her AIRC, choosing her most recent scan. She turned to Rick, putting a hand on his arm before he got into the water. "Rick, I need to know you have my back. If something goes wrong, I need to know you won't just leave me down there."

"I'm not going to let you die, but I can't promise any heroic stunt like Cam."

With the permission from the officials, the team stepped off the edge of the bridge and plunged into the frigid Spring water. The shock of the water nearly took the breath from her, but Maria was used to this, or she knew she should be at least. She looked around at the other two and saw a similar look of shock on their faces. "So, what's the plan? We won't be able to communicate down there to each other or to our AIMs." She touched her leg gingerly, glad for the waterproof wrap to keep her wound dry.

"We keep our eyes on each other at all times. We'll signal if we're too cold or if we're finding it too difficult. We can't afford another injury, Maria, so don't try to prove yourself with this challenge." Rick's voice wavered, his lower jaw already reacting to the cold water. "AIMs will go for oxygen every thirty seconds unless we find we need it sooner. Ready?"

The team nodded and after giving their commands to their AIMs, they took a breath and submerged themselves beneath the waves.

Cam watched his team disappear beneath the water as he sat on the hood of the rental car.

"We still expect you to come to the training area, even with Maria back."

He glanced to the side as Mark leaned against the vehicle. "How did the trials go last night?"

"Henk thinks he's finalized the new substance and chip. We just need you to train it and go through the time progressions before we know for sure. This could be it." Mark nodded towards the bridge. "Should she be doing that so soon after being cleared?"

"As long as we get a full score, I couldn't care less."

"It's funny that you think you can lie to me so easily." Mark grinned and clapped Cam on the shoulder as he walked away. "Keep her away from the lab this time. You're good. You've always been good, but you can't afford to let your secret out. None of us can. I'll see you later tonight."

He had tried not to think about the Maria situation. It was as if she was not even on the team. He had been free to go out at night drinking, going to the lab, everything he had done – well, mostly everything – before she had been signed. Since she was benched, he had thrown himself into the experiments, working late with his colleagues, even missing team meetings. He knew he should not be jeopardizing the team that way, but it was keeping him sane, keeping his mind busy. He needed that. He wished he had something to occupy him while he waited for his team to surface as memories of the sound of gushing water swallowing him played in his mind.

In the frigid dimness of the water, Ryan looked around, seeing his captain signal down to where Maria's AIM had swum. They had been down for less than fifteen seconds but he could already feel his lungs burning. He pushed the feeling aside, knowing part of it was panic, and followed his team-mates deeper beneath the surface. The headlamps they wore shone straight beams through the water, illuminating the massive concrete supports for the bridge. Further down along the bridge, other groups of beams shone in the water, some rising back to the surface in defeat.

Ryan squeezed his eyes together briefly, trying to help them to focus long enough to get to Maria's AIM. He saw Rick stop and wave, signalling to wait until the AIMs came back with their oxygen containers and felt a rush of relief. One set of thirty seconds gone. Glancing down to where the third AIM was, he realized that it was waiting down at their goal and the rush of relief left him. The force of the current was not rough enough that they had to compensate, but once they went down further they would have to swim hard to stay together and stay on target. *A timed challenge? Really? We'll be lucky if we even finish,* Ryan thought to himself, using the concrete support as a brace until the AIMs came back down to them.

The fish came back quickly, holding a line in their mouths with a small oxygen cylinder trailing behind. They went to Ryan and Maria first, the captain making sure that his team got the oxygen they needed. Rick was thankful that he was a strong swimmer, and likely would not need oxygen for another ten seconds but with how far down they seemed to need to go, even he was slightly nervous. Even within the first minute of the challenge, various teams had given up. Revolution had never failed a challenge in its ten years of existence. There were some challenges in which they obtained the minimum points, but they never failed completely. They were not about to start.

Rick grabbed at the cylinder and breathed in the oxygen he needed for the next thirty seconds. At this rate, they would be lucky to get a minimum score, but it would be better than nothing. With a motion of his arm, he swam down further with his team, keeping close to the concrete support. At least around there, the current would only slam them into the concrete rather than sweep them away down the strait. Going down slowly, he could feel the pressure of the water begin to press against every inch of his body. Just a bit further down. He swam a bit lower, letting his teammates wait for the oxygen while he continued. He could hold his breath a little longer.

Cam continued to sit on the hood of the car, his eyes intently glued to the surface of the water where his team had submerged themselves. Three minutes. It had been three minutes. No other team had lasted that long. Seven teams had come and gone since Cam had been waiting. Something had to be wrong. Something always went wrong during water challenges. Usually he loved the media attention his team received, but now they were making him nervous. When the team's progress was updated online, the sports media in the area arrived on the scene. Cam knew they were only there to see someone hurt.

Four minutes.

Five minutes.

Three hundred seconds had never felt so long to Cam before. All of a sudden, he heard a quiet 'ding' sound from his AIRC. One hundred points for Revolution. He jumped off from the car when he saw his team pop up from beneath the waves, welcomed by the officials and other teams erupting into applause.

"Yes!" Cam shouted, pumping a fist into the air before he jogged down to the entrance of the walkway, shoving a few people out of the way in the process. He felt a hand push him aside and before he could shout a response he noticed the bold red cross on the man's shirt. Cam's eyes widened at the realization that the crowd had quietened, and he ran after the medic.

"Twenty-nine, thirty!"

He broke through the ring of watchers as a medic moved away from compressing Rick's chest and moved to his mouth to perform rescue breaths. His eyes went over to Maria and Ryan who were each wrapped in thick blankets. He heard her scream Rick's name, her face twisted in agony as she continued to try to reach out to Rick, only to be held back by Ryan.

"We have a pulse! Get him on the stretcher."

His eyes shot back to Rick as he coughed up the water from his lungs. Cam wiped his face with his hand, watching as the medics strapped Rick to a stretcher and moved past him. Suddenly he was aware of Maria about to pass him, going after Rick. Before she could get by, he grabbed her and pushed her back gently.

"Stop. Maria, just stop. Let them do their job. Ryan, would you do something?" Cam waited until Ryan managed to pull her back and hold her against his body. The new team dynamics were slowly taking shape, each player had a new role. Everything was so different now. He leaned against the railing, grateful that the officials were keeping the crowds back to give them space. Other teams were not even approaching them. He shook his head, running his hands through his hair. "I don't understand. You guys were down there for a while, but...I don't understand."

Ryan looked down at Maria as she buried her face in his chest. He shook his head with a shrug. "I don't know. Everything was fine. We were getting the oxygen in time. The current got stronger, and Rick went down lower than us. We waited for the AIMs but Rick kept going." He paused, catching his breath. "We scanned the barcode and then, he just disappeared. He just…Maria found him crashed against the pillar and she and his AIM brought him up to the surface."

Cam looked at Maria and motioned back towards land. "Come on." He held his arm out, letting his team-mates go down the walkway ahead of him as the crowds of fans and teams parted for them.

"He'll only need to be here overnight. He's fine, but we want to be absolutely sure before we let him go and compete in any more challenges. He doesn't seem to have a concussion, but he has a few bruised ribs from being slammed against the concrete. Nothing to be too concerned with."

Ryan glanced at his two team-mates before smiling lightly to the doctor. "Thanks." He watched him nod and leave the three outside the hospital room Rick was sharing with another patient. "Well, at least we can leave in the morning." When neither said anything, he put a hand on Maria's arm and tipped her head up with his other. "You heard the doctor. He's fine. But maybe it was a mistake to join this team. You guys are always getting hurt," he teased with a laugh.

"That's because the people on this team take stupid risks," Cam pointed out, earning a glare from Maria. "But it's the reason we're so good. No one ever got anywhere without taking a few risks." He caught Maria's eyes before going into Rick's room. "So, what happened to not dying?" Cam's voice travelled out the room into the hallway.

Ryan kept his hand on Maria's arm to stop her from going inside after Cam. "Hey, you okay?" He pulled her against him when she shook her head. He smiled, feeling her close to him again. "He'll be out tomorrow morning. Don't worry. He'll be fine, and we'll be one big, happy team."

Maria laughed as she rested her cheek against his chest. "You've gone crazy since I've been away." She looked up at him, not bothering to hold back a soft smile. "Why can't I just meet a guy from a different team? Why does it always have to be a teammate?"

He grinned and glanced around before he kissed her lightly. His grin grew. Each kiss felt like the first, back at her apartment in Kitchener. "Because apparently no one ever got anywhere without taking a few risks."

She took a small step away from him and lowered her voice. "Ryan, look-"

"Sorry. I just-"

"I know."

"Hey," came Cam's voice.

Maria stepped back from Ryan quickly and saw Cam back into the hall with them. She cleared her throat nervously. "How does he look?"

"Beat up." He looked at Ryan but could not even make eye contact. Why was it so hard for people on this team to not keep secrets? He was no exception. He leaned against the door frame. "What happened out there, seriously?"

She looked away and shrugged. "We scanned the barcode and then I guess a current separated us. I saw Ryan's headlamp but I couldn't see Rick's." She paused and shut her eyes. He should not have gone so far ahead of them.

He watched her for a minute. "If I had been a second late in Niagara Falls, you'd be dead. If you had found Rick a second later, he'd be dead." He reached out and squeezed her shoulder gently. "I guess we're finally working as a team. Besides, we got full points. We'll be fine."

CHAPTER 21

Ryan tapped his fingers on his knee along with the music as Cam drove to the Charlottetown airport. He looked at Cam when he turned the music down. He noticed a strained look on his face, a look he had seen more than a few times since the accident.

"What's on your mind?"

Cam hesitated briefly before he started. "I know I've been a jerk to you lately, more than a jerk, but you could've told me. Even if you were trying to hide it from Rick or the public, at least I deserved to know."

He could not tell if Cam was upset, or disappointed. "What are you talking about?"

"You and Maria. I saw you guys outside Rick's hospital room the other day."

Ryan's eyes widened as his face flushed. "We're not together." He saw Cam nod, but the nod was too slight to convince Ryan he believed him. He was right though, he did deserve to know. "We talked about it, though, being together. Almost had her convinced, but who was I kidding?"

"I don't see anything stopping you guys."

"She doesn't think it's over with you." He forced a small smile when Cam whipped his head to face him. "I'm fine with that, I guess. She asked for time to figure things out, and I'm willing to give her whatever she needs." Ryan watched Cam's eyes focus on the road, his eyebrows furrowed in forced concentration.

"She broke up with me. She's made it very clear we can't be together. And I'm not about to go crawling back to her. Even if she begged, I probably wouldn't even take her back."

Ryan looked out the window and watched as other cars drifted behind them as Cam sped by. He could not help but notice that Cam had not mentioned that Maria had slept with someone else, as though it did not matter anymore. But he and Maria had spent some time together, and had talked a bit about the possibility of a relationship before the team had parted temporarily. It had not been until that week that Maria had decided to stop things before they went further. Ryan had been glad for Cam's absence that night, not needing to make a fool of himself in front of him. At least they both knew where the other stood so there was no more guessing, and now he could really concentrate on working as a part of the team. They were going to make it work.

"How are you? Sick of that question going around the team yet?" Maria asked her captain while they followed close behind Cam's vehicle down the highway.

"Tired, but I can compete today, thankfully. I don't know how you or my dad dealt with it. I hated just being in that bed, knowing I couldn't compete." Rick grimaced, slightly nervous from Maria's driving. Not that she was a bad driver...that he would ever say.

"I meant how are you doing overall? There's been a lot going on. Cam and I never caused this much trouble for your dad but you seem to be handling it fine."

Rick looked out the window. Three years had been long enough to become close with her, and long enough to learn that she would not take anything less than the truth. "I'm glad I've seemed that way. Truth is, it's close to killing me. I hate being away from Brittany and Adam right now, but I can't stand not competing. My dad's been out of the hospital and he says he's okay but my mom, she's still worried about him. Talks about him being tired all the time. If he was still captain, we'd be getting perfect scores on every challenge, Ryan would be fully trained, and you and Cam would've worked things out."

She was quiet long enough for Rick to think he had offended her. He swore quietly and before he could apologize, she spoke.

"You've been an amazing husband to Brittany. I've seen you with her, and with Adam, and you're an amazing dad. Ryan is being trained by Cam who, I hate to say it, is the best person to train him. Your dad is fine, and doing better than most people after a heart attack. I should know." She closed her eyes briefly. Time had yet to heal some wounds. "Cam and I, your dad would never be able to do anything to help us work things out. It's completely our problem, and now we're just trying to deal with it. That's what's been affecting our challenges, not your ability as a captain. I take responsibility for that, so don't beat yourself up over it. You're an amazing captain; don't you ever think otherwise."

Rick nodded, but remained silent as he thought about what she said. He had always known Maria to be frank and while he may not agree with what she said, he was relieved. He had been so concerned with what he had been doing wrong that he had ignored what he had done right. As long as someone else had recognized that he had done his job, he guessed that was what mattered. They had been getting full scores at the past few challenges. Maybe he was not doing such a bad job. Maybe this would be their year.

"So what's been going on with you?"

Maria shrugged. "Other than the Cam drama?"

He watched her face as her eyes flitted around the road in front of them, and into the mirrors. "I've never seen you on a health kick like this. You might be trying to hide it from everyone, but you can't hide it from me. You don't eat fast food anymore, you work out three times a day now, even on challenge days, and I found out your AIM's been tracking your weight."

She glared at the AIM in the back seat who felt no emotion for its actions. "I'm an athlete. I'm trying to stay in shape."

"Maria."

She sighed. "I've gained weight."

"So? A few extra pounds won't hurt you."

"I've gained ten pounds in the last four and a half months." She should not even be complaining, she knew. It was normal, but not for an athlete. "No matter what I do, it's never good enough."

He reached over and put a hand on her knee as he watched her face cloud with frustration and desperation. "What are we talking about, here? Because it doesn't sound like your weight."

"It's everything, I guess. All of us. We work and train our butts off. Individually we have the highest stats in the game, but we haven't gotten higher than the third spot."

Rick nodded and squeezed her knee before removing his hand. "I get it. Believe me. Just make sure you don't overdo it. As long as you're healthy, I don't care what you weigh. We'll get there, eventually." He watched her for a moment more before he continued. "So, since I'm such an amazing captain-"

"And husband, and friend."

"You're going to get a perfect score at this challenge, right?"

Maria laughed and poked him in the arm. "You got it, boss."

By the time Revolution arrived back in Ontario for the Toronto challenge, sports channels were announcing the arrival of other CST teams. Ryan looked around at the other vehicles transporting groups into the main staging area. He felt as if this was his first challenge all over again. This was the first month end challenge of the season, where teams from all across Canada would compete directly against each other.

"Are you ready for this?"

Ryan nodded without looking at Cam. "Going to have to be. This isn't really much worse than other challenges, is it?" When Cam hesitated, he looked at him, knowing he was showing every bit of anxiety that he felt.

"It feels like it is, because we'll be on the same level as other teams. There's more pressure, but no, it's not usually much more extreme than other challenges. It'll be in qualifying stages, which is only done in the month and season end challenges."

"What moves us on? Best time?"

"Usually. It's normally a variation of that." Cam glanced over at Ryan and gave him a half smile. "Hey, you had the courage to kiss my ex in front of me. Buck up. It's just a challenge."

He laughed and felt his face flush again. "Yeah, that was pretty much suicide, wasn't it?"

"It was," he said cheerfully, but his face changed in an instant, and he shot a warning look at Ryan. "Don't do it again." Cam stared at him long enough to make his point before he was guided into a parking space designated for his team. Maria and Rick were standing next to their already parked car. "Since when do you speed, Maria?" he asked when he stepped out of the truck.

"Since our flight was delayed." Maria threw her bag onto her back and headed towards the starting area with her team. "Are we ready for this?"

"Ready when you are," he answered.

Ryan glanced at Cam in time to see him hold his gaze with Maria for a moment as they reached the start. "Nothing stopping us?" he whispered.

Cam eyed Maria with a shrug. "Nothing other than three years of history." He gave him a smug look before Rick rounded them up. It was time to plan.

"Welcome to the tenth anniversary Toronto Challenge. There are three stages for this challenge. The top fifty percent of teams from the first stage will move on to the second stage. From that, the top third will move on to the final stage. As in other years, if you fail a stage, no points will be distributed for that portion. A stage must be completed to earn points," the announcer spoke out to the crowd of athletes and fans who were controlled by a wire fence. "Each team now has the details of the first stage in their AIRCs for their reference. The first stage is a relay obstacle course; one leg per team member. For teams with three members, they will begin at the second leg with a time penalty. Good luck!"

Rick moved his team to their starting area to talk. "Alright, it looks like each leg pretty much plays to our strengths. Cam, there's one leg which requires stamina and strength it looks like. I don't think I can do it."

"Don't worry about it. I'll do it."

"Good. I'll take this first leg. Maria, I'll give you the actual obstacle leg of it. Ryan, you'll have the last leg. If we do our jobs right, you won't feel too much pressure. It's a retrieving leg. We won't know exactly what we're dealing with until we get there."

Rick took a look at each of his team-mates and gave a small nod. "You guys have really impressed me this season. Despite the fighting, and injuries, and other personal issues, we're still ranked at the top. No matter how we finish this challenge, even if we don't finish, I'll still be proud of you."

Cam rolled his eyes. "When did you get so sentimental? It's disgusting. I'll see you guys later." Before he began walking to his leg's start, he held a hand out to Rick. "Good luck, Captain."

Rick watched as his team walked away and he could not help but smile. Maybe they really did have a chance at this. He slipped his AIRC from his pocket and flipped through his scans. Ahead of him, the leg looked relatively easy, for him at least. He selected an osprey from his list and watched his AIM transform from a robin into the larger bird of prey.

"Teams, ready!"

"Pay attention to me, and the end of the maze," Rick said to his AIM as he slipped on a blindfold at the same time as the other teams. "Try to lead me over clear ground, and give me slack if I have to go down a hill. If you have to, communicate through the AIRC but we should be able to do this without."

"Understood," the AIM replied through the remote console.

"Go!"

Rick felt the rope in his hand move as his AIM flew up into the sky. Around him, the only sounds were from the cheering crowds. The teams were silent for the moment, listening and waiting for their AIMs. It was an eerie feeling, not being able to see and barely any sound around him. A moment later, he felt the rope pull taut as his AIM led him forward into the maze constructed by the CST in the Serena Gundy Park in the heart of the city.

It would have been a simple challenge if he did not have to wear the blindfold, but now he had to trust that his AIM would lead him the quickest way out of the maze, and safely. He heard the sounds of the other teams walking near him, but still there was no one talking to their AIM. The park itself was thick with trees and hiking trails, so Rick was not sure how his AIM was going to guide him without the rope getting caught on the trees. He would have to trust his AIM, and he knew it would need a lot of endurance to continue to fly slowly and long enough for Rick to finish this leg.

His AIM began to pull harder on the rope, leading Rick from side to side around corners, enough so that Rick began to jog. Usually he did not agree with paved trails in parks, but now he was thankful so much money had gone into the park when it was first built. As he thought about the smoothness of the path, a quick jerk on the rope sent Rick stumbling a few steps before he caught his balance. He laughed before he could wonder if anyone saw the mistake.

"How are we doing?" Rick asked into his AIRC quietly, not wanting other teams to be distracted by him.

"Falling behind."

"Then let's go!" It frustrated him sometimes that the AIMs were not sentient. It would really help if they could take the initiative to pick up the pace when they began to fall behind.

The rope pulled taut again, and Rick could feel his AIM pull harder to pick up speed. It made him feel like a stubborn old dog being led around by his leash. Maybe that was not so far from the truth. His AIM led him around what he felt was a corner and a blast of noise hit him: teams yelling at their AIMs, robotic noises from AIRCs, and the sounds of screaming fans.

Alright, now people can see me stumble.

He had no idea how much farther he had to go. Being able to hear everyone else did not mean much in regards to finishing. It was a strange challenge, having to walk around a maze. It might have been more impressive had he been able to see it, but the fans could see it so that might make up for it. All of a sudden, his rope went slack. He stopped, almost stumbling again from the change of pace. Was he at the end? If his AIM was talking to him, he could not hear it over the crowd. He felt a few strange tugs on the rope, heard the crowd cheer louder, and then his rope went taut again. Without seeing, he guessed his AIM had either begun to lose power, or had become entangled with another AIM.

"Rick! You're almost there! Come on!"

Rick followed the rope as his AIM led him, hopefully, to the finish. He had not stopped jogging and normally that would not have bothered him, but after the incident in Charlottetown he still was not feeling one hundred percent well. Hearing the voice of his team-mate spurred him on to quicken his jog until he felt someone take his arm.

He stopped and whipped off his blindfold to see Cam wrapping up the loose rope quickly as the osprey landed next to Rick's feet.

"You good?"

"Yeah, go!" Rick said, pushing Cam a bit to get him to start his leg of the obstacle stage. He cheered along with the rest of the crowd, and stopped when he took a look around. He was the last one to show up, which was not the way to begin this challenge, especially as a captain. But he trusted the rest of his team. They would make up the time.

Cam took off at a run through the trees, leaving the main trail, his AIM running beside him in the form of the grey wolf he scanned near the beginning of the season. Thankfully, he was one of the better runners and despite being the last person to leave this leg of the stage, he was quickly catching up and glad to have the wolf at his side. He tried to forget about the fact that Rick had been the last out of hundreds of teams to finish his leg. Instead, he concentrated on what he needed to do.

"Can you get up ahead and see what's coming?" Cam called out to his AIM. All he knew to do was run, and run fast. Beyond that, he had no idea. He watched as the wolf pulled ahead of him, causing a few other athletes to veer away as though they forgot it was not a real wolf. Cam smiled. *If only they knew.*

He had known he would have to make up for Rick's leg, but for likely the first time in his professional career, he let it go. Rick was still recovering, and Cam could not fault him for that. People apparently called that growth. No, personal growth was forgetting about the robotic cameras along the path. He had not even posed for them while he waiting for Rick. There was no time for that; not during this challenge. There was too much on the line, and they had too much to prove.

"Wall ahead."

"What?" Cam yelled through the AIRC attached to his belt. "What do you mean a wall?"

"What do you think?"

"Watch it," he warned. Now he remembered why he paid attention to the location of the cameras. Rounding a bend of trees, he stopped suddenly. He was, in fact, faced with a large wooden structure which acted as a wall. Thankfully, he had caught up to the majority of the teams who were now struggling to get over the wall. He grabbed his AIRC quickly and selected the first bird in his list. "Go over to the other side and check it out."

He watched as the cardinal flew over the wall and then he looked around at the other teams. Some were trying to climb with their own strength, and some were getting their AIMs to help them up a bit with a boost. There were two teams with ropes, and Cam recognized them as top contenders...at least in Ontario. The teams were in the top twenty at least, which was pretty decent so they knew what they were doing. Nothing compared to his top five rank, though.

"I need more strength. Bird form."

Cam swore and switched his AIM from a cardinal to a hawk. "Hurry up!"

The hawk soared back over the wall and dropped one end of a rope at Cam's feet. "Your turn."

"Shut up. You know better in challenges. Any other surprises for me?" Cam snapped as he grabbed the rope and hauled himself up the wall.

"Just the end of the leg."

"Good," he replied with a grunt as he took large steps up the side of the wall, using the rope as leverage. This was the first time he really had to use much of his muscles in the season, other than in Niagara Falls, but he was definitely glad that he had taken this leg. The time Rick lost in the first leg was nothing compared to what he would have lost in this one.

As his hand gripped the top of the wall, it slipped but tightened around the rope as he went down a short distance. He swore again as the rope burned the flesh of his palm. Within seconds, his hand was back on the top of the wall and he pulled his upper body over the top. Through squinted eyes, he saw only a few teams on the other side of the wall and single team-mates waiting for their partners to finish their leg. Cam swung his legs over the wall and let himself fall on the other side, curling his body to roll when he hit the ground. It took him a moment to catch his breath before he stood and raced towards Maria, who was standing across a small field. He glanced at his sides as he ran and grinned, seeing he had caught up with the front of the pack. With a triumphant yell, he slapped Maria's hand in the trade off and watched her flip through her scans.

"You know what you're doing?" he asked between his gasps for air.

"Hell yeah." She flashed him a grin as she grabbed the withers of the horse her AIM had transformed into, and then pulled herself up onto the bare back. "If I'm doing an obstacle leg, I'm going to do it right. See you at the finish line." She grinned again before she kicked at the sides of the horse she had trained to react to the physical prompt.

Cam leaned forward, holding his hands against his knees as he caught his breath, watching Maria ride off down the path others were running themselves. He looked over and gave out a frustrated sigh as Jack approached him. "I told you to stay away from us."

"Just wanted to wish you good luck, but I guess you don't need it. Looks like you're testing something new out, aren't you? Or is there just something different about your AIM?" Jack gave him a smirk before he looked over at Cam's AIM. "See you at the finish line," he said as his team-mate finally finished the first leg.

He rolled his eyes as Jack left, but looked down at the hawk that had landed at his feet. "Probably wasn't the best time to work with your coding."

"Probably not."

CHAPTER 22

Maria glanced over her shoulder as she rode away from Cam, but quickly turned her attention back to the obstacles ahead. When she had seen what lay ahead of her, she knew she had to use her horse scan. It was a strange feeling to ride a horse, or an AIM version of a horse, without reins. No saddle, no problem. But no reins? This was going to be all leg work. She could use verbal commands, and normally she would, but she had trained for this. And Cam had said it was stupid to spend so much time training the horse. She loved when she was able to prove him wrong.

"*'Spread the training out equally,'* he said," Maria muttered as she led the horse down the path at a full gallop. No reason to go slow until the obstacles showed up. She made a sharp turn and immediately slowed the AIM to a canter and went over the first obstacle which, thankfully for her, looked very similar to an equestrian jump. At least the height of it made it seem like it. As she landed, she guessed it was almost a metre high. She could not help but grin as she patted the neck of the AIM. "And he made fun of me for keeping up with my riding. So what if you're not a real horse? I still need to know how to ride you without a saddle."

She did not mind that the AIM did not respond. What was it supposed to say, anyhow? AIMs did not have a mind of their own, or opinions. Maria frowned when the path marked for the leg went off the main path and into the forest. This was not going to be good. In the split second she had to make her choice, she kept the horse scan active and leaned down against the neck of the AIM. Normally, she hated wearing a helmet when she rode, but right then, she understood the benefits of wearing one while riding in a forest. She pressed her left thigh against the barrel of the horse, urging it right to miss a tree. Jumping in here would be interesting. There would be no way they would make such a high jump with so little head room.

The teams ahead of her had used mostly large dogs, which would make more sense in the forest but even if the dog, or other type of canine, could run fast, it was all up to the athlete. In her case, it was a combination of athlete and AIM. If the athlete did not train the AIM for obstacles such as this, there would be a lot of yelling and voice commands. That was exactly what she heard up ahead.

Maria smiled to herself as she saw a congested group of athletes with their AIMS – mostly large dogs as she had suspected, although there was a horse as well – and slowed her AIM down to a trot so she would be able to manoeuvre around them. She gave them a little wave, and grinned to the camera that had found its way into the forest, before taking off again. With a glance over her shoulder, she saw one participant try to jump onto the back of the horse as if he had not thought of it before, and as if he had never ridden before.

"Well, this is going relatively-" She stopped and shut her eyes briefly as a sharp pain came from her abdomen. She swore, but then opened her eyes when the AIM slowed to a trot. "What are you doing?"

"Do you need assistance?"

"No, I'm fine. Keep going." Her AIM would not ask again, but she knew it would continue to monitor her. All she needed at that moment was to finish the challenge. She could worry about the future moments when they won.

She ducked again as the AIM bulldozed under a low branch, and then jumped over a fallen tree. She knew there were cameras set up everywhere in the forest, programmed to follow any movement of the athletes and if it had been quiet, Maria would have been able to hear their gentle whirring noise as they flitted around her. The only sound she heard was hooves crunching the branches and leaves covering the ground, and the comforting rhythm of the horse breathing heavily as they sped along.

Every now and then as she looked to the side, Maria could see small groups of fans lined along the edge of the forest, either trying to peer in at the athletes and their AIMs, or watching the action on the plasma screens set up around the course. She smiled, egotistically knowing that the majority of the fans would be watching her team as they came up from behind.

Another jump and another turn around a bend brought the end of the leg in view. Maria glanced behind her as she urged her AIM into another full gallop. Two other teams so far had caught on and were riding horses behind her, not as successfully as her, she noted. *See, real animals are still good for something.* She spotted Ryan up ahead at the edge of a field which looked similar to the one in which she had begun.

"Alright, give it all you got," she said to the AIM. It stretched out its neck even further as it ran, pushing the limits of the scan Maria had obtained. Hearing a growl, she looked down to the ground and saw a wolf running beside her AIM. She looked around for an owner but no one was anywhere close to her. She swore when the wolf jumped up, snapping its jaws at her ankle. She steered her AIM away from the wolf and looked around, surprised that real animals had been allowed on the field. A wolf seemed out of place in the middle of Toronto, but she knew an AIM would never do that.

"Energy low," her AIM warned as they neared the finish.

"Keep going!"

She had never pushed her AIM so hard – that was always Cam's specialty – but now that the end of her leg was in sight and there was a rogue animal on the field, it was necessary. She knew that if she was riding a real horse, it would be close to passing out. And if it passed out, that usually meant…

Maria squealed as the AIM beneath her fell over and transformed into a smaller default form. She was propelled through the air and did not have enough time to tuck her legs before she hit the ground hard with her stomach, her arms at least going out before her face planted into the ground. She groaned before she heard the sound of the wolf growl behind her. She swore as she got her legs underneath her and jumped up. Looking around, she found her AIM in the form of a swallow and knew it would be safe long enough for her to finish the leg. Behind her AIM and the wolf, Maria saw the athletes on horses gain ground. Behind them, there came another group of athletes with their AIMs. She swore, feeling as though ambushed in a war.

She took off at a run as the crowd cheered, ignoring the wolf which continued to follow her. It veered away suddenly, and disappeared within the crowd of athletes gaining ground on her. She would have loved to enjoy this, all of the attention her team was getting, but there would hopefully be time for that later. She saw Ryan waiting, ready to take off as soon as she got to him, his face more intense with focus and determination than she had ever seen. She slapped his hand.

"Go!" she yelled at him, letting him take off at a run as if he had absorbed her momentum. Other teams quickly came up from behind her as she dropped to her knees and dramatically lay on her back. They would make it. They had made up enough time and caught up with the top third of the teams, and they only needed to be in the top half. As she gasped for air, Maria grinned with a single thought in her mind. They were back.

With the feel of Maria's hand on his, Ryan took off towards the retrieving area. He took his AIRC from his pocket as he ran, selecting the golden retriever from his list. It was not an extraordinary choice, but until he knew what he would have to do, he would go with his first instinct. Since there had been a few teams start ahead of him, Ryan had been able to see what he might have to expect. Of course, he had watched the CST challenges on TV for years, but this...this was so much different. As soon as Maria had touched his hand, he was off, and it felt great. This was his chance to show what he could do. What that was, he was not quite sure yet. He would know soon enough.

"Any idea what we're looking for?" he asked his AIM as he ran into the main retrieving area, where a group of other athletes were already working with their AIMs.

"How should I know? This is my first time too."

Ryan looked at his AIM. "Excuse me? I thought we talked about the attitude."

"Shall I scan the area for something that can tell us what to look for?"

He stopped and looked around him. "I don't know. In small challenges, we look for barcodes, right? Sometimes only you in your animal form can see it." In the small field, there was not much to see. Random AIMs were running everywhere, mostly dogs trying to catch a scent. Why had Rick chosen him to go last? Ryan was strong; he could have done the second leg. Cam was clearly the best person on the team at the moment. He was the anchor; he would be able to win it for them. All of the time Cam and Maria had made up and gained was going to be lost because he had absolutely no idea what he was doing. He looked up into the sky in frustration, trying to clear his mind. Above him, AIMs in the form of bird scans were flying, trying to find something.

Ryan's eyes went wide and he spun around wildly, trying to look for something. "TV! You can always see it on TV. Where are the cameras?"

"In the trees," his AIM answered as it started off towards the edge of the field with Ryan close behind. It seemed to have anticipated what Ryan would want.

He had noticed some teams in the area he was running towards, but everyone seemed so confused he had not thought they were actually on to something. When they stood at the bottom of a tree, Ryan quickly switched his AIM from the golden retriever to its usual squirrel form. "The birds can't see it. It has to be in the trees. Try to get as high up as possible."

"And then?"

"I don't know. Do squirrel things. Jump around. Try to find something out of the ordinary. It might even be a barcode. Let me know if you need to be something bigger to carry it back," Ryan told his AIM. The squirrel clambered up the tree and disappeared into the branches. The early spring had only brought the buds of leaves, but it was still enough to hide the small AIM form as it climbed up. He was grateful that Cam had helped him train his AIM in the squirrel form. It definitely needed the training for today.

Ryan took a few steps back and shielded his eyes from the sun so he could try to watch his AIM. He let a few seconds pass before he checked up on it. "Anything yet?" He was not used to completely relying on his AIM to complete a challenge, not that he had much experience in that area. His AIM did not respond, which was not usual. Had it run out of energy like Maria's? "Are you still there?"

For that brief moment, Ryan felt everyone's eyes on him as if he was the only person out on the field. He became deaf to the cheers from the crowd and the shouts from the athletes as they tried to guide their AIMs from the ground. He only heard the emptiness that should have been filled by his AIM's 'voice.'

"Got it. Coming down with a barcode."

Ryan breathed a sigh of relief. Now all he cared about was getting to that finish line. Within seconds, a grey squirrel was at his feet, holding a small strip of metal in its mouth.

"That's it?"

"Well, I think you have to actually cross the finish line."

He took the barcode and changed his AIM back into a dog. "Are you supposed to be this snarky?" Did he really want the answer to that? "Come on," he said before he took off towards the finish line, his AIM close at his heels.

He was not the first one to finish, or even in the top five. Top ten would have been nice, but at least they were within the top third. And that was more than enough to get his team through to the next stage of the challenge. Ahead, he saw the rest of his team waiting for him and although he was too far away to hear them, he knew they were cheering him on.

"Push it, if you can," Ryan called out to his AIM when he noticed someone come from behind and began running alongside him. Now it felt more like a competition. He had no idea who the other athlete was, or which of the two the crowd was cheering for, but they crossed the finish line at the same time to the same eruption of cheers. Ryan stumbled as he crossed, stopping quickly as his team went to greet him.

He grinned as Rick grabbed his arm and pulled him into what he always called a 'man hug.' "We did it!"

Rick laughed. "Now only two more stages to go. Think you can handle it?"

Ryan nodded with a glance towards Maria. "I'm ready for anything." He looked at Cam as he tried to catch his breath as quickly as possible. "Bring it on." He was ready for anything now.

CHAPTER 23

Revolution stood at the base of the CN tower an hour after they completed the first stage. Now they were looking at the second. Rick turned to his team while the officials finalised the stage.

"This shouldn't be too difficult for us, but we need to make sure we use our strongest AIMs, and hopefully we've trained them well," he said as he looked back up the tower.

Ryan looked up at the platform which was placed a quarter of the way to the top of the structure. It had once been the tallest free standing building, and world renowned Canadian building. How things changed. Now it was probably only the fifth tallest, thanks to the buildings in Asia. As Ryan looked up, he found he did not really care about those buildings. The thought of ascending this one was a daunting concept, and the looks on the face of his teammates told him they felt the same way. Even Maria. With her recent climbing history, Ryan could not blame her. They would have to ascend a full hundred and forty metres, which did not seem like much, but from where he stood it may as well be the distance to the moon.

"All teams to their starting positions."

Maria pulled Cam aside as her team began gearing up. "Something happened in the last stage."

"Yeah, we killed it!"

"No, well, yes, but that's not what I meant." She looked around and lowered her voice. "I think an AIM tried to attack me on the field."

He raised an eyebrow. "What are you talking about? The wolf that got on the field?"

"It had a light on its neck, Cam."

He swore and looked around as if trying to find someone. "Well, did it actually hurt you?"

"No, but-"

"Then it's just another team trying to freak you out. AIMs can't actually hurt you, remember? That doesn't mean it can't scare you and get close."

Maria grabbed his arm as he began walking away. "Cam, it attacked my AIM too. It was low on energy and found itself in danger so it went into its default mode. That's why I fell."

Cam sighed. "Look, I don't know what happened, okay? There are a lot of things going on right now, and most of them I'm not a part of. If it was because of the things I do, I'll find out if someone knows about it."

She was not fully satisfied with his answer, but she finally realized something. She had always assumed he knew everything that happened in the Underground, as if everything was related to him or it was directly his fault. She had never thought of the Underground as a massive organization. She had always figured it was similar to a gang. Maybe there was more to it. He had mentioned that Jack worked for a different organization. Was there more than one Underground? More than one faction? She followed Cam to their starting position and hurriedly slipped on her harness, once again frowning when she could not get it to her usual adjustments.

Rick looked at his team as they finished with their safety harnesses. "Let's not have any accidents this time, okay?" He smiled at Maria, who gave him a sarcastic roll of the eyes, before focusing on the stage ahead. Their AIMs were already at the platform, waiting as birds to bring down their end of the cable. After the Niagara Falls challenge, the CST had stepped up their security for climbing challenges. No one other than the athletes was allowed near the base of the tower, and officials triple-checked the ropes and cables.

"Ready. Start!"

The teams all turned their heads towards the platform to see their AIMs take flight in unison, forming a dark ring around the structure as they plummeted down towards their owners. Revolution prepared as Cam's AIM reached them first. He grabbed onto the rope as the AIM disappeared on its way back to the platform. He slipped the rope through his carabiners and ascenders and paused, waiting for his AIM to reach the platform once again and for CST officials to check his rope and knots. They were taking no chances this time.

Cam could feel his heart pounding, but had no idea how to slow it. Why had he thought it would be a good idea to test the new programming with his AIM during this challenge, when so much was hinging on it? And if an AIM had actually attacked Maria, he needed to keep an eye out for that AIM as well.

He glanced at Maria. "I won't be able to catch you this time."

"We'll be fine." Her rope grew taut which signalled her to begin the ascent. "Besides, I can't keep going into these challenges thinking you'll catch me if I fall." She began pumping her arm and leg alternately, pulling herself up with the ascenders.

Cam watched her travel up, slowly at first but she soon gained speed, and pulled out his AIRC when he realized he was the last of his team to begin, despite being the first to get set up. "What's going on?"

"There was a problem. It's fixed. Transforming now."

As the rope pulled taut, Cam looked around at the other athletes who also had slow starts. Twenty metres away, he saw Jack still on the ground, grinning at him. That would explain the problem. He swore when he realized that Jack was more than just his AIM's problem. After four years, he was beginning to lose whatever control he had over his own secret.

The final group began their ascent to a loud roar from the crowd which encircled the base of the tower. Cam grinned at the attention. This is what he lived for. Well, hopefully he would live. He was not quite sure how comfortable he felt at that moment, completely relying on his AIM to hold the rope while he climbed. Thankfully, they would not have to climb the entire way, or else the majority of the athletes would not even make it. Cam's fear was when the AIMs would have to pull them the rest of the way. Around him, he noticed a few teams being lowered slightly already. He looked up to see his team with a solid lead over many others. It did not matter how far ahead they climbed, though, unless Cam was with them.

"When I get to the halfway point, you're going to have to bring me up as quickly as possible. I got separated from the rest of my team because of your *problems*," Cam called out through the AIRC.

"My problems are your problems, and it may be a big one. There's a hacker."

Cam swore and pumped his arm and leg harder, climbing the rope as quickly as he could. "Keep an eye on it. Make sure it doesn't get near any other AIMs."

"That's what I was doing."

A hacker was not a good sign. Cam knew that the only reason Jack had brought along a hacked AIM was because of him. He swore again. It had come to this.

"I really didn't want to fight him again." He tuned out the sound of the fans for the first time in his life and concentrated on getting to the halfway point. If Jack was willing to risk the life of all of these other athletes just to get to him, then there was a big problem. When it had been between just the two of them, that was one thing, but to put these other people in the middle of it? To risk the lives of his team-mates? And for what? He swore again, frustrated that Maria had been right. *It was never supposed to get this far.*

Ryan looked down as he and his two team-mates approached the halfway point. They had been climbing for close to ten minutes, and Cam still had not caught up to them. "Is he alright?"

"He had a slow start. He'll catch up," Maria said, but the waver in her voice betrayed her nerves.

He wanted to reach out to her, to comfort her, but of course letting go of the rope was a bad idea, despite the caribiners and harness. "You'll be fine. All of our AIMs are helping each other, like we trained them to. You're not going to fall."

"I'm worried about Cam. His AIM is the quickest out of our four. Something's going on up there but my AIM hasn't noticed anything. It isn't reporting anything, at least."

Ryan thought for a brief moment before he called out through his AIRC. "Is everything alright with Cam's AIM?"

"There was suspicious activity which needed to be dealt with," came the reply.

He heard Maria swear as she stopped right at the halfway point. "What does that mean?"

"It means that Cam needs to hurry the hell up." She held onto the ascender with one hand as she pressed a touch screen button on her AIRC. "Cam, get up here, now. I don't know what's going on at the platform but I do *not* want us down here while your AIM fixes it."

They both heard Cam swear through the AIRC. "Yeah, I'm coming."

"Everything alright?"

Ryan looked at Rick who had just pulled himself up to their level. "Yeah, we're just trying to get Cam to hurry up." He looked at his captain and saw the strain on his face. It had been a good move on their part to have Cam do the most physical leg of the first stage and it had helped to give Rick a rest, but it was already beginning to take a toll on him. Ryan did not like the fact that he could tell just how difficult this was for the captain. "He's right below us, and then our AIMs get to do the heavy lifting."

"Excuse me? Heavy lifting?"

He grinned at Maria as she glared back at him. "Hey, you said yourself that you've gained weight."

"Doesn't mean I'm heavy," she replied tersely in a way Ryan hoped was playful.

He looked to his side as Cam pulled his way up the rope and stopped next to them, sweat glistening on his forehead and his eyes narrowed in either frustration or anger. Ryan could never really tell with him. "Ready?"

"Get us up!' Rick called out before Cam could even reply.

Ryan had no idea what to expect for this next part of the challenge. He did not even really understand the difficulty in this stage, other than the climbing of course. That was difficult for them, but what did it show about their AIMs? That they could hold onto a rope while they climbed up? Suddenly, he was jerked on his rope as he was pulled up along with the rest of his team. It was still difficult, having to hold onto the ascenders as they were hauled up. There was not even a safety net set up below them. Either there were people up on the platform watching out for them, or the officials put a lot of trust into the abilities of the AIMs. Ryan did not feel safe either way, for some reason.

He looked over at Maria and checked out her face. It was stony, rigid in concentration. But there was something else there. Anger? Maybe even a little bit of disappointment? He could understand that. They went from being in the top ten teams to somewhere in the middle. They needed to be in the top third of this batch to make it through to the next stage.

"Is there any way we can get them to go faster?" he asked his captain, who looked as though he was simply trying to keep his body straight.

Rick nodded but looked over at his team-mates before he said anything to his AIM. "Are they all able to go faster than what we told them?"

"If we climb," Maria answered.

"Let's just get this stage finished. I'm sick of being behind everyone," Cam called out as he nodded to Rick.

"Alright. AIMs, let's do this! Guys, keep climbing!"

Their ropes began rising faster to the platform as the team's AIMs pulled harder at the same time as they continued to climb. Ryan dared a glance at his captain, noticing the strain he was putting on his body. But they all had to finish at the same time. There was no time to rest. His other team-mates did not seem to be struggling too much, but Cam had already been struggling to catch up with them, and that fall Maria had taken from her AIM could not have been easy on her body. Ryan was just glad her AIM had charged enough energy to handle this challenge. Then a thought hit him. *What if it hasn't? What if this was too much for any of our AIMs? The CST wouldn't intentionally create a challenge that couldn't be completed, would they? Especially one as dangerous as this?*

He shook his head and continued to ascend up the rope. The sound of the crowd below had been lost, so when he looked forward he was startled to see a face staring back at him. He focused more and realized that they had been climbing just in front of the glass panels which encased the glass elevators. It seemed that the officials had opened up the elevators for fans and had stopped them at intervals. He could not imagine how expensive those tickets had been. Even though he could not hear the fans cheering below, Ryan could look into the faces of these fans. The group of people in front of him smiled and waved. A few small children jumped up and down as they pointed out the window at the team, one pointing at Cam and the other pointed at him.

Ryan glanced over at Cam and saw that he had noticed the fans as well. His team-mate grinned, but of course could not wave. Instead, he continued up the rope, instantly refocusing back on the challenge. It was a strange feeling, to go faster than he knew he should be. It was almost as if he was running on a moving sidewalk in an airport.

In a moment of insanity, Ryan looked down and instantly felt the world spinning around him. He was not the greatest judge of distance, or height, but after the twenty minutes of climbing they had to be pretty high from the ground. In his second moment of insanity, he looked down again and saw that there were more teams below them than he remembered. Finally, a moment of brilliance came upon him, and Ryan looked up. They were almost there. Again, he took a look at his team-mates and noticed the look on Maria's face. Cam had noticed too.

Cam leaned a bit over in between moving his arms with the ascenders. "Hey, are you alright?" He raised an eyebrow when she nodded, but her face was still twisted in a very obvious excruciating pain. "Maria, are you okay?"

"I said I'm fine. We're almost done. We're almost done."

"Pull us faster!" Cam called out, his tone earning the attention of his captain, who finally noticed Maria.

"What's wrong?"

"Cramp, that's all. Just hurry up," she snapped as she continued to pull herself up the rope as the AIMs did their part. She cried out as her arm reached out, and she instantly jerked it back towards her abdomen. After a brief second, she got back into a rhythm of ascending.

Cam watched her for another brief moment before he continued up after her, not wanting to allow the other teams to catch up. By now they were easily in the top third, and he planned on keeping it that way. As he brought his arm up, he felt a strong grip wrap around it and he looked up to face an official leaning over the side of the platform. He had not even noticed how close they were to the finish. With the other man's help, he pulled himself up onto the platform at the same time as his other teammates. He looked around at the other teams that had finished, and then looked back over the edge. It was a good thing he was not afraid of heights, not the way Ryan seemed to be. For some reason, the kid kept looking down over the edge which then resulted in his entire body shaking. He did not care how far down the ground was. All he cared about was that two thirds of the teams were still down there.

"Congratulations. You'll be moving on to the third stage," an official said hurriedly as he moved on to another team that was just finishing the climb. "Congratulations…"

Cam looked to the rest of his team with a grin. "How awesome was that?" he yelled over the wind. With how the gales could be at that height, they were lucky the weather was calm. He slapped the two other men on the back but looked at Maria, who still seemed to be in pain as she knelt on the ground. "You sure it's just a cramp? Should a medic come take a look at you?"

She shook her head, her eyes squeezed shut briefly. "I'm fine. Falling off the horse and then doing this wasn't the greatest idea. I'll be fine, don't worry. In another hour, I'll be ready for the next stage." She took in a deep breath and stood up. She glanced around and stepped towards him as her eyes narrowed slightly. "Go figure out what your AIM had to take care of. If it affects our team, or if it puts any other team in danger, so help me, Cameron, I will-"

"I'll take care of it," he assured her. "It's the first monthly challenge. There's always going to be some shady people."

"Make sure that you take care of it."

"I will."

CHAPTER 24

"So, you're sure it's nothing to worry about?" Maria held the phone to her ear, looking around her as she spoke. The pains were getting too difficult to ignore, and harder to hide.

"Hey, Maria!"

She turned around quickly and saw Rick waving at her. "Okay, thanks Dr. Andrews. Bye," she finished quickly. Maria slipped the phone back into her pocket as Rick came over to her. "Yeah, what's up?"

"Have you seen Cam? We're starting soon and I haven't even seen him since the last stage ended." He looked around him, as if to emphasize his point.

"I'll take a look for him. Have you tried calling his cell, or getting a hold of him through the AIRC?" she asked as she began walking from her captain.

"Yeah. He picked up the cell and immediately hung up." Rick shrugged and ran a hand through his hair. "The last two stages went so well, I can't see what would make him go back to being…well, being him. Just make sure he's okay. I don't think he's going to like what the next stage is."

Maria wandered away and looked around at the other teams that had progressed to this final stage. There were a few new ones who had made it this far, which was a nice surprise. Usually, they would only see the same teams in the last stage of a major challenge like this. Of course, she saw those regular teams as well, but new teams meant new competition. She knew how the top teams acted, how they functioned and she knew their weaknesses. These new up and coming teams, she had no idea how they would perform in this stage.

She continued to look around for her missing team-mate, not sure why she had even gone to look for him in the first place. Maybe she was just used to that. For the past three years, it had been her job to look after him and make sure he kept out of trouble. It turned out he had already gotten himself into trouble a year before she had even joined the team. Turning another corner around a building, she saw Cam standing with a woman a little ways ahead. Squinting slightly, she could see that it was not just any girl.

Emily Richardson. Emily Richardson standing far too close to Cam to make Maria comfortable. She scolded herself. She had lost the right to be jealous when she slept with Jack. She looked at Cam and felt somewhat relieved to see him look slightly more than furious. Even from where she stood, she could tell he was yelling. His wide gestures were another clue. He was not a hand-talker, but boy, could his arms wave when he was angry.

It hit her, at that moment. She was in on it. Whatever Cam's AIM had sensed up on that platform, Emily had something to do with it, and by extension, Jack. By an even further extension, it all came back to the Underground. She remembered that Cam had mentioned that Jack did not work in the Underground, but in another organization. The thought of more than one illegal organization made her nervous. She watched them for a moment, and wanted to try to read their lips but she knew better than to try to learn anything. Less knowledge is always better. At least that's what her father had taught her from his military experience dealing with hostile groups.

Cam pointed at Emily before pointing off in the distance which seemed to dismiss her, and she left in the direction he had pointed. Maria looked around but decided not to hide herself as Cam turned in her direction and head over to her. He stopped briefly when he saw her, shook his head and continued walking.

"So I guess you dealt with it?" Maria asked as he got closer.

"I told you I would." He did not stop as he addressed her. His sharp tone told Maria she should not talk about it anymore, but something had to be said.

"Cameron, come on. This is ridiculous. How can you be okay with having a dangerous AIM on the course?" she asked as she followed him back to their team.

"It's not dangerous, that's how. I can deal with it."

"There were people who could have fallen because their AIMs were attacked by another AIM. I heard people talking about it, Cameron. It attacked me in the first stage."

"Maria." He stopped suddenly and turned to look at her. "I know it attacked you, but you didn't get hurt, and you won't get hurt. For the first time in our relationship, could you please just trust me?"

She had expected his voice to be harsh and cold. Instead it was soft and almost warm. "I do trust you."

"Then please act like it. I know what I'm doing."

With his eyes so focused on her, she almost felt as though she was in a trance. He had not looked at her with such desperation in a long time. She nodded and then shook her head as if to shake away the confusion. "I just don't want anything to happen. We're so close to winning this thing."

Cam laughed and put an arm around her shoulder. "You mean I'm so close to winning this thing."

She gave him a grin as they reached the rest of the team. "Yeah, about that. We need to talk about the next stage."

His arm dropped away from her quickly as Ryan looked towards them. "Sorry. I had to take care of a few things," he called out to the rest of his team. He did not recognize the worried looks on their faces. "So, where's the set up area?"

Cam swore as they stood at the starting line for the final stage of the challenge. He walked in a small circle and waved his hand. "We can use a handicap."

"Are you kidding me? We have to do this." Rick shook his head in frustration. "You're going to have to suck it up."

"Four years. I've gone four years without having to do a water challenge. I'm not about to change that."

"You'll be in a boat. You'll be fine!"

Cam snorted. "Oh yeah, boats worked real well for you at the Owen Sound challenge, didn't they?"

"Teams, please make your way to your designated starting area!" a voice announced over a loudspeaker, nearly drowned out by the sound of the teams and fans combined.

"I can't do this. I don't care if we're in boats." Cam's voice was frantic, something his team knew he hated to show.

Maria looked at Rick and motioned towards one boat. "You and Ryan can take that one. I'll go with Cam."

"The handicap is fine. I'm not getting in that boat."

She glanced at Cam before looking back at Rick. "Go. I'll take care of it." She headed for one canoe along the waterfront with their team name on it and grabbed Cam's wrist as she walked by him. "Come on." She let go only when they arrived at the side of the boat. She busied herself with the contents of the boat, readying it for the challenge. Maria glanced at Cam and tapped her foot. "Well, get in."

"Maria…"

"Alright, you get to listen to me now." She stepped towards him with a sigh. "I know you're hesitant. I know better than anyone why. I was the one who found you on that beach after you almost drowned. I was the one who waited with you to make sure you didn't die overnight while the medics tried to find us. Believe me, I understand your concern. But we need this. Rick needs this. And I think you need this too. You've been so concerned with whatever work it is that you're doing because we haven't been doing well in challenges. I get that, I really do." Maria paused and looked back to the boat.

"You wanted me to trust you. Now I'm asking you to trust me. I won't let anything happen to you. If the boat gets tipped, I'll make sure you don't go under. Do you trust me?"

He looked at her with surprise, and both realized she had not asked that in a very long time. He waited a moment as if thinking before he nodded.

"Yeah, I do."

She nodded. "Alright. Then get in the boat." She watched as he took in a breath and got into the canoe, hiding his nerves expertly, and he sat down quickly.

"Teams, ready!"

Maria turned around to look at Cam, paddle in hand. The paddles were simply to assist their AIM in pulling them across the channel. "You ready for this?" She gave him a reassuring smile when he nodded. "You'll be great. You're Cam Tylar, after all. No one's expecting you to go through with this. Imagine all of the interviews you'll get!" She laughed when his face suddenly turned thoughtful. "Yeah, just keep that thought in your head."

She held her paddle ready as Cam copied her gesture. Both of their AIMs were ready in the forms of fish in the water. It had been a difficult decision. If they'd had whales, it may have been easier to pull the boat to the island across the small channel harbour, but being in a freshwater lake did not allow for that.

They had to use the biggest fish they had, which also meant that they would have to do some of the work. Maria's only concern was that they had no idea where they were going. Their AIMs had been programmed with the coordinates, but they were rough estimates, and if they did not find the exact finishing area, they would not get the points.

Maria readied herself and she mentally evaluated her teammates. Rick had been given enough time to rest from the last stage, and Ryan seemed to be a strong enough paddler. At least he had experience with a canoe, unlike when she had to teach him how to kayak. It seemed so long ago now.

"Go!"

Their boat jerked forward and Maria instinctively looked behind her to make sure Cam had not been too startled by the motion. She kicked herself for taking the front, but even with his phobia of the water, he was still the stronger of the two and he would be able to paddle faster. It was not as though he did not have any experience in the water. He just did not have any good experiences. She could still remember finding him on that beach four years ago after his AIM had been attacked in the ocean. They had both been competing separately in an open competition in the Caribbean and at one point during a water stage, his AIM had been attacked. Well, he had said it was attacked, but she was not sure he really knew what had happened. He had not been back in the water since. At least not sober.

Teams began to pull ahead of their boat easily and Maria shouted over her shoulder to Cam. "We need to paddle if we want to stay ahead." From the corner of her eye, she saw him dip the paddle into the water hesitantly before taking a strong stroke. She looked over to the other Revolution canoe and called out to them as well. "Paddle?"

"Yeah! We have to go all out for this one," Rick called back. He and Ryan had already begun paddling, but Maria and Cam were already pulling ahead. "We're going to have to push our AIMs too. If they run out of energy, we'll still be able to finish this stage. They can still get us in the right area."

With twenty-five teams all starting at once, the harbour seemed crowded as they crossed towards the island which housed the Tommy Thompson Park. The entry into the small inlet was big enough for only ten teams at a time, so they would have to step it up if they wanted to be in the first group of teams to approach the island.

Maria looked around as she paddled, her arms moving fluidly up and down with the paddle, in and out of the water. Every now and then she glanced behind to Cam and saw his intent stare on the island ahead of them. She doubted he was even looking at the water. She smiled when his eyes met hers and she turned forward. She was proud of him for doing this. He had tried to confront his fear for years. During the summers, she had tried taking him to the beach. He would go, and stay on the sand. The closest he ever got was recently in Owen Sound when he had helped his team take the kayaks from the water. Maybe people could get over their fears. Maybe people could change. Just maybe.

"How are you doing?" she called back over her shoulder as her arms began to tire. Her AIM had not tried to communicate with her yet, which she thought was a good sign. They were keeping up with the head of the teams so even if the AIMs tired soon, they still had a far enough lead to finish well.

"Determined to finish this thing."

"Well, maybe we'll have to go onto land to finish rather than stay in the water."

"I don't know if I'm that lucky."

She looked over at Rick and Ryan and noticed they were only slightly behind them. "Hey, you guys alright?"

"My AIM doesn't seem to be responding too well. It may not have recharged fully after the last stage," Ryan yelled. He had stopped paddling and was fiddling with his AIRC, leaving Rick to do the majority of the paddling. It was not the best idea, especially after the strain he went through in the last stage, but Ryan had to get his AIM under control to finish the challenge.

"Give it a rest and try to make up for it with the paddling. You guys are still doing great!" Maria looked ahead to see that they were indeed one of the first few teams to pass into the small bay in the centre of the island. *Where are they taking us?*

It had only been ten minutes, but Maria knew that the entire water experience would seem like a lifetime to Cam, who was breathing heavily. He was a fit person, a very fit and athletic person – something Maria had always noticed. He did not get tired easily, but the strain of his fear and the challenge was getting to him.

"We're almost there," Maria said to him as she stopped paddling. They were coming close to the shore alongside eleven other canoes, which was a good sign. There was a land component to this challenge, but that also meant more reliance on the AIM that they had already pushed much too hard that day.

"The water's calmer in here," Cam said with only a slight waver to his voice. He set his paddle down on the inside of the canoe and took a look at his AIRC. His eyebrows furrowed and he looked around as if expecting to see something.

"What is it?"

He shook his head. "Nothing. Just trying to get my bearings."

With the same jerk as when they had started, the canoe jolted to a stop as they ran into the beach. Maria jumped swiftly from the canoe and into the shallow water. She pulled the boat forward out of the water as Rick did the same for his canoe beside her. As soon as there was no water around the sides, Cam jumped out and switched his AIM from a fish to the wolf he had used before.

"Ready?" he asked as his team-mates switched their AIMs as well, except for Ryan who kept tapping at his AIRC furiously. Cam raised an eyebrow, and then noticed his AIM move towards the water where Ryan's AIM was. "Everything okay?"

Finally, a wolf appeared in the shallow water and walked onto the beach, shaking the water from its fur and Ryan nodded. "Yeah. I think there's something wrong with my AIRC though. It's still not connecting properly to my AIM."

"We'll figure it out later. Let's just finish this challenge first," Rick said quickly and headed after his AIM.

Cam looked at Ryan's AIM as it sniffed the air and kept its distance from the other AIMs, almost as if it was afraid of them. Or found them as threats.

He kept an eye on the AIM as he followed the rest of his team as a line of fans came into view along the beach. He grinned and waved as they ran past them. He would have loved to stop and take in what he had just accomplished. Four years since he had been on the water, and now, he had done it. There would be time to self-reflect later. He just had to concentrate on finishing the challenge, and to make sure that nothing, and no one stood in their way.

CHAPTER 25

The team ran down a small dirt path, following their AIMs as closely as they could. Ryan looked around as they went, but he kept a careful eye on his AIM. It was running alongside the other AIMs but it seemed to be following the pack rather than taking an active role. He hoped that if it was running low on energy, it would last until the end of the challenge. They were so close.

"Is there any way our AIMs can lead us but without using so much energy?" Maria asked as if she had read his mind. "We pushed them pretty hard in the water."

"Yeah, but then we'd slow down. We should have this finished soon," Rick replied as he kept track of his AIM through his console. He glanced over at Ryan. "Everything alright?"

He shrugged as he tapped away at his AIRC. "I think so. I'm going to have to get my AIRC checked out. The screen's lagging."

The team stopped when a bear suddenly lumbered onto the path. They stiffened and watched the bear sniff the air in their direction. Ryan looked over the bear for the blinking light. He finally found it on its neck, but for some reason he still felt uneasy about the way it blocked the path.

"Who does that belong to?" His voice was quiet as if the AIM would attack if he spoke any louder.

"Who do you think?"

Jack walked out from the bushes with a sneer on his face.

"You realize that you can be disqualified for sabotaging another team's ability to complete a challenge, right? But why would I think you'd let that stop you?" Rick stepped forward.

"I couldn't care less about that. What I do care about is showing people what happens when they cross me," Jack growled looking pointedly at Cam. "You almost got me disqualified earlier, Tylar. That wasn't very sportsmanlike."

"You were the one who brought in a hacked AIM," Cam spat back. His AIM stepped in front of him. It bore its teeth with a snarl in warning.

He laughed arrogantly. If anyone could laugh like that, it was Jack. "You really think that intimidates me?" He nodded as he turned to his AIM. The bear let out a low growl before it took a step forward.

Cam's AIM growled back, mirroring the bear's movement.

"This is stupid," Maria said. "The AIM's can't do anything to each other. We don't have time to see which one of you is the bigger man."

The bear roared louder. Maria stepped back. She used to believe that AIMs could not hurt humans but after the wolf had attacked her, she was beginning to doubt that. She was beginning to doubt a lot of things at the moment. She collected herself and slowly advanced.

"I wouldn't do that," Jack warned as he revealed a small handgun from underneath his jacket. "This is between me and Cam."

Maria's eyes narrowed but she felt her face pale. She had told Cam it would come to this. Before she could react, Ryan stepped in front of Maria without a word, only a stare towards Jack.

"Ryan, don't be stupid," Cam said. He turned his attention quickly towards Maria.

He was trembling slightly, but Ryan held his ground. "It's not like he'll actually do anything with cameras around." He took his eyes from Jack quickly when his AIM rubbed up against his leg and sniffed him. He wanted to push the AIM away, but he was not sure what Jack would do if he made any more movements.

"Do you see any cameras?" Jack asked with a laugh.

He had not noticed before now, but Jack was right. Ryan could not see any cameras. They must have gone a considerable way off the correct path. Unless the cameras had been…dealt with.

"Ryan, get Maria out of here." Cam continued to stare at Jack with his AIM at his side.

"We're not leaving you," Ryan replied, but could not hide the slight waver in his voice. His AIRC began making strange sounds. "*Error…. error…*"

"Jack, don't be an idiot. You guys can deal with this later, after the challenge." Maria looked between Cam and Jack, staying behind her human shield.

"Oh no," Jack replied. "This is actually the best way to get to him. Make him worry about people he cares about. It's the only time he's actually useful. Isn't that right, Cam?"

"Come on." She stepped from behind Ryan. *This is getting ridiculous. We're running out of time.*

"You had your chance." Jack pulled out the gun and pointed it towards Ryan and Maria. His AIM took a few more steps forward and bellowed.

Maria held her hands up. "Jack, you don't want to do this. You know I can get that gun from you within three steps, and I know you don't want to shoot me just to get at Cam." She took a tentative step forward. "And you know that once I get that gun from you, my aim is much better than yours. I don't care what kind of practice you think you've had."

Cam swore and pushed Maria back. "Rick, would you get your team out of here?"

Until now, Rick had been in a silent trance. He watched the scene play out in front of him as if he was not a part of it. But then Cam addressed him. He needed to get his team out of there. But that meant his whole team.

"Cam, let's go," he said quietly, staring at the gun.

"*System overload…*"

Ryan looked down at his AIRC quickly. The stats on his AIRC were fluctuating sporadically.

Suddenly Ryan's AIM began to growl. It moved away from its position at his side and turned towards the team. There was something different. Its eyes were alight. And Ryan could not find the blinking light on its neck. It slowly walked towards the bear, its ears pointed back and its hair was raised.

"You think I don't know it can't do anything to me?" Jack asked mockingly.

But no one responded. No one seemed sure anymore.

Ryan's AIRC continued its chant. "*Error... error...*" The stats were maxing out.

Another low growl from the AIM made the group freeze.

"Guys? My AIRC lost connection with my AIM," Ryan said quietly. "Its stats went off the charts, and the screen keeps filling with error messages."

Cam swore and grabbed Ryan's AIRC. The wolf snapped at him from a distance as a warning, but Cam's AIM moved itself quickly in front of Cam. "What did you do to it?"

"I didn't do anything!"

He swore again as he flipped furiously through various screens on the AIRC, his eyes flickering every now and then to the wolf. He forgot about Jack. This was worse. His eyes narrowed and he pointed to the animal. "Ryan, is this the AIM we gave you?"

"Yeah, of course!"

"One at a time, go back down the path. Don't run until you're around the bend of trees," he said to his team, his focus solely on the wolf before them.

"Yeah, as Jack points a gun at us. That's a smart idea," Maria snapped.

The wolf began to advance on the team slowly, ignoring the bear completely.

"Enough of this!" Jack aimed the gun towards the wolf. "This is ridiculous," he said as he cocked the hammer.

Cam looked at Jack and his eyes widened. "No!" He lunged for Jack. He grabbed for the gun, but Jack held him away. Cam twisted himself around Jack's arm barrier. He pushed the gun upwards in the split second Jack pulled the trigger. He looked quickly at the wolf to see the result of the shot.

The AIM was only startled by the sound. After a few seconds, it took a few steps forward in defiance.

"Don't you dare shoot it."

Jack looked at Cam for a moment before he grinned. "Competing with a rogue, are you?"

"I didn't know what it was. I'm surprised you people even acknowledge their existence," he snapped as he pushed himself away from him. He swore and looked back to his team, desperately trying to think of a solution. He could not destroy the AIM, but there was no way he could get it back under control in the time they had to complete the challenge. Not in front of his team-mates. He had to leave it.

"We have to get out of here. I'll come back for the AIM later. Jack, get out of here. Make sure no one comes back down this path." He took a step back towards Jack and spoke in a low voice. "And if you *ever* aim a gun at her again, I will not hesitate sending you to the hospital again. But next time it'll be in a body bag. My aim's gotten a lot better." With that final word of warning, he watched as Jack moved away from the group slowly, keeping his AIM between himself and the wolf.

He looked at his team and finally noticed they were all staring at him, the wolf being largely ignored for the moment. "Let's go. Just move slowly."

"What happened to my AIM?" Ryan asked as they moved down the path backwards, watching as Cam's AIM circled his own as if about to fight.

"It got disconnected, that's all. It'll be fixed later."

"How exactly does an AIM become disconnected, and how do you know it'll be fixed?" Rick suddenly realized he was afraid of the answer. He had known Cam for five years, but there was so much he did not know about the man.

"Because he'll be the one who reconnects it," Maria said quietly, coming to the quick realization.

Cam's eyes met hers. "I can't do it right now, but yeah, that's my job: to reconnect dangerous AIMs."

Maria swore as they made it around the bend in the path. She turned around and looked at her other team-mates, and noticed that neither of them seemed to understand. Maybe that was a good thing. Rick seemed to be trying, but she was not about to connect the dots for him. Within seconds of turning around the bend, growls erupted ahead of them along with the sound of the wolves scuffling on the ground.

A short ringing noise from their AIRCs brought them from their confusion and light panic from the sound of the AIMs fighting mere metres away from them. The noise made them each look at their consoles. Maria's heart fell as she looked at the screen.

"Attempt failed," Ryan read. His face lined with confusion, the concept not processing. "No points."

Maria wiped her face and shoved her console back into her pocket. She looked at Cam. Now she was angry.

"We've never not been able to complete a major challenge. You even got into a boat," Rick said, addressing Cam. His confused daze turned into a fit of frustration as he swore and quickly transformed his AIM into a default mode.

"We still got a good amount of points from the other stages…" Ryan's voice trailed off, unsure whether or not to continue speaking.

Rick shook his head and headed back to the water where a larger boat with officials was waiting to pick up teams who had not yet made it across the harbour. "Let's just get a hotel and figure out our next move." He looked at Cam briefly before he got onto the boat. There would be a long conversation later.

Ryan followed close behind his captain, and his hand brushed against Maria's briefly as he passed her.

Maria looked at Cam as he stared at his AIRC. She sighed and stepped towards him. "At least you got on a boat." When he did not reply she glanced around. "Guess you have a phone call to make?"

"I thought Ryan's AIM was normal. I checked its code myself. Its registration code said it was made by the CST, not the Underground. I checked the code," Cam said softly. "When AIMs turn like that, it's the Underground that make them go back to normal. *I'm* the one who makes them safe for people to use. So if you think I'm a terrible person for choosing that job over my relationship with you, then screw you. I'm done defending myself."

He started down towards the dock, but stopped when Maria put a hand on his arm.

"I'm not asking you to defend yourself. I'm just proud of you for getting into that boat."

He looked at her and suddenly noticed the confliction on her face. She was angry because it was his fault Jack ambushed them. Without that interruption they would have finished the challenge. And for the second time in a month, she had a gun pointed at her because of him. But now, now she at least knew part of what he did in the Underground. It meant she would be in more danger, but he could see that she could not hate his work anymore even if she barely understood what had happened to Ryan's AIM. And he had gotten on a boat.

He sighed and motioned towards the other half of their team. "Well, you get to see me do it again." He forced a smile as they met up with Rick and Ryan. It was hard for Cam to convince himself that it was not his fault that they lost the challenge, but of course it was. It was not Jack's fault, even though he desperately wanted to blame him. Cam had no one else to blame but himself. As he stepped onto the second boat he had been on in four years, his AIM stepped to his side. Its fur was matted and what would have looked like bite marks on a real animal were on its neck.

Cam looked down with a teasing grin. "You like me."

"I tolerate you more than I do most humans. Besides, I'm stuck with you."

"Well don't be so loud about it," Cam warned, hoping no one had heard that interaction. His AIM seemed to be the only thing he could do right. He could not even help his team finish a challenge. He dreaded the team meeting he knew Rick would hold later. He just had to take it one minute at a time until then. That was all he could do without taking off.

Just take it one minute at a time.

"Do we really need to talk about what happened?" Maria asked as she paced around her hotel room. They had been much too late in booking a hotel, and had ended up with the last two hotel rooms.

All the men shared one room and Maria, as the only female, got the other.

"We need to figure out what to do with Ryan's AIM, but yeah, we need to talk about why we couldn't finish the challenge." Rick watched as she paced, and then he held his head in his hands. "I want to say I'm proud of what we accomplished, and I can for the first two stages but that last stage? What the hell was that? And where the hell is Cam?"

"He went back to the park to get Ryan's AIM," she said softly before she stopped in front of the window.

"I don't understand why I couldn't go get it. It's my AIM," Ryan asked, standing next to Maria.

"Cam's been working with AIMs longer than any of us, even you Rick. If there's anyone who can deal with a malfunctioning AIM, it's him. We're just going to have to trust him."

"Why?" Rick stood up quickly. "What's the deal with him and Jack? He came looking for Cam with a gun. What the hell was that about?"

"Yeah, I saw it. He pointed it at me, remember?" she snapped. She sighed as she looked at Rick. It was very rare for her to snap and become angry with Rick. She opened her mouth to speak, but a cry came out instead as her abdomen constricted with an agonizing pain.

"Maria?"

She shut her eyes tight as she hugged her abdomen. "I'm fine. I just…" She paused to wait for the pain to subside. "Let's just have a meeting in the morning when Cam's around. Some time to calm down will be best, for all of us."

Rick stood up and looked down into her face. "You okay?" He watched her as she wordlessly nodded before he headed for the door. "See you in the morning. It'll be a new day. We'll just wait for then." He raised a hand in farewell before he left Ryan and Maria alone in the room.

Maria looked back to the window as Ryan put a hand on her back. "I'm really okay. I just pushed myself too hard today."

"You were amazing," he said before he kissed the side of her head. He paused for a moment before he continued. "Why was Jack after Cam?"

"Rivalry, I guess."

"That was more than just Scanning rivalry back there. Was it...was it over you?"

Maria laughed and looked up at him. "No, it had nothing to do with me. That was entirely between Cam and Jack."

"He pointed a gun at you."

"And you put yourself in front of me."

"If anything had happened to you–" He was cut off by Maria's lips on his. Before he could properly respond, she pulled away.

"Thank you."

He relaxed as she leaned against him. "You should get some rest. It's been a long day."

She nodded after a moment and walked with him to the door, her key card in her hand. "I'm going to take a walk inside the hotel first. I need to just move." She smiled when he kissed her cheek.

"See you in the morning."

She sat in the lobby for what she felt was hours before she finally saw Cam walk through the front doors with an unfamiliar woman and a man she recognized after a moment as Mark. She stood and watched the three speak for a moment before the two left Cam at the front desk.

Maria stepped up to him quickly after he got the key card for his room. As she got closer, she saw the tiredness on his face.

"Everything go okay?"

He looked to her, startled by her sudden appearance. He motioned down towards the two AIMs following him quietly and obediently. He did not say anything as he headed towards the elevator, and remained silent as they got in.

"Cam–"

"Why aren't you with him?"

Maria's eyes widened in surprise. "What?"

"I talked to Ryan. Maria, we both know we're not getting back together at this point. It's been two months…two months." He stabbed at the button for his floor. "You care about him?"

She hesitated. "I think so."

"Then I'll stay out of the way."

"It's complicated."

"How? The guy can handle that you still have feelings for me." Their eyes met. "They'll go away."

"Cam, I'm–"

"Look, you saw most of what I do in the Underground so that's out of the way. Fine. But things are wrapping up with certain projects and situations are becoming more intense. You saw that today too."

"Cameron…"

"Things are just going to get worse."

"Lucas Cameron Tylar, would you please listen to me?"

He spun to look at her, his eyes narrowed until he saw the pained look on her face. But he could not let her talk. He did not want to hear it. She sounded too much like his mother.

"I can't keep you safe." He sighed and shrugged his shoulders in defeat. "I can't keep you from getting hurt," he said as the elevator doors opened. He stepped out and shot her a look over his shoulder. "Have a good night."

She closed her eyes as the doors shut between them. She would have to try again in the morning. She had made up her mind to tell him, especially with how situations were playing out. Maria knew he could not protect her from getting hurt, but she had to tell him. She would tell him in the morning, and she would make him listen.

CHAPTER 26

Rick groaned, rolling over as he heard his cell phone ringing. "Five more minutes…" When the ringing continued, he groaned louder and grabbed his phone, holding it to his ear. "Yeah?" His voice was slurred groggily.

"Shut up! I'm trying to sleep!" Cam yelled as he threw a pillow at Rick.

Rick turned the light on and sat up quickly, deflecting the pillow easily. "Yeah, this is Rick. You said Maria Kier?"

"Tell her to shut up too! And turn the light off!"

Rick listened carefully to the woman on the other end of the phone. His eyes quickly went over to Cam, wide with surprise, before he covered his face with his hand and nodded to whatever she was saying. "Which hospital did you say you're calling from?" he asked after a few moments.

Cam re-opened his eyes and sat up slowly. Rick was not talking to Maria, but about her with someone at a hospital. Why was she at the hospital? It was a good five minutes before Rick even moved or spoke again.

"Does she want him in with her? …Okay, let her know we'll be right there." He hung up the phone and swung his legs around to the other side of the bed to face the other two members of his team. "Cam, did you miss a call?"

With a flustered look, Cam grabbed his phone from the nightstand and saw that he had missed three calls. Two from an unknown number, the hospital most likely. The first had been from Maria. Two hours ago. He looked back at Rick with a moment of realization. They were both Maria's emergency contacts. "Where is she?"

"Maria's in the hospital. She's asking for us. For you."

"What happened? We saw her just before she went to sleep, didn't we?" Ryan asked. He was now wide awake as well.

"Maria's in labour." Rick spoke slowly as if he were trying to understand the words.

"She's..." Cam started.

"Cam, it's a stillbirth. The baby died," he said as gently as possible.

Cam and Ryan merely stared at their captain for a minute before he finally found his words, and the strength to voice them. "How...how far along is, was she?"

"About eighteen weeks."

Cam stood and turned away, putting his hands behind his head. The other two stayed silent, waiting for Cam to get over the initial shock. Neither wanted to say anything, but both knew what that timeline meant. Eighteen weeks was well before the break-up. After a moment, he took an audible deep breath and turned back around, and began to dress quickly.

"Cam," Rick said, following his lead, "if you're going, you have to be there. I mean really be there."

Cam looked at Ryan and saw the look of utter confusion and hurt on his face. But it was not about him. "I know. I will."

"We're looking for Maria Kier," Rick said as Revolution arrived at the hospital. Ryan and Cam stood back a bit, trying not to crowd around the receptionist. Cam tried not to look around, or do anything really. He just listened to Rick and the nurse. One thing at a time; that was all he could handle for the moment. Just one thing.

The nurse tapped away at the keyboard and ran a short nail down the monitor and then across. "She's still in the delivery room. Looks like she's been there for a few hours now. If you'll have a seat in the waiting room, I'll have someone let you know when you can see her."

Rick nodded slowly. "The delivery room…okay, thanks." He looked over his shoulder at Cam briefly. "She doesn't…she doesn't want anyone in there?"

Her lips formed a thin line and she shook her head. "She asked for someone at first, but I think she's more scared and hurt than lonely right now." She glanced around Rick. As quiet as they had been with their relationship, the public had heard rumours that Maria and Cam had been together. The nurse had certainly assumed the baby's paternity. "If he wants to go in, I'm sure she won't kick him out," she said quietly.

He nodded his thanks, and the three walked into the waiting room. A few people were sitting there already. Some sat reading three month old magazines while others watched the TV, barely focusing on the images.

Cam stayed standing while the other two sat on the other side of the room from the others waiting. The longer it took people to recognize them, the better. "I have to…I can't just sit here."

"What if she's out soon?" Ryan asked.

"I'll be there, I just can't be here. I can't be here while she's in there. I just, I can't," he said before walking off with his hands in his pockets.

Ryan looked at Rick, who had his head hanging down with his hands at the side of his face. "She's going to be okay," he said after a minute.

Rick nodded. "I know. I just never want to understand what's going through Cam's head right now. With everything going on: The CST, my dad, everything, and now a miscarriage. Stillbirth, even. It's hard, and I wish this didn't have to happen to them. She didn't even tell us she was pregnant." His head sank down to his knees and he rested his hands behind his neck. "She didn't even tell Cam."

Cam wandered down the halls, looking straight ahead as he went. If he looked around, he would begin thinking too much. He passed a nurse's station and ignored the woman calling out to him. He stopped suddenly when he heard a scream. A scream of pain mixed with sobs. He allowed himself to look around and found himself deep within the maternity ward.

"Are you going in?"

He turned to face a woman holding out an offering in her hands. "Excuse me?"

"Mr. Tylar, you'll need these if you're going in with her."

He took the pile of hospital clothing wordlessly, staring at her as she walked back to her station. He should have kept looking straight ahead. He looked at the sign of the delivery room next to him and leaned his back against the wall. He closed his eyes as he heard another scream. He slid down the wall and let himself sit on the ground. Where he should have heard the cries of a woman and a baby, he heard only a woman and a man.

A few hours later, and with Cam still gone, Ryan shoved Rick awake when he saw a doctor walking towards them.

"Is she okay?" Ryan asked as he jumped out of his seat before Rick could even stand up.

"Physically, Miss Kier is fine, considering. No complications so far, but I'd like to have her stay for another forty-eight hours so she can have the chance to speak with a counsellor and to get documents in order. She's awake now, but her body is still exhausted after going through labour, even though it wasn't full term. I will warn you that this is not going to be an easy road for her. You can come see her now if you'd like."

The two followed the doctor down a few halls into the maternity ward. Rick walked into the room first, followed by Ryan. He stood next to the bed and put a hand on Maria's arm.

"Maria?"

Maria turned over in the bed and looked up at him, her face still tear-stained, and her eyes were red and puffy. "Sorry you had to get up before seven."

Rick laughed as he knelt by the bed and put his other hand at the top of her head, rubbing her forehead with his thumb. "How are you? Physically?"

She shrugged. "Sore. I didn't get any pain meds. My mom always told me I'd want them and I couldn't handle…handle it without drugs. Always have to prove her wrong."

He smiled lightly, but it faded as he shook his head. "You didn't tell any of us."

"No."

"You didn't tell Cam."

She shook her head and glanced at Ryan as if taking a mental headcount, and then briefly to the door. "I'm glad you two came."

"He came. He'll be here," Ryan said, stepping closer to her bed. He took her hand in his.

"Are you mad?"

"Why would we be mad? If anything, I can't believe you were cleared." He paused. "But I do like my sleep."

Maria laughed, but her eyes went back to the door quickly and stayed there, seeing movement behind Rick.

Rick looked over his shoulder to see Cam leaning against the door frame, his hands shoved into his pockets. He could not read his face, not because it was emotionless, but because there were too many for even Cam to know what they were. He nodded quickly before standing up.

"We'll be back in a bit, okay?"

She looked at Cam once the others had left, wanting to look away, but it was like a car crash happening in front of her. She did not want to see the devastation, but her eyes were stuck. He came into the room slowly, but stopped at the chair next to the bed and sat down. She watched him prop his head up with his elbows on his knees, his fists intertwined in front of his mouth as he looked straight back at her. They stayed like that for a few minutes, just looking at each other. She let out a sigh and opened her mouth to speak when Cam beat her to it.

"You didn't tell me. You had all this time. You had chances to tell me in private. You went through all of those challenges. You didn't tell me."

She could not believe how much hurt was in his voice. "I haven't known long."

"You were pregnant with my child. You went through *labour* with *my* child. I heard you...I was outside the door as you went through labour with *our* child."

He had been there. Maybe he had not come in, but he had been there. She couldn't take it anymore. She had done so well at holding back her hormones, making sure no one saw her cry or flip out, but the walls she spent the past month building came crashing down with her shaky sobs.

Maria covered her face with her hands, turning into the pillow as if to hide from Cam. How could she have a conversation with him? How could she ever possibly be okay again? She had been in a delivery room. She had pushed through the contractions. She'd been through the process that usually brought life into the world – for nothing. She continued to sob even after she felt his hand on her arm, recognizing it as his way of trying to comfort her. She took a few deep breaths, trying to control her breathing and her emotions, and had to attempt this three times before she felt as though she could reduce the sobs to mere tears streaming down her face.

She wiped her face, still feeling Cam's hand on her arm. When she finally looked at him, Maria saw him wiping his own face as well and that was when it hit her. He actually cared. He had just found out he had a child and then a minute later, he found out that his child had died before it could even become a child. How could she tell him that she had heard a heartbeat when he would never be able to hear that too? How could she tell him that she had felt the baby kick whenever he had been near her, when he would never feel the kick against his hand on her stomach? Maybe in the future, but never for his first, never for this child with Maria.

Any anger Cam felt now was justified, to him of course. He had already missed out on so much, and Cam felt that was the worst of it all. He would never get any of that back. She had taken that away from him. She had not even given him a chance to be a dad. But he couldn't show his anger, not yet, not in front of her tear-stained face. He pushed his anger aside, and it gave way to a feeling of deep loss, which he found ridiculous. How could he grieve something, someone, how could he miss someone who was never born? How could he mourn the loss of someone he never knew? But Cam knew that was exactly what he, and Maria, were grieving for. And all he could do was put his hand on her arm to comfort her. Words would mean nothing, no profession of feelings he knew would never go away, no words of encouragement would ease any pain. But that touch meant they shared something, a loss only they could feel.

"When...when did you find out?" Cam asked after a while. His voice was soft and detached. It was the only way he could speak.

"Just after Niagara Falls. It was why I wasn't cleared in the first place. I mean, I had thought I might be for a while, especially with my weight gain, but I didn't find out for sure until Niagara Falls," Maria answered slowly. She attempted to sit up a bit more in the bed but stopped, not having the energy. "They saw it in my blood tests, and they wanted to run more tests to make sure she was healthy before I began competing again."

Cam's eyes widened as he looked at her quickly. "She?" he breathed. "It was a girl?"

Maria nodded. "I didn't know before today. I wanted to wait. I wanted it to be a surprise." She let out a soft sigh. "Cam, I tried to tell you. I wanted to, but we fight, and then we're fine, then–"

"She was the complication. She was the reason you wouldn't date Ryan." He nodded as if he finally understood. "And then in the elevator, you tried to tell me." He laughed at himself. "You've never called me by my first name, let alone my full name. I should've just shut up."

"It wouldn't have made a difference, Cam. You would've had an evening knowing I was pregnant and who knows how you would've reacted to that. And then a few hours later..." Her voice trailed off as a nurse stepped into the room hesitantly.

"I'm sorry for interrupting." The woman smiled sadly as she stepped to the side of Maria's bed and stood next to the chair Cam sat in. "Unfortunately, I have some forms I'll need you to fill out, Maria. Are you okay to talk about this?"

She glanced at Cam and saw that his eyes were closed, but his hand slid down her arm to hold her hand. "As much as I can be."

"This first one is for the birth certificate, which I know isn't right, but we need it for records and it's the only way to register a stillbirth now. This second one is the release form for her body. We'll bring her to any cemetery or funeral home for you. All of the expenses are covered by the hospital, so you don't have to worry about that."

Maria's eyes widened. She pushed the papers away from her as she shook her head. "No. What are you talking about?"

"She has to be buried. There doesn't have to be a service, but she has to be brought somewhere. I'm so sorry. If either of you want to see her, just let me know," the nurse said soothingly as Maria continued to shake her head in disbelief.

"No. No, no, no…I can't. I can't do this, I can't." She felt Cam's hand tighten around hers.

"I think we should do it."

Maria looked at Cam to find his eyes looking back into hers. "What?"

"We should have a small service. I think…I think it'll be good for us, to see her."

The nurse gave a small nod and left the papers on the bed with Maria. "Take your time, Maria." As the nurse left, she stepped out of the way of Ryan as he made his way into the room.

He looked back and forth between the two and took a small step backwards. "I can come back later."

Cam shook his head and stood up, letting go of her hand. "No, it's fine. I need to walk." He began to take a step away from the bed but stopped and looked back to Maria. "Is that alright?" He left when she nodded.

Maria watched as Cam left and Ryan took his seat. She looked at him with the blank face she was already sick of wearing. But she could not wear anything else.

"So, I guess things kind of make sense now." Ryan did not look directly at her. "Of course you wouldn't think things were over with him. You…you were carrying his child."

"Ryan, I couldn't tell you before I told Cam."

He nodded. "Yeah, I know. I just...I think we're all trying to digest this." He paused for a moment and then finally looked at her. "I wouldn't have run."

She smiled. "I know."

He nodded again and cleared his throat. "How are you?"

"A little more than broken." There was a pause. "Cam wants to have a funeral for her."

Ryan pushed past the reference to the baby's sex. Reassuring him was the last thing Maria needed to worry about. "You don't?"

"I don't know. It's easier to not think about it, I think." She closed her eyes for a moment before she grabbed the papers the nurse had left behind. "Going to have to face something eventually. It might as well be this." She looked at him. "Do you mind giving me a minute?" She waited until he left before she reached over to her purse and pulled out her cell phone.

"Hi, may I speak to Colonel Madden?"

Rick walked up next to Cam and put his hand on Cam's shoulder. "I wouldn't have thought I'd find you here."

Cam shrugged, staring through the glass window at the newborns. Their cries could be heard faintly through the glass. "Ryan's talking to her." He paused. "I'm sorry about the challenge. Rick, I've done a lot of things I shouldn't have."

"Cam, your kid just died."

"We should've finished the challenge. It was my fault."

"Cam, just stop."

He shook his head. "A nurse brought me in to see her. She's so...she's so small." He rested a closed fist against the glass. "It's not fair, Rick."

"I know."

Half an hour later, Ryan left Maria's room once again but stopped suddenly when he ran into Rick and Cam.

"Hey."

"Hey," Rick replied and motioned towards Cam. "I found him wandering around the-"

"We said we wouldn't talk about it," Cam snapped. He looked into Maria's room. "She still awake?"

Maria looked up from the papers as Cam came back into the room alone. She glanced back down, suddenly embarrassed when she saw him looking at the papers. She tried to protest when he took the papers from her. "Cam…"

"You chose a name."

"I was going to wait until you came back. It's not set in stone." She swore and covered her face. "Cam…"

"My mom's name." He nodded before he looked at Maria. "It's perfect."

Maria's hands slid down her face and she watched him for a moment. She had thought she would never feel so destroyed as when her dad had died, would never feel so helpless. She had been the one who organized everything, from the funeral to dealing with the lawyer for his estate. Thinking about planning yet another funeral, for a life she had never known, was devastating. But she realized then that she hadn't been alone. Cam had been there to help her through every step, having to have done the same the year before when his mother had passed. And he was here with her again. She didn't have to go through this alone.

"I think you were right. About the service. I think it'll be good." Her eyes widened briefly. "The challenges."

"Maria, you're allowed to not think about the competition." Cam sat back down in the seat. Neither could believe his suggestion. The sport was everything to him, or rather, it had been. Things changed so quickly. "Rick already talked to the board. We'll go on a break for a few weeks to get everything settled. It's…it's pretty much understood you won't be competing for the rest of the season."

"I want to."

"The things you did already this season, you probably shouldn't have done. I honestly can't believe they cleared you." Cam shook his head and his eyes narrowed as he focused on a spot on her bed. "I can't believe you even did the challenges after you found out."

"What else was I supposed to do?"

"Tell us you were pregnant. You were gone for two weeks. We could've managed. We will manage. I even went in the water today…yesterday."

"Cam, I wasn't about to quit. You wouldn't have wanted me to. I know you, and I know that you're probably thinking this is my fault, that I lost the baby because of the challenges-"

"You're really going to tell me it isn't your fault?" He closed his eyes and shook his head. "I didn't mean that."

"Yes, you did."

Cam looked up at Maria, but she kept her eyes away from him. "You fell pretty hard."

"I wouldn't have fallen if that AIM hadn't attacked me."

He hesitated and shook his head again. "I'm sorry. It's a lot, right now."

"I know."

He nodded and glanced out the doorway. "Guess we should talk to the guys about all of this." He looked back at Maria with a sigh. "I'm sorry, Maria."

"Me too."

CHAPTER 27

Revolution walked away from the small, open hole in the manicured ground close to a week after the incident. The name Lucy Elizabeth Tylar was engraved on a small piece of granite set next to Maria's father. Maria forced herself to keep walking away without looking back over her shoulder. All she had wanted to do was fall to the ground and stay there until her own hole had to be dug. She looked to her side quickly when she felt Cam's hand on her back, leading her away from the plot. She smiled lightly, acknowledging the comforting gesture. She knew it was not just for her. He needed it too, as much as he was trying to hide it. He had been so strong that morning. Too strong.

"Owen, I'm really glad you're here," Maria said softly.

"Me too."

Maria looked away quickly. His once youthful smile now looked like that of an old man. She hated herself for not visiting him when she had last been in Kitchener, but it had been hard to do it. The heart attack had really taken a toll on the man's body, and she had not noticed until that day. Then again, everything seemed so much worse on the day she and Cam buried their daughter.

As they walked back toward the vehicles, the sound of voices wafted towards them. They continued walking and suddenly, they saw news vans surrounded by a group of people. The reporters caught sight of Revolution and their voices grew louder as they came streaming towards the team.

"Maria! Cam! How are you feeling right now?"

"Owen, does this mean you'll be coming back to the team?"

Cam swore and stepped in front of Maria as the freelance reporters came up to them.

"What does this mean for the team, Cam?"

Cam swore again. "It means you get the hell out of our face."

"Maria, who was the father? What are you going to do now?"

"Who the hell do you think was the father?" Cam yelled and took Maria by the arm, seeing her face fill with tears. "We're getting out of here." He put her into the backseat of a car as Ryan slid into the driver's seat. He looked back over his shoulder and saw Owen and Rick herding the reporters away. Owen had always been good at taking care of them. As he was about to follow Maria, he noticed another car parked a little further down the small paved lane. He hesitated for a moment and looked down when Maria grabbed his hand.

"I'll meet you guys at the hotel," he said as he stuck his head down into the car.

Maria looked over her shoulder and let go of his hand when she saw the car. "Go."

He looked down at her quickly. The hesitation and reluctance was clear through the pained look in his eyes. "I won't be long."

"Do what you have to do." Two weeks earlier, she never would have said anything like that. So much could happen in an instant. So many people could change just as quickly.

Cam walked slowly over to the parked vehicle and although Rick and Owen would have questions, with the tone of the morning so far, no one would bother to ask. He slid into the passenger seat of the car and held his face in his hands.

"You have the best timing. You really do," he muttered, his voice muffled through his fingers.

"I'm so sorry, Cam. I really didn't want to come, but Henk's in a panic."

"Sandra, I really can't do this right now."

"The McCarthys have agreed to meet with us."

Cam lowered his head onto the dashboard, his chest rising with deep breaths. "How much time do we have?" he asked after a minute.

"A year."

He laughed but kept his head down.

"But we need to have everything ready, including working AIMs and at least three fully programmed AIMs."

"I can't do that in a year. That last batch Henk came up with wasn't as finalized as he thought. I can't do it."

"You can if you do it full time." Sandra looked at Cam when he finally lifted his head and turned his attention to an open hole in the manicured lawn. "Are you sure you want to do this?"

Cam kept his eyes looking out through the window. "I have to. I can't keep this away from them anymore. I can't keep her, any of them, safe. Maria's been right about me all along. I'm a liability to the team."

"When are you going to tell them?"

"Today," he answered with determination in his voice. "This day sucks already. There's not much worse that can happen than burying my kid."

"I'm so sorry, Cam."

"Who else knows?"

"Everyone. Teams are talking about it too, which is probably why the reporters showed up."

Cam nodded and clicked in the seatbelt. "Hotel first, then we go the lab."

"We can give you more time. There's no rush right now."

"I don't need more time. I need you to drive me to the hotel."

Ryan sat next to Maria in Owen's hotel room. He had heard Cam say he would not be long but it had been almost half an hour. He put his hand briefly on Maria's and smiled which she tried to return. He did not expect anything more from her.

"Alright, well I guess Cam doesn't need to be here for all of this," Owen started. "I've been in touch with our sponsors and the board, and they've all agreed to allow Maria the rest of the season off, to have some time. It's your decision, Maria, of course. If you decide to continue the season, your doctors won't clear you for a month. There's no rush to make the decision." He sat down on the other side of Maria. "I know that this is all a lot to take in, and I know that there's nothing you'd like better to do than curl into a ball and hide for the rest of your life. But I also know you well enough to know that if you don't stay busy, you'll collapse. So, whatever you do, just make sure it's something."

Maria nodded as she continued to look down at her lap. "I think I need the time. I just don't know about Cam, if he needs me around or if it'd be better if I just disappear for a while. Before the season started, I applied for a job in the army." She paused and looked at her team-mates. "I've talked to the Base Commander, but I don't know what I'm doing, if I can come back to the team."

"Well, you'll have to discuss with Cam what he needs but I agree with you. I think you need the time. With that being said, we need to figure out how the rest of the challenges work." Owen grinned and looked at his son. "Old habits, I suppose."

"I don't mind," Rick replied. "It's good to not feel like the captain for a few minutes. But you're right. To be honest, before the Toronto challenge, I wouldn't have thought we could compete with just three people, but Cam impressed me and I think that if he focuses on getting over his fear of water, it'll help him work through this." He paused when there was a knock at the door and Ryan got up to answer it.

Cam walked into the room and let the door close behind him. "Sorry I took longer than I said."

"Everything okay?" Owen asked.

"No, not really." Cam looked around at the people in the room and he motioned towards Ryan. "Might as well sit down. I need to say something." He waited until Ryan was sitting. They were all staring at him. He would have to look at them as he said this. Cam was already being a coward, in his opinion; there was no point in getting any lower.

"It was my fault we failed that challenge. Jack was after me for things that I'm doing outside the CST, so he tried to get to the team first. His AIM attacked Maria during her leg of the challenge, which was why she fell and…" He looked at Maria briefly. "It was my fault he came after us. I guess the cops found out about his AIM, so they're after him now."

"What *things* are you doing?" Owen asked. He raised a fatherly eyebrow when Cam hesitated.

"It doesn't really matter to you guys anymore." He sighed. "I'm resigning," Cam said as he brought his head up to face the others.

There was a brief silence before Rick spoke out. "What are you talking about?"

"I've resigned. I signed the documents a few days ago, and the board already has them," he said quickly as he rubbed the back of his neck. "I let my agent go, too. I know Maria's going to be out for the rest of the season and this is going to affect the entire team, but I think it's for the best."

Rick and Ryan both looked over at Maria, who simply stared at Cam. It was obvious how hard she had to try to hold back, to not say anything right then. Ryan spoke up before Maria had the chance to burst.

"I don't understand. I mean, I know a lot's happened, but is this really the right decision? For everyone?"

"I can't do this. I can't be here. I talked to the board before I made any decision. It's been done." Cam sighed with a shake of his head. "I'm sorry for putting you all in this position, I really am. I know how difficult of a time we had when Owen was benched, and I hate doing it to you again." He paused as he looked at them and shrugged his shoulders as if there was nothing else to say. "Good luck," he said before he moved back to the door and left the room.

Maria was not sure how long she had been holding her breath when she finally let it out. She shook her head violently, as if Cam could see it from the hallway. "No." She got up before any of the other team-mates could stop her and ran out into the hallway. "Cam!" She called out after him again when he did not stop, walking towards him.

"Lucas!" she screamed at him, finally succeeding in getting him to stop and turn around, using that name for the second time in her life. As she got closer to him, Maria could see him shaking his head.

"Don't, Maria."

"What are you doing?"

"I can't be here. I just can't look at you," Cam said with exasperation.

Maria's forehead furrowed as she looked up at him. "What are you talking about?"

"Maria, I can't look at you and not think about what happened. I can't look at you and not think about the baby we lost. I know I shouldn't be backing out. I know I should be stronger, but I'm not. I can't do this. You took *so* much away from me, and I can't be here anymore. I can't look at you and not think about the danger I bring to this team."

"Cameron, please," Maria pleaded, stepping closer to him.

"There is a tombstone out there with the name of my daughter," he said as he raised his voice slightly, pointing his arm out as though pointing straight at the granite. "That's all you let me have of her. A grave." The anger he felt in the hospital began to come back. How could she play the victim when they were both hurting? How could she not see how much he needed to just get away from her, to stop thinking about an AIM attacking her?

She shook her head and looked up at him, taking a breath in preparation to speak. "I know this is hard for you, all of this, but you can't just leave. I know leaving the competition is killing you inside, I know that it's the last thing you want to do." She paused to think about his decision. "I guess that should tell me how much you're hurting."

Cam shut his eyes as he stepped forward and leaned his forehead against hers. It wasn't supposed to be this hard. He was supposed to be gone by now. The plan was to quit in order to focus on his research, to make sure that his work was finished. To make sure that this, what had happened, never happened to another person. It was supposed to be easy. "I'm so sorry, Maria. I'm sorry that all of this is happening, and I'm sorry I'm doing this to the team but we both know that this team was falling apart even before this all happened. Even if I wanted to try to pull this team back together, I can't."

"Cam."

Cam shook his head as he stepped away from her. "Goodbye."

Maria felt her breath catch in her throat. How could there be so much finality in one word? So much pain? She closed her eyes, willed herself to hold back the tears, and to hold back everything else she wanted to say.

"Goodbye," she said, finally looking back at him and almost had to catch herself as he moved away from her and started back down the hallway. Maria watched him leave as she slid down against the wall, and stayed there as she stared down the empty hallway long after Rick and Ryan joined her. Finally, she looked over at her team-mates with a tear-stained face.

"What do we do now?"

Rick sighed and slid down next to her. "We push forward. We train harder than ever, and we push forward." He looked at her as she leaned her head on his shoulder. You're going to have to reply to that job offer with the army."

"I know. But for now, we push forward."

Cam slammed the heavy metal door behind him as he entered the crowded warehouse. He looked around as he walked down an aisle and noticed everyone watch him as he passed, stopping their conversations as he came into view. He opened a door at the end of the aisle and noticed that Sandra had followed close behind him. He looked at a middle-aged man sitting in front of a microscope, holding a petri dish with carefully gloved hands.

The man looked up at him and slowly put down the dish. "L.J, you don't have to be here. You can take some time."

He shook his head with determination. For the first time in a week, he felt he was in the right place, and making the right decision. He had never felt so firm on the ground.

"We have a year. Let's get to work."

ACKNOWLEDGMENTS

Above all, I thank God for the strength and motivation to finish this novel, and for His peace. All of my gifts and talents come from Him. To Him be the glory.

To my friends and family, thank you for being so supportive as I went through this journey, and for your patience as I endlessly talked about my book and characters. I can't promise I'll ever stop talking about it.

Thank you to my beta-readers for doing the final read-through. Your comments have been so valuable. On that note, there have been dozens of people who read through very early stages of this novel, specifically members of Authonomy.com, and Diane who had some great suggestions early on.

I wouldn't have been able to put this all together without my wonderful supporters on Kickstarter. Thank you for believing in this novel and sharing in my passion to bring Scanning to the world.

Not only did Becky act as a beta-reader, she was the woman who designed my publishing logo, and she did such a fantastic job! She was so patient as I asked for alterations and tweaks, and in the end she designed something that really represents me as a self-publisher.

And of course to Ben, for whom this book is dedicated. You are my partner, and my best friend. Thank you for your encouragement, support, your logistics, your unwavering love, your love of animals, and for your blessing to continue your idea.

ABOUT THE AUTHOR

Nichole Sotzek has a B.A Honours in Near Eastern Archaeology and Medieval Studies. Her husband developed the idea for the novel as a child, and in 2010 the two began collaborating on 'Revealing the Revolution' until he gave her full control of the novel and concept a few months later. Nichole is currently working on the following books in the series. When she's not writing, she spends most of her time outside with her husband, scanning.

Manufactured by Amazon.ca
Bolton, ON